Death on Portal Mesa

Love to Mary —
Happy Reading!

JACK F. KIRKEBY

Jack

This book is a work of modern, western fiction and any resemblance to persons, living or dead, or places, events or locales is purely coincidental. The characters are productions of the author's imagination and used fictitiously.

Published by Jack F. Kirkeby
Mission Viejo, California, 92692

All questions or requests concerning the publication or copyright of this book should be directed to the publisher by email to info@jackkirkeby.com.

For more information about the author and his other projects, visit www.JackKirkeby.com. This book is also available for purchase as an E-book at Amazon.com, the Apple Store, BarnesAndNoble.com and most major E-retailers.

Cover Design by Mark Worcester
Book Consultant: Mark Worcester, DeJureMedia.com

Library of Congress Control Number: 2013908956
ISBN: 0615806325
ISBN-13: 978-0615806327
Printed in the United States of America.
First Printing, June 2013.

Death on Portal Mesa
Kirkeby, Jack F.
1. Wyoming—Fiction, 2. Ranching—Fiction, 3. Arapaho—Fiction

CONTENTS

Acknowledgements

To my beloved wife, Priscilla Kirkeby, I owe much for her tireless support and professional editing during the writing of this novel.

And to my son-in-law and good friend, Mark Worcester, I owe much for the book cover design, and the publishing of this book.

Without these two this writing would not be in print.

Death on Portal Mesa

1 | AN UNTIMELY DEATH

Tuesday, May 10, 1952

George Red Fox Bentley could run, perhaps better and faster than anyone else on the track team. Now in his senior year at the University of Vermont, he was considering his three options: To make a career of track and field, enter the business world or return home to his father's ranch in Wyoming, and become a rancher. The decision was taken out of his hands when Coach Jones met him as he finished his fourth lap of the quarter mile track. He handed George a telegram, "This was received by Administration just a few moments ago. It's marked urgent."

George, still breathing fast from his run, gasped "Thanks," then tore open the envelope. The message read:

> YOUR FATHER WAS KILLED IN A HUNTING ACCIDENT THIS MORNING. PLEASE RETURN TO RANCH ASAP.

The message was signed: Pete.

George looked up at Coach Jones with unseeing eyes and an emotionless face. "My father has been killed." He turned away quickly, not willing to share his emotions. This personal tragedy was too great; a part of him was lost forever. He walked off the field in shock, numb to everything around him.

Still in a daze, he began putting his affairs in order for an early departure for the ranch. Packing was simple, saying good-bye to his many friends was not. His thoughts went to Joan LaCross. Joan and he had a 'sometimes relationship' which had just cycled on again. They had been together the night before, and he still felt her warmth. He dialed her number and listened to her soft "Hello."

"Joan? This is George, my Father has just been killed."

"Oh, I'm so very sorry. Would you like me to come over?"

"I'd like that very much."

"I'll see you in a few moments."

Next, George called the captain of the College Rifle Team. This was difficult, as he knew he was needed for next week's interstate competition. He had no choice and all he could do was wish the team well. George sensed the end of something that had been a meaningful part of his life—leaving a community of books, professors, papers, and other familiar activities of his scholastic time.

Joan came, wearing a soft rose-colored cashmere sweater and a plaid skirt to match. She wore rose-colored socks, with saddle shoes, and no jewelry. It was this lovely unpretentious look that George was attracted to. Her presence overshadowed his sadness for the moment, and they embraced. Finally she said, "Will you be leaving for Wyoming?"

"I'm booked on a flight tomorrow morning."

"I understand your need to go, but I hate to have you away from me at this time. You'll be so far away." She paused, and then said, "I guess that's selfish of me."

"I'll miss you too."

"Do you plan on returning to finish school?"

"I suppose not, at least not in the foreseeable future. With Dad gone there is no one to run the ranch, and I probably will be plenty busy for some time catching up on things."

"Will you write to me?"

"Of course, can you pick me up by eight in the morning, and drive me to the airport?"

"Sure, can I do anything, help you pack, or something?"

"I'd like you to have dinner with me tonight."

"Certainly, I'll pick you up, at six."

Joan started to go, then turned toward him. She reached up and kissed him lightly, finding little warmth. Now that he was leaving for the West, with no promise to return, Joan felt alarm and discovered strong feelings she was unaware of until now. His love had been tender and physically fulfilling, but he had avoided any mention of a life together. Tonight she wanted desperately to be with him, but sensed it would not be a good experience. She knew he would prefer to be alone with his thoughts. She would not interfere with this.

George, as elected president of the Student Council, was well known at the university. As an athlete, he was a member of the boxing team in his freshman and sophomore years, and excelled at track and field for his entire college experience. A little over six foot two inches, and with trim hard muscles, George had the classic look, high cheek bones leading to piercing eyes, set under jet black eyebrows. His black hair had just a tinge of red when viewed in the sun, and was kept as long as the athletic department would allow.

A private person, he seemed to reject familiarity, being careful not to reveal any of his inner thoughts or feelings. It was that privacy of self that his friends found frustrating and puzzling. No one was to know how deeply he was hurt over the death of his only remaining parent. He had no brothers or sisters, and now the last of his family was gone. Joan LaCross had come closer to penetrating that shell than anyone, but his feelings for her were short of total commitment. He was honest about that.

Wednesday, May 11, 1952

Joan's 1946 Plymouth coupe stopped in front of George's apartment just before eight. She sat for a moment contemplating the complexities of this man. One thing she knew for certain: She was in love with George, and would take him any way he came.

George came quickly down the steps, stowing his gear in the rear seat, and slipped in beside Joan. She looked at her man for a moment, then said an affectionate "Good Morning Sweetie."

He responded with a warm smile and, "Hi."

En route to the airport, Joan asked, "Were you very close to your father?"

"Yes, he was all I had for a family."

Joan glanced at her rider in frustration, thinking: George needs help and won't let me in. She remained silent.

On arrival at the airport, Joan dropped George, his one overstuffed piece of luggage and his rifle in its leather case off at the terminal entrance. She watched his broad shouldered muscular frame disappear in the crowd, then left to park the car. George headed for the ticket window and they both arrived at the gate about the same time. They stared at each other and she reached up and kissed him, again hoping for some sign of warmth and love. There was none.

"Well I guess this is good-bye for now then."

"Good-bye Joan."

"Bye-bye George."

Joan waited until the plane lifted off on its flight to the West. She walked slowly out of the terminal, her mind going over the last twenty-four hours, and its impact on her life. Would she see him again? Her intuition told her that he was not coming back. She knew he cared for her, but at this point it was not love. She already missed his gentle strength.

George's flight home was filled with memories. His mother, White Dove, was the daughter of an Arapaho Chief, and his father, a Scottish immigrant, pioneer and finally a staunch American; both gone now, but very much alive in his thoughts. Regretfully, he had been away at college for the last five years of his father's life, but just knowing that he was there, had been important to George.

The world George was about to enter **was** far removed from the college campus and its regimen. It had been just under five years since he left for college and except for a rare visit home, he lived the student life with its demands. He felt sad and puzzled at his father's death, and was determined to find out why this happened. His father had always been a careful man, not prone to mistakes or accidents. The last time they were together he was strong, healthy, and alert of mind.

Glencoe, the county seat of Contra County, had a small air strip just outside of town. George had called ahead to Pete, the ranch foreman, and asked him to pick him up. When the air-taxi circled the field, George picked out the oversized garage acting as a hanger, the wind sock and a lone figure waiting for the plane to land, who turned out to be Pete. George took the big step down from the plane before the steps could be set up. The day was cold and the wind was strong, adding to his depression. Pete's pleasant, familiar face greeted him. It helped a lot.

The years had been good to Pete. The squat bowlegged ranch hand was still young looking; sporting a fine reddish-colored mustache, thick dark hair cut low in the back, and wearing his familiar checkered shirt. After a bearish hug they climbed into the ranch pick-up and started for the Arrow—B Ranch.

"What happened, Pete?"

"I'm not sure, George, maybe you can figure it out. First off, we're down to just me. Bob retired two months ago, and your Dad and I were trying to get by with just the two of us until the fall round-up. Marie reckons she's cooked long enough, and is leaving next week.

"I don't get much outa Bill Williams, the Sheriff, he seems stuck on this being an accident." Pete continued, "That herd of elk passed by on its way to some mountain meadows for summer graze, and your Dad went off to see if he could bag one. That was early yesterday morning. About noon that big gray of his came wandering in home without Dick aboard. I took and back-tracked up the trail and found your Dad."

"Where is he now…at the Ranch?"

"Yeah. Soon as the Sheriff said it was OK, I put him on that hoss of his and brought 'im home."

"How do you think he died?"

"Damned if I can figure it out, I sure don't think the way the Sheriff does."

"So what does he think?"

"Wal, from what he told me, your Dad came riding up this draw on Portal Mesa, the one that is about five miles south of the ranch, fired one shot at somethin' or someone, got shucked off'n his hoss, landed on his head and broke his neck."

"That's what the Sheriff believes?"

"Yep."

George looked at Pete for a minute or two then said, "Unbelievable. An excellent horseman, a man known for his caution, fires a rifle, falls off his cow pony head first yet, and breaks his neck. This could never happen. Where's Dad's rifle now?"

"The Sheriff has it locked up. He says it's evidence."

"That must mean that he's not sure. I guess I'll have to pay him a visit in the morning."

The highway had turned into Main Street in Walnut when George said, "You'd better stop in town and let me talk to the undertaker."

"Okay George." Pete had been thinking to bring up the subject of the body, now two days old and still in the house, but was trying to be delicate about it. "You know me and your Dad go back a long way. I've lost a good friend away too soon. This shouldn'a happened."

The meeting with the undertaker was short, testy, and business like. The rancher asked for minimal service, burial to be on the ranch next to White Dove, his mother; and was to take place on Friday, two days from now. Richard Bentley's body was to stay at the ranch.

The undertaker objected to everything. He said,

"Preparation of the body is best done at my place, and it's closer to the cemetery where most people wish to be laid to rest, and Friday is not a good day for me."

"I guess I didn't make myself clear, I am the customer, you give the service. Please give those services as I am requesting; then submit your charges. They will be paid if the service is adequate."

The undertaker nodded his head in assent. After all, he thought to himself, I'm dealing with a half breed and I have to expect this kind of thing.

Pete listened with interest to this young person he had watched grow from the day of his birth. He left for college a young teen-ager and returned a strong determined person. He sounded much like his father.

The drive to the ranch took a little under an hour. It seemed like forever to George, who had been on the road since eight that morning: two commercial airlines, one commuter air taxi and then this. His mood was somber just like the weather which was looking more and more like rain, or perhaps a late snow. Pete filled him in on everything he knew, which wasn't much. In time the truck drove under the ranch sign, carved on an old slab of weathered cedar, an arrow pointing to a capital B. This also served as the ranch brand. When they drove into the yard, Charlie, the aging ranch dog, let out a series of yelps and barks destined to frighten all interlopers to death. Pete said, "Guess we better introduce you to Charlie again. I don't reckon he'll remember you after all this time. He's been downright cranky lately, guess he's gitten old."

"From what I can remember, Charlie always was a bit ornery."

"That's a fact."

The big red Irish Setter continued his symphony of barks, yelps, howls and growls, then quieted and sniffed George thoroughly from top to bottom, finally sitting with a panting grin to be petted.

It was early nightfall and a single light shone from the

kitchen of the ranch house. Marie came to the window and let out a squeal of welcome home to George, then ran around and opened the front door. She was still Marie: warm, homey, concerned, and tireless in her effort to do for her family [the Bentleys]. She gave George a big hug and then with tears in her eyes she told of her sorrow over the death of Mr. Bentley.

George entered his father's bedroom and gazed down at the man he called Dad, his eyes now closed, his voice stilled forever, his smile gone. A feeling of sadness and despair gripped the son. Visions of their times together flashed through his mind … times away from the people in the everyday world, private times when a father shared the natural world with his son. His loneliness was complete.

Thursday, May 12

It was 8 o'clock when George finally reached the Sheriff. An authoritative voice announced, "Sheriff Bill Williams here."

"Hello Sheriff, this is George Bentley, Richard Bentley's son. I'd like to get together with you to discuss my father's death."

"Tomorrow will be fine, be here at nine."

"The funeral is set for tomorrow, how about Saturday."

"This office is closed on Saturdays."

"Would you mind making an exception to that. I really don't care to wait over a week-end on the matter of my father's death."

"Look Bentley, I'm out of town until next Tuesday. You can be at my office at nine on Tuesday or at nine on Tuesday." With that he hung up.

George looked at the receiver for a moment, thinking some not so nice phrases. The operator came in with a cheery "Hello, are you off the line?"

"Almost, what's your name?"

"Dorothy."

"Dorothy, will you connect me with Chief Running Deer on the reservation please."

"Sure honey, hold on for a minute."

"This is Chief Running Deer."

"Grandfather, this is George, I just arrived at the ranch."

The Chief said "I have been expecting your call; our sadness is great. We shall all miss your Father."

"Grandfather, the funeral is set for tomorrow at 1 P.M; please know that you would be missed if you did not come."

"May we have a half hour alone with your father? There are certain things we must do for a fallen one such as he."

"Yes Grandfather, that will be fine." George hung up the phone. He recalled the last of many visits to the small Arapaho village. He was just eighteen, and was to leave for college the next day. Chief Running Deer, his grandfather, and George sat across from each other. "Red Fox, it is good that you enter a house of wisdom. You will do well. Learn quickly, but do not forget from where you came. Your father has taught you the ways of the West. Your mother had given you much in the area of compassion and love before she left us. And now you will see the ways, and wisdoms of the East. You will go far, my grandson."

Many years ago, Richard Bentley had been adopted into the tribe. He was known as "White Owl" for his wisdom. Many times he stood in defense of tribal members, and they would miss him. His son, George, was a favorite with the Chief, and on one of those visits to the tribe, George was given his Indian name, Red Fox.

The undertaker arrived about 9:30 and took about two hours to prepare the body of Richard Bentley which was placed in a simple casket made of local woods and moved to the central living area of the ranch house for viewing. The grave was dug by two men from town in preparation for Friday's burial rites.

George's sleep that night was troubled by unanswered questions and the life and tasks that lay ahead. When he left the ranch, five years ago, he had just turned eighteen. Now he must run that ranch. It was one-thirty A. M., when he turned out the bedside lamp, and another hour before sleep finally took hold.

Friday, May 13

Four came from the Council of Elders. Somber and impressed with their importance and the solemnity of the moment, they sequestered to the opened casket to perform the Tribal Rites. In a little under 45 minutes they silently filed out of the room, and informed Chief Running Deer that all was right, now, White Owl could be put to rest. The casket remained open for viewing until early afternoon, then it was closed and moved to the gravesite. The minister from the Glencoe Presbyterian Church conducted a short service with Pete giving the eulogy:

"Richard Bentley left his native Scotland at the age of fifteen. He immigrated to the United States in 1920, started this ranch in 1922, and married White Dove in 1926. In the ensuing years, he built the respect of all of us. Those who worked with him knew him as a friend, tolerant with our mistakes and a true western man. His love for his adopted country is well known. We shall all miss Richard Bentley."

Following the burial rites, a reception was held in the ranch house. Neighboring ranchers and friends began arriving at one for the service and continued until eight in the evening. Ranchers, townspeople and friends united in showing their respect for the deceased. They came with food and drink. They came to console and to join in the sadness. But they came, mostly to tell what they had felt for Richard Bentley. Each looked at George, and took stock.

At the reception, George met Sheriff Bill Williams for the first time. The Sheriff extended his hand and said, "I'm Bill Williams, the Sheriff. I am sorry for your loss."

"Thank you Sheriff. How long have you known my father?"

"Only since I moved here, six months ago. From the

several times we talked, and from what I learned from the local residents, I gained respect and a personal liking for your father."

"I am puzzled about my father's death. I understand that you consider it to be an accident?"

"We can discuss this on Tuesday." With that, the Sheriff turned and left.

Pete walked up and asked, "What was that all about?"

"Like you said, our esteemed Sheriff doesn't seem very cooperative."

Pete chuckled, "So, what else is new?"

"Pete, I'm having trouble accepting that Dad died from an accident. My father taught me to 'Take risks only when they are necessary in the pursuit of your goal'. Risks he would take when required, for sure; otherwise, he was Mr. Conservative. If there's something that you can think of concerning Dad's death, anything at all, let's hear it."

"George, I don't believe it either. What I have is a hunch and some wild guesswork. What you need are facts. I don't have any of those things." Pete's weather- beaten face showed puzzlement. "I'll help all I can." He continued, "I want to see that gun that could unseat an experienced horseman riding on a very reliable horse, acquainted and fond of the rider."

"You didn't see it when you picked up Dad?"

"It was nowhere in sight when I found the body."

George scratched his head, "That's sure strange. Where did the Sheriff find it?"

"Don't know, I didn't ask him."

"Pete, I've been gone a long time. The next few weeks will be a learning process for me. I expect to make a mistake or two. Step in when necessary. I will appreciate that.

"We'll try going it with just the two of us until the fall round-up and then see what happens. By the way, I went out to the corral this morning and had a look at Nellie. She sure looks good. Has she been ridden much?"

"We try to exercise all the stock once a week, Boss, but

lately, with just the two of us, I'm afraid that schedule was messed up a bit."

"Pete, call me George for now. I haven't earned the title of Boss–yet."

2 | RANCH LIFE

Richard Bentley had picked the site of his ranch house carefully. There was a commanding view of the valley floor from the living room and kitchen. Looking to the left one could clearly see the slanting formation called Leaning Mesa, three to four square miles of heavily wooded and nearly inaccessible tableland. Five or six miles to the right stood Portal Mesa, a sloping shoulder of the mountains in the west. It was this formation that provided access to the mountains beyond. Up this incline, native elk made their annual migration into the mountains and greener pastures. From the two bedrooms in the rear, a view of the mountains dominated all else with its grandeur. The bunk-house, tool shed, garage, corral, and barn were all located below ranch house level, on the upper valley floor. A five thousand gallon water tank was nestled in a cleft in the mountains, some 200 feet above the ranch house.

Saturday, May 14

George awoke at seven, feeling that he should have been up earlier. A little embarrassed, he went into the kitchen to find Marie almost ready to put the breakfast things away. He invited her to sit with him for a second cup of coffee, and in time, asked, “Marie, I understand your reasons for leaving, and I don’t wish to change that, but could you see your way clear to stay for another week or two. It would give me time to find someone to take your place.”

Marie wiped her hands on her apron and said, “Of course, Mr. Bentley, I’ll stay for two weeks if you like.”

“Well that’s just fine, I sure appreciate that. Oh, I won’t be here for lunch or dinner on Monday. I’m going into Glencoe and won’t be back until late. All my old ranch clothes and gear don’t fit, and I need to buy some new ones. I’ll need a shopping list too. I might as well be useful while I’m at it.”

Pete was feeding the horses when George walked up. “Good morning Pete, I guess I overslept. Ranch life isn’t quite the same as what I’ve been doing.”

“If I remember right, you played this game pretty well. I’m not worried.”

“Pete, I’m curious to know why Bob left?”

“Search me, it just up and happened. There’s somethin else, your Dad’s been gittin offers on the ranch lately.”

“How long ago did that start?”

“About three months ago. You’ll find some mail on that subject on your father’s desk.”

George glanced quickly at Pete, “Knowing Dad, I bet that went over like a lead balloon.”

“You got that right.”

“Pete, I’m going into Glencoe on Monday to buy clothes and see the family lawyer. Is there anything I need to pick up while I’m in town?”

“There might be. I’ll phone an order into Peterson’s. Check with ’im on your way home.”

Monday, May 16

George entered the office of Emery Forbes, noting the tired gold leaf letters on the door, announcing EMERY

WAYNE FORBES, Attorney at Law. He pushed open the door, and a blast of hot, stale air came rushing out, bespeaking of old varnish and stale cigar smoke. The outer office, that once contained a part time secretary, was unoccupied. George stuck his head into the inner office. "Emery?"

The bespectacled lawyer either could no longer see very well, or didn't recognize George, responded with an irritated, "I am Emery Forbes, what do you want?"

"Mr. Forbes, I'm George Bentley."

"Oh–you look different from the last time I saw you. I've been waiting for you to come. My condolences and sympathy for your loss."

"Thank you, I would like to see my father's papers."

"Papers, oh–I'll need a death certificate of course, and proof of who you are."

"Isn't that getting a little sticky? You know my father's dead, and you have known me since I was born."

"That's the law."

"Well where in hell do I get one, and how do you expect me to get my birth certificate locked up in your files?"

"The family doctor usually, although you may have to check with the Sheriff as a doctor may not have been called. I suspect you will have to wait until tomorrow to find anyone."

George walked out of the stuffy office scratching his scalp in a state of total frustration. Saying to himself, "It's a lot of miles out to the ranch and back, only to face idiots, who have nothing to do but think of ways to keep things from getting done. Everything around here seems to be on someone else's time table." He drove the two blocks to Sears & Roebuck, where he bought denim wear, boots and a hat. The hat, a black broad brimmed Stetson, was altered to include two leather laces to tie under the chin. Envisioning the cold winters, and long days out on the range, he added some long johns, flannel shirts, and a heavy sheepskin jacket.

Paying for all this became somewhat of an issue, as he

didn't have access to the ranch charge account or his father's credit. They finally settled on half cash and the rest in a month. This pretty well stripped him of his ready cash, and he still had ranch supplies to pick-up. He considered just walking out, but he needed the clothes he had selected. Going to another store would just take more of his time, and besides, maybe the same thing would happen again. He picked up his purchases, climbed into the pick-up, and headed for Walnut.

Walnut, where most of the local ranches including the Arrow—B did business, lay in a direct line from Glencoe to the ranch. It was a town of about 400 families. Main Street boasted of thirteen buildings: two churches, one saloon, one general store, two gas stations, a feed store, a grade school, a small hotel, cafe, post office, sheriff's office and jail. The only reason for it being there was to service the surrounding ranches and mines. The remains of a motel consisting of eight Indian teepees, an office and a parking lot was stark evidence of better times; as did the several closed signs and boarded up store fronts. When the interstate highway system was built, Walnut was bypassed. George drove directly to Rosey's Cafe. It had been five years since his last visit here, and he was anxious to renew an old friendship. The jukebox was gone and Rosey had added two more tables. A beautiful spread of antelope horns graced one end of the room and the storied rams head at the other. It was this trophy ram's head and horns that Rosey had to show for her hunting skills, the story of which was chronicled on the back of the menu, a reprint of a news article written fifteen years ago. Rosey herself didn't look like much, but she was loved by everyone in the county. Her charisma could charm the belligerence out of a female grizzly bear with cubs, her love for people was unbounded. Her memory was accurate but kind.

It was lunch time and five of the six tables were occupied, all strangers to George. When he sat down, Rosey came over with a steaming cup of coffee and said, "Wow, you sure have changed. The last time I saw you, you were nothing but a skinny kid, and now you are downright handsome and you look strong as an ox."

"It's sure good to see you Rosey, you look great."

"I'm so very sorry about your Dad, he was one of my favorite people."

"Thanks Rosey. When can we sit and talk for a few moments?"

"I'll be out of customers about 2:30, will you still be in town?"

"Sure, and for now, send me out one of your blue plate specials."

A short time later, Rosey came out from behind the counter with an oversized plate, heaped high with mashed potatoes, grilled pork chops, gravy and canned peas. The ubiquitous piece of apple pie followed, along with more steaming coffee.

"This one's on the house George, I'm sure glad to see you."

"Holy cow, Rosey, if this is lunch, what do you serve for dinner? I'm going to be fat as a pig if I do this thing very often."

George finished his lunch and headed for the general store. He walked up the three steps into the store, and entered a bit of the past, complete with antique cash register atop a worn wooden counter. Square glass jars were lined up behind the counter and what had to be an apple barrel stood to the left. The balance of the shelves behind the counter contained canned goods. Flour and other staples were in bins along half of the back wall. Clothes, harness gear, and tools took up the left half of the store. "Hello Mr. Peterson, do you remember me, George, Richard Bentley's son?"

The bespectacled store owner ignored the question and uttered a high pitched "What can I do for you sonny?"

"I have some supplies to pick up for the Arrow—B, and my name is Mr. Bentley."

"Oh yes, the foreman, Peter White, called in to say you were coming. Your things are ready."

George left Peterson's, and drove over to Bud's Blacksmith shop. Bud was gone and the new owner did more business in flushing out car radiators than blacksmithing; at least this person was friendly and chatted a bit about local happenings. His name was Carl, and he still did a little shoeing and some other metal work.

Rosey had already turned the clean-up duties over to her one employee when George returned. She sat them both in the end booth directly under the mounted ram's horns. Rosey commented, "You don't look so hot, Dearie."

"I didn't know it showed, I never could hide anything from you."

"Don't tell me, let me guess; you've been made to feel less than welcome around here."

"Uh huh."

"OK kid, now you're going to find out what you're made of. Your father faced these people down a long time ago, and it looks like it's your turn. You'll get no help from anybody, and they expect you to fall flat on your face.

"Now nothing goes on in this end of the county that I don't hear about, so take it from Aunty Rosey; watch out, hang in there, and come by when things seem nutty."

"That's nice to know. I'll keep it in mind. I'm not sure whether it's my Indian half or just plain Wyomingism, whatever, the townspeople look at me as if I was a sheepherder or something. Yours is the only friendly face I've seen around here."

"Give 'em time George, these folks, for the most part, are OK. My guess is that, once they know you, they'll come around. There's one thing that comes to mind though, your father got awful mad when someone tried to buy the ranch."

George laughed out loud. "Knowing my Dad I would expect he got more than mad. Who tried to buy the Arrow—B from Dad?"

Rosey chuckled, "The offer came through Jones Realty, and your Dad almost sent Mr. Jones to the hospital. Jones filed a complaint, but it didn't stick as it happened on ranch property."

"Dad always was rather sensitive about the ranch. I think I'll have a talk with Mr. Jones."

"The Sheriff got into the act too, so you might ask him first."

"I have an appointment to see our esteemed lawman in the morning. I seem to have ruffled his feathers a bit. Maybe he'll have simmered down enough by then for us to have a meaningful conversation. I need to find out a few things."

Rosey got up, looked hard at this young man she had watched grow and said, "George, are you wondering about your father's accident?"

"I don't believe it was an accident."

"I don't either. Watch your back."

Tuesday, May 17

George was waiting in front of the Sheriff's office when Bill Williams drove up. The Sheriff unlocked the front door and the two men entered. "Sit down while I put the coffee on."

The Sheriff's office was a chunk of the once large open room, originally a general store. It was to the left as you entered the building. To the right was a row of jail cells, each secured with flat bolt mechanisms. To the rear was a staircase leading to the second floor. The gun rack was behind the sheriff's desk, and was secured with a bar and padlock. The Sheriff went to the locked gun rack, opened it and removed the gun that Richard Bentley had been carrying when he was killed. It was wrapped in a piece of khaki colored canvas kept snug with two brown shoe laces.

"Now is this what you wanted to see? It's not available to anyone until the investigation is over."

"Oh, so you are not entirely satisfied that my father's death was an accident?"

"I didn't say one way or the other. You'll get a copy of the official report in due time."

George looked hard at the Sheriff. "A prominent man is killed. His son wants to know what the Sheriff's office can tell him about it, and you waffle around with platitudes."

"The conduct of this office concerning any investigation is privy until I say so."

"Privy information my ass. It was my father that was killed. I didn't come down here to look at a gun from a distance; hell, I know what it looks like. "My father was too good a horseman to be thrown and break his neck. If the Law believes this, you're not doing your job."

"Simmer down George–your attitude is lousy, and if you want cooperation and help you had better change it."

"Well my lousy attitude is because everyone I talk to keeps his mouth shut about what happened. Can you tell me anything about an altercation between my dad and Mr. Jones of Glencoe?"

"That's a matter of public record, and available to you. If you wish, I'll run you off a copy. Anything else?"

"I need a copy of the death certificate. Can you tell me where I can get one?"

"A death certificate should have been initiated by your family doctor. If he needs verification of time and date, I'll supply them."

"Would you mind starting on this as soon as possible. Our family doctor is Dr. Morrison. I'm dead in the water until a death certificate is made available."

"I'll take care of it today. In the meantime, leave investigating to the authorities. This is our job, not yours. I don't need some half-baked kid sounding off and cluttering things up."

"And, Mr. Williams, as a public servant, your attitude stinks. I'm committed to go by the rules and obey the law, but I've come 3,000 miles to find my father has been killed under strange circumstances. The Sheriff isn't asking how or why, and apparently nobody else is either. I think I deserve better than that."

The Sheriff put his coffee cup down, took a long look at

George, as if he had just seen him for the first time and said, "OK, I guess I asked for that. Alright then, I am investigating your father's death. There are no clues to indicate any foul play. All I have to go on is a hunch, no hard evidence. I'll keep you posted if anything turns up; just don't come in here hard-assed making unsubstantiated remarks about me and my job. I don't cotton to that.

"One thing that interests me, is the day before the accident your father came into town and bought some ammunition for that rifle of his. That's not much, but it's all I have.

"Your Father was a legend around the county. We all liked him, but it's a fact of life that when a person gets too successful or well liked, there are always those who wish to tear him down. Your father would not be torn down."

"I know, and neither will I. I'm sorry I mouthed off. I'll try to control this temper of mine a little better. Can you tell me anything more about that rifle?"

"No."

"Please call me when a copy of that Jones report is available."

"I'll do that. In the meantime, good luck."

Thursday, May 19

George finally reached Dr. Morrison, the family doctor, by phone, "Hello Doctor, this is George Bentley."

"Hello George, I just now heard of your father's death. I've been away on a fishing trip. You must be very sad. Is there anything I can do?"

"Well yes Doctor. I need a death certificate; the Sheriff has all the details. Can you prepare one for me?"

"Yes of course, where should I send it when I'm finished?"

"Send a copy to Emery Forbes and a copy to me."

George hung up and went out to the barn where Pete was feeding the horses. "Pete, I guess we'd better start making a ranch hand out of me again. You sure can't do it alone; and I hope we can handle things between us until the fall round-up like you and Dad planned. Let's get saddled up and go see what there is that needs fixing."

"Sounds good to me boss. We should start over near Portal Mesa, then work south all the way to Leaning Mesa. For today, we'll probably do more looking than fixing."

Nellie had not been ridden much lately, and bounced around a bit before George could put a saddle on her. Pete, watching this performance, thought of offering to help, but didn't.

After several false starts, George's sense of humor had almost run out, when he recalled the first time his Dad took him to the corral and said, "Do it" He was about seven and up till then there had been someone to "Do it" for him." He thought he caught a smile on Pete's face, which he decided to ignore. Nellie finally settled down and came over and sniffed around George a bit. After a gentle conversation from George she succumbed, and let herself be saddled and mounted.

The two men rode south for about an hour climbing gradually to the shoulder of the mountain, then turned west, counting stock as they went along. George observed, "Some of these cattle sure are in rugged spots. We'll need more manpower to get 'em out."

"That's a fact, especially as these cows of yours seem to like shoulder high cactus and chaparral."

"Yeah and I'm going to have to get my language skills back again. Cows probably don't understand Vermont University talk." They rode on in silence for a while. "Why don't you show me where you found Dad while we're up this way."

"Okay, it's not too far from here." Pete found the trail into the mountains in short order, and they started on up. It was a long climb to where the land leveled off. This was Portal Mesa: a five or six acre almost level piece of land, strewn with jeep size boulders. A solitary ponderosa stood like a sentinel on the west end. Close by could be seen the trail head: the gateway into the mountains beyond. The horses were pretty well winded and were glad to stop for a rest. The riders had brought water for their horses and sat down while the animals nibbled on spring grass and drank. Pete said, "Marie stuffed some lunch in my saddle bags. Do you want some now or shall we wait until noon?"

"Let's wait, it's shaping up to become a long day."

"That's true; say how's your rear holding up after no riding for five years?"

"I have an idea I'll be sleeping on my stomach tonight. Is it much farther?"

"I guess about 20 minutes. Do you see that tall ponderosa ahead?"

"I see it."

"That's close to where I found him. The trail swings wide around that tree, then starts a switch-back up into the higher elevations. This trail follows the old elk migration route."

"I know the trail, Dad and I have been up that way many times together."

The two riders followed the trail to a point opposite the huge ponderosa, standing like a sentinel at the entrance to the uplands. Pete pointed to a spot on the rocks "I found him layin' across that rock."

"Where did you find the gun?"

"I didn't. The Sheriff did. I guess I must be gittin' old–or somethin'."

George got off his horse and studied the scene very carefully. "How did the body get away over here? This is at least thirty-five feet from the trail."

Pete scratched his head, "Unless he rode over here to look at something, or–to talk to someone. He was on the hunt, so maybe he saw some elk and wanted a better shot."

"Pete, that doesn't play either. That herd usually makes a horrific mess when it goes by. The ground around here looks mighty peaceful. Let's mosey around a bit, and see what we can find. You cross over the trail and go uphill, I'll work on this side. Look for something out of place."

It was well after twelve when George called stop. He had found a great lunch spot, and Marie's lunch came out. Pete was removing some rocks to make eating flatter when he saw something shiny in the corner of his eye. He looked a little closer and reached over and picked up a shiny brass shell casing. He passed it to George.

George rolled the shell casing in his hand, "That's dumb luck for you. Where do you suppose the bullet went that came out of this? There's no tarnish so it's quite recent. If it was Dad's he must have come alive after he broke his neck and ejected it and we know that didn't happen. Let's keep this to ourselves Pete; in the meantime I'll try to get the Sheriff to allow me to look at that rifle."

"I've got the same hunch you have George, and I don't like it much. Shall we keep looking or come back in the morning?"

"No, it's getting late and I don't like riding trail in the dark."

Single file riding is not conducive to much conversation, but when the trail finally widened George came alongside Pete, "I think I figured out how Dad came up with a broken neck."

"I'm listening."

"When a man is hung, like in the old days, he breaks his neck, right?"

"Go on."

"Broken necks don't just happen. There seems no natural cause for Dad to have a broken neck. Perhaps someone helped this happen."

"Our Sheriff will never buy that one."

George reined in Nellie, looked across at Pete and said, "A broken neck by virtue of a hanging is unique, and leaves certain characteristics that are recognizable to the trained pathologist. If this evidence is present, it will prove Dad was hanged. I'm going to hire a specialist from wherever I have to, have him take another look at the body and find out.

We'll return in the morning and have a look at that convenient branch on the ponderosa. The body could have been moved from the scene to make it look more like a riding accident, and to stop one of us from looking too close."

Pete shook his head, "All that activity has got to have left some sign, and this place looked as if it had never seen horses, elk, or people."

"That's a fact. Do we own any tree climbing spikes?"

"Hanging in the barn."

Wednesday, May 17

The night had been short of a nightmare, unsettling and brutal to George. In spite of the physical strain of five hours in the saddle, which he was unaccustomed to, he could not sleep. It was nothing but an iron will that found him back in the saddle again the next morning. Marie must have been up all night. Breakfast was ready and a lunch packed when the two men got up. It was cold and dark when they left for the mountain trail. The horses were perky and kept up a lively pace. The ache in George's behind soon tapered off to a dull numbness and he began to regain his skills and endurance, sidelined while he was in college. Pete picketed the two horses while George slipped on the pair of tree climbing cleats, and clumsily made his way to the first branch. What he saw sent cold chills through his body and a sick feeling. The rope burns on the bark were well defined and quite new. Something or someone had to have swung at the end of a rope, and recently.

George looked down at Pete, who was standing with his hat pushed back looking upward, "There are definitely rope burns up here. Let's look around for signs on the ground."

The search was disappointing. Whoever had caused the marks on the branch had been careful to remove any sign of activity underneath.

George climbed up the tree trunk once more and looked again at the crease crossing the branch and visualized a human being hanging from this tree limb. He saw a vision of his father swinging by the neck. It was a nightmarish dream that he would never forget.

3 | THE WILL

It was late afternoon when George and Pete started the return trip to the Arrow—B. The search of the area around where the body had been found failed to produce any additional clues. Pete shook his head and said, "Jesus, somebody's done a good job. People and animals leave sign in their passing. There's nothin' here. Even the mess I made when I collected your Dad is missing. The Sheriff must have left some mess, and even that seems to have been cleaned up… Somebody's been here?"

George, talking to himself out loud, said, "And that somebody sure has gone to a lot of trouble to make this look like an accident. They also know a bit about covering their tracks. This takes a fair amount of skill, like as my ancestors might've had.

"What's really bothering me is that everyone in town seems to know something is wrong and won't talk about it. I feel sometimes like I'm being watched from the sidelines. Sort of waiting for me to fall or fail or go away maybe. Lots of question and very few answers. There's a lot of things I don't understand about all of this, but we can't do much about it at this point."

George turned to Pete, "Let's get on the trail, it's getting late."

Pete cinched up his saddle, mounted up, looked across at his boss and said, "I think somebody wants your ranch . . .real bad."

"Yeah, well I sure don't figure on giving it up," George took the reins, rubbed Nellie on the nose, and patted her on the neck. He swung into the saddle and faced Pete. "Why do you think someone wants this ranch Pete?"

"First there's the offer on the ranch, which your Dad turned down. Then your Dad gets killed. The killer couldn't make a deal with Dick, and thinks you might be easier to do business with."

"Maybe you're right. We need to find out the who and why, and convince them that it's not a profitable idea. In the meantime we better get in and run the ranch. We'll start hiring for the fall round-up in a week or two. We'll be shorthanded as hell, but I need time to find just the right people. I don't expect any trouble, but you never know. We better watch for any sign of intruder on ranch property. I'll ask the Sheriff to keep an eye open for strangers in town. They've killed once, and they won't hesitate to kill again."

"Kinda reminds me of when I first started workin' for your Dad. Everything went OK until he married your Mother, and then mysterious things started to happen. It was a tough go for a year or two."

"Rosey kind of hinted there was some trouble, and that I might see some of it, now that Dad's gone. I think this is something different. I'm beginning to think that most of those stiff-necked people from town are just measuring up the Indian in me. They will have to make up their own minds in their own time about that. If we are right, and there are, in fact, some bad guys out there trying to steal this ranch, it is separate and above the prejudice in town. They may be bigoted, but I don't think they're criminals."

"Your Dad wouldn't put up with no one talking down to your Mom. Everybody around here finally grew to like her. But that's kind of the way it is here: each of us had to prove ourselves before we were accepted."

George said, "Just maybe I can get something out of Jones when I talk to him. He seems in the loop somehow. In the meantime, as I said before, be careful."

Dr. Morrison called to say that the death certificate was ready, and that he had forwarded a copy to Forbes. Monday morning found George in Forbes' office, nursing a cup of coffee and looking across the desk at attorney Forbes shuffle papers.

Emery Forbes finally looked at his client and said, "Mister Bentley, I have everything ready for you. I'll read the will first, and then go to other matters."

"Emery, would you mind skipping over the legal guff, and tell me what I have. Then give me a copy. I can read."

"I guess I can do that, although this is unusual. Your father might have done something like that, though, come to think of it. Since you are the only living descendant, I can tell you that you inherited the ranch, along with all of the assets and all of the debts, if there are any. The will also provides a retirement income for Peter White and Marie Carpenter. Emery shifted his horn rimmed reading glasses down, and tipped his head. He peered intently at George and added, "It's interesting, but your dad came in and made some changes to the will shortly before his death."

"Were there any major changes?"

"Well, the one that seems significant was concerning Bob Gibson. As you know, he worked for your father for 25 years. The will directed the estate to set up a trust fund for Peter White, Bob Gibson and Marie Carpenter. It was a substantial amount for their respective retirements. The update, signed just three weeks before your father's death, disbanded the fund for Bob Gibson, deleted all mention of Bob, but left Marie and Pete as it was."

"Do you have any clues as to why?"

"Your father wasn't one to explain anything."

"Okay Emery, put my name on what's mine and continue the two trust funds as they are. Then send me copies, along with such legal documents I need to conduct business for the ranch. If you can think of anything that might shed light on the Bob Gibson deletion, please call me. Oh, and what other papers do you have that are mine?"

"The balance of the documents you want are in a safety deposit box in the bank in Glencoe."

George left Forbes' office deep in thought, and headed for the ranch. His father had been a man of strong will, however, for him to deny a long-time employee his retirement benefits was out of character for Richard Bentley. Something very traumatic must have caused this action. One more unanswered question. He remembered Bob as an employee of his father, he remembered Pete as a good friend. That was the difference.

George needed to find out as much as possible about the finances of ranching, and how Richard Bentley did business. His father had added a small office, just off the kitchen. George had been in there before, but had not taken the time to do more than browse. Since money is the usual cause for criminal acts, there just might be some answers in the ranch financial records that could help explain things. Reading through twenty-five years of ledgers was not his idea of a fun trip, but a necessary one. By the time he got back to the ranch, he had pretty well decided to take the time to do the job.

Up to now, George had been sleeping in the bunkhouse. It was time to move into the main ranch house. After the undertaker removed the body from the master bedroom, Marie had cleaned and aired the whole house. When George entered his Dad's bedroom he found, to his surprise, everything neat, clean and fresh. He turned to Marie and said, "My goodness Marie, when did you have time to do this?"

Marie beamed and answered, "When you were out taking care of the ranch and business, I thought I would make it nice. I hope you didn't mind me going into his room. There were some mail and papers scattered about. I put them all together and in the top bureau drawer."

"That was just fine Marie. It's made it much easier for me to do what I have to do. Do you still plan on leaving the end of next week?"

"Yes Mister Bentley, I made these plans over a year ago, and I have tickets all paid for to start my traveling."

"Dad left instructions in the will to provide you with some retirement income. It will be some time before I know just how much. I'll advance you whatever you need, until I have some answers as to how much it will be. It's important that you keep me posted as to your whereabouts."

"Oh! Your father has always been very generous to me. Yes I will keep you informed. I know I will be spending some time in Florida. I have a friend that lives there. I can give you that address now."

After supper George began the task of reading the ranch records and papers. The aggregate of papers was stuffed into the seven drawers of the handmade desk, one of which was stuck, and when George finally got it loose by brute force, it landed upside down on the floor. Of course, the contents spewed everywhere. The virtue of patience was missing in George as he surveyed the small office. Peering in where the drawer had been to find out what made it stick, George found a small key taped to the back of the desk. It turned out to be a key to the safety deposit box. With it, on a small square of note paper, was written 'First National Bank of Glencoe' #110'.

Armed with a copy of his father's death certificate, the key to the safety deposit box, and his own birth certificate, George entered the Glencoe First National Bank and approached the lone figure sitting behind a dinky sized desk directly below a sign announcing: LOANS.

"I'm George Bentley"

"What can I do for you Mister Bentley?"

"I would like to get into my father's safety deposit box. Here's my father's death certificate, my birth certificate, and the key to the box."

"I have authority to open any box to the person whose

name is shown for that box. You don't fit that category."

"Perhaps you missed the point. My father is dead, I am the son, who needs to have access to my father's papers in order to run my ranch."

"I understand your problem, but I have no authority in this matter."

"If you understood the problem, you would tell me who does have authority."

"Oh. Mister Willows, the bank president,–I think."

"Fine, I'd like to see him."

"He's out of town right now."

"Do you have a manager?"

"I'm acting manager while Mister Willows is away."

George glared at the little man before him, "Just what kind of managing can you do when you have no authority? What is your name?"

"It was a full two weeks before George was awarded permission to open the safety deposit box. It contained family documents, a copy of the upgraded will, three thousand dollars in cash, and a disclaimer that read:

I, Bob Gibson, do hereby relinquish all claims to the Bentley ranch or other Bentley holdings, stocks, bonds or cash and bank accounts.

The document was dated March 13, 1952. It was signed by Bob Gibson. The embossed mark of a notary public, registered in the state of Wyoming, verified the signature.

4 | A COLLEGE SWEETHEART

In his first weeks of busy, frustrating and sometimes traumatic activities, George had neither the time, nor the inclination to concern himself with the people and activities at college. Ten days after his arrival at the ranch, he received a card of condolence from Joan. There was a short note inside:

> This place doesn't seem the same with you gone. I'm going through the paces of graduation month, but I'm sort of lackluster about it. I guess I miss you more than I thought I would. Your leaving was so sudden. I'm having a hard time getting used to it.
>
> The Rifle Team did well, but missed top honors, and most people here felt you would have made a difference, however they do understand your reasons for leaving when you did.
>
> There has been talk about awarding you an absentee degree, due to your fine scholastic record, and the circumstances of your departure. I hope they do that. You have certainly earned it.
>
> All my love, Joan

George pondered Joan's note in depth. Could Joan be

making more of their relationship than he was? Joan had been a good friend, and he missed having her near, however that chemistry that draws people together, and makes lasting relationships, just wasn't there, for him, at least. Now Joan seemed to have different thoughts on the matter, and that's what bothered him. The timing was lousy anyway. George considered it unfair to Joan to let her think there was marriage and lifelong commitment between them. He contemplated being straight forward about it. That was his way. Then, thoughts of White Dove, his mother, and her teachings of compassion crossed his mind. She would have counseled him to be kind, to consider Joan's feelings, and to do it now. Like… let her down gently. In the end, George did nothing, and hoped the Joan problem would go away. And then the second letter arrived about a week later.

It had been a lousy day. The locals treated him like some kind of varmint, and nobody seemed interested in finding out the ifs and buts involved in his father's death. In short, George was used to making decisions, and executing same quickly. He was frustrated in everything he tried to do here.

Rural Free Delivery promised delivery of mail to the ranch, not when it would be delivered. So, whenever you were in town, you automatically stopped by the post office to pick up any mail that was there. The post office, which bragged to be the smallest US Post office in America, was in fact, about the size of a large telephone booth. Martha, the postmistress, weighed around 250 pounds, and barely fit through the door. She was just closing up for the day when George drove up.

George said, "I'm George Bentley, I'd like to pick up the mail for the Arrow— B Ranch."

Martha glowered at him, then looked at her watch and said, "This post office closes at 4:30, but I'll make an exception this time." She shifted her mass back in again and found the Arrow—B mail. She sniffed at the top letter, then, handing the mail to George she said, "I'm sure you want this one, it's from Vermont and smells nice."

George was not impressed with the personal interest the postal clerk was taking in his mail, and wondered how long it would be before the rest of Walnut knew he had received a letter that smelled nice? He thanked Martha and climbed into his pick-up, then opened Joan's letter, it was four pages long and contained mostly newsy things related to the college. It also included the following:

> I'm coming out to see you this summer. I'll be riding with a friend of mine, and he's not sure when he will be making the trip. It will probably be sometime in late July or early August. I'll call you when I know more.
>
> I know that you must be terribly busy, but you did promise to write. I need to know what's happening to the man in my life. You have become very important to me. Also please include your phone number.
>
> Love, Joan

George was feeling more uncomfortable about Joan all the time. He folded the letter, then drove on out to the ranch, all the time muttering to himself about how stupid he was when it came to women.

That evening the new owner of the Arrow—B sat at his desk in the living room, and tried to compose a "gentle" letter to Joan, and after three or four tries, all of which ended up in the fireplace, he went to bed.

Procrastination was not George's usual approach to things, but in this case it was made easy by long days on the range, and little time for anything else. So the third letter came. Pete brought the mail in, and when he handed it to George, he remarked with a grin, "Here's the mail, that one on top sure smells nice."

"Damn it Pete, you too?"

"Jeez, what did I do, step on a nerve or something?"

"Well I guess you weren't to know. I'm a little touchy these days. I got a problem that won't go away. That letter is part of the problem."

"Sorry, I'll try to keep my big mouth shut after this."

"That's OK." George took the mail into the office, and opened Joan's letter:

> Dearest,
>
> Happy news. Plans are that I should arrive 1st week in August. I haven't heard from you yet, I guess the mail is slow…

George groaned and reached for a calendar. Putting Joan up on the ranch presented somewhat of a problem. He was definitely not a prude, but did not want Joan, or any other woman for that matter living with him at this time. That option was for a wife, and love, and commitment. He went over again his remembrance of their times together, and couldn't recall having told her he loved her. His conduct might not have been the most honorable, but that was a mutual thing… he thought.

George sat down and started to write:

> Dear Joan,
>
> I really don't have a good excuse for not writing before this, for which I am sorry. I'll bring you up to date on the events of the last three weeks, and maybe that will help you understand. I also suggest that this is not a good time for a visit to the ranch.
>
> First, I believe that my father was murdered. At least all signs point that way, and the Sheriff is finally convinced of this, which he wasn't in the beginning. In addition, one of my employees seems to have disappeared. And thirdly someone is trying to buy this ranch, offering big bucks.
>
> Out here, the law is responsible for very large chunks of real estate. When they need help, they recruit from the local ranchers and townspeople. What I'm saying, Joan, is there may be some trouble here, and I'm in the middle of it. For this reason alone, I would not wish you to stay at the ranch, and would have to put you up in a motel

somewhere. Perhaps when I have some answers, you could come for a visit.

In the meantime, I remain your good friend, who misses you.

George.

George let his letter age for two days, reread it several times, and then put it out for the postman to pick up.

5 | BETTY

On the day of George's appointment with the Sheriff, he came early and stopped in at Rosey's Cafe. The one customer, sitting at the counter talking with Rosey, looked about 25. She wore western clothes: a plaid shirt tucked into form fitting jeans, and from what he could see, she was wearing riding boots. Her Spanish style hat rested on a nearby seat. Auburn, shoulder length hair, worn in a carefree manner framed her lightly tanned face. Large luminous eyes, that dared and promised, smiled in consort with her lips.

George said, "Hi Rosey" not taking his eyes off the person at the counter, who now stared back.

Rosey looked at them both and laughed, "George, meet Betty. Betty meet George."

They both said "Hi" then Betty removed her hat from the seat next to her.

George took the empty seat. "Thanks."

"I'm sorry to hear about your father. It must be a difficult time for you."

"Thank you for that.... I was not ready for this."

"I don't think anyone is ever ready to lose a parent." Betty felt uncomfortable talking sideways. "Ah, why don't we sit at a table?"

They moved to the table under the Ram's head.

"Do you live close by?" George was facing her now, and decided that her eyes were deep ocean blue.

"With my Dad on the Harris Ranch, about 15 miles south of here."

"Harris? I don't recognize the name. I guess there have been some changes while I've been away. How long have you lived here?"

"Dad bought the ranch about two years ago, and I moved in with him last July–Are you going to live on the Arrow–B?"

"Yeah, I kinda think Dad would've liked that, and besides, I don't think I could stand city life for long."

"Do you have any brothers or sisters?"

"No. What about you?"

"There's just Dad and me. I lost my husband two years ago, and Mom died when I was 15."

George looked at his watch, then got up to go. "Life seems very unfair sometimes. I'm sorry Betty, I have an appointment with the Sheriff right now. May I call you?"

"I'd like that."

When Rosey and Betty were alone again, Rosey came out and sat opposite Betty "OK Sweetie, what would you like to know? I've known George since he was born."

Betty laughed, "Rosey, you're kind of intuitive you know. Just tell me everything. Like does he have a steady date or something?"

"Well, no one around these parts, but I don't know much about the last five years while he was in college. His Father used to come in and show me newspaper clippings. He was a miler on the college athletic team, and a good one too. He also did some boxing, but I think his true love was the college rifle team. His Dad was sure proud of that.

"George's mother was the daughter of Chief Running Deer. She died when George was twelve. His grandfather, the Chief, is a good friend of mine. He visits me every few months, when he comes to town. I think you'll like him."

"Please go on."

"That's all for now Bet. I have customers coming in. We'll continue this the next time you come to town." Rosey chuckled "He sure perked up when he saw you. I think you turned him on." Betty blushed right through her tan, and Rosey laughed as Betty went out the door.

* * *

On their first date Betty and George drove into Glencoe, had dinner and went to the movies. The drive was about 90 minutes each way. They drove in silence for about ten minutes when Betty said, "Tell me about your college."

"There's not much to tell, I left the ranch for the University of Vermont in 1947. I looked at the world and books for the next five years, and left school, a month before graduation, when Dad was killed."

Betty looked over at George and said, "Oh, that's too bad. Will you try to get your degree through the mail, or return and finish up sometime later?"

"I'm not sure, at this point."

Betty remembered Rosey saying something about his modesty, but not his close mouth. They rode in silence for a few miles. "When did you find out about your father's death?"

"About noon, the day it happened. I was out on the athletic field when the coach handed me the telegram."

"And?"

"It wasn't a good time for me, if that's what you are asking."

"I'm sorry I didn't mean to pry."

George glanced over at his passenger, "You didn't, and thank you for asking."

They rode in silence for a half an hour.

"George, pull over to the side of the road please."

The car stopped. The world became silent.

Betty said "Let's start this trip over. Only this time, shall we communicate? That's what people do, you know." She was now facing George, "We need to find out about each other, and we can't do it this way."

George turned and looked into her eyes. "Betty, you are so beautiful you've made me speechless." He reached over and took her hand, then drew her to him.

Betty kissed him lightly in return. "You're silly, and you have me stumbling all over the place for words." She pushed him gently away, and said, "We'd better get on our way or we'll miss the movie."

George started the car; there was much silence, but there was also much said in that silence. Betty was a little frightened. She wasn't sure what was happening to herself. Could she again feel strongly for someone? Dared she hope to love another person as she had Paul? Her thoughts traveled to the day they met. She was just turned fourteen. He was fifteen. They were friends, they were schoolmates, and they became adults together. It was hard to think of ever being apart. The tragedy of his death left her numb. Now, two years later, she had finally accepted Paul's death, and that life has to go on.

Betty snuggled against George, feeling his strength, scenting his manness and knowing something special was happening in her life. She, for the moment, accepted the silence.

George was experiencing emotions the like of nothing he had ever known. The warmth and magic of love, and wanting to be with, and a part of, another human being. His thoughts were mixed, with remembrances of his absent family. He couldn't share this time with his mother and father. How he would have wished his father and Betty to know each other. His mother and Betty would have enjoyed a fine relationship too. He was sad for the moment.

The road was straight, the sun lay low in the west, hanging just above the mountain crests. He looked to the right. Betty's face picked up the last rays of the setting sun, smiling eyes, wide open and honest returned his stare. She glanced at the road ahead, "If we are to spend much more time together, hadn't you better look at the road once in a while?" George turned back to watching the road, "I could solve that problem by stopping for a few moments, but then we want to get to the movies. Don't we?"

Betty nodded, and put her head back on his shoulder.

* * *

Not that George didn't think about Betty more or less most of the time, but affairs of the ranch could not wait. So, it was a full ten days before he drove up the three hundred foot private road to the Harris ranch house. Nellie occupied one side of a two-horse trailer which was attached to George's pickup, and when Betty came out to meet him, he said, "Hi Betty," took her hand then told her of his plans to do a mountain ride picnic thing.

Betty looked past his shoulder at the horse trailer and offered, "Why didn't you let me know about OUR plans when we talked on the phone? I like the idea just fine, but it's nice to have choices?"

George said, "It was supposed to be a surprise." Thinking, 'I have to start thinking in twos.'

Betty, now feeling a little off balance, said, "This is really a nice idea," then reached up and kissed him.

George went out to the corral and threw a rope around Betty's horse, led him up and into the horse trailer alongside Nellie and turned to meet Betty who was carrying a saddle…They drove to the trail head for Portal Mesa, and saddled up for the trip. The two riders climbed through the desert chaparral, then the scrub pines and up onto the mesa. The trail was narrow which meant single file, and little conversation. They stopped under the shade of a pinion pine, a few feet from a running brook. George dismounted, and came around to help Betty. She stood beside her mount, facing him with just the touch of a smile. For George, the world stood still and his heart throbbed. He took the reins from her hand then led the two horses to a lush grassy meadow. They wouldn't stray from the fresh spring grass and a nearby running brook.

Betty spread a blanket on the ground, and laid out the lunch. They sat together facing the panorama of the valley below. A soft summer breeze was touching each.

Betty took George's hand and said, "I married my lifelong sweetheart when I was twenty. We lived in Provo, Utah. He was killed in a hunting accident about two years ago, and I haven't felt much like dating since. One day I was talking to Rosey, and she convinced me to take another look at who I am. I decided to join the living again. It was hard for me at first because I had been living in a kind of nether world since the accident. I guess I must have been a real bore to those around me. Rosey is some kind of person. Very understanding, very compassionate, and very wise. She's been a good friend."

George said, "I've known Rosey since I was born and I agree, she's something else. I wonder why she has never married?"

"Rosey gives so much of herself to everyone, maybe that's why."

George turned and faced Betty, "You are the only person I have ever brought to this spot. I've saved this for somebody special."

"Are you saying that I am special to you?"

"With a capital S."

"Do you always make up your mind about women this fast? After all, this is only our second date."

"Only when I'm sure."

It was a lazy time. Quiescent to the fullest.

Betty said, "I love it here. This is a time and place of beauty and peace. You have made me feel very special bringing me here."

George answered, "You are."

In time they started for home. The horses picked their way carefully down the rough trail. The dozen or so switchbacks, afforded each rider eye contact but little conversation on the way to the valley below. When they arrived at the trail head, where the horse trailer waited, George led each animal into its stall, lifted the gate, climbed into the pickup with Betty, and started for the Harris ranch.

Steve Harris was waiting for them. "George, you'll stay for dinner of course?"

"Thank you, I'd like that. I'll see to the horses, and clean up."

Betty and her father, Steve, went into the house. Steve said to his daughter, "You like him very much, don't you?"

"Yes, Dad, maybe too much." She stood in the doorway watching George care for the horses. He's gentle and fun to be with. He seems to like me — a lot."

"Your instincts have always served you well daughter . Perhaps nothing will equal what you had with Paul, but he wouldn't have wanted you to give up living."

"Maybe it's happening a little fast for me."

"Trust your instincts daughter."

George was still feeling her good night kiss when he drove into the Arrow—B yard.

* * *

On one of those dinner/movie dates, George said, "Betty, you seem as bored with this movie as I am, let's head back home."

"It's not very good, I admit. Let's watch one or two more scenes, and see if anything happens." Betty had been edging toward an evening when they 'didn't go to a movie', but she didn't want to make it too easy for George either. She let another fifteen minutes slide by. "All right honey, if this movie really bores you, I guess we might as well be traveling on home."

They drove in silence for a few moments and George said, "Would you like to see the ranch?"

Betty had read George pretty well, and was enjoying his discomfort. She was a little surprised when he pulled out of town, half expecting him to suggest a motel or something. And maybe a bit disappointed too. "So how can I see a ranch in the dark?"

"There's a full moon out there."

"Well I guess it's all right."

Charlie was there to meet them when they drove up. He went through his usual investigations and pretty well sniffed Betty to pieces, then sat in front of her for a petting.

George had been careful not to make Betty uncomfortable. He wanted this to be something very mutual, very meaningful to each, and more than a moment of pleasure. As they approached the ranch house, he was still a little concerned that Betty might feel she was being rushed. He parked the truck, came around and opened the door for her, then, taking her hand, led her up the steps and through the door into the ranch house.

They both knew the time was now, and it would be something special and the beginning of a strong romantic time for each.

6 | THE RIFLE

Morning found George sitting across from Sheriff Williams, sipping coffee on a hot June day. The Sheriff, having no one in lock-up, would have stayed at home if it weren't for this appointment with George. There was no air conditioning in the Sheriff's office, and at 9 a.m. it was already a humid 88 degrees. The Richard Bentley case had sort of bogged down, and the Sheriff saw no reason to stir things up. George Red Fox Bentley had other ideas. Every instinct in his body told him an unknown assassin killed his father. He did not intend to let the Sheriff forget the Bentleys. He was, like a dog with a bone.

The Sheriff looked over the top of his steaming coffee cup, "What's on your mind George?"

"I'd like to see my father's rifle."

The Sheriff didn't move from his chair, "We've been through all of this once already. I haven't seen anything new concerning this case."

"Well maybe if you were out there pounding the bushes you might stumble onto something. Speaking of bushes, we found this out near where my Dad was killed." George handed the spent cartridge casing to the Sheriff.

The Sheriff bristled, put his coffee cup down, "So what's

unusual about a used 30 caliber shell casing. There must be a quarter million of these things in this valley, with all the hunting that goes on around here. You'll have to do something better than that, George."

George was trying to stay under control. He thought it better for the Sheriff to discover how new the casing was, and to see if it was right for his father's gun. He waited. "Ah, we found that about thirty feet from where the body was found, a few days after the day my father died."

The Sheriff took another sip of coffee, wiped the sweat off his forehead, and picked up the shell casing. And turned it over in his hand. "Let's see if it fits your father's rifle." He got up, went to the gun cabinet, and brought the rifle over to his desk. Taking a handkerchief he pulled back the bolt. There was a live round in the chamber. Removing the magazine, he counted nine rounds that normally held ten. He sniffed the breach of the rifle, and concluded that it had recently been fired. "That's interesting. What's your idea on this one?"

"I suspect that casing came out of this rifle. You can prove it by matching the firing pin marks of this one with another fired from the same rifle."

"This, even I can figure out. Give me a scenario that will support your 'murder theory'."

"Well for starters, if Dad fired off his rifle, got shucked off his horse, landed on his head and broke his neck, how did this shell casing get thirty feet away? Now for a second thought, you might consider this: Everything looks too neat around the crime scene. There are no signs of man or animal ever being in that area. Even your tracks weren't there. We've had no rain since then to wash out tracks and such, and we can't even find the mess that Pete made when he picked up the body. Someone's been there since the day the body was found–cleaning up. This is curious, particularly to me. Something only my ancestors would be capable of. Now for thirds, there are some strange rope burns on the lower limb of that lone ponderosa standing at the beginning of the trail head." George gave just a touch of a smile "None of which includes my gut feelings, which you rightfully choose to ignore."

"So what do rope burns on a tree limb mean?"

"Something or somebody hung there a short time ago. Like old time hanging? My father did die of a broken neck, didn't he?

"The assumption that Dad fired a round, fell off his horse on his head, broke his neck; then chucked the empty cartridge out of that rifle you have of mine, is not in the realm of possibilities. Oh, and then got up, moved himself over forty feet from where he discharged his rifle. Or something?"

The Sheriff had been rolling the shell casing around in his hand. He looked up at George, "This rifle has been fired recently, and there is one round missing from the magazine. This does pose some unanswered questions. Don't get your hopes up. This doesn't prove anything.

"I'll send this rifle and that casing in to the city lab for analysis. This will take a couple of weeks, so have patience, I'll call you when the results are in."

"Great. By the way, where did you find the rifle?"

"About ten feet from the body."

"That's sure strange, Pete couldn't find it, and he was there before you were."

"Go on."

"Pete tells me he did a good deal of looking around the crime scene when he picked up the body. This is just one more sign that there has been tampering, with evidence. Why? What is somebody afraid of?"

The Sheriff felt a bit like he was losing control, and was trying to control his temptation to throw this persistent person out of his office said, "George, I think you have been reading too many Westerns lately. Look, you've stirred this thing up nicely. Now let me do my job."

George left the sheriff's office considering what his rights as a private citizen were concerning, 'inaction by an elected official'. He considered going to Forbes for some legal advice, but gave up that idea quick like, as he wasn't sure where he stood with anyone around these parts, including the town barrister. He concluded, waiting on the report on his father's rifle was in order. Then go from there.

* * *

It was hot out on the range. Both George and Pete were out daily but rarely together, as there was much to do, and it took both of them riding separately to keep ahead of the chores. Marie left, so preparing meals became somewhat of a problem. Pete became pretty good at opening cans and cooking from the freezer. Both of them knew this would last just so long before they got totally bored with the idea. Marie was going to be hard to replace. George placed ads in the local weekly paper, with no response, so far.

The Sheriff mailed a copy of the complaint filed by Mr. Jones. According to the report, the Realtor made an unsolicited call on Richard Bentley at the ranch. After a short meeting, Mr. Bentley said, "No." Mr. Jones persisted. Mr. Bentley hit him in the nose, and threw him off the ranch. That was simple enough and quite believable knowing Richard Bentley; but it didn't answer any of the outstanding questions concerning the crime.

Toward the middle of June, the Sheriff called the Arrow—B. George picked up the phone on the second ring: "Hello."

"George?"

"Speaking."

"Bill Williams here, I just received the information back about your father's rifle."

"Great, what do we have?"

"We have a firing pin match. There were no fingerprints at all, which looks like this rifle has been wiped clean. This office will proceed with the investigation."

"Well that sounds like progress. I have a favor to ask of you. I think one more link in this puzzle is Bob Gibson, a former employee of the Arrow—B. I need to find this man and talk with him."

"George, if you have some reason to suspect this person of some criminal act, and it makes sense to me, I'd like to hear about it, and I will try to locate him. If not, leave the investigation to this office. I'll be available for such a discussion tomorrow."

"How about Rosey's tomorrow for lunch?"

"Twelve noon sounds good." The Sheriff hesitated, "I need to talk with you about some other things, anyway. Also I'd like to return your rifle, we're through with it for now. I went out and took a look at those rope burns on the ponderosa. Very strange, as you say. What made you look up there?"

"You know, I questioned the accident theory from the start. I had to find some evidence to disprove this idea. Necks don't usually break when riders fall off horses. That's the only tree up there."

The Sheriff was silent for a moment. "You must have had one lousy night's sleep after figuring that one out. I sure hope your theory is wrong. See you tomorrow at noon."

The Sheriff was already seated in Rosey's Cafe when George arrived. He paused on the steps, slapped the dust out of his hat then walked through the door and said a cheery hello to Rosey. Seating himself opposite the big man, he said, "Bob Gibson worked for my Dad for twenty-five years. Just three months ago, my father canceled a long-standing retirement account he had set up for Bob, and I found this disclaimer in the ranch safety deposit box." He handed the Sheriff a copy of the disclaimer. "Now this is not at all like my Dad. There had to be something going on which Dad couldn't tolerate. Now add to that the pressure applied to my Dad to sell the ranch."

"It does look like something is going on. I'll put out some feelers and see if we can locate this man. What does he look like? Do we have any pictures?"

"Ah, I just happened to have one of those things." George passed the Sheriff a snap shot of Bob working a horse in the Arrow—B corral.

"You know George, you could get downright irritating. Don't you ever miss anything?"

"Not if I can help it. Thanks."

* * *

Mr. Jones called and asked to meet with George. He agreed and a meeting was set up for a Saturday morning at the ranch. After a cup of coffee and Jones had offered his condolences for the death of Richard Bentley, he said, "Would you be interested in selling the Arrow—B?"

"No, why do you ask?"

"I've had an inquiry from an eastern firm. They will pay a good price."

"Why this ranch, in particular, do you know?"

"I don't know. Does a million dollars interest you?"

"Let me make this very clear, this ranch is not for sale. I understand you once approached my father with an offer. Tell me, who is making these wild offers for this particular piece of real estate that can't be worth half that?"

"The buyer wishes to remain anonymous."

"And he won't disclose what he wants this property for?"

"No, he specifically said, no questions. That's your final answer then?"

"Yes, now I think you had better leave, or I'll act like Richard Bentley."

"According to the law, I am obligated to present any offer of purchase to the owner, regardless of the price. This I have done, and I don't want any trouble. Good-bye Mr. Bentley."

George watched Mr. Jones' white Buick convertible drive off down the road. He was rapidly running out of clues concerning the killing of his father. He was feeling frustrations borne of his failure to resolve this mystery.

Pete was in the barn doing some busy work when he heard the shots. They came from somewhere up near the water tower. He went to find George, but couldn't find him.

Then, shoving his pistol into his belt, he started for the source of the shots. He found George behind the water tower, firing his rifle at a small paper target some 200 yards distant. It didn't take an expert to know how good his boss was with that rifle. He never seemed to miss. Pete called out, "I heard shots, I thought I'd better take a look."

"Hello Pete, I guess I should have told you I was coming out here. This is what I do sometimes when I need to 'get away from it all'. Or something."

"I take it your visit with Jones was not very good."

"Right. Why don't you join me?"

"I don't know much about that long gun you're using. My favorite is this here pistol."

"It shoots doesn't it, so let's see it shoot."

"I usually practice on rabbits and snakes when I'm out riding."

"Let's see now, you're on a bouncing horse, you have a short barreled weapon, which has limited accuracy at best, your target is moving. You sure like to give the critters an even break."

"OK, it's getting dark, let's get some practice in earlier in the day. I have a spot down yonder that I use all the time."

George said, "That sounds reasonable. Let's go eat."

7 | THE FRIENDLY SIDEWINDER

George awoke from total darkness and sat up. His head felt terrible, his throat dry and sore and he had little or no memory. Looking about he saw nothing but endless desert: sage, prickly pear and an occasional saguaro cactus standing high against the surrounding desert shrub. He lapsed into a semi sleep, with uneasy dreams of his ancestors, dreams of his grandfather leaving him alone in the desert to make his way. Lessons of survival, harsh disciplines born of the desert environment, inherent with the people who live there. Forcing himself into consciousness, he explored his aching head and found an ugly gash with blood oozing out.

He was thirsty, terribly thirsty. Crawling at first, and then managing a few steps he headed for the nearest saguaro. He knew there was water there. Thorns stuck out from everywhere. The man struggled against the armored plant, knocking down the thorns with a stone, and then carving out a bite sized chunk. The taste was bitter, but there was water.

The merciless sun hung high in the sky. The man took shade from the cactus, gradually piecing together the events of yesterday. Two things were certain: first that he was expected to die, and second that his survival depended on himself alone. No one else knew where he was. He remembered leaving the ranch for Walnut to pick up some supplies. Then it all came back in a rush: Spotting a downed steer just off the road, he stopped to take a look and two men jumped out of the bushes and held him at gun-point. He was bound and placed in the passenger side of his truck. One of his assailants climbed onto a motorcycle. The other drove his truck. They proceeded south a few miles then turned right on an old dirt mining road angling off toward the mountains. The two vehicles traveled for about fifty miles. Then all went blank.

Evening came and with it some relief from the 100 degree heat. Taking as much of the cactus as he could carry, he retraced his steps to where it all started. The familiar tracks of his truck went in both directions. He chose to follow the tracks leading to his abductors. To return to the highway was unthinkable, as it was over 50 miles. He walked all night and when dawn arrived, the sun returned and with it the terrible heat. There were rocks now that afforded some shade. George slept until his hunger woke him up. Man can exist for four days without food and still be physically effective. It has been almost two days since he had anything to eat. That left two days in which he must have food or face his enemies too weak to be effective against them.

The next two days and nights were some kind of hell. Traveling by night, hiding from the sun and the eyes of his enemies by day, George followed the tire tracks and slowly made his way across the desert. He tasted the prickly pear, some desert berries and an occasional lizard. When he needed water he tapped the cactus. Toward evening of the third day he spotted a distant light. Instincts born of a thousand years and an iron will prepared this man for what lay ahead. There was no moon this night and travel was slow. At daybreak he saw a small shack and alongside was parked his truck and the motorcycle. Keeping his truck between himself and the shack he reached in and removed the keys from the ignition then lifted up the hood and removed the rotor from the distributor, replacing the distributor cap. The motorcycle was easy, with no ignition leads it wasn't going anywhere. He melted back into the desert to watch. It was a full two hours before the occupants stirred. By the time the two men were finished with some kind of breakfast and threw out the slops another hour had passed. George was desperately fighting to stay awake, and almost dozed off several times. He felt sickish from lack of water and food.

The two men moved out of the cabin. The taller of the two said, "Let's deliver the truck, and collect our money and get the hell out of here. I wonder why it was so important that we steal this particular truck. It sure isn't much to look at."

"Beats me, Sam, this heap isn't worth the $5,000.00 we're getting paid for it. I'll drive the truck; you take the motorcycle."

Sam said, "Your driving scares the shit out of me. But go ahead, only hold it down to something under 80 on these lousy roads."

Art said, " Hey, fork over the keys."

"They're in the ignition."

"The hell they are, you come and find 'em."

Sam was sure he had left the keys in the ignition, but he wasn't ready to call Art down, "Come on, they must be in the shack somewhere." After they had searched the cabin and surrounding ground, Sam hot-wired the ignition. Finding that this didn't work, he lifted up the hood. It took him almost an hour to find out the distributor rotor was missing. A cold chill went through him, "We've got a problem; someone's screwed up this engine, It ain't goin' nowhere." He went over to the motorcycle and found more bad news.

George Red Fox Bentley took this time to enter the cabin and take what food and water was handy, then slip unseen behind the shack and once again melt into the chaparral. He drank and ate, then moved away into a spot that gave him a view of the shack. He needed sleep desperately, but that he couldn't do right now. Once again he thought of the time spent with his grandfather, Running Deer. He had been tested then and he was being tested now. Those times were something special, learning of the desert, of the creatures that lived within, and learning to survive in this hostile environment with nothing but his two hands. It was remembering those times and the lessons of survival that kept him alive. He fought sleep and watched and listened.

Sam said, "I'm going in to make a pot of coffee. Take a look around. Be sure you have your gun and be careful." He entered the cabin and came right out again. "What did you do with that bottle of water?"

"I haven't even been in the cabin."

"Well, if you haven't and I haven't, who the hell has?"

Sam said, "I'm going off and around to see if I can catch the son of a bitch. For Christ sake, stay here."

Art was standing in the doorway when he heard Sam scream. "Come here quick, and be careful, I'm looking right at the eyes of a sidewinder."

Art picked up a shovel and headed toward Sam's voice. It took some time to find Sam. He was clinging to a large upright rock with a desert sidewinder resting across his boot. After a couple of misses, Art finally hit the snake behind the head and killed it.

"Jeez, what took you so long, I could have been killed waiting for you."

"Shut-up Sam, you're lucky I was here."

The two men returned to the cabin to find their 5-gallon can of water had been tipped over and the contents running out the front door. Looking around, they saw that their blankets and the rest of the food were gone.

"I'll kill him, I'll kill him. He's got to be close by." Sam yelled, as he started off in the bushes waving his gun.

George headed for the shelter of the rocks. He climbed steadily until he was about two miles from the shack. He found an old mine shaft and cautiously entered . It was now about noon, and he settled down for some rest. Some fourteen hours later he awoke. Refreshing himself with food and water taken from the shack, he retraced his steps back to the dark cabin. George could hear snores coming from within. He went over to the truck and replaced the missing part, then further disabling the motorcycle he took another look at the cabin. No sign of any one awake there. Piling some tumbleweed against the side of the cabin, he caught it on fire. He then climbed into the truck and drove off.

8 | A TALL TALE

George found the Sheriff at Rosey's Cafe with a six inch stack of hot cakes, and a huge coffee mug, resting on the metal trimmed linoleum counter in front of him.

Rosey saw him first and said, "Are we glad to see you. Jesus, you look awful."

The Sheriff turned, looked George over and said, "You sure got my attention this time; what happened, did you run into a grizzly bear? Do you want me to call Doc Morrison?"

"Let's talk first." George collapsed onto a stool, turned to Rosey, "Would you get me some food and coffee."

"Oh my God Bill, look at his head. Yuh need a doctor." She picked up the phone and said, "Dorothy, get Doc Morrison on the phone, we need him fast at my place."

The operator put in the call, then called Rosey back, "He's on his way, Rosey, tell me what's goin' on."

"George just showed up, he looks awful bad. I'll tell yuh more later."

Rosey served up some coffee and food, and watched George wolf it down, "When was the last time you had a good meal anyway?"

"I guess it's been six or seven days, and am I glad to be here."

"Sheriff, two men jumped me a week ago and left me in the desert for dead. I wasn't. They're out at Lemke's old mining shack, which caught on fire. I don't think they'll be too hard to pick up as they are out of food, water, blankets and transportation. They are armed, however, so look out. I'll file a complaint before I leave town for the ranch." George turned to Rosey, "Does Betty know I've been missing?"

"Sure honey, you'd better call her, she's been worrying herself sick."

"Uh huh, can I use your phone?"

"Sure."

George lifted the receiver and listened to Dorothy, "This is the operator, Dorothy speaking."

"Dorothy, please get me the Harris ranch."

"Oh is this you George? I'm ringing now. Are you O K?"

"Not exactly, Dorothy, can I have this conversation with Betty in private, please."

"Yes, of course, Dearie."

Betty picked up the phone. "Hello."

"Hi Betty, this is George."

"Where are you? The whole county has been searching. Were you locked up?"

"It's a long story, but I'm okay. I can't see you until tomorrow. Can we have dinner together tomorrow night?"

"I'd like to see you now. Why do I have to wait until tomorrow?"

"I have some business to take care of and I need to do it tonight."

'How about after the business is done? I'd really like to see you."

"No, I can't sweetheart, can I pick you up at 5:30 tomorrow evening then?"

Betty paused for almost a minute before she answered, "Well all right, but that's a long time to wait."

"I'll explain everything when I see you. I love you Betty."

The short silence before "I love you too," came over the

phone, gave George some concern. He did not want Betty to see him: all scratches, wounds and fatigued. Besides he was sleeping sitting up, craved food, and looked like one of the walking dead. He hung up the phone, and turned to more of Rosey's offerings. As usual they were more than adequate.

Rosey lived alone in a small house a block from the cafe. After George had eaten, she piled him in his truck and took him to her place. George showered and then lay down on Rosey's bed for a moment and immediately fell into a sound sleep. Dr. Morrison came over, took one look at George's head and woke him up long enough to stitch up his head wound, after which George fell asleep again.

The following morning, George walked over to the Sheriff's office and filed a complaint. The Sheriff said, "Okay, let's take it from the top, you didn't give me anything to go on last night."

"Sheriff, I was driving into town, when I spotted a downed steer. I stopped to investigate and two men jumped me. They put me in my truck. One drove my truck, the other rode a motorcycle. We went about 50 miles south into the desert over some dirt roads. They stopped, and one of them held me at gun point, while the other hit me over the head with the barrel of his pistol, and knocked me cold.

"I came to several hours later. I followed their tracks, which led to Lemke's old mining shack. I got my truck back, stole their food and water, disabled their bike and headed for here.

"They talked about getting $5,000 for the job, which sounds like somebody wants me dead. I'm slightly offended at not being worth more than $5,000. All joking aside, these guys are serious about this thing, and whoever is doing the bank-rolling won't stop just because we have these two in jail.

"I got awfully upset when Jones offered me one million dollars for the ranch. It seems that my father turned down a similar offer, and then got killed. Now along come these two idiots who left me to die, then talk about how they expect to get paid for it. These rummies are small potatoes, and just might be frightened enough to talk about it. I hope."

The Sheriff asked, "Have you ever seen either of these two before?"

"They're total strangers to me. They remind me of two city type hoods. They sound like they were hired to do this one job. Like murder, and then vanish.

"As far as I know, they both have pistols. They should be ready to surrender, however, to anyone with water and food. I don't think they're used to the desert life, and I expect you'll have little trouble."

"Let's see now, you're wounded, crawl around the desert for four days, attack and overcome two armed men with your bare hands. Then you disable their transportation, and steal their food and water. Well that seems like just an average day's work. I don't even want to hear how the shack burned down. Now you want me to believe all that shit, and I must be going crazy, because I almost do. I had a nice peaceful county until you came, and it seems you brought a whole passel of crimes along with you."

The Sheriff sighed and said, "I'll call you at the ranch when I get those two behind bars. That is, if this isn't all a myth."

George kind of grinned and said, "Honest Injun, Sheriff, that's just the way it happened."

"That really does it. 'Honest Injun?' Oh my God, and I have to put up with this. Okay, I'll go out and take a look, based on the condition of your head and the complaint. I must have a hole in my head to believe any of it."

* * *

Out at Lemke's shack, Sam and Art scrambled out of the burning building in time to save nothing but their skins. They spent the rest of the night in each other's arms for warmth, on the ground, nestled up against a rock. Morning found them both totally miserable. Sam screamed, "I'll kill him! I'll kill him! Nobody can do this to me and get away with it."

"Aw shut up Sam. Save it for later, we got problems, like no water or food. And in about two hours it'll be 110 in the shade, which we don't have any of. I don't think I want to meet the guy who did this anyway. He's uncanny. Even the snakes are on his side." Art, leaning against a large rock scratched his head and said, "You don't suppose the guy you cold cocked back there is the shithead did this to us?"

Sam scratched his head and said, "I don't think so, I hit him hard enough to crack his skull, besides, that was over twenty miles and he was on foot. He's got to be buzzard meat by now."

"Well that's the only way I can figger it. It ain't gonna stop either. I want out of this place, money or not. I got the jitters here!"

Sam said, "I don't feel very welcome either. Go take another look at that bike, I'm goin' up to that old mine shaft, we have to have shade for today. If we can't get that bike working, we'll have to walk out of here at night, when it's cool."

After removing rocks, tumbleweed and debris from the entrance, Sam stepped into the old mine shaft. He lit his zippo cigarette lighter and examined the surrounding circle of light. Off in one corner he found several candles. Stepping out of the entrance, He called out, "Art, I'm going on in."

Art answered, "Wait for me. This bike ain't goin' nowhere."

The two men lit a candle and walked to the far end of the mine. Off to one side, nestled into the rock was an alcove containing some supplies. The mine, naturally cool, provided a perfect refrigerator, and the former owner had left some "just in case" food. There was no water, but there were several dozen cans of peaches, canned meat, and beans. It looked like the owner intended to come back someday, and these were emergency supplies.

Sam went back out and took another look at their motorcycle. George had done a good job. That bike is a wipe-out. "Art, come 'ere. Look at that dust cloud moving along the road, and coming this way." Sam climbed up on a rock and said, "I can see three separate cars coming. Whoever that bastard is that messed us up last night has got to rot in hell, I hope."

Art said, "It must be the law, coming out to pick us up, they think. I have no intention of being caught. There's no doubt we would end up dead, if not by the law, then the Big Man would see to it. Our only chance is to hole up here in the mine, and hope they don't see us."

Art said, "I didn't want to go on this one anyway, that lousy 5,000 bucks wasn't enough for this kind of shit. I was colder than a rattlesnake's belly all night, and now I'm fryin.

"Shut up your whimperin' Sam, yuh make me sick. I gotta think."

"Well yuh better hurry up about it, we ain't got much time."

"Okay, we don't have much choice, let's get in there and hide in a corner or somethin'."

9 | TO CATCH A PAIR

Bill Williams watched George climb into his truck and head for the Arrow—B. Until now, the most serious problems he had faced as sheriff was caring for the town drunk or reminding the hot rod boys to slow down. Not that Bill wasn't tough, he was the product of almost ten years in the Marines as company commander. He was used to giving orders and expecting them to be carried out. He had always been the boss, and so far, civilian life had not changed that concept. He was a western man, and got along well with the local ranchers and miners. Now he was to be tested.

George had said they would be easy to collar. Three days without food or water in the desert should soften up just about anybody. Or… on the other hand, they were armed. The Sheriff considered his options, one of which was to call for assistance from the State Police. This seemed reasonable, and would improve the odds a bit, just in case. He picked up the phone and dialed State Police Headquarters in Glencoe, and was put through to the Chief's office. "Chief, this is Sheriff Williams in Walnut."

"Hello Bill, what can I do for you?"

"I have two fugitives, wanted in connection with a kidnapping and attempted murder out here, and I need back-up to make the arrest. They are armed, but may be harmless as they have spent three days of miserable time in our desert."

The Chief said, "Hold on a minute Bill… Okay, are you ready to go on this thing?"

"As of right now Chief."

"How about two squad cars and four bodies, say in about two hours?"

"Sounds good to me, have them meet me at my office. Oh, we'll be going into the desert, they'll need water and some food. It's going to be hot out here."

The Sheriff then called his deputy. "Leon, there's two men out at Lemke's shack we need to pick up. The State Police are on their way to help. As soon they get here we'll head out for the desert. Come into the office ASAP. It'll be hot, bring some water."

The Sheriff called Rosey and asked her to have four lunches ready for them to take on their trip, then went to the office. Deputy Roberts was waiting, "Leon, the two persons who attacked and kidnapped George Bentley last week are holed up out in Lemke's old mining shack, or what's left of it that is. We'll be heading out that way shortly."

The Wyoming State Police arrived, and after a short conference, the three vehicles started south into the desert. The Sheriff would be in charge of the caravan and direct operations. The air was dry and the desert simmered, promising temperatures in the 100 plus range by mid-afternoon. The trip took just under an hour and a half, with the Sheriff's station wagon leading. The two following vehicles drove through clouds of dust thrown up by the lead vehicle and combined with the heat to made it pure misery for the four police officers, and by the time they arrived at Lemke's shack they were not very amiable. The officer in charge of the two police vehicles put in a call to their Chief back in Glencoe.

"This is Daniel in car three. Do you read me?"

"This is Chief Richardson, go ahead."

"Chief, this is a shitty job. We've been breathing dust

from the Sheriff's station wagon for the last hour, it's over a hundred degrees, and we ain't there yet. How much crap do you want us to take out here?"

Chief Richardson sighed impatiently, and said, "Dan, just do your job. Call me when you have the suspects in custody." And closed the microphone.

Dan's' partner said, "That sure got us nowhere. I wonder how long he'd put up with this?"

Dan said, "Probably not very long. I don't really like taking orders from Williams. He's not our boss."

A short time later, the Sheriff's car slowed, and the disabled motorcycle looking forlorn in the dust, came into view. To the right, the remains of the burned out shack was stark evidence of the drama that had taken place the night before. There was no sign of its former occupants.

With a great deal of caution, the six lawmen searched the area, and came up empty. It was now approaching 110 degrees, the desert sun had chased all living things to shelter, either underground or into whatever shade the low shrub provided. Two humans, without water would be cooked unless they could find shade fast. The Sheriff concluded that since they weren't visible here, they must have found shelter close by.

He considered his options. There weren't many. The Chief of police would not expect his four officers to stay too long, and could pull them out of there at any time. He looked at the four grumbling State Police officers, and decided they would be worth more with a little rest in the air conditioned patrol vehicles, and ordered them to do just that. He turned to Leon, who seemed to be all right, and said, "Let's see if we can track these guys in the desert sand."

Leon answered, "They're either dead or holed up in one of those abandoned mines up ahead."

"I think you're right, let's take a look." They circled the burned out shack and found a set of footprints leading up toward the mountains. Big Bill Williams squatted over the tracks examining them carefully and said, "There are two persons, they are wearing city shoes, probably oxfords, the tracks are staggered indicating they're tired, and no effort was made to hide them."

The tracks led directly to one of the several mine shafts along the base of the mountains. Approaching carefully the two men headed for the entrance, and were greeted by gunfire. Both men ducked behind some large rocks, and prepared to return fire.

The Sheriff called out, "This is the Law, you're both under arrest, come out with your hands up."

Art said, "Screw you Sheriff, come on in and arrest us."

The Sheriff said, "Leon, fire some shots at the mine entrance, I'll move on up."

Leon Roberts had been a deputy for only three months. His total knowledge of law enforcement was a six month crash course sponsored by the state college system. Now he was expected to lean around a rock and rapid fire his rifle, while the men in the mine took pot shots at him. The rock he was behind was growing smaller by the minute and he was wondering just why he had decided on this for a profession.

The Sheriff looked at his deputy. Leon didn't move, he was scared to death. He sighed and thought to himself, This is not a western movie and he was not John Wayne.

When the four officers heard the gunfire, they piled out of their squad cars and joined the Sheriff and Leon. Carefully that is. The Sheriff said, "They're holed up in that mine up ahead, would you guys give me some cover. I wanta get alongside the entrance."

A big burley state policeman, named, Dan, that seemed to be in charge, scratched his neck, paused, then said, "What are you going to do when you get there?"

"Well Dan, I hope to start a fire with that there tumble weed that you see piled up against the hillside, and stuff it into the mine. If we get enough smoke blowing in there, the suspects 'ill come out."

"Jesus, that's the hard way. How about some tear gas?"

"Great. I don't have any, do you?"

"Back in the squad car, I'll go get it."

Back in the mine, Sam said, "That about makes up my mind Art, there's six of them and only two of us. Tear gas will get us out fast. Let's make a deal."

Art, replied, "Sam, we for sure are going up for murder and kidnapping. That's big time stuff. Think about it, before we make that kind of decision."

"Believe me I am, but if we can get in the hands of the police instead of this Sheriff, the Big Man can probably get us out. I don't want to surrender to that Sheriff. He looks mean."

Sam said, "OK, I'll go for it, if we can be sure to end up in police custody."

State trooper, Daniel Crowley returned with a canister of tear gas, showed the Sheriff how to activate it, and said wryly, "All you have to do is get this inside the mine shaft."

"I got it, now how about some cover fire from the boys while I run for the side of the mine entrance?"

"We can do that, it's your life, good luck." With that the State Police began firing at the mine entrance. On cue, the sheriff dashed forward, and plastered himself up against the side of the entrance to the mine tunnel.

A voice called from inside the mine, "Hold your fire, we're coming out to surrender." The gunfire stopped and a kind of whitish looking piece of cloth was projected out the mine entrance.

The Sheriff said, "Throw out your weapons, walk out nice and slow like, you're under arrest."

Two hand guns came airborne out of the mine, and the two fugitives followed. The four state police officers came forward brandishing their weapons. The two fugitives then walked forward with their hands up surrendering to the state police.

Back at their vehicles, Dan called his chief, "We have the two fugitives in hand. The Sheriff wants them put in his jail. Is this okay?"

The Chief answered, "Who made the arrest?"

"We did."

"You'd better bring them in here then. Let me talk to the Sheriff."

The Sheriff had been listening in. Hello Chief, this is Bill. First off, we were all in on the arrest. Second, I want to question these two."

"Bill, your jail scares me. It's older than I am, and wouldn't hold a lame chicken overnight. I think we need better security than that. You can come over here and do your thing."

"I don't have a choice, do I? Hang on to these two." As soon as the State Police left, Bill picked up the phone and dialed the Arrow—B. After four or five rings, Pete answered, "Hello, this is the Arrow—B."

"This is the Sheriff, is George handy?"

"He's out on the range, do you want him to call you back?"

"Yeah, as soon as he gets back."

George rode in about six, and called the Sheriff, and of course he was gone for the day. He tried his house. There was no answer there either. He called again after eight the next morning and the Sheriff answered, "Bill Williams here."

"You called?"

"Hello George, I have some good news and some bad news. The good news is that we have those two rummies in custody. The bad news is that the State Police insisted on taking the prisoners."

"How did that happen?"

"I requested back up support from the Wyoming State Police. Those dead beats, the ones that I was not supposed to have any trouble with, got lucky and found food and water in the back of one of those abandoned mines. The two of them got cornered in that first mine. It had no rear exit. The two of them came out, and surrendered directly to the State Police. I argued with the Chief. He said he doesn't like my jail."

George laughed. "What jail? Is there any way we can

question these two?"

"I'm checking with the DA now on that one."

"Do you know what they were booked on?"

"Your complaint said, attempted murder and kidnapping. That's what I indicated to the arresting officers. I also gave them a copy of your complaint. Besides that, they have a resisting arrest charge."

"That sounds reasonable. How about you and me tripping over to Glencoe in the morning for a conversation with the DA and see if he will allow us to interrogate?"

"You're trying to do my job again…Not too hot an idea George, but I happen to be in a good mood and I'll let it go. Okay, make it to my office by 8 a.m. We'll go into Glencoe as you suggest."

"Great, but I have a shaky feeling about waiting that long."

"Patience, my lad, nothing happens over a weekend around here."

George hung up the phone, thinking negative thoughts like…I sure hope those idiots don't figure a way not to be there when we arrive. This latest attempt on my life and/or the attempt to steal or buy the ranch is making me nervous. And, I am getting downright mad. That's bad as I might do something irrational, and that I don't want to do.

* * *

It was close to 5:30, as promised, when George drove the big blue ranch pick-up into the front driveway of the Harris ranch to pick up Betty. He had gone to great lengths to disguise his injuries and cover up the stitches on his head. He intuitively knew that Betty might be distressed over his narrow escape; and considering the trauma she had gone through with her husband's death, he felt he should spare her this.

Betty was standing in the doorway when he walked up. "Hi, it's sure good to see you" and reached up to meet his embrace. Their kiss was long and loving.

"Betty I've missed you terribly."

"I've been frightened; with no word for a full week and not knowing what might have happened."

George related the events of the past week, glossing over the danger parts of his ordeal. He thought he noted a kind of closing down on the part of Betty, and again felt how much he loved her, and needed her in his life. Betty became silent, and as they walked back to the pick-up, George could feel her trembling hand. "What's the matter sweetheart?"

"I sense that you were in a great deal of danger. I care so much for you, I can't handle that."

"It's over, Betty. It's just a small thing in our lives. It won't happen again. It's finished."

She looked up at him then, gathering her emotions, wanting to erase her fears. She smiled and said, "Well okay, I'm hungry, let's go to dinner."

* * *

Monday finally came. George and Bill climbed into the Sheriff's station wagon and headed for Glencoe. They pulled up in front of the State Police Headquarters building and made their way through the reception desk, a police sergeant and a secretary, to the Chief.

After introductions, the Chief asked, "What can I do for you gentlemen?"

The Sheriff said, "We need to talk to those two suspects that were picked up out near Walnut last week."

"They just left here. They're out on bail."

George bristled, "I didn't know bail could be set for attempted murder suspects."

"The Judge set bail at $100,000 each. That should have been enough."

Bill said, "Just how do you find a judge over a week-end around here Chief?"

"You don't, this one came in at nine this morning, which

in itself is unusual; heard the appeal for bail, set the amount, all in the space of thirty minutes. The next thing I heard, they were gone."

George said, "Those two raised $200,000?"

"Yup."

Bill said, "Can they be brought in for questioning?"

The Chief answered, "Yes, if you can show good cause, and we can find them."

George shifted his 190 pounds of solid muscle, tilted his head and parted his hair where the eleven stitches showed so the Chief could see, and said, "Is this just cause enough?"

"They did that?"

"They did that, stole my vehicle, kidnapped me dumped me in the desert to die and thought nothing about it. It's all in the complaint. I'd like to know what kind of a judge would read the complaint, plus the resisting arrest charge and possibly justify setting any bail at all."

The Chief squirmed around in his swivel chair, drummed his knuckles on his desk top and said, "I did not read the complaint, and since these prisoners were released legally, I don't think any part of the law has been broken on our part. It is interesting, though, that a district judge, known for being late all the time got here so fast. Even more strange is how someone could raise $200,000 by 9:30 a.m. on a Monday morning." He then rummaged through the papers in his in-basket until he found a copy of the complaint. Scanning the sheet before him, he turned to the Sheriff and asked, "Why do you need to question these two?"

"We've had strange things happen in and around Walnut lately. It's almost a crime wave, and these two could possibly tell us something about this and maybe why. I am requesting from your agency any cooperation you can give, in bringing these two in for questioning. I am also suggesting that you consider bringing this matter to the attention of the District Attorney. There may be some wrong doings on the part of the Judicial."

"Suggest it all you want Sheriff, you're talking about the

untouchables. I'll do what I can though, and I'll also try to find out why you were left out of the loop. In the meantime, and for what it's worth, I offer my apologies for this office."

The return trip to Walnut found both men deep in thought. George finally said, "Bill, there is evil going on here, and it has come from the outside. I doubt that we will ever see those two again."

"I have somewhat the same feeling, just what is your theory?"

George answered, "If someone is willing to part with 200,000 dollars for their release, they don't want them to talk. That means the next time you hear the news, those two will be dead. We have the questionable act of a district judge, who is obviously taking orders from out of state. The acceptance of a large sum of cash, without verification as to where it came from, and finally the release of known criminals back on the street again, a very unusual happening. This sounds like some kind of pay-off."

The Sheriff was silent for a time and then said, "George, everything you said sounds reasonable; however, I don't believe the Chief's involved. This goes deeper than his office, as you said. I don't have much experience beyond his office. Also there's got to be a connection to your father's death."

George shifted around and looked at his driver. "What you are saying, if I read you right, is this is the end of the trail as far as your office is concerned."

"Negative, I believe we have run out of clues, and will just have to wait for something else to happen."

"That's very comforting Bill; these clues you're talking about are a bit close to home. The last clue nearly cost me my life, and hurt like hell."

"Got any other ideas, I'm open to suggestions?"

"No, not really."

"Well, let's hope we're wrong. The Chief put out an APB on the suspects before we left, and maybe they will pick them up before anything else happens. I wish you weren't so god damned right all the time."

"I do seem to attract the criminal element around here. I sure hope they don't get serious about this thing."

The Sheriff groaned, and said, "Jokes I don't need. My first concern is keeping you alive until we get to the bottom of things."

* * *

Bill and George had been back a week from their visit to State Police headquarters and the Sheriff had just settled into a new adventure novel, his feet resting on his desk, that familiar coffee cup and one of Rosey's pork chop sandwiches on a low table alongside. The week had netted nothing in the line of answers and gratefully the Sheriff had not received any phone calls from George. When the phone rang he unconcernedly answered, "This is the Sheriff."

"Bill Williams?"

"Speaking."

"This is the Chief of Police in Glencoe. We've had no luck finding those two suspects. I do, however, have a hunch you might be interested in; it has to do with a Chicago killing I heard about. Two men, fitting the description of those two that jumped bail last week, were found dead in a back alley on Chicago's South side.

"Hm, timing's about right too. How did they die?"

"That's the weird part of it, they both had broken necks."

"Now I'm interested, Chief, that's how Richard Bentley was killed out here. Do you think you might be able to arrange for me to see the bodies before they get stashed away in the ground or something?"

"I'll call right now, and call you right back."

The phone rang about ten minutes later. "Bill, here's the deal: You will need to be in Chicago tomorrow for sure. It's all set up for you to view the bodies, my secretary will fill you in on the details. Don't hang up, she'll be on this line in a minute."

"Thanks for the help, Chief. I'll call you when I return."

* * *

A little over four hours after the Sheriff left Wyoming, he found himself in the Windy City airport. He took a taxi from the airport to the city morgue, and found the coroner expecting him and cooperative.

"How long do you expect to be in town, Sheriff?"

"Just long enough to look at these two bodies, and perhaps have a chat with your homicide department."

"Well then, when we're through here, I'll steer you to wherever you want to go. Follow me."

The two men wound their way through stairs, aisles and doors, all cold, and in time stopped in front of a row of man-sized slide in body drawers. Inserting his key into a lock, the coroner slid two six foot drawers out into view. He exposed the bodies for the Sheriff to see. The blast of cold air that came sluicing out with the body drawers complemented the chill that traversed his spine when he viewed the faces of the dead men. The Sheriff knew now he was dealing with tough, determined, big city criminals. This had become a real life drama of killing and greed. It involved his county, it was nasty and it would not go away. He said, "Thanks, that's all I need to see. Could we stop off at your office for a moment?"

"Sure, I'm right down the hall."

The coroner's office was kind of an oasis in a desert of cold halls, cold-storage areas and records depot. Bill found himself sitting across a littered desk facing the coroner, sipping a cup of Lipton tea.

The Coroner broke the silence, "You have some specific questions you want to ask?"

Bill said, "Yes, as a matter of fact, I would like to know something about hanging as related to broken necks. Are there different kinds of broken necks?"

The Coroner thought for a moment, then said, "If I read you right, you are asking if it is possible to tell if a person with a broken neck was hanged or if he fell off a wall."

"That's what I'm asking."

"Yes, with some reservations."

"Can this be determined by autopsy?"

"In general, yes. It is not considered a must as far as the usual autopsy."

"Thank you, please tell me how to get to Homicide from here."

A few minutes later the Sheriff was sitting in front of a Chicago homicide detective. He asked, "Is it your intention to pursue an investigation into the deaths of the two men who were found with broken necks in a Chicago back alley two days ago?"

"We aren't too excited about it, they both were wanted criminals. Just what is your interest in this?"

"These two men were collected in my county. Each was being sought for attempted murder, kidnapping and more. They each jumped $100,000 bail and were wanted for questioning in my county.

"We have an ongoing murder investigation which is tied to these two men. I need to know if there were any gang connections, and or what these connections were to events taking place in Contra County, Wyoming. I have no investigative powers outside of my County, so what I request is just that, a request. Frankly, I need help."

"That's a bundle of trouble. I see your point. I'll do what I can, within the constraints of my office. If I find out anything, I'll let you know. You should be aware, however that this office considers these cases not worthy of spending too much time and money on."

The trip back to Walnut took forever. On the plane Sheriff Williams tried reading a magazine but his mind kept recounting the body boxes, the smell of death, and the visage of the lowly figures of the dead criminals. From there he saw the figure of Richard Bentley swaying in the wind from a rope, under the big ponderosa. He tried working crossword puzzles. That didn't help either. By the time he deplaned, and slipped behind the wheel of his station wagon, his nerves were raw. But when he drove into his garage, he had resolved one question: He would not be frightened off. This was his job.

Whoever was behind this, was serious. They have killed three people already and would kill again to accomplish their purpose. When he took the job of Sheriff, it looked like a cushy job. It wasn't, and now he is faced with crime of the first degree. Not looking forward to telephoning George Bentley, the Sheriff knew he must, and had better get to it now. He placed a call to the Bentley Ranch.

"George here."

"George, this is Bill Williams. I have just returned from Chicago, where I viewed the bodies of the two suspects we had in custody. They were known, Chicago hoods and all here are glad to see them dead."

"Nuts, how'd they die?"

"They both came up with broken necks."

"And I suppose nobody in Chicago is at all excited about the deaths of two known criminals?"

"Exactly."

"Seems we're running out of leads like you said."

"From the way things have been going, I suspect that won't be a problem. More will develop, nothing has changed, the persons we are up against will undoubtedly try again."

"That's a certainty. Well I have a ranch to run, and that's what I intend to do. I think I will sit back and see what happens."

"I expected you might take that attitude. It'll just be my luck to hear that you'd been bushwhacked or something, and leave me with another crime. Just try to stay alive please."

10 | MODERN RUSTLERS

The next few days seemed quiet enough. George was beginning to ask himself how his father and Pete, both in their fifties, could keep up with the multitude of chores, and still get out on the range to work with the herd. He began thinking in terms of hiring another hand to replace Bob. And then there was the fall round-up. He would be hiring then for sure.

It was with these thoughts in mind that he drove his pickup out to the farthest reaches of his ranch early one morning. The road was dusty dry and the wheels of his pick-up threw up billowing brown clouds. Up ahead he spotted vultures wheeling high in the pristine blue sky. The big birds circled and dropped to the ground, taking off again then circling once more. George drove off the road heading directly for the birds, crossing a dry wash and coming up over a slight rise. Before him lay the remains of a butchered steer. A half dozen turkey vultures hopped in and around the carcass. The stench was horrible. He fired a round from his rifle, stepped out of the truck, and moved up wind. The vultures on the ground complained bitterly, took off, and hung up in the sky with the others. There were tire tracks and foot prints everywhere and when he read the sign he concluded there was more than one steer involved, perhaps three. A single shot in the head had caused this one to fall. It looked like two more had met the same fate, and were heaved onto a waiting truck bed. The heavily laden truck left deep tire tracks and George picked out the footprints of at least three men. He followed the tire tracks until they ended at the state highway.

* * *

George found the Sheriff reading a book, with his feet planted firmly on his desk. He looked up and asked, "What brings you into town George?"

"There's rustling going on out my way."

"Maybe one of your Indian friends needed a meal or two."

"The Tribe, as you call it, knows that all they need to do is ask. They wouldn't steal from this ranch."

"I guess I'd have to agree, someone else's ranch maybe, but not yours. My guess is it's a one timer. They won't be back."

George grimaced, "I can't understand why you feel it's necessary to select the Tribe as being suspect every time something goes wrong. Have you ever been out to the village? Or is it just easier to sit on your ass and bleep?"

"All right, simmer down George. Where's your sense of humor, I was only kidding."

Two intense dark eyes looked hard at the Sheriff. "Humor noted. Now let's go see what the non-Indians have done, I'm driving."

Bill considered George for a moment, "Okay, let's go then."

On the way out, Bill asked George, "Anything new on your Dad's death?"

"Considering we both felt something would start soon, this bit of cattle rustling sure looks like one more link in the chain."

The Sheriff sighed, "I agree, it sort of points that way."

"By the way, I've decided to have Dad's body exhumed. Does the Law get involved here?"

"I really don't know. You better check with your attorney. Who's going to do the autopsy?"

"I've been talking to a man from Chicago."

"And?"

"The Chicago coroner is waiting for a break in his schedule. I expect it'll be sometime next week."

George parked some distance away from the vulture guarded kill, so not to disturb any tracks or tire marks. He waited by the truck while Bill read the signs.

"Crap, the stink is awful; let's get outa here. I sure hope these are some smart city boys that needed a steak or two, or a stake, whatever. I think they're long gone. I need to have you sign a complaint."

"I think it's connected to the other happenings. It's started all over again. Another invitation for me to quit, only this one doesn't hurt so much." George reached up and touched that four inch scar on his head.

"I hate it when you say things like that. You could be right. You seem to be that way quite often."

The Sheriff took note of the rifle stowed in the truck, and now noticed a pistol as well. "I see you've added to your arsenal."

"You told me to stay alive."

"And I suppose Pete's packing that pistol of his too."

"We do target practice together. He's pretty good with that thing, for a man his age."

"This was supposed to be such a peaceful county, and I find ranchers taking up arms? I can see your point though."

"Well Sheriff, you're liable to see a lot more of this kind of thing if the Law doesn't do something soon. My Father is killed, I'm beaten half to death, suspects are allowed to walk out of jail, and nothing happens from this office. Now, I have rustling going, and you don't feel it's worthy of investigating. What d' you expect us to do?"

"All right George, calm down. I didn't say I'm not

concerned. I'm running an office with two men trying to police 5,000 square miles of territory. For the first time in ten or fifteen years, there's real trouble here. I've appealed for some help, to the Board of Supervisors, the State Police, and I'll go to the Governor if I have to."

"Well, I'm losing patience fast. These vermin might get lucky on their next try, whatever that may be. From now on you can expect some old fashioned frontier justice out of the Arrow—B, legal or otherwise."

The two men drove back to the office in silence. George impatiently filled out the necessary paper work, and handed it to the Sheriff. Bill walked out with George, and watched him climb into the ranch pickup. "George, be careful. I can't help from here, and I also can't make you my only priority. I am concerned, and will try to get some more help. In the meantime, I suggest you get someone to watch your back. Hire somebody, if you have to. Try to stay within the law. I have to carry out the law when it's broken."

George grimaced. There was no law against doing a little investigating on his own, and that he intended to do.

During the twenty mile drive to his ranch, his thoughts traveled to other times: the growing years, the lessons and disciplines of the West learned from his father; and those special times spent with his grandfather. He thought of the compassion and love he learned from his mother, the daughter of Chief Running Deer, his grandfather.

His mother, White Dove, and his father, Richard, built this ranch. They were frontier people, facing a much greater challenge than he was facing now. They had prevailed, and so would he. They were both gone, now he was responsible. The Arrow—B stood for something. He was the new guardian.

Sheriff Bill Williams sat in thought. He was losing control, something he didn't like. He had just been dressed down by a man fifteen years his junior. This hurt even worse. He knew that George had every right to say what he said, but that didn't make it any easier.

Someone was rustling cattle in his jurisdiction, and that was unacceptable. He picked up the phone and called his friend Chuck, the sheriff of Bar County which bordered Contra County on the east. "Hi Chuck, I want to chat a bit: how about my place around ten tomorrow?"

"Hello Bill, ten o'clock's out, but I can make a twelve o'clock lunch. You buy'n'?"

"Yeah, I'll buy, how about Rosey's?"

"Okay , I'll see you there."

* * *

Rosey's Cafe was a little like the town hall. Everything that went on in the county came under scrutiny at Rosey's, and every one of the locals participated in the discussions that took place. The dining room didn't lend itself to private conversations very well, and Rosey kept herself and the rest of Walnut well informed. Nobody really minded though, as that was the way of things in Contra County. The two lawmen sat opposite each other at a table under a fine set of antelope horns. Each had a heaping bowl of Rosey's beef stew, steaming and thick. Bill said, "We got a problem, there's rustling going on over in the Leaning Mesa area and awfully close to the county line. Have you heard anything?"

Chuck Steele's round ruddy face looked up in surprise. "You serious? I haven't heard the word rustling for over ten years."

"Dead serious, I went out and took a look. It looked like three men in an oversized pickup. They came in the night, shot and butchered three steers, piled the meat onto the truck and drove off."

"Well, so the Tribe needed a bit of meat."

"I don't think so. This happened on the Bentley Ranch, and they wouldn't steal from there for any reason."

"Bill, I have no clue to this at all. I sure hope they stay out of my County; especially as my people almost feel they don't need a Sheriff at all. I have one part time deputy, and I supply my own vehicle."

"I sure know what you are talking about. I'm under staffed and under equipped too." Bill shoved his empty bowl off to the side. "Chuck, this could be part of the ongoing attempt to gain control of the Arrow—B. Since this happened close to our mutual border I'm almost positive they drove into your county to escape. I think they'll try again. Can you kind of keep an eye open for me?"

"I can sure do that, but this is a big lot of real estate to cover."

"Thanks for that. Every little bit helps." Bill turned to Rosey, I need a check and, oh yes; you can tell all."

* * *

The Arapaho lived in a small valley on the far side of the mountains, to the north of the George Bentley holdings. George had not been there for a long time, and as he neared the reservation he was filled with anticipation and memories. He left his truck at the ranch and was riding Nellie. Behind trotted a young stallion, a gift for the Chief. He rode up to the council building, dismounted, hung the reins over a rail, and untied the stallion from Nellie's saddle horn. A voice from behind said, "Welcome, Red Fox, I've been expecting you."

George turned, "Hello Grandfather, I've been looking forward to coming." He led the stallion to the Chief and said, "This is a gift from the Arrow—B."

The Chief took the rope from George, and with glistening eyes, patted and caressed his gift. Talking softly he continued to touch his new friend. He recalled earlier days, when, as a young buck, he rode the range and the mountains of this land. Turning to his grandson, "Red Fox, you have brought me a fine gift. Come and tell me of yourself."

George entered the council chambers with his grandfather. When they were seated, the chief said, "It is with great pleasure that I welcome you to our lodge."

The Chief looked much the same as when George had last seen him. Intense eyes peering from a weathered, kindly face, strong, and demanding respect from those around him. The pleasantries lasted an hour. George finally said, "We have cattle rustlers operating on the Arrow—B. They come at night in a pickup, make their kill, load up, and drive off."

The Chief sat in silence while his grandson related the events of the last forty eight hours. When George was finished, the Chief asked, "Are we suspect?"

"Not at this time, but it seems that the Sheriff is anxious to make it so."

"What reason does he have?"

"None, really, but he dislikes anyone who is not 100% white, which of course includes me."

"Red Fox, I would recommend tolerance, and understanding in dealing with misguided white folks. For the most part we are treated well. It hasn't always been this way."

"Thank you Grandfather. Your counsel is good. I have missed your support and your strength. I hope you will visit the Arrow—B soon."

"I will expect to, at a time when you are more settled."

"I must leave now, Grandfather, I'll inform you of any news concerning the cattle rustling."

George headed back to his ranch. He thought of his father, who, at the age of fifteen, emigrated from Scotland, traveled to the sparsely populated Far West, and filed a claim on forty acres of semi desert. In the ensuing years he added to those acres, built the ranch buildings, and overcame the extreme prejudices against his marriage to White Dove, the Chief's daughter. George concluded that what he was going through was minor compared to those of his father.

Riding out of the valley and around the end of Leaning Mesa, George was greeted by a flock of circling vultures. It took nearly an hour to pick his way through the desert shrub and boulders to where the kill lay. It looked much as before, the thieves taking all the beef their vehicle could carry. George spoke his thoughts aloud, "This had to be a truck with, say, two and a half ton capacity or more and probably had some kind of hoist. He spoke aloud, "These guys are greedy." He dismounted, and examined the ground around the pile of dismembered animal parts. He spoke out loud, "Damn, I wonder if Dad had any of this going on."

He climbed back on Nellie, and headed for the ranch. Riding 'easy in the saddle', George gave note to the commitment of his enemies. They had shown a willingness to pay a high price to achieve their goal. It was unlikely that they would give up in their attempt to acquire the Arrow—B. Something that had troubled George from the start was how these eastern city criminals were able to come to what should be, an unfamiliar hostile land, and move about with ease. This had given rise to the suspicion that they must have a local connection. He speculated that real estate broker Jones from Glencoe was involved. He doubted, though, that the land peddler had the western man guts to be part of this conspiracy. There had to be someone else. Someone that knew the country. Someone familiar to the locals. Someone with an ear to everything that happens here.

Nellie trotted into the ranch yard, eager for a rest and some oats. George let her head over to the barn and practically invite him to get off, and take care of her needs, which he did of course.

When he entered the ranch house, Pete called from the kitchen, "Come and get it or I'll throw it out."

George washed up, then started in on the steak and potatoes. "They're at it again Pete, three more steers over near Leaning Mesa."

Pete stopped a fork full of steak half way to his mouth, and asked, "Buzzards again?"

"Just like the last time. I don't think we can stop it unless we get some more bodies working the range, and I'll have to do that awfully fast or I'll go broke. This is getting expensive. I'll head in to see the Sheriff in the morning, and while I'm there I'd better put some feelers out for some ranch hands. Can you think of anything we need while I'm in town?"

"Not unless they have some new kind of rat trap, made for catching two legged rats."

"I have some ideas on that one, have patience."

"Okay, I'll clean up here, then I'm headed for the bunk house. See you in the morning."

George managed to arrive in town in time for coffee at Rosey's. The Sheriff was there reading the local paper over breakfast. "Howdy Bill, are you open for business, or do I have to wait until you get to the office?"

The Sheriff looked up at the tall raw boned ranch owner and inwardly grimaced; he really didn't want this problem and this guy was bound to bring more bad news. "I've notified our neighbors over in Bar County, and that's all I can do at this point. Bring me some more evidence, something concrete to work on."

George, holding himself in rein, said, "Oh, I intend to, I just lost three more steers last night, same pattern as before, only this time they used a pretty large truck with a hoist."

"Shit, the office will be open in fifteen minutes, you can come over there and file a complaint."

"You're not coming over to look?"

The sheriff gave George a dark look and said, "There you go again, trying to run this office."

"I don't think it's the office that needs running. Rustlers and the like don't frequent offices."

"You know George, if you weren't such a smart ass, you might get a whole lot more help. When I stop to think about it, you just told me what a lousy job I'm doing."

"Losing cattle, and money, for the benefit of thieves makes one a bit testy, especially when much of it goes to feeding the buzzards. I guess I got a bit out of line."

"Apology accepted, sit down, have some coffee. I'll be ready to leave in about ten minutes."

George and the Sheriff made the trip to the kill site. The Sheriff said "This is beginning to look like what we were thinking a few weeks ago. More clues! Since this is happening mostly to you, it seems kind of pointed…someone's trying to make you poor enough to sell. The other complaints I have received have been close to your spread, and could be mistakes."

"That's the conclusion I came to. I think I'll hire some more hands, and try to stop my bleeding. It's a little soon for the fall round-up, but I can't stand much more of this."

"If I find out anything, I'll let you know." The Sheriff pulled out his pipe, started to stuff tobacco in, and said, "Keep it clean George."

* * *

The moon was out in full, the night air crisp and George was headed out toward Leaning Mesa when he heard rifle shots. Ever diminishing echoes erased the night's silence. The man and horse climbed as far up Leaning Mesa as they could and halted. He could see for miles from here. Headlights were moving bumpily toward the road but too far for George to catch up with. The vehicle turned left, heading across the county line. George rode on back to the ranch house and was greeted by a young brave sent by Running Deer with a message which read: "Suggest you check Bar County, no action on reservation lands.

* * *

Sheriff Bill Williams looked up from his novel and grunted out, "Not again?" George, in spite of his losses, was getting some kind of pleasure out of seeing the Sheriff agonize over 'rustling' in his county. "Uh huh, I got hit again last night, the truck turned left and drove into the next county."

"You saw the vehicle? What kind of truck? How about a license number?"

"Too far away."

"So, fill out a complaint. You know the routine."

"This stupid paperwork isn't solving the problem."

"All right, then don't file a complaint. At this point there's not much else we can do. I'm in touch with the State Police, the county supervisors, whom I report to, and if I have to, I'll go to the Governor. If you can figure a way to give me a little more lead time, maybe I can do something. By the time I get to the crime scene, I'm three days late."

George drove away wondering just why the sheriff was avoiding any effort to solve this problem. He headed for the county line, and after a short time, found what he was looking for-: a large boulder to hide behind, a view of the road and grass for his horse. He headed for the Arrow—B where he traded in his truck for Nellie. Just short of two hours later found George propped up against a boulder, watching the road. He was chewing on some jerky and drinking from his canteen when he heard the rumble of a far off truck headed his way. It was almost daylight when headlights showed over the low hill to his left. And then they were there!

George's' rifle barked three times aimed low for a tire. The truck swerved and then went over on its side skidding along to a noisy stop, the cargo of beef hurled over and onto the truck cab trapping its occupants inside. He carefully approached the truck from the underside of the cab, then called out, "Is anybody hurt in there?"

"Na but we're gonna need help gitten out."

George said, "I don't reckon to be too helpful until you throw out your weapons."

"We don't have any."

"Bullshit, your lien' through your teeth." George went over to Nellie and walked her over to the overturned vehicle. He tied a loop around one of the beeves then cinched a pair of half hitches to Nellie's saddle horn. Talking softly he backed Nellie up and pulled the carcass off the truck door. Retrieving his rope, he cut three, three foot, pieces, then called out, "Okay, one at a time, remember, I can hit a running rabbit at 100 yards with this thing. If any of you'd like to test this out, be my guest."

George heard some whispering, then a voice said, "I'm coming out, don't shoot."

The truck door opened gingerly and a head stuck out. George said, "Now crawl out carefully, and walk over to me. The man did as he was told. George watching, saw the cab door edge upward again. He placed a shot from his rifle across the door. It dropped shut. "I said one at a time fellows. Now you lie face down." Again the man did as he was told. George straddled his prisoner, and tied his hands behind his back, then to Nellie's saddle horn. In time, all three men lay on the ground. He then tied the three together then to Nellie's saddle horn, mounted, ordered the three to stand up and start walking.

The Sun was just coming up over the horizon when the cavalcade started. It was a full ten miles into town.

* * *

George walked into the sheriffs' office with three rustlers in tow. The Sheriff, a bit startled, said, "What's this all about?"

"These are the three rustlers we've been looking for; they seem a little tired. It may be the early morning ten mile hike that did it."

"Did you catch them in the act?"

George winked at the Sheriff, "Do we hang 'em tonight, or is it better to wait for the sun to rise tomorrow?"

After the three were locked up, the two men went out to the spot where the truck lay along with its stolen beeves. The Sheriff crawled into the cab and found three pistols and a rifle. All had silencers, and the rifle had a scope.

"Geez, how did you do this, George?"

"Most cooperative people I've ever seen," George said, with a straight face.

"Ouch, I should know better than to expect a straight answer. You are alone on a horse, you stop a speeding vehicle, with three heavily armed men inside, capture them, tie them up, and walk them ten miles into the Sheriff's office." The Sheriff crawled out of the truck cab taking the vehicle registration papers and all the hardware. "Then you tell me about how cooperative they were. George, your stories get worse and worse."

It was about half way back to town when the sheriff broke the silence and said "I need to find where this beef is ending up. As you said, I can't solve anything sitting here. That means spending some time away. Leon can't cut the mustard, and would fall apart if I left him to run the office–I don't suppose you'd be interested in being deputized?"

George, caught off guard and suddenly finding something to like in this man answered "I try to do my part and what is necessary as a citizen, if this is a requirement, I'll go for it."

"Fine, we'll take care of the swearing in when we get in town; in the meantime start to think like a lawman. Now I figure to do some traveling for the next week or two. I can let Leon sit and answer the phone. That will leave you clear to investigate, or whatever you need to do."

"Do you suppose it's possible to get anything intelligent out of those three idiots we have in jail?"

"Well maybe in the past we could have gotten away with a little pressure here and there, but today I'd have the whole state descend on me if I so much as twisted an arm. So we'll have to play it cozy and careful like until we can build up something for the DA. My concern is stopping this operation ASAP. It's in my territory and I don't like it much. These jerks act like the world owes them a living, and "you" count for nothing! Can one of your hands take over if you have to be gone for any length of time?"

"I only have one right now, but I'll work it out. Oh by the way, is there any chance that I might be able to recoup any or all of my losses, now that we have these guys in jail?"

"Very likely not, unless we manage to find those responsible; these guys are just small potatoes, and will, quote "know their rights". What do you think are your losses to date?"

"Something like $5,000."

"Wow, and that's just what we know about from one

rancher and there are about two dozen ranchers in this county alone. I had a call yesterday from Dick Jarvis, he thinks he is missing some stock."

11 | A CUP OF COFFEE AT ROSEY'S

Bill and George returned from the site of the overturned truck early in the evening. They decided to question the prisoners in the morning. The Sheriff turned to his deputy, "Leon, you take the early watch. I'll relieve you at one."

"Yes sir."

Bill looked over at George, "You're welcome to spend the night at my house. You sure don't need a 20 mile horseback ride starting at 8 PM."

"You sure Martha won't mind?"

"Are you kidding, she'll be glad to have someone to talk to besides me.

She's been bugging me to bring you home for the last month. There's grass out in the back yard for Nellie."

* * *

Rosey was closing up for the night when two strangers walked in the door. She said, "I'm sorry, I'm closed for the night."

One of the men took a large pistol from under his coat, "Listen very carefully, sister. Pick up your phone, and call the Sheriff's office. Tell him you have an unruly customer, and you need help." The man waved the big ugly gun in her face. "Do it now!"

Rosey hesitated a moment, and the man ground the barrel of his pistol in her ear. "All right, all right, just get that thing out of my ear." She lifted the receiver off its hook. The operator answered, "Hello, is this you Rosey?"

"Yeah, it's me, get me the Sheriff's office ..fast."

"Sure, hold on, I'm ringing now. Is there something wrong?"

"Hell yes there's something wrong, hurry it up will yuh."

Leon answered the phone, listened, and said, "Hang in there, Rosey, I'll be right over." He locked up the office, jumped in his car, and with tires screeching, sped over to Rosey's Cafe.

Rosey, with a puzzled expression on her face, met him at the door. "I don't know what's going on, these two gorillas came in here and forced me to call you. Then, after I hung up, they vamoosed."

"I'd better stick around, Rosey, they might be back. Did you recognize either one of 'em?"

"They were strangers to me. Where's Bill?"

"He and George went home to Bill's house to catch some sleep. I'm guarding the prisoners. Bill will relieve me at one." They're going to question the suspects in the morning, before George goes back to the ranch."

"Go sit down, I'll pour you some coffee and cut you a piece of apple pie."

Leon sat with his back to the wall. He loosened the flap on his service revolver, and watched the front door. Rosey delivered up some coffee and pie, then, "Leon, you don't suppose all that gun in my face phone call was to get you away from the jail or something?"

Leon got a frightened look on his face. He jumped up from the table, sprinted out to his car, and tore down the street to the jail. Pushing open the door, he found the office in a shambles. "Oh shit,"

He picked up the phone and called the Sheriff's house.

After a half a dozen rings, the Sheriff answered in a raspy voice. "This is the Sheriff."

"Bill, this is Leon, there's been a jail break."

"Holy Christ, I'll be right over."

George, asleep in the guest bedroom, woke up when the phone rang. He looked out the bedroom door to see Bill hurriedly pulling on his pants and running for the front door. "You look madder than a wet chicken. Leon miss his teddy bear or something?"

"Sometimes your jokes really stink. There was a jail break."

"Damn. Are you saying the prisoners are gone?"

"That's what jail breaks are usually for. Let's get going."

Deputy Roberts, looking a bit sheepish, met the two men when they drove up. The Sheriff and George entered the building, through the splintered front door. Files and desk drawers were scattered all over the floor. The jail door hung open, and the gun cabinet glass was shattered. The mangled padlock lay nearby on the floor.

The Sheriff turned to Leon, "Where in hell were you when all this happened?"

"Rosey called to ask me to come right over, she was having trouble with a customer, and when I returned it was like this."

"And I suppose when you got to Rosey's place, the trouble was gone and you stayed to have a cup of coffee?"

"Well yeah, but how did you know that?"

"Easy, that's just the dumb thing you might do. Did it ever occur to you that someone wanted you away from the jail for few minutes?"

"Well yes, just when Rosey set the coffee down in front of me."

The Sheriff looked angrily at Leon, "your first job was here. Anything else you should check with me. You also knew how lousy this jail is, we've discussed it enough times. Don't you know how to use the phone?"

"I was gonna call you, but everything happened so fast. It

sounded like Rosey was in real trouble."

"I suppose we're lucky; if you'd a been here you mighta been killed–This bunch play rough." He picked up the phone, and called State Police headquarters in Glencoe. The desk Sergeant that answered took the information and promised to have his chief call in the morning.

Bill sighed, then, "Sergeant, this is not a tomorrow thing. Find your Chief now."

"Well, hold on, I'll see what I can do."

A few minutes later, "Hello Bill. What's the trouble?"

"We just had a jail break out here. Can you do an APB, and maybe a road block or two?"

The Chief sort of half laughed. "I been telling you for years to do something about that fourteenth century jail. Did the town drunk escape or something?"

"At this point your humor leaves me cold. I had three suspects in custody. They were caught rustling cattle from the Bentley ranch. We were to question them in the morning. I thought maybe they might be headed your way."

"My apologies Bill, I'll get right on it. Give the desk sergeant what info you have. I'll clear it with him."

"The Sheriff hung up the phone then wearily turned to Leon, "We're not going to do anything with this mess tonight. I'll sleep here, you go on home. We'll clean up in the morning. Get back here early."

George, quiet up to now, was still looking at the havoc caused by the fugitives. "This is sure a rotten break. These guys'll be back stealing my cattle by tomorrow night. I suppose, while they were about it, they took their personal effects: weapons, ID etc. We probably don't even know their names–I guarantee the next time I get my hands on any of these vermin, they're going to pay big." He looked over at the unhappy Sheriff, and added, "before the 'Law' gets their hands on them!"

The Sheriff set up the office cot, got some blankets out of a drawer, "I understand your sentiments, but I won't be party to any kind of frontier justice either."

"The way I see it, I have two choices: Use methods that are less than legit or give away my ranch. I think giving in to this Chicago Mafia would hurt everyone in the valley. I'll not do that. So, unless you give me some awfully good reasons, you can expect some strange and interesting treatment of criminals attacking the Arrow—B.

The Sheriff said, "Notwithstanding your promise, and the implication of strong arm tactics, the real question is what are they going to throw at you next? And we know there will be a next."

"It sort of seems that way doesn't it? Something else is bothering me, Bill; how did their buddies know they were in jail so fast? Is someone here on the take?"

"Good question. Go on over to my house, and finish your sleep. I'll have to sleep here.

"Okay, but I'm going to call the ranch and fill Pete in on what's going on. Just in case they decide to do something out there tonight–on their way home."

The next morning, Martha sat George down at the kitchen table and served up some hot cakes,

"Don't bother with me, Martha."

"Shush, I'm glad to have you here. I wanted to see the man that Bill's been talking about. You're all I hear about anymore."

George thanked Martha for the breakfast, and promised to stop for dinner sometime soon. He went out to the back yard where Nellie was breakfasting on that early summer grass, put a saddle on her, then rode down to the Sheriff's office.

Leon and the Sheriff were cleaning up the mess, when George walked in. It wasn't a time for conversation, which would only result in telling each other what they both knew already. Leon seemed subdued, almost to the point that he might give up this 'being a lawman' business altogether. The Sheriff was in a foul mood, not having much sleep to show for the night on a cot in the office.

The Sheriff's thoughts went back to when he was a

company commander in the Marine Corps. There, military protocol was clear, neat, and concise. "Leon left his post, and the book would prescribe punishment." Here, he had choices: fire Leon for derelict of duty, and try to find someone to take his place. Not an easy job. Or, try to bring his deputy up out of his funk, and rebuild his self-esteem to where he could function again. Also not easy.

This was not the Marine Corps! The Sheriff looked over at Leon, then said to the tall rancher he was sworn to uphold the law for. "George, we goofed. You deserved better than that."

Suddenly, the air cleared, and the friendship became stronger. George chuckled, "I can just hear Law Enforcement around here laughing their heads off at your expense. This story will be echoed for months: And of course the local Gazette will headline something like: Local Rancher Captures Suspected Rustlers-Sheriff Williams Lets Them Go".

The Sheriff groaned "Thanks for reminding me. I deserve whatever they throw at me, but I'll survive."

"Kind of a good thing I had the night to simmer down, Bill. I was plenty mad last night–I'm headin' out for my ranch. I don't want Pete out there alone right now.

"However, the Law is failing to do what they are hired for. If you can't protect the citizen, then the Citizen will have to do the job. I've delivered five criminals into your hands. Between you and the courts, I have nothing to show for it. The criminals are gone, and the threat is still out there.

"Sheriff, I need some more riders. If you hear of some hands lookin' for work, send them on over."

The Sheriff was silent for a moment, "I haven't heard of anyone lately. Why don't you check with Rosey; she hears everything before I do."

"Yeah, I think you're right. I'll talk to her."

The Sheriff, whose mood was not improving any with time, considered George's comment concerning the Law. He knew George was right, but that didn't make it any easier.

His dark silence did not go unnoticed by George.

He looked around at the disarray. You know Bill, this may just be the wake-up call the County Supervisors need, maybe they might do something now." He paused, "This is hard evidence they can't ignore.

"While I think of it, consider this scenario: Information seems to travel faster than the speed of light around here. It can only do that through the telephone. Dorothy listens in on some of our conversations, and picks up on most everything that goes on. Perhaps she has a friend, also a switchboard operator, in Glencoe. The two of them pass gossip back and forth. Her friend is not so morally attuned to our well-being as Dorothy is, and makes out with the bad guys."

"You may have a point, George; certainly, they seem to know every little thing that happens. I think I'll have a chat with Dorothy, and see what I can find out." The Sheriff paused for a moment, then in a matter of fact voice said, "I agree with what you said about the Law. This office is not equipped or manned to handle this kind of a problem. The best I can do is have a conversation with the County Supervisors at their next meeting. I don't think they have any notion what's going on here. This is like a bit of big time crime, from Chicago or New York. They're trying to take over."

"When's their next meeting?"

"Supposed to be this week. I'll be there."

George, looking somber, climbed back on Nellie and started for the Arrow—B.

* * *

George and Pete just sat down to dinner, when Charlie started barking. George asked, "Now what's the matter with that dumb dog? It sounds like he ran into a porcupine of something."

"I don't think so, it's more than the usual fuss he makes."

Pete got up, reached for the ranch shot gun, and headed out the front door.

George followed him, picking up his rifle as he went outside. First they heard the roar of an engine, then a truck came speeding out from behind the barn. There was the sound of breaking glass as the truck pulled away. Suddenly a fire started in the ranch pickup. Charlie nearly went crazy, racing after the departing truck. Aiming high, to avoid hitting his dog, George pumped six fast shots into the back window of the speeding vehicle. The truck didn't slow, and was soon out of range.

Pete and George turned their attention to the burning pickup. The smell of gasoline permeated the night air. They hastily backed away, watching helplessly as the flames licked at the truck's gas tank. The resulting explosion was deafening. Flames shot in all directions. The horses in the corral screamed. A corner of the barn caught on fire. The men fought the fire and saved the barn. The horses were racing around the corral, rising up on their hind feet, pounding the rails to get away from the fire. It took the better part of the evening to subdue the frightened beasts. The two men walked into the house and looked at the cold food waiting from dinner, George said, "I really don't feel hungry, this is one more thing to add to the list. He picked up the phone to call the Sheriff. The phone was dead.

"Pete, things are getting rough here and I wouldn't blame you if you left for now. If you wish to stay, I'll be mighty grateful. You will always have a job here whichever way you decide."

"Boss, these scum bums make me mad. I haven't used a gun for years, but I reckon I haven't forgot how. I'm stayin' around, through hell or high water."

"Thanks Pete, you make me feel right fine. Watch yourself, stay inside the law and let's ride this one out."

Charlie came charging up, his tail whipping the air, panting, and uttering soft noises. He could not be intimidated.

12 | A STUBBORN MAN

Betty Harris drove into town to pick up groceries and mail. As she often did, she stopped at Rosey's Cafe for a cup of coffee and some gossip. Rosey was cleaning up from her breakfast business. "Hi Rosey."

"Hello Betty, I'll be out in a minute."

Rosey came out from behind the counter, wiping her hands on her apron. She poured them each a cup of coffee, then sat down opposite her friend. "Hi. Gee you look good—positively radiant. You in love or something?"

"You're the most intuitive person I ever met. I didn't think it showed. Now tell me what's going on, I haven't heard much lately. You know how close-mouthed George is."

"Oh, well let's see, first off George captured three rustlers, walked them ten miles into town, and turned them over to the Sheriff."

"By himself?"

"That's what Leon told me. George has everyone talking around here, but the bad news is, there was a jail break, and the prisoners escaped."

"You mean, George, a private citizen, captures three outlaws, and the Law lets them escape. That sounds like the last time. George lives through some kind of hell, the criminals were captured, then, the court let them go."

"When you put it that way it sounds terrible. I know the Sheriff was embarrassed

by this one. He really likes George, although it didn't start out that way. He asked him to be a deputy by the way."

"You mean 'Deputy' like old time Sheriff's helper?"

"You got that right honey."

"He didn't accept did he?"

"Uh huh."

"Well that makes me mad. I lost my love of a lifetime from a gun. Now I'm given a second chance, and George goes and does a dumb thing like that."

"Well, the Sheriff can't handle it alone; and you know Leon couldn't stop a nine year old fist fight. Besides it's all happening on Arrow—B land. George can't let this one go.

"The Sheriff asked the County Supervisors to hire some more people and buy some new equipment for the office. Well you know what that means: Lots of talk. Put off to next month's meeting, and hope the problem will go away."

"This isn't fair, Rosey."

Rosey took a long look at her friend, and said, "I sure agree with that, Betty, and what I'm going to tell you, won't make you feel any better either. This is big time stuff, these guys are playing hard ball. I think there will be some nasties to look forward to. I just had a taste of it. They came in here and took over. Made me call the sheriff's office to get Leon out of the way while they broke up the jail, and released the prisoners. This one brute stuck a cannon in my ear. It still hurts. "

Betty sighed, "I guess there's no use trying to persuade that stubborn man of mine to move or something. You know, he was offered a million dollars for the ranch. Something about the honor of the Arrow—B, and he didn't want to let his father and mother down."

"Really? He turned down a million dollars? He sounds more like his old man all the time." Rosey reached over and took Betty's hand. "Hang in there kid. George is uncanny. He can stand a whole lot of trouble. For sure he won't stand by and let someone run over him like these rustlers are trying to do."

"I know that, Rosey, that's what worries me. He won't bend at all. He'll stick in there through hell or high water. I just want him alive when he comes off the high water. Gotta go Rosey. Thanks for the info. Please keep me posted."

Rosey watched Betty as she went out the door; her thoughts going to their first meeting, nearly two years ago. It was the beginning of a strong friendship. At first Betty was reluctant to talk about herself, but in time told of her marriage, then the death of her husband, and the resulting sadness that claimed her very soul. Now she saw Betty as a whole person again, partaking of the joys of life. Betty and George were two fine people. It was good to have them for friends.

* * *

George rode Nellie into town and went directly to the sheriff's office. Bill took the news of the truck burning with a groan. "I guess things were too peaceful around here, something had to screw it up. Is that the only vehicle you have?"

"I intended to buy a back-up soon. This will just make it happen sooner."

"What will you do for transportation in the meantime?"

"Who knows, I might discover horses again."

George headed for Rosey's and found her leaning on the counter supporting most of her 160 pounds on her elbows. "Hi Rosey, how about some steak and eggs?"

"Hello George, Betty just left, and I kind of think you're in trouble."

"Oh, so what did I do, forget her birthday or something?"

"I think she expects you to stop playing sheriff."

"Make my eggs over light–how much trouble?"

"Well, the way I see it, Betty's in love with you, and is worried that something might happen to you."

"And I'm nuts about her, but you know I have to see this thing through Rosey—I guess I'll ride out and talk to Betty."

"Sounds like a plan to me. Tell me about the truck burning?"

"They came out of nowhere, heaved a Molotov cocktail into the cab of my truck, and that's all she wrote. By the way, I need three or four more hands. Will you keep your eyes open? Don't be too fussy, I'll sort them out."

"Sure honey, I'll call you. Take care, watch your back, and remember you have a lot of people who care about you."

* * *

The trip out to the Harris Ranch took about two hours. Mr. Harris met him out at the gate. "Hi George, I hear you are having a peck of troubles. I kind of thought that rustling was a thing of the past."

"It appears not, is Betty home?"

"Sure is, I'll tell her you're here."

Betty came out and said a cold "Hello."

"Hi, Rosey tells me that I have a problem."

"That's right George, I am not going to be a grieving widow again, just because you want to play soldier and get yourself killed. I've been through that once already!"

"Betty, you don't understand, these guys are trying to wipe out my ranch. They're vicious. I had visitors last night; they burned up the ranch pickup. I'm in this thing whether I want to or not. What you are asking is against everything I know and believe in."

"Then there's no way I can talk you out of this?"

"Betty, they're trying to eat up my ranch."

"Well I knew it would do no good, but I had to try. Stay for dinner?"

"Thanks, I thought you'd never ask."

Steve joined in and said, "George, can you stay for the

night?"

"I think not. I don't want to leave Pete alone at night."

"Okay then, you have two other choices, either leave Nellie here and drive our ranch wagon home, or we can trailer Nellie to your place and I'll drive home from there."

"Well if it's OK with you, Steve, I'd appreciate having your ranch wagon, I need some way to drive into Glencoe to look at new trucks."

Mr. Harris stood up, slipped his arm around his daughter and said, "I also have an extra ranch hand I can loan you for a week or two. Would that help?"

"It sure would. I have feelers out for some more ranch hands, but that maybe won't happen instantly. Your offer is very welcome."

"It's settled then, I'll send Spike out in the morning on your horse. You'll like him, he's great with horses."

After dinner, Betty followed George out to the ranch station wagon. Her kiss was long and her embrace strong and assuring. As they parted she said, "I need you in my life, don't let anything happen to you."

"That's not a problem, You've given me a great deal to stay alive for. We'll ride this one out together. Betty, I love you."

13 | SURVIVAL

It was dark when George arrived at the Arrow—B. Charlie made a lot of noise until he found out who was in the strange vehicle. This brought Pete out with his shotgun. George said, "I like the greeting. Gives me a real warm feeling."

"Well the warm feeling was meant for someone else. You know that dog's going to bust a lung someday. After that fire last night he's been acting like a young pup. I'd sure miss him if anything were to happen to him. Where's Nellie?"

"Spike's coming out with her in the morning, and will stay with us for a week or two, or at least until I can hire some more help. Steve Harris also loaned us his station wagon."

"Damned if that isn't the first break we've had around here. I hope it's a sign of things to come. I know Spike. We get along great. Get any help from the Sheriff?"

"Not much, he's trying to get the County Supervisors to come up with some money, and they have a budget problem all the time as it is. I suspect we're going to have to do it ourselves. It's not our Sheriff's fault. He didn't build the jail." George continued wryly, "He'll be taking a lot of flak from Law Enforcement all over the country, when they hear that a civilian brought in three fugitives, who then broke out of jail. Anything new here?"

"I got the telephone line fixed where it had been cut, and I called the Sheriff as you asked. He said you'd already gone."

"Pete, I've been thinking about those bums driving up to the ranch buildings like they did. I'm sure they will try it again. Maybe if we discourage them a bit they won't be so eager to try stunts like that again. Supposing we dig a three foot trench across the road, right where it enters ranch property. We make it with square sides, about three feet deep, and cover it some way. These idiots come charging in here on their next trip, they don't even slow down and the front of the truck drops into a void. That ought to break an axle don't you think?"

Pete shoved his hat to the back of his head, got a smile on his face, "You know George, you just got a trench digging volunteer."

"I kind of thought you might like that idea." George looked at his good friend, his mind filled with memories of their long association. "Tell me Pete, how come you never married?"

"Your Dad kept bugging me about that one. I guess I got so comfortable here on this ranch and all. George, I was working this ranch when you were born. It means a lot to me. I don't want to see it go down the drain. Now I want to see this thing through. I won't leave unless you fire me. Maybe if this gets straightened out. . ."

"I sure am grateful for that sentiment. It's good to have you on my side. Uh, you kind of like Rosey don't you?"

"Wal maybe I like her a lot, but I don't think there's anything in return, besides as I just said—-."

"Yeah, I know what you just said. I think I'll stay up and give Charlie some help for the rest of the night. Tomorrow we'll have three of us and we can set up some careful ways."

"Sounds like a winner to me boss. I'll give you some relief in the early hours."

* * *

When Nellie, with Spike on board, arrived, she nosed right on up to George, ignoring Spike's commands completely. Spike, trying to get off, had to wait for the big bay to stop where she wanted to. George took the reins from Spike, "Hi, go on in, Pete's waiting for you with some grub. I'll take care of Nellie."

Spike groaned, "That sure is one strong willed hoss. She's been telling me what to do and which way to go ever since I got on board."

George smiled, and said, "I don't know what's got into her lately, she's gotten sort of one-mannish." Spike watched George handle his horse. He stripped off her saddle, then rubbed her down with a handful of straw, and fed her some oats, all the time talking to her in a soft voice.

Spike walked into the kitchen where Pete was assembling some lunch. "Hi Pete, it's been a long time."

"Hello pardner, sure am glad to see you."

"Right, say that boss of yours sure can handle that hoss of his."

Pete chuckled, "I'm surprised she let you ride her, but then you always were a natural when it came to horses. Sit down."

"She wouldn't let me on top for twenty minutes."

"That must of been a joy."

"It was. Tell me what's been going on, I hear everything third hand."

"Well this George Bentley seems to have inherited all of his father's resourcefulness and skills. He gets into more trouble than a maverick steer, but always seems to get out of it. He's tough as nails, and has more savvy at his age then I do now."

"I take it that you like him then?"

"Shor do, and I intend to stay around for as long as he needs me. He and this ranch are in a peck of trouble, and I intend to help all I can."

George walked in and sat down to flap jacks and bacon.

When the lunch was finished he said, "Spike, it's sure good to have you here. Until we get more ranch hands, the three of us have to keep this ranch from being destroyed. The herd will have to fend for itself for now. Pete will fill you in on the bad stuff that's been going on. I have no doubt there will be more attempts to sabotage and destroy what's here. Try not to go anyplace alone. Be armed at all times, and keep your eyes open. Pete take Spike out to the gate, and you two start on that slit trench. See if you can disguise it when it's done. I'm expecting some nocturnal visitors, and we want to be ready to greet them."

The Bentley property skirts the north-south county road, and the entrance to the ranch was situated right at the junction of this county highway and the quarter mile private road leading to the ranch buildings. Pete and Spike were out at the gate, working on the slit trench when George answered the double ring of the phone. Dorothy answered his curt hello. "Hello Mr. Bentley, the Sheriff wants to talk to you. Hold for a minute."

The Sheriff came on the line, "George, the State Police found a truck, with lots of broken glass and blood all over the seats, upstate somewhere. It also came complete with empty gas can, rags and bottles. There was no sign of the occupants. The vehicle turns out to have been stolen a week ago from a Chicago meat processing center near the Chicago Stock Yards."

"I take it someone will be following up on this?"

"To the extent that the Chicago Police feel it is in the interest of Chicago residents. I talked with Chief Richardson in Glencoe, he said he'll talk to his counterpart in Chicago, but he doubts they are interested enough to do much. These types of auto thefts leave few clues."

"Hm, must have been someone shooting at the truck as it sped away."

The Sheriff chuckled. "You wouldn't know anything about that, of course?"

"Not me. Is Richardson going to leave it at that, or

investigate further from this end?"

"I don't know George. They're dusting for fingerprints. They might tie it into some known hoods. I suspect another body will show up someplace. He said there was an awful lot of blood."

"Well, I intend to make it very expensive for those who are responsible for this attempt to destroy me, or take away that what is mine. By the way, if you drive over here for any reason, call first. It'll be healthier that way."

George hung up the phone deep in thought. He considered the possibility that someone might die at his hands. Already two, and possibly a third, had paid the price. His enemies seemed to have no concern over taking a life. This bothered him, but it was a risk he had to take if he were to prevail. He thought then of his love for Betty, and their plans and future. He must resolve the problems surrounding his ranch and fast.

* * *

When Pete came out of the bunkhouse at daybreak he spotted a dozen big buzzards hovering high in the sky a couple a miles south. Fascinated he watched as others gathered and started their dives to the ground, each taking its turn then soaring aloft, waiting for another shot at whatever was out there. He entered the ranch house and woke George. "Hey Boss, they're at it again, another vulture convention."

George popped out of bed and went out to look. "Let's ride over there together, Spike can hold down the fort. They're long gone, but we better take a look anyway. These vermin are getting me plenty sore. I'll saddle up while you make some coffee and breakfast."

The two men rode to where the vultures were, dismounted and studied the scene. Pete leaned over and picked up an empty shell casing lying on the ground. Turning it over in his hand, he handed it to George. "Here's something."

"I don't understand why we didn't hear this Pete, the rifle this came out of makes plenty of noise, especially in this clear air."

"That does seem a bit strange, do you suppose they used silencers?"

"Maybe. That kind of sounds like big city racketeer style."

Back at the ranch George called the Sheriff, "I got hit again last night."

Bill said, "I think I'll pay you a visit."

"Fine, make it later this afternoon, I'm gone 'til about three. Did you talk to Dorothy about listening in?"

"Yes, and the matter is taken care of. I'll fill you in when I see you."

"I had a reason for asking. I have a surprise for our nighttime visitors. You know what a tank trap was in the war? Well we have one across the gate where you enter our property. When you get there, honk or fire a shot or something. Someone will meet you at the gate."

The Sheriff drove up around four in the afternoon. As advised he leaned on his horn, and waited. Pete and Spike had done a pretty good job of camouflage, and the Sheriff had a bit of trouble finding the trap across the driveway. Doing an end run wouldn't work as the remains of an ancient lava flow butted up against one side of the gate. The other side sloped off into a small arroyo. George drove out and met Bill where he was waiting. He laid a heavy piece of plywood over the trench as a bridge. "Come on in, you're just in time for grub, such as it is."

Bill looked at the hole he could have driven into, "Damn, you guys mean business. I'd sure hate to drive into that thing. He drove carefully over the temporary bridge, then up to the ranch yard. George picked up the plywood bridge, and followed. "Sure glad you warned me. The next thing I know you'll be planting land mines around here."

"Well, I figure this'll only work for one time, but it should make a dent in their truck supply anyway. Who knows, maybe we can catch one or two of them. Speaking of land mines, do you know of a good source?"

"I was only joking. You wouldn't–or would you?" The Sheriff looked into two intense black eyes, that told him nothing, and said, "I guess you'd better not tell me every little thing you have in mind. How are you and Pete getting along without Marie?"

"Not well, housekeeping and cooking isn't my bag. I have a woman that comes out once a week and digs me out. She's due tomorrow. I guess Marie felt no longer needed when Dad was killed. Would you believe that woman sent me a steak in the mail. She's afraid I'm not getting proper nourishment or something."

"How was the steak?"

"Well aged. George laughed. What's been happening? I know you've been out of town."

"I went to both Glencoe and the state capitol and I got more questions than answers. I thought it was time we talked."

"Sounds good to me, why don't you stay for the night."

"Okay, I'll give my wife a call. Anything new happen here?"

"Nothing seems to have changed. I lost three last night. How are the other ranchers doing?"

"I've had three complaints besides yours. Same MO. I suspect the rustlers thought they were rustling your cattle. I'm convinced this is a 'Wipe out the Arrow—B program', starting with your dad's death."

"I think you're right. I intend to defend this ranch, whatever it takes, and for as long as my money holds out. Under these circumstances, I prefer not to be tied down to too many rules that I need to follow as a deputy. This is a rough bunch, and I will hang in there tough. I think that's the only language they'll understand. C'mon in, let's go eat."

After dinner the two men sat opposite each other at the hand fashioned kitchen table, a reminder of George's father's skills. Bill looked around at this warm comfortable home, reflecting the personality of a loving person. "Tell me about your mother, George. I quickly learned to like your dad in the few short months I knew him."

George started dealing gin rummy. It was nice to be asked about his parents. It didn't happen very often. "Mother was the daughter of Chief Running Deer. She was gentle, loving and very knowledgeable in the skills and arts of her people. She made each of us a bit better. Her death was very traumatic for both dad and her father as well as for myself. We all miss her."

"How old were you when she died?"

"Twelve."

"Some of the good guys in this world die too soon. How do you think your mother and father would have handled something like what you are going through?"

"In the early days around here, they did. They hung in there tough." George paused, then, "There was prejudice here in its worst form."

The gin rummy game proceeded in silence for a bit, then, "I can't officially agree with what you are setting up here. I guess that if our positions were reversed, I'd do the same thing."

"Bill, I'm not about to roll over like a puppy dog."

"Yah, I figured that."

"How'd you make out with Dorothy?" George asked.

"Oh that was interesting. This was my first visit to our telephone switchboard. They're using equipment that's a hundred years old. In fact, we must be the only place left in the U. S. not using an automatic dialing system.

"I felt all along that Dorothy wasn't the problem. When I spoke to her about passing information to a friend, she was very upset with herself. She agreed to keep our conversations confidential. She gave me the name of her counterpart in Glencoe. I asked Chief Richardson to see if he can find out who she has been passing information to. He said he would."

"Gin."

"I don't suppose you have another deck of cards, these

seem to be biased?"

"Uh huh, try one of these. Did you ask Dorothy if there has been any information coming her way that might be helpful to us here?"

The Sheriff selected a deck of cards from a box that George offered. He shuffled several times, and dealt two gin-rummy hands. "I asked. She'll come through, she likes you."

"That's nice."

"Yah, well since all the rest of the women in this valley are going gaga over you, it's no surprise."

"I'm putting on three more ranch hands for sure, and maybe a couple more. I expect that will allow me to watch my borders better. I need to protect my property. This thing is like a gopher: plug up one hole, and he digs another. Have you considered aircraft for spotting and squad cars for follow-up?"

"That's what I've been away checking on. All of these things take money and until the Supervisors decide there is a problem, and vote to do something about it, my office is kind of powerless."

"What about the State Police?"

"That's another option being considered.

"George, this problem is not going to go away until we get to the city bosses that order, and bank-roll these crimes. That's what I've been working on. You said it yourself 'as long as your money holds out'. Well, these guys seem to have an unlimited bank roll, and human resources to boot. How long will your money hold out?"

"I'm okay for a while yet."

The Sheriff paused, then, "On the positive side, you have some very strong allies now. I think Chief Richardson has come around. He doesn't enjoy even thinking about crime from the east coming out here. Your neighboring ranchers are beginning to pressure the Board to take some action, and I have a feeling they'll be looking for someone to blame." Which will be me, of course. I expect to tell them to shut up and listen, or fire me."

George looked across at his friend for a moment, thinking, he was glad to be a friend of Bill Williams, the Sheriff. The past few weeks had been tough. A wake-up call perhaps, to what was coming. He would have toughed it out, of course, but he now felt he had an ally, and maybe there was a light at the end of the tunnel. George said, "I think I know how to keep them off my land. I'll try to keep it clean, but this bunch had better stop messing with this rancher.—I'm all out of patience."

"Be careful. You know it's my sworn duty to uphold the law. I suppose if you had anything planned, legal that is, I would be the first to know?"

Each took a moment to study the other.

"I'm going to protect my ranch. So far, the Law hasn't been able to do that. If I break the law in this effort, so be it. You'll have to catch me at it."

George called Rosey's, "Hi Rosey, how are things? Got anything for me?"

"Hello George. Not yet but I've passed the word around."

"I've changed my mind a bit, make that three instead of one. And Rosey, don't be too fussy."

Rosey asked, "How did your visit to the Harris Ranch go?"

"I do have a problem, but we worked it out for now. This is difficult for me. Betty's feelings are strong and positive, yet she still carries the pain of losing her first love. I understand her concerns. We both know it will be dangerous. Betty is coming to grips with that. It's hard for her. Your concern, Rosey, is noted. Thank you for that."

Rosey was silent for a moment, "Sweetie, if I can help in any way, let me know."

"Thanks, you're a good friend."

Turning away from the phone he said to the Sheriff, "Am I stepping outside the law if I hire a couple of braves from the Tribe and house them in my bunkhouse?"

"I'm not sure, you'll have to ask the Bureau of Indian

Affairs man. He has an office in town."

"Thanks, I think I'll do that. Do you have any comment on this idea, I noticed you sort of twitched when I mentioned the Tribe?"

"We both know my sentiments on that matter. I'll play it strictly by the law however, and that goes for you too."

"I wouldn't expect anything less– Gin."

"Shit, what do I owe you?"

"Ah let's see, it comes to $11.50."

"You always lucky at this?"

* * *

The Sheriff left for town at six a.m. and George headed for the Indian village shortly after. Chief Running Deer listened without comment as George related some of the events unfolding in the County. When George asked for the services of two Tribal members the chief answered, "This is a matter I need to discuss in council. I'll do that, and inform you of our decision." The answer was not unexpected. The Chief would deliberate and confer with the Tribal Elders. They would discuss this matter with their representative to the Bureau of Indian Affairs and, above all, they would protect the interests of their people. George guessed it would take a week, perhaps two, and he needed them now.

It was late in the afternoon when George rode his horse into the ranch yard. Pete came out to meet him and said, "I have some good news, Rosey is sending two people out to be interviewed for those jobs. They'll be here for supper."

"Great. Anything else happen?"

"Nope, nothing ever does in daylight."

"Sounds like our guests are coming now. How's grub coming?"

"Fine, it will be on the table after everyone washes up."

George met the two horsemen as they rode up. One turned out to be a woman, which was a surprise. She bounced off her horse, "Howdy, I'm Mary Ellen, this is Carl.

We're here about a job."

"Hello to you both, I'm George Bentley. Come right in, dinner's on the table."

During dinner there was little talk and when the dishes were cleared away, George said, "Tell me about yourself Mary-Ellen."

"Not much to tell, Mr. Bentley, I left East New York when I was twelve and came to live with my uncle Tom, here in Wyoming. I have been learning about the West ever since. I can cook, ride, shoot and do all those other things that you hire ranch hands for."

"The bunk house is not really set up for coed living."

"I can handle that, just tell your other hands to keep their paws off."

"For tonight, you can stay in the ranch house, I'll sleep in the bunk house with the rest of the pawed types." Turning to the young man waiting to be interviewed he said, "What's your story Carl?"

"I kind of guess, from the conversation, that I really don't fit here. I don't do most of these ranchy type things."

"Do you want a job?"

"Well sure. But I don't want to take your money if I can't do the work."

"You seem to be able to ride OK. Let's try it for a week and see how we get along."

George answered the ringing phone with a curt "Hello." Rosey's voice came on the line.

"George, I just sent one more out. His name is Don Jones. He has a somewhat colorful life style. Some people don't like him, but I do. He's good with guns and cattle.

"Great, here's my heavyweight. Thanks Rosey, I owe you one." George hung up the phone and turned to Pete. "As soon as you get everyone a place to sleep and blankets and stuff, come in and see me."

Pete came up the ranch house stairs, and through the open door with a big grin on his face. "Boss, it sure is good to see some people around here. Now maybe we can get a handle on this thing."

"I don't think much is going to change right away, Pete, These guys won't give up just because we hire a few more ranch hands. They have killed before, and they will try to kill again. So watch out!

"In the morning send Carl into town to pick up some lumber. We need to wall off a part of the bunk house so Mary Ellen can have some privacy. I think the ranch wagon will hold what you need. Start the rest at the jobs they do best. Plan to rotate all of us, at guard duty. Post a schedule some place where we can all read it. That includes me."

The phone rang. Dorothy said, "Mr. Bentley, I have Chief Running Deer on the line."

"This is Red Fox, Grandfather."

"The Council has agreed that two of our people will be made available to you, as you requested. You are warned that physical contact between whites and members of the Tribe must be avoided."

"I assure you of that, Grandfather. How soon will they be here?"

"These two have their own ponies, and could ride over tomorrow morning."

"That will be very helpful, Grandfather. Please extend my thanks to the Council."

"They are very mindful of the many times White Owl came to our defense."

George hung up the receiver, and turned to Pete. "We're getting two men from the Tribe. They should be here some time tomorrow morning. When they arrive, find them space in the bunk house and see that they stow their gear etc. Their names are Sam and Tony. I'll want to see the three of you as soon as you get them settled in.

14 | STRATEGY

Morning found George studying the Richard Bentley ledgers. Of particular interest was the fall payroll. He needed to know more about administrating the ranch when fully staffed, as it would be for the fall round-up. He wanted to find out: when things should be done, who would buy his stock, how negotiations took place, how long it would take, and any and all bits of information he could find. Of course Pete would know most of this, but George preferred to do things on his own as much as possible.

His father had not kept any kind of a diary, but was accurate to a tee when it came to his accounts. George began plotting ranch expenses for the last five years. Something off balance caught his eye. A sudden increase in winter feed costs was easily visible on his set of graphs. Wages were fairly stable. He plotted sales for the corresponding years, and they remained at a constant level. Scratching his head, he reviewed the items in question, and confirmed the anomaly.

A strong "Come in" greeted Pete's knock. He, Sam, and Tony entered. George looked up from the pile of ledgers, and got up and greeted his new employees. "Pete, let's get some coffee in here, we have a lot to talk about." He turned to Sam and Tony, "Welcome to the Arrow-B, it's good to have you here." The three moved over to the dining room table. "Do either or both of you speak in our native tongue?"

"We both attended reservation schools, and were required to do so."

"Did Chief Running Deer tell you what this is about?"

Sam who seemed to be answering for the two of them said, "Our Chief told us only that we were to report to you and be available for some difficult duty."

Pete came with the coffee, and joined them. George said, "This is a private conversation among the four of us. You may share what you hear with only one person. That would be Chief Running Deer. Something else too, Pete is the ranch foreman. That is, he directs all of us in matters of the ranch operation. This includes telling us when and how you do our jobs.

"Sam, you and Tony will be our Eyes and Ears. One of you will be stationed atop Leaning Mesa; the other will stay here at the ranch. I expect you will want to take turns. Nearly the entire Bentley Ranch will be visible from the Mesa. One of you will be stationed up there to watch for intruders onto ranch property. When any unusual activity happens, the lookout will inform the ranch.

"I've given thought to the use of smoke signals, as hayseed as that idea may sound, but I think a better idea would be citizen band radio. Tony, you and I will go into town tomorrow, and hopefully find what we need to do the job. Sam, you'd better go out to the reservation and inform Chief Running Deer of all we have discussed. Pick up what special items and clothing the two of you will need for an extended camp out. I don't want to use the phone, as I want this to be a surprise to the would be rustlers.

"For the purpose of security, when using the new equipment, use the Arapaho tongue only. I doubt that anyone from Chicago will figure that out. Tony, I'll see you in the morning–early."

Alone again, George continued reviewing the ranch records. It took him until noon to finish a set of graphs showing a break-down of ranch expenses covering 1947 through 1952. Most items, such as government land-leasing fees, utilities, and payroll, remained pretty much the same. George could understand seasonal payroll fluctuations, and from these he gained an insight to how many employees he would need throughout the year. Graphs of winter feed costs, general maintenance of property and machinery, however, took a jump in 1950, and climbed again in 1951. The differences were significant, and confirmed his earlier finding.

The cheery clanging sound of Mary Ellen hitting the rusty triangle, hanging outside, brought George and the others to the long table for lunch. He was still thinking dollars when lunch was served. The mashed potatoes, canned peas and pork chops kept everyone busy chewing with not much chance for talk. Mary Ellen kept serving seconds until she, in total frustration, said, "That's it you rummies, there ain't any more."

George beckoned to Pete, "Come on into the office for a minute; I need some help with a problem." The two men got up from the table and went into the office. George looked across his desk piled high with ledgers and papers at his friend. "Maybe you can help me understand why ranch expenses increased so much in the last two years?"

Pete hesitated, then looking embarrassed, said, "I don't think I can help much, Bob always handled everything concerning money. My arithmetic is so bad, I let him handle the numbers. I kept out of things. Is there something wrong?"

"Would there be a reason why our winter feed bill should double over the last two years?"

"None that I can think of. Bob ordered all the feed and other stuff."

"And I suppose he also went into town, picked up and paid for or charged things?"

"Except when your Dad did it."

"Dad never told you why Bob left?"

"You know how close mouthed he was."

"Yeah, I know, which reminds me, I see we carried one more rider throughout the year than we had with just you, and Bob. Do you know why he cut back?"

"Other than that your Dad was quite thrifty, and whenever someone left he didn't rush to hire someone else."

"OK Pete, do you suppose Bob could have been siphoning money off the ranch accounts somehow, and Dad caught him at it and that's why he got fired?"

"Now that you mention it, I reckon it could have happened that way. I'd have to rule out him killing Dick though. I couldn't believe that."

"All right, I know now, there was something going on starting a year or so ago. I guess I won't know the answer until we talk with Bob. We have a ranch to run, rustlers to deal with, and a serious enemy somewhere out there. We'd better get on with it."

Pete got up to leave. He was quiet and somber looking. He turned and looked his boss in the eye. "Bob was never a mixer. He liked poker, and didn't seem to mind if he lost. He took his vacations somewhere to the west of here. Once I took him to the airport and he took a plane to Reno, Nevada. None of us could get very close to him."

"Thanks Pete."

The sign on the front of the Glencoe War Surplus store boasted: "Everything from battleships to bullets." When George and Tony entered they had to walk around a Navy drop boat to reach the counter, and George laughed at the reference. The aisles were about two feet wide, so one had to move sideways to pass through. Items of every conceivable nature filled shelves from floor to ceiling. The proprietor came out of a three by four foot office and said a cheery "Hello, when you find what you want, you can come over here and pay for it," all the time eyeing Tony as if he were looking at some kind of an un-human being.

George looked down at the 5 foot 4 inch storeowner and said, "Do you have a problem with the way we look?" The voice was commanding. It came from an awfully big man, and the storeowner selected discretion to be in order at this point.

"No, no not at all, what can I help you find?"

"Do you have any citizen band radio equipment?"

"Third aisle, top shelf, left side."

The two men left the store with what they needed, and headed for the radio store in town. The store owner was cordial, and said, "What can I do for you?"

George said, "I need some extra batteries, and some advice and information. The storeowner of your War Surplus store where I bought this didn't seem to know anything.

The young man chuckled, "He doesn't. I'll help you any way I can. What do you need to know?"

"Well for one, how much battery will I need to operate two CB's for say, two weeks."

The technician did some calculations, and said, "Let's say you used this 1 hour a day, the batteries should last for a month. Two hours, two weeks. Call that an educated guess."

"That suits me fine. Now show us how it works."

George and Tony left the radio store and went to the Bureau of Mines office. Here they picked up some maps of the county. The topographical map of the area around Walnut clearly showed the major landmarks, including both Leaning Mesa and Portal Mesa.

Their next stop was the Dodge dealership. It took George all of fifteen minutes to decide on what he wanted. Ordering from a catalogue, he groaned when informed there was a 30 day wait on delivery. "I know it's not your fault, but does everything happen tomorrow around here?"

"If it would help, I can supply you with a loaner."

"That would help things a lot. Can I have it today?"

"It'll be ready shortly."

The reservation was situated on Butte Creek and was shielded from Long Valley by Leaning Mesa. The Tribal council building dominated the residence and school buildings and that's where Sam found Chief Running Deer in discussion with several of the Tribal Elders. He fidgeted around the outside of the group, waiting to be recognized and finally summed up his courage and interrupted the proceedings. Speaking in the Arapaho tongue, he informed his Chief that he must see him alone, and that he had a message from his grandson, Red Fox. He was instructed to sit with patience until the council meeting was over. In time, Sam was admitted to a private audience with Chief Running Deer.

"Sam, it is not usual to interrupt a council meeting, what was so important that caused you to do so?"

"I have an important message from Red Fox."

"And what is that message?"

"Red Fox wants you to know that Tony or myself will be camping at the top of Leaning Mesa. The other of us will remain below at the ranch. We will talk to each other by radio. He also instructed me to use only the Arapaho tongue, no English."

"Did you remind him that the upper reaches of Leaning Mesa contain Tribal artifacts and they are sacred to our Nation?"

"No, I did not."

"Well do so when you see him next."

The Chief paused, looking at Sam intently then smiled and said, "This should be interesting, you will have to live in the old ways for a period of time. Is there anything else I should know?"

"Red Fox made it clear that no one was to know of this plan. No one at all. He also asked me to select those items I would need for a two to three week stay in the wilderness of Leaning Mesa."

"Tony, you are to do as Red Fox has chosen. You are to consider him as a member of our Tribe. Remember, however, there is to be no physical contact with the white folks. You will inform Red Fox that I agree with his plan. Also be careful not to disturb our sacred burial places in the mountains.

"Leave here in the darkness of night. Today I will select those items you will need for such a stay in the mountains. They will be ready for you when you leave tonight."

* * *

Pete had trouble with Mary Ellen. Not putting her on the guard duty list was a mistake, and she told him so. In fact she said, "If you want breakfast tomorrow morning, my name better be on that list."

Pete, thinking dark negative thoughts about a new ranch hand telling him how to ram rod, looked into two blazing eyes, and remembered the savory aroma of those pork chops, "Oh, I didn't think you needed the extra duty, with the early breakfast and all; but if you really need to do this thing, you can start us off tonight."

That's how come Mary Ellen was out front, wrapped in a blanket, with Charlie sort of snoring at her feet at two a.m. that night. She held a rifle across her knees, and a clapper to hit the rusty triangle if need be. She had calmed down, and accepted Pete's explanation. "Nobody was going to coddle her. She would not be treated like some kind of a soft female from the city." Then all hell broke loose: She heard the screeching of brakes, metal crunching, and angry men's voices coming across the night air, loud and clear. Charlie produced a series of barks at about 300 per minute, and at the same time, Mary Ellen started rapping on the triangle. The Arrow—B came to life.

15 | AMBUSH

Mary Ellen was in the Rusty Bucket with the motor running when George came out the door, rifle in hand. He jumped in and they headed for the ranch entrance gate. Ahead they could see headlights speeding north. A second set held firm at the gate. lighting a short strip on the ranch road. They approached the car cautiously. The vehicle, a 1950 Chrysler Sedan had no front wheels, the hood lying flat to the ground. One passenger sat in the front right side. He was slumped over with his head resting on the dashboard. George reached in through the open window placing his index finger on the injured man and found pulse. "We'd better get this man to a hospital fast. I think he suffered a concussion when his head hit the windshield. There's no use going after that other vehicle, by the time we get this wreck out of the way, they'll be long gone." George reached in and checked the unconscious man for weapons. He removed a hand gun, then turned to Mary Ellen and said, "Mary Ellen, stay with this guy. I'll go call Doc Morrison. You better hold your rifle on him, just in case he wakes up or something. These are nasty people we're dealing with, watch out."

Heading back to the ranch George slowed to talk to Pete driving the ranch wagon. "Boss, how'd you get up here so fast?"

"Mary Ellen was ready for me. I'm calling Doc Morrison; there's an injured man up ahead. Stay with Mary Ellen, and see if you can figure how to get our gate cleared. Oh, and watch that prisoner. He might come to life or something."

Pete grinned and said, "It worked eh?"

"Just like we planned."

"Carl was talking to the Sheriff when I left. He should be here in a while."

Back at the ranch house, George called Doctor Morrison, who was grumpy from Grumpville. Walnut's only doctor finally settled down and said, "I just wish that someone would get sick or have a baby sometime other than 2 a.m. I guess I can be out there in half an hour. In the meantime, lay the patient with his head slightly lower than his feet. Keep him warm and pray."

George would do what the doctor suggested, but wasn't so sure about the pray bit, as there was a five gallon can of gasoline in the back of the disabled vehicle obviously to be used on his spread. He returned to the crash scene, and noted to the others, "This makes me real mad. I feel bad about this injured man, but he asked for it. By now, the gangsters that are bank rolling this thing must be paying real high prices. They should be running out of street bums by now. "Okay, let's go to work. Someone make a soft level place for our would be arsonist. Someone else get some blankets from the ranch, and then we need to move this wreck out of the way."

The Sheriff and Deputy Roberts arrived, followed by Doc Morrison. The Sheriff said, "Jeesh, you did a number on that car." He reached in and pulled out the gasoline container. You know this bunch is nasty. The supervisors better listen this time. If something bad is allowed to happen, they'll face some very angry ranchers. By the way, I've had several people call and offer their support."

George said, "That's nice, I've always felt good about my neighbors, and this is very welcome. I hope, however, that they don't have to get into this mess. It really is my problem. This won't work a second time, I guess I'll have to go to plan B."

The Sheriff shuddered a bit and said, I'm afraid to ask what Plan B is. I need an invitation to spend a few nights at the Arrow—B. Some of the things I hear around here frighten me."

"You got it."

Doc Morrison went directly to the unconscious man, took a fast look, and said, "We need to get this man to the hospital fast."

The Sheriff said, "It's also got to be a lock-up hospital."

"That's your problem, mine is to keep him alive. He needs to be transported by ambulance to the hospital in Glencoe."

George interrupted, "Let's get to the ranch and make some phone calls. He turned to Don Jones, "Stay here and guard this idiot. We'll be back as soon as possible. In case you haven't heard, we are famous for losing people who get in jail. Don't let anything happen to this one. We need him."

The Sheriff placed a call to Chief Richardson of the Wyoming State Police. The Chief was not very friendly at first, but who is at 3 a.m. on any morning.

"Chief, this is Bill Williams, sorry to wake you but I have a situation out here that I need your help with. This is another chapter in the Richard Bentley case. I have a prisoner who is unconscious, and needs to be in the hospital. He was injured when he tried to torch George Bentley's ranch. I want this man kept alive, and that means 24-hour guard duty. His so-called friends will shoot him dead in a second if they can. Now chief, we need to question this man. Obviously not practical at this time, we'll have to wait and hope that he regains consciousness, and soon."

"Do you have a doctor out there?"

"Doc Morrison's with him now. Will you need to talk with Doc?"

"No Bill, what I need is some sleep. I'll get on this, first thing in the morning. I understand what you're into. Call me when you have some answers or when you need anything else."

"Thanks. I'll direct the ambulance to report to you, they should be there in about three hours." Bill hung up the receiver, and said to George. "It's all set up for tomorrow morning. I'll take the prisoner myself."

George edged the Sheriff away from the others present and said, "This much is clear, by the time that ambulance gets here, the whole world will know that this man is alive. He won't be allowed to reach Glencoe if you don't have lots of firepower along. I can loan you Don Jones, and you better take Roberts too."

The Sheriff knew that George was right. One more screw-up of the law, and he would rightfully be fired. Besides, when it came to situations involving firearms, more is always better than less. "I sure agree with that thought. I would rather have you along than either or both of those two, but that can't be. You have to stay here."

Chief Richardson hung up the phone, and turned out the light. Sleep eluded him as the impact of what was happening began to sink in. This department had screwed up once over this Bentley thing, and he sure didn't want a repeat. He got back out of bed and called the Sergeant on duty. "This is Chief Richardson, Sergeant, I want two squad cars, with two well-armed officers in each ready in half an hour at the station."

"OK Chief, who should I call?"

"I don't give a shit who or where you get them. You figure that out, and fast."

"Yes Sir."

The Chief threw some clothes on, said a fast goodbye to Betsy, his wife, and rushed out the door. He pulled up to the station about the same time as three officers arrived. "Where in hell is the other one?" He looked at the duty officer, who picked up the phone to find out. The soft feminine voice that answered said, "He's in the shower, he should be there in thirty minutes."

The Chief grabbed the phone, "Listen this is the Chief, if he isn't here in ten minutes he's fired." He turned to the three officers standing by and said, "Two of you head down highway 16 to Walnut and meet the ambulance coming north. Give escort all the way to the hospital. When you get there, back up will be waiting. Be prepared, there may be gunfire. The injured man is to be protected. He also may come to, and be dangerous. Now take off."

The fourth officer came, still putting clothes on, The Chief said, "You two get on the highway to Walnut. Set up some place a few miles outside of town along the road. Stop all vehicles until the ambulance comes, then help escort to the hospital. Now be aware, if you have trouble, it'll be real. We're dealing with killers."

It was just on five-thirty when the ambulance arrived at the Arrow—B. The still unconscious suspect was placed aboard, and Don Jones climbed in with him. The Sheriff and deputy Roberts rode in the Sheriff's pickup. The two vehicles, with the ambulance leading, headed for Glencoe. About half way to town, the first squad car met the oncoming ambulance, and took lead position in the caravan. In the meantime squad car number two found a spot about three miles out of town. They parked in plain sight with lights flashing, lit some flares, and waited. The half-light of daybreak revealed the long lonely road. The rising sun caught the tops of the mountains in the west. The two men waited in a silent world.

It came as a pesky, almost not there, buzz, like that of a housefly in your bedroom at night. Then it mellowed to a far away roar. The sound of an approaching vehicle. One of the officers contacted headquarters. And suddenly they were there. Gunfire sputtered, the officers sought shelter. The vehicle sped past spraying bullets at the tires of the squad car. The two officers stood up, and fired their rifles after the retreating vehicle, with no noticeable effect. They turned to their squad car, and found it totally disabled. They called headquarters.

Chief Richardson picked up the phone on his desk, listened to the police report coming from the radio room. "Holy crap, get hold of car number two and tell them what happened. In the meantime this station is on alert. I want all officers to report in as of now. Hold it, I'll talk to them myself. Get em on the line, I 'll be right down."

The Chief ran down to the radio room, took the mike from the operator. "This is the Chief, you heard?"

"Yeah, we heard. We'll be ready."

"Stop the caravan. Get the Sheriff up on the radio fast. I want to talk to him."

The Sheriff came on the radio. "What's the problem Chief?"

"Bill, all hell is goin' to break loose down there shortly. Here's the situation. A car full of Chicago racketeer types with automatic weapons are headed your way. Take charge. Do what you have to keep everybody alive. I'll send out more back up. Put that officer back on."

"I'm here, Chief."

"The Sheriff is in charge out there. Do what he tells you, and watch out. These guys will be shooting when they get there."

"I got it, Chief."

The Sheriff considered his forces. One city police vehicle, with two officers armed with one repeating rifle, a shotgun and two handguns. One ambulance, containing the injured man plus a well-armed Don Jones. He and Roberts each had repeating rifles, and he wore his revolver. That seemed like a lot of firepower, but would it keep people alive when a speeding vehicle was spewing bullets from automatic weapons. The two officers in the other vehicle were lucky. No one got killed. One thing was clear: they were better off stopped than moving.

Up ahead the road ascended over a low hill. The Sheriff chose a spot just below the crest of the hill to set up his forces. He gave orders quickly, allowing no objections.

"Place the injured man on his stretcher, out of the ambulance, on the ground behind whatever cover you can find. I want the ambulance on the west side of the road, empty. The patrol car and my pick-up on the other side of the road." To the ambulance driver he said, "You get yourself out of sight someplace. Stay close to the injured man. Everyone else take cover behind the patrol car and my pickup. We don't have much time. Do it!"

The Sheriff had everyone in position just in time to hear the far off sound of a speeding vehicle, unmistakable in an otherwise soundless morning, alerting the waiting law enforcement party of the oncoming car. It seemed forever before the top of the vehicle showed above the crest of the hill. It came, fast and deliberate. The car slowed, the occupants opened fire on the ambulance, ripping into the side of the vehicle with a vicious snarl of metal against metal, then sped on.

Don Jones was the first to react, aiming for the gas tank as the car sped by, he fired his rifle, pumping out six fast shots before the vehicle was out of range. The car swerved, spewing gasoline over the road, then caught on fire, and careened down the hill. The gas tank blew with a roar. A huge orange ball of fire shot skyward.

The men covered their faces and eyes to shield them from the intense heat, but the momentum of the burning vehicle soon carried it away.

Sheriff Bill Williams was not unused to gunfire. He had not seen anything like this. "Holy Christ, Don, you sure did a number on that car. I doubt if anyone's still alive."

"You told me they'd come a shootin'. I never heard a waitin 'til you got shot at."

The burning remains of the vehicle were too hot to go near. One of the officers got on the radio to his boss, "Chief, you better talk to the Sheriff."

"Chief, we have one burning vehicle, condition of occupants likely dead. It looks like there will be three bodies when the fire subsides. All of our personnel, including the patient are okay."

"Jesus, when will you be starting for the hospital? I won't even ask how you did this."

The Sheriff looked at Don reloading his rifle. "I don't know if the ambulance is even drivable. If not we'll have to transport the patient in my pickup. One way or another we should be there in forty-five minutes. I think our troubles are over for the day.

"We'll be ready. Ten Four."

The Sheriff turned to Don. "That's the fastest bit o shootin I've ever seen. Anything special about that rifle?"

"Well yeah, I sort o tinkered with it a bit. When they're new, they don't work to suit me."

The two police officers walked down to the burning car and confirmed that there were three bodies inside. The caravan, minus the ambulance, had an uneventful trip to the hospital. The Wyoming State Police took over the custody of the unconscious suspect, and arranged for the disposition of the burnt-out car and bodies.

Sitting in Chief Richardson's office, the Sheriff was put through to the Arrow—B. "Hello–George?"

"Howdy Bill, did you make it?"

"Just as planned, ah–with the help of Don."

"You want to expand on that?"

"Nah, your troubles are over for the day, I'll fill in the details when I see you."

"When will that be?"

"How about Rosey's in a couple of hours?"

"Sure, I'll be there."

16 | JOAN'S IN TOWN

Rosey was picking up the breakfast mess, filling sugar bowls, salt cellars and the like, when a slick looking roadster stopped in front of the cafe. She peered out through the curtains, thinking what a beautiful girl. Two people got out of the car and came into the diner. Rosey looked into two blue gray eyes that smiled, and trusted. "I'm just cleaning up the breakfast things, and lunch won't be ready for two hours."

The girl, who looked in her early twenties, sat down on a bar stool and said, "That's okay. I can come back at lunchtime. This is Walnut, Wyoming, isn't it?"

"The one and only. You look a long way from home."

"I am. My home's in Vermont." She turned to her companion and said, "Well, this is it. Thanks for the lift. Bye. The two young people embraced. She gave him a peck of a kiss. "Good luck to you."

The young man went out to the car, pulled two suitcases out of the rumble seat and brought them into the diner. He smiled and said, "Bye-bye Joan, give my best to George." He went out the door, climbed into his car, and drove off.

The young woman moved her suitcases out of the way, and said, "My name is Joan LaCross, and I'm looking for the

Arrow—B Ranch. I take it you're Rosey?"

"I sure am. Have a seat while I finish cleaning up from breakfast. Want some coffee? It's just fresh. I made it for me–to go on."

"Thanks, coffee sounds great. It's good to sit down on something that doesn't move for a change. You must know George Bentley, he told me you were his favorite person from home, and to be sure and see you if ever I came out this way."

"Comes in here all the time." Joan had that rare simple beauty that made a person stare, and Rosey did just that. She put down her sugar bowl, and sat across from Joan. "George is a special person around here. We all like him very much. Tell me, where did you two meet?"

Joan needed someone to talk to. George wrote a short story around Rosey, a western cafe owner, for a class assignment. The subject for the story sat across from her. Joan read that story in the school journal. It was like knowing a person long before you meet. She was not disappointed at what she saw. "You know Rosey, I've looked forward to meeting you for a long time–we went to the same college. I met him almost five years ago.

"When he left college he kind of stepped out of my life. I'm not sure whether it was because of all the trouble at the ranch, or that he didn't feel he wanted to have me in his life any more. That's why I'm here. I need to know."

Rosey, making full eye contact, felt the sincerity of this young person. However she responded, it must be with the truth, and it must not interfere. The obvious conflict between Betty, her best friend, and this lovely person sitting across from her, was troubling. "Has George told you any of the details of the events happening here?"

"Not really. His letters are rare, and he doesn't say anything about the dangerous stuff. I finally subscribed to the Glencoe Weekly Journal. That helped a little, but it didn't get close enough to the action to tell me much."

"Yes, that's George all right." Rosey paused "You must

be in love with him to come all the way out here to see him. Considering this is a sort of nothing spot, and not even on most maps, you're kinda gutsy for a city girl."

"I've never met anyone like you Rosey. In the space of just a few minutes, you've made me say things I wouldn't say to someone I've known all my life. Yes, I'm in love with him, damn it. He's nearly driven me crazy, not writing or calling me hardly."

Rosey got up to pour the coffee. She busied herself with little things: making toast, bringing out the jam and butter, while she thought of the dilemma facing her. Finally she sat down again. "George is faced with a determined enemy, who wants to take over his ranch. He has been pistol whipped, and shot at. Now he has someone trying to rustle cattle from his spread. Last week they tried to burn him out. Maybe that's why you haven't heard from him much."

"Wow, you have some real nasties out here in Wyoming. It sounds a lot like a Western movie. George is really in a lot of danger then? Can't the police do anything?"

"I guess things are different here than where you come from. Our Sheriff has some 12,000 square miles to police. When there is trouble, the ranchers usually help out. By the way, where did you plan to spend the night?"

"I planned on calling George. How far away is the ranch?"

"About twenty miles. And there are no taxis. Why don't you stay with me for tonight? You can call George now, and make arrangements for tomorrow. Go ahead and use my phone."

"That's too much trouble for you. Aren't there any hotels here?"

"Not really, this town is for ranchers and miners. We don't have visitors like yourself more than once or twice a year."

"Sure you don't mind?"

"I'd like the company. You can use my phone. Just pick up the receiver, and ask Dorothy for the Arrow—B."

"Thanks Rosey."

Joan placed the call. A winded female voice answered, "Hello, this is Mary Ellen at the Arrow—B."

"May I speak to George Bentley please?"

"He's out on the range somewhere, can I have him call you?"

"Please do. This is Joan LaCross, and I'm at Rosey's Cafe." She hung up the receiver. Joan, with a blank look on her face, turned to Rosey. "Well, I might as well make myself useful. Can I help? Who's Mary Ellen?"

"Sure honey, I'll get you an apron." Rosey sensed the young woman's concern, and empathized. "Mary Ellen works for the Arrow—B. She does the cooking, and a whole bunch of other things. You'll like her." Rosey got up and brought coffee and toast to the table. She studied the woman sitting across from her. Joan wore no cosmetics, she didn't need any. Her hair hung carefree, just touching the top of her shoulders. A short sleeved blouse of fine cotton, unbuttoned down a ways, revealed much of her neck and just a bit of her breasts. Rosey saw eyes, open and innocent. They said it all. This person was hurting pretty bad. "Where do your folks live?"

"Northern Vermont. They live on a farm. My family has lived there for over a hundred years. It's kind of James Fenimore Cooper country. How long have you known George?"

"His mother, White Dove, brought him here when he was a week old."

"He's never told me any of these interesting things. In five years, all I was able to find out was that he lived on a ranch. I didn't even know what state it was in until his father died."

Rosey laughed, "Let's get started on the lunch. I have help coming in at noon. The breakfast trade is not that great, but the lunch business is good. I'm not sure if people come in here for my cooking or the gossip. This is the town gossip center. If someone wants to spread a rumor, or hear one, they come here."

"Well, it must be your cooking. According to George, you are the best in the West."

Lunch time came and Joan helped where she could. George hadn't called by three o'clock, so she wandered down Main Street, stopping in the general store for a look around. She took her time, and walked the full length of the street, finding even the blacksmith shop interesting. She ended up in the public library, located in the Sheriff's office building which also contained the jail. The librarian introduced herself as Peggy. Book checkout was on the honor system, and residents, ranchers and miners simply picked out their selection, signed the checkout card and left. Joan selected a romance, sat down and started to read.

Rosey was getting ready for her dinner crowd when Betty walked in. Startled, she dropped her pitcher of iced tea. It made a terrible tinkling, clattering, noise, and a mess on the floor.

Betty asked, "Are you all right Rosey, you look like you've seen a ghost or something?"

"Yeah, I'm fine. I don't know what made me do that. Must have something on my mind. Staying for dinner?"

"Can't stay. I picked up some medicine from the Vet. Dad's waiting to dose a sick cow. Anything new?"

Rosey was trying to form an answer to that question, when, mercifully, the phone rang. She leaned over the counter and retrieved the receiver from its cradle. "Hello, this is Rosey."

"Hi, Rosey. Someone called from there. I was to call back?"

"That can wait. Betty's here. Want to talk to her?"

"Put her on."

"Hi George. I don't see much of you these days. Can we get together soon?"

"I miss you too Sweetheart. It seems that running a ranch is sort of a busy job."

"Damn it George, after we're married you'll have to share

your life with me. No, I've got that wrong. Before we get married you'll have to learn to share your life with me." Her eyes flashed at the telephone she held in her hand. "You make me feel real wanted.

"I hear about that car with the injured man, the truck burning, the ambulance incident, all from someone else. You'd think I'd be the first to know what's going on with the man I want to marry. I'm usually the last. If you keep protecting me from every little thing that happens around here, it'll be a long wait for our next date. All I get from you is running a ranch is a busy job."

"Okay Betty, simmer down. What do you want to know?"

Betty looked hard at Rosey. She said to the phone, "George, I just want to be part of your life. Don't leave me out."

"Betty, you are my life. Things just seem to happen so fast out here, that I don't seem to have time to phone even."

"Now you tell me you don't have time to phone me. Keep it up George. You're doing great."

"Okay, I'm sorry I didn't mean that. When can I see you, or are you too mad for that even?"

"Can you come over for dinner tonight?"

"I have to meet with the Sheriff at four. Soon as I'm through there I'll come on over."

Betty hung up the phone, and grimaced at Rosey, "That man is terrible. He treats me like I'm a soft city girl that needs protection or something. I finally found out about that hit on the head and the week in the desert tracking down the culprits that did it. From someone else, of course. He drives me batty with this modesty stuff. I wonder if it will be this way after we're married."

"That's kind of newsy you know. Did he actually propose?"

"Yeah, sort of. He talks about our future life together. I think he won't pop the question until he gets this Arrow—B trouble settled, and he has resolved the mystery of his father's death."

"Betty, don't kid yourself, this guy's in love with you. Rosey took Betty's hand, looking into her moist eyes, and said, "That's the way George is. You won't be able to change that."

Betty touched the corner of each of her eyes with a napkin she pulled from a holder sitting on the counter. "I gotta go. Thanks for listening. Be talking to you soon. Bye."

Ten minutes after Betty walked out the door, Joan walked in. "Gosh, what a quaint little town you work in. Do you live here too?"

"All my life. Oh, George called from the Arrow—B. He's home now, why don't you call him?

"Joan reached across the counter, and lifted the receiver from its cradle. Three thousand miles and nearly four months had separated her from her man. Now that the moment was upon her, she was dizzy with anticipation. Butterflies flopped their way around her middle, and she said in a shaky voice, "Dorothy, will you get me the Arrow—B please."

"Sure Honey, hang on a minute."

"Hello George, this is Joan. I'm in Walnut."

George recognized Joan's soft pleasant voice. He hesitated a moment. "Hello yourself. I thought you were to let me know when you were coming?"

This was not the kind of reception Joan expected "This was an all of a sudden thing. I had fifteen minutes to pack, and we were on our way."

"Are you, at Rosey's?"

"Yeah, and she asked me to spend the night here."

"Joan, this is a bit of a dilemma. The ranch is not a safe place to be right now. The nearest motel is 85 miles away.– Didn't you get my letter?"

"Sure. I got your letter. You didn't say not to come, and I'm willing to take whatever risk there is. I need to be near you."

"It'll be nice to see you too. I'll drive in to Walnut tomorrow and meet you at Rosey's. She's a wonderful person to be with. Enjoy."

"She sure is. I can see why you used to talk about her so much. What time can I expect you tomorrow?"

"Around eight, I guess. We can have breakfast together. Good night Joan, I'll see you in the morning." George hung up the phone. He sat in thought.

Pete's firm knock on the door interrupted his thoughts [mostly about that last phone call]. "Come in."

"Hi. We just received our first message from Sam. He's on top of Leaning Mesa, as you planned. Tony informs me that everything is set up. Radios are working fine. Visibility from the mesa is great. He can see almost the whole valley. They'll both sleep days, and do duty after dark."

"Tony can do double duty then. I guess you'll have him act as night shift guard, while he listens for a call from Sam?"

"I'm counting on it. Now maybe the rest of us can get more sleep. Have you heard from the ambulance?"

"Yep. The prisoner's all tucked in to a hospital bed, with 24-hour guard. Pete, the Sheriff will be here around four. When I'm through talking to Bill, I'm heading for the Harris Ranch for dinner. Keep me informed."

"Okay Boss."

Pete went out the door, and George went back to his reflections. He contemplated telling Betty right off about Joan–she's already mad at me, maybe I'd better wait for things to calm down a bit. I suppose Betty'll want me to explain why I didn't say something three months ago? But then, if she found out that a former girl friend of mine is in town, from someone else–How did I get into this mess?

When the Sheriff and Don arrived at the Arrow—B, they brought George up to date on the ambulance trip to the hospital. The Sheriff told of rapid-fire weapons spraying bullets from a speeding vehicle into the ambulance, and police cars.

George commented, "We're lucky none of you was killed. That's mean stuff."

The Sheriff said, "These were modern versions of the

Tommy Gun of gangster fame. Don took less than half a second to fire his weapon, who knows what that is, at the fleeing car. He was accurate, fast, and deadly. If it weren't for him, these vermin would have returned and wiped us out." The Sheriff shuddered, "He saved our necks."

He continued, "George, at last count, five people are dead, and maybe six. The seventh is in the hospital and may die. This kind of thing doesn't happen unless the stakes are very high. Someone, maybe from Chicago, is putting up big bucks to get what they want. Frankly, I don't know how to stop it. I'm filing my report with the County Board tomorrow in person. I'm asking for four additional deputies, and two patrol cars. The trouble is, I don't have a clue as to what to do with them, if I get 'em. The area we have to police is too big."

George nodded, "I think you guys did a great job. These bums took the chance and paid the price. You all fired your weapons in self-defense." George paused, and looked intently at the Sheriff. "Maybe I can help. I think I know a way to stay ahead of them. I can give you early warning on anyone entering the county at night. Can you take it from there with the four deputies?"

George went to his desk, picked up a map, and spread it out. "Bill, here's a map of the county. Notice the grid lines, and how they are numbered. There are two more maps the same as this one, which is yours. I will inform you of any activity going on, and give you a grid number telling you just where the activity is."

"Now, if you can do that–I'll take it from there. How are you going to do this?"

"Yours is not to know. I guarantee it's legal."

"When do you intend to start this legal thing, that I can't know about?"

"Tonight."

The Sheriff got up, folded his new map, and headed for the door. "Be careful–I'll be ready to move when you call."

"Right. As soon as we get word of trouble, you'll be

called."

Alone again, George returned to thinking about the Joan/Betty dilemma. This time he made up his mind to tell Betty tonight. He climbed into the Rusty Bucket and headed for the Harris Ranch.

Steve Harris liked George from the start. When Betty owned up to being in love with George, he was delighted. He knew his daughter and her moods pretty well, and George seemed to make her blossom. When she got back from her trip into town, she handed over the mail and a bottle of medicine to her Dad, hardly even seeing him, and with only an abstract Hi. Steve watched her put on an apron, and start the dinner in silence.

"Okay. What is it?"

Betty turned her head, and looked at her father. Her eyes were glistening with denied tears. "Oh, that man of mine is impossible. Is there something in the rules that says a man can't share his problems with his woman? By the way, he's coming over to dinner tonight."

"That's nice. You can tell him all this to his face."

"I guess I kinda did. He called Rosey, and asked to talk to me."

"So what did you tell him?"

"Only that it might be a long wait for our next date.

"That was a bitchy thing to do."

"I guess I shouldn't expect any sympathy from either of you two men. You'd stick together no matter what."

Betty was standing on the front porch when George drove up. "I saw your headlights turn into our road. I'm glad you're here." She tilted her head and moved into his arms. Their embrace was long and tender. "Dinner's about ready, I just have to take it out of the oven. Go sit down. I'll call Dad."

During dinner George related recent events around the Arrow—B. He wasn't very good at it and knew it.

Betty asked, "Anything else happen that I should know about?"

George had planned to tell Betty about Joan, but not until they were alone.

"Only that the locals are fed up to their chins with the violence that's going on. I'm beginning to find a friend here and there–Oh yes, a friend of mine from college showed up in Walnut today."

Betty looked up from her dinner, "Where is he now, at the ranch?"

"Ah no, she's staying with Rosey tonight."

"Oh, it's a girl friend?"

"Well, she was."

"How much of a girl friend?"

Steve Harris got up from the table, "I have to check on a lame horse." He hurried out the door.

Betty was beginning to enjoy George's discomfort. "It doesn't seem very hospitable of you, not to invite her to the ranch. Why didn't you ask her to come out with you tonight. We could have met."

"I don't think that's very funny."

"Didn't you know she was coming?"

"Yes I knew, I tried to tell her not to come. She came anyway. Her name is Joan."

"So, how many letters have you two been writing to each other. How many calls on the phone?"

"Betty, you're being unfair."

"I know it. I just can't help myself. I'm sorry." Betty smiled. Her man had agonized over how to tell her of a former love. She got up and came over to him. Sitting on his knees, she kissed him. "Now tell me about the ambulance trip."

Steve chose that moment to rejoin Betty and George at the table. "Stay for the night George?"

"I'd like that, but I have something going that should help the Law do its job. As you know, our esteemed Sheriff has been short of enough personnel to do much, or unlucky or something. I need to be at the ranch, particularly at night. Do you mind if I keep Spike for a while longer?"

"Not at all, I'd be over there myself if I could leave here."

"Thanks for that Steve. I'd better start for home."

Betty made no attempt to leave George's knees. She had her arms around his neck, "Go on about the ambulance ride."

"This one was our Sheriff's show. He planned and executed a strategy that was successful. Don Jones did the rest. Unfortunately, three of the four criminals died. The other is in the hospital. Also Chief Richardson was very cooperative."

"That's it? You weren't there?"

George said, with a smile on his face, "No, dammit, I missed this one."

Betty shuddered. "I wish you wouldn't make jokes like this. I can't stand the thought of something happening to you."

George drove to the ranch, still wondering what to do with Joan. She couldn't stay long with Rosey. He concluded that a trip to Walnut to try to figure something out was a must.

Together with Betty again, was a wonderfully warm happening in spite of her barbed remarks about Joan [being here]. Her presence stayed in his mind. Betty was love itself. Special in his life. To be nurtured, and held, gently but positively. An integral part of his existence.

17 | FALSE ALARM

Somewhere in the South Side of Chicago, the leaders of the illicit Black Mariah Gang gathered to review family business activities. Among the items discussed was that of the acquisition of some Wyoming properties. The gathering of sixteen family members was, as usual, called by Frank, who by seniority and succession was the 'Top Banana'.

After some family matters, such as an upcoming wedding, were dispensed with, Frank turned to his son, "Okay Junior, tell us once again, this man Bentley won't sell. He has managed to make all of us look like idiots, and you can't find someone to handle him. By now he should be dead. Can't you do anything right?"

Junior, stared hard at his Father, "Somehow he managed to avoid everything we threw at him. So far, we've lost the two dummies sent out to kill him last month, another was killed when we tried to set the ranch on fire, and three more died when we tried again. There's a seventh man in the hospital in a coma. God help us if he wakes up. We can't get near him, they have cops all over the place."

Frank screamed, "You have an unlimited bank account. Doesn't anybody want money?"

"I'm telling you Papa, this guy's tough. He lived through a

hit on the head that would have killed a three hundred pound gorilla, crawled for forty miles in the desert sun without water to get at our boys, stole their truck and motorcycle, then left them for the Sheriff to pick up. They were armed, and he wasn't. He's got two eyes in back of his head, and misses nothing. Now I'm having trouble finding anyone to go out there."

"Junior, you haven't learned a thing in twenty-four years. If you want to get a job done, do it yourself. You don't seem to be able to pick someone with intelligence to do it. I want this man dead."

The young man glared at his Father with hate in his eyes. "Alone?"

"No, I've got a couple of hit men in mind. They'll keep you from running away. Go get the job done!"

The discussion continued. One senior member of the syndicate said, "This is getting expensive. I think we should reexamine our needs here."

Frank gave a black look at the person who dared question his authority, "Nobody, but nobody is going to do this to us. I don't see why it's so difficult to send a man out there to hide in the bushes and shoot 'im as he rides by. If I didn't have a bunch of idiots working for me, the job would have been finished three months ago. This organization needs that ranch to further our interests and complete our master plan. Once we get Bentley out of there, the rest will be easy."

Junior shifted his slight body to an upright position, "Papa, how about sending Muscles out there? He'd love killing this one."

"That's a tempting idea. Breaking Bentley's neck would suit me fine. However, we can't take a chance. This hit must be for sure, and soon."

* * *

The County Board of Supervisors met on Monday morning in the Sheriff's office. Two of the members had arrived early to review the condition of the recently repaired office and jail. They were both from nearby ranches, and at this time of year, getting ready for fall round-up and making preparations for the cold of winter on the range.

They were impatient to get this meeting over, and return to their ranches. They also didn't like spending taxpayer money for repairing the damaged sheriff's office and jail. In short, they expected their elected Sheriff to handle this sort of thing. The other three members of the Board arrived, and they were not exactly happy about what was going on either.

The meeting came to order after coffee and doughnuts, courtesy of Rosey's Cafe, with Charlie Adams, a local rancher, presiding. After the minutes of the last meeting were read, the chairman noted the request for additional personnel in the sheriff's office. "We took no action on this item last month, and the problem didn't go away." He poured himself another cup of coffee, "Bill, give us a status report."

The Sheriff stood and said, "In order to understand what's going on, I'll take you back to last May. One of our long time residents was murdered. Subsequently, an anonymous offer to buy the Arrow—B was made. The offer came through Jones Realty, and was for an amount of one million dollars, twice the known value of the ranch. The offer was refused. Then the new owner of the Arrow—B, George Bentley, was viciously attacked. We apprehended the perpetrators. Some questionable judge in Glencoe let them out on $100,000.00 bail. They were promptly found dead in Chicago. The size of the bail bond, and the manner of death looks like big time gangland activities, and is the first indication that this might be an attempt by a Chicago syndicate to establish operations in our county. In plain language, take over the county like they have in some cities."

"You know this for a fact?"

"Yes Charlie, if you check my expense account, you'll find items pertaining to a trip to the Chicago morgue. I found two bodies in their morgue ice box. I verified that these two bodies belonged to the two suspects we arrested on a variety of counts here. You will recall that these two were released on bail from jail in Glenco."

A second board member said incredulously, "Someone raised $200,000 to bail out these men?"

"That's right, and all this took place within 30 minutes in the Glencoe courthouse, just as court opened in the morning. The DA is investigating."

"Now we have rustling on the Arrow—B. George Bentley, a private citizen, captured three rustlers, and turned them over to the Law. We let them break out of jail. Last week these scum set fire to the Arrow—B pickup, and would have torched the barn and buildings except for the vigilance of ranch personnel. Since then four criminals drove into a trap set by Arrow—B punchers. Three men were killed, and one injured in that scuffle."

The Sheriff paused, "There's more; the State Police lost one patrol car, riddled with bullets, and the Ace Ambulance Co. had an ambulance shot up. Miraculously, to date, we have not lost any of our people."

A third member of the Board asked, "What do these criminals want from us? Maybe, we should find this out. You say the owner of the Arrow—B is in the center of all this. Does he have a problem? Aren't we interfering into a private affair?"

The Sheriff stood tall, glaring down at the Board member "You should know George Bentley, the owner of the Arrow—B. He is a respected rancher in our county. His father was killed on my watch. He deserves better than that."

The Sheriff continued, "There's big time criminal activity taking place in our county. To date, six have died and possibly seven. The man in the hospital might as well be dead. If he recovers and we aren't careful, his friends'll finish him off so he won't talk. We hope he'll come to, and we can question him.

"The ranchers in the county are pissed. They see all this happening, and expect my office to handle it. The Arrow—B is an armed camp, and some of the rest of the ranchers are dusting off their guns. This office has neither the manpower nor the equipment to handle this kind of criminal activity."

"Sheriff, what about the State Police?"

"The State Police are too far from the action, and don't have enough equipment and manpower to handle their everyday assignments, and our problems too. They have been very cooperative to this point. I don't think they can do much more."

"We don't have budget for a larger Sheriff's office. Personnel and equipment are expensive."

The Sheriff sighed. "You don't seem to understand. A Chicago gang is trying to take control of your county. You either deal with it now, or after they are fully entrenched here. Measure your costs against having to fight this scum later."

The Board Chairman said, "I'm beginning to see your point. Is this all in your report?"

"And more, Charlie. There's also a shopping list of what I think we need."

Another Board member commented, "The voters are going to scream. Their taxes will go up, and with it, their blood pressure."

"In case you haven't heard, the voters are screaming right now about our failure to stop the violence that's going on. Furthermore, while we're understaffed, we take the risk of someone on our side being killed."

"How do you plan to utilize the additional forces?"

"George Bentley has set up an early warning system at his own expense. He will pass information to me. I'll dispatch the units to the scene." The State Police have agreed to assist if needed. They too don't want eastern gangland interests to settle into our state. In addition I'll be watching for out of state vehicles entering our county. With the extra units, I can do this."

"Okay Sheriff, I think we have all the information we need. This Board will be in touch, when we figure out what we can do."

The Sheriff glared at the seated Board members. "That's

the word I received last month. We don't have any time left. Word of their latest failure will have already reached Syndicate headquarters by now, and I expect more visitors from Chicago in the next few days."

The Chairman stood up, "We'll call you this afternoon Sheriff. You've spelled it out just fine."

* * *

George could stand a lot of trouble, but this Joan and Betty thing, he didn't need. For the first time since arriving at the ranch, he felt depressed. He was bone tired, and couldn't sleep. By morning he felt terrible and really didn't relish a trip to town. He finally concluded there was no way out, and he would have to deal with it. Skipping breakfast, he climbed into the Rusty Bucket, and headed for town. Driving directly to Rosey's, he entered the cafe.

For reasons known only to the gods, half of the town of Walnut decided to have breakfast at Rosey's on this particular day. A breathless Joan came out from the kitchen with a load of meals on each arm. She gave him one of her winning smiles, and eyed him to the one empty table. "Gosh it's good to see you George. I'll be with you as soon as I can."

George took the preferred seat, and in time Joan brought him a cup of coffee and the hand written menu. "Rosey needs help, as you can see. I'll be back in a second to take your order." She hurried away before George could answer.

Somehow, Joan had found time to buy some western clothes. She was a knockout anyway, and the new look just seemed to complement her natural beauty. George looked around to see who was in the diner. He couldn't help envisioning some of the thoughts that must be in the heads of his fellow ranchers being served. He laughed to himself, shook his head, and began to study the menu. He had just made his choice when he heard a voice from the booth behind him, "Where'd Rosey get that new hand? That's the best looking filly I've seen in a month of Sundays." A companion voice answered, "That can't be real, I could become unfaithful to Margaret over something like that." The first voice answered, "You wouldn't know what to do with one like that."

Joan came up to take George's order, "Hi sweetheart, I'll be off at ten. We can visit for an hour. I have to be back at eleven. Rosey's help called in sick this morning. Love you."

"Pancakes, bacon, and two eggs over light will be fine. I'll wait."

The first voice whistled then said, "He sure knows where the body's buried."

George turned and looked into the eyes of the rancher sitting behind, who now stared back and said, "Go get 'er kid."

George turned back to his coffee, thinking, It would be a lot easier if Joan wasn't so god damned good looking? Joan came with his breakfast. It was huge. George groaned, "Rosey thinks I don't get anything to eat at the ranch. She tries to make up for it when I come in. How've you been Joan?"

"Fine. I'll talk to you later." She smiled and hurried on.

George had his face in the plate full of food, when a voice from behind said, "Howdy George, what brings you into town?"

George raised his head. "Sit down Sheriff. I had some business that needed doing."

The Sheriff sat down opposite George, and began to relate his day in court with the County Board of Supervisors, when Joan came up with a cup of coffee. She handed the Sheriff a menu and said, "Aren't you going to introduce me to your friend, George?"

The Sheriff looked up at Joan, "Yes George, please introduce us."

"Joan, this is the Sheriff. Bill, meet Joan."

Joan looked hard at the Sheriff, "Is this the Sheriff you told me about in your letters?"

"This is him."

"George seems to like you. That makes you okay for my money."

"Thanks. Where are you from, Joan?"

"My home's in Vermont. I met George in college."

The Sheriff was not above appreciating a good looking woman, and this was one of those kinds of things. "You live with your folks?"

"Except when I was at college."

All kinds of thoughts were popping around in the Sheriff's mind. "Have you been planning this trip for long?"

"Not really."

"Are you staying at the Arrow—B?"

"If I get invited, George seems to think it's too dangerous. That I can handle, the danger, that is." She gave George an inquiring impish look, and thought he looked a bit uncomfortable.

The Sheriff was beginning to appreciate what was happening. He doubted that George had told Betty about Joan. "Yes George, why don't you invite Joan out to the ranch?"

Joan moved away, and started serving other customers again. George scowled over at his friend across the table, who was smiling like a Cheshire cat. "You don't think I have enough trouble. You have to add to it."

"I was just trying to be helpful."

"Joan showing up here was a complete surprise to me–I'd just as soon you weren't so helpful."

"Most of the men around here would give their eye teeth to have a woman like that. You have two, and you're complaining."

"Yeah, well two is sometimes not better than one."

Rosey answered the ringing phone. She listened, then called out, "George, it's for you."

George took the offered telephone, listened, then said, "I'll be there in 25 minutes. Get things ready." He turned to the Sheriff, and said, "We're going to have visitors. They're in quadrant 25, headed toward the Arrow—B. I'm going to the ranch.

The Sheriff took his map out of his pocket, spread it out, and located the indicated position. He ran out the door, climbed into his pick-up, and headed out after George.

When George arrived at the ranch he went directly to Tony. "What's going on Tony?"

"I'm glad you're here Mr. Bentley. Sam called to report a truck traveling toward the Arrow—B. He first noticed a moving dust cloud, then made out the shape of a truck."

"Can you get him on the radio?"

"I can try, he might be out watching the truck. It was traveling on the dirt road that skirts the mountains."

George watched as Tony tried to reach Sam. There was no response. Tony asked, "Should I keep trying?"

"No, just wait for him to call."

George went outside and found Pete. "Where do you have Don today?"

"He's over in the Leaning Mesa area. Do you need him?"

"Tony called and said there's someone heading this way. We need to meet them. The Sheriff's on his way, but I like to cover him. Trouble can often be avoided if we have enough visible manpower.–Leave Spike in charge, pick up your rifle, and come with me."

George and Pete headed for the oncoming truck. They spotted two fast moving dust clouds up ahead. The lead vehicle slowed. They closed on the two speeding cars. As the second dust cloud became a vehicle, all three cars stopped within a few feet of each other. The Sheriff jumped out from the following vehicle, brandishing a shot gun. Within seconds George and Pete were out of their vehicle, looking down the sights of their weapons at the interloping truck.

The Sheriff called out, "Just ease out of there with your hands up. This is Sheriff Williams."

The one occupant of the pickup, a slender woman of about 35, did as requested. The Sheriff lowered his weapon. "Harriet, what the hell are you doing way out here?"

She dropped her arms, "What's your problem Bill. Is it

against the law to visit a neighbor anymore? Damn you. You scarred me half to death."

"Sorry about that, we were expecting someone else. Who're you going to visit?"

"Well, I was going to the Arrow—B, with some apple pies. I guess I should have called first."

An embarrassed George said, "We weren't sure who was coming down this road. We've had some trouble lately, and we're trying to keep outsiders away. Please come back to the ranch with us."

Harriet looked at the Sheriff. How about introducing us Bill. I keep hearing about this hombre, and now I want a proper introduction."

"Harriet meet George, George meet Harriet."

Harriet folded her arms, and took a long look at George, "So this is who the whole valley is talking about. I knew your Dad. He was some kind of a gentleman, but he could also hang tough if he had to. From what I'm hearing, you take after your paw pretty well."

"Well thank you for that. He seems to have had a lot of friends here."

Harriet noted the three well-armed men. "What kind of trouble?"

George lied, "I seem to be losing a few cows lately, that's all."

"Baloney, I hear more than that from Dorothy, and she's been awfully quiet since one of you got to 'er. What's going on guys? You're carrying enough firepower to hold off an army."

18 | A WALK IN THE MOONLIGHT

Harriet left the three apple pies with George, and headed for her own ranch. Bill waited for her to leave then started in again on George. "You seem a bit greedy. Every female in the valley, including my wife, is falling for you; then you bring in an outsider like Joan. Now you have 'em driving 30 miles to bring you apple pies."

"Oh shut up. I went into Walnut this morning to tell Joan about Betty, and this emergency came along. So I still have the problem. I can't do this sort of thing on the telephone, so now I'll have to go into town again tomorrow–are you coming back to the ranch?"

Bill chuckled, "No, I think I'll give my one woman a break, and go home for the night." He studied his friend for a moment. "In spite of the false alarm, I think you have a good idea with this early warning system. Most of the ranchers around here are watching out for strange vehicles coming into the area and with all the women in the valley gaga over you; I think we can get somewhere." Bill climbed into his vehicle, looked up at George and said, " If I screw up and allow something to happen to you, they'll kill me."

"Yours is not to worry, I'll take care." George got into the truck with Pete. "I sure don't have to worry about getting bored in this County of ours. It's been wild. Good night my friend."

The next morning George and Pete drove into Walnut. He dropped Pete off at the general store to pick up some supplies, then drove over to Rosey's Cafe. The diner was empty of customers. Rosey spotted him and called out, "Sit down honey, Joan will be here in a minute." She came out from the kitchen with a cup of coffee shaking her head. "This girl 's in love with you, George."

"Rosey, you know I love Betty. I tried to tell Joan by letter, post card, and telephone. Nothing worked."

"Well if I know you like I think I do, you're trying to be nice, and haven't really told Joan anything. You can't do it this way George. Just come out and say it. You probably haven't told her that you don't love her, or that you have found someone else. Joan's a strong fine young woman. She will survive, believe me. Tell her! You look miserable, how long have you been agonizing over this?"

"Longer than I would like to admit. I need to get it straightened out."

"Here comes your girl. Good luck."

George stood up and met a cheerful Joan.

Joan kissed him lightly. "What was all the rush about last night? I was just getting ready to come out from the kitchen, and you were gone."

"I got a call from the ranch. I needed to be there fast."

"That tells me a lot. Would you care to expand on that a bit?" Joan sat down opposite George. "Your letters didn't tell me anything either. I guess I'm expecting too much to ask why the man in my life keeps everything interesting to himself."

"Okay, okay. We've been losing a few cows lately. The lookout thought he spotted something, and when we went out to look it turned out to be a false alarm."

"You mean rustling, like in a western novel. You get on your horse, and ride off after the bad guys with your Winchester and pistols?"

George laughed and remembered why he liked Joan so much. She had this great sense of humor, usually tells it as it is, and was ready to like most everyone she met. She would always be on the cutting edge of life, willing to try anything new. "Well, we do have pickups and Sheriffs, and police now. Let's talk about us."

"Yeah, well I've been trying to get you to do that for five years. What's the big hurry now? I want to see the ranch. Can't we do the 'us talking' out there? Rosey said I could take the day off. Oh, I guess I forgot to tell you, Rosey wants me to stay. She says she needs me, and wants the company. I like it here."

George reached up and scratched his head. "All right, grab a hat. It's going to be hot."

"You'll have to stop off at Rosey's house, that's where I keep all my hats."

After picking up Joan's overnight bag, they drove over to the general store, picked up Pete and a load of supplies. Joan took an instant liking to the short, bowlegged ranch foreman. She noted his shyness, smiled, and tried to put him at ease.

Pete stumbled around for words, and finally mumbled out, "Howdy ma'am. George told me you were in town. Shore am glad you could come."

Joan, now sandwiched between the two men, faced a warm smile at Pete and said, "Hi. Old close-mouth hasn't told me much about the ranch, but he sure has said a lot of nice things about you."

George started driving. Pete returned Joan's smile. "He's like a son to me, I was here when he was born."

"I'm very excited. I can't believe I'm finally going to see the ranch. I thought this day would never get here. How long a trip is it?"

"Be there in 30 minutes." Pete didn't really look at Joan, he kind of sensed her, keeping his eyes looking forward. This woman was like nothing he had ever been close to before.

There were bumps in the road, and one time Joan landed right smack in the middle of Pete's lap. She didn't seem in a hurry to get off, so they rode that way for a mile or so. That's when he discovered what his boss' problem was. This much woman could drive a man crazy.

The Rusty Bucket moaned and groaned its way to the ranch. Conversation was virtually impossible. When they arrived, Pete helped Joan get out of the truck. He felt her warmth through the hand he held, which he held too long. Oh, if I was just a bit younger.

A woman came out to meet the truck as it arrived. "Dinner's ready, come and get it." She saw Joan, "Come with me Honey, I've got a place for ladies to wash up. I'm Mary Ellen. I cook, among other things."

"Hi. I'm Joan. The food smells great." She followed Mary Ellen, who had somehow found a way to transform a corner of the bunk house, with its attendant smells of horses, old leather, tobacco, and just plain sweat, into an island of comfort. "I've never been on a ranch before; for that matter, I've never been out of Vermont before. This is very exciting."

Mary Ellen showed Joan the soap and towels, "I'm from New York. Came west when I was twelve. I love it here. Hope you can stay a while. I need someone to talk to–ah, when you're ready, come on out to the cook shack. I have to put the food out. This is quite something, as this bunch of cayhoots will eat everything in sight, if I wasn't there. I'll save you something."

When Joan entered the cook shack, she was greeted by seven members of the Arrow–B, all seated at a long table. They all rose. She laughed. "This looks like some kind of a conspiracy." Joan took a seat. "I'm Joan."

Introductions were made, and the meal continued. In a short time Joan had seven new friends. Word had passed around that this was someone special to their boss. There was already speculation concerning Joan and Betty.

George, of course, would like to see the whole matter vanish. It wouldn't. He got up from the table and checked the watch schedule. It was his night, and with a sigh he said,

"Joan, you'll sleep in the ranch house. I'll be on duty tonight."

"Sounds serious. Does anyone get hurt or killed in this war you're fighting?" Joan added impishly, "All night?"

"No, we're just careful, that's all." George ignored the invitation.

"Yeah, well Rosey seems to think differently."

George reached down and took Joan's hand. He helped her up from the bench. "Let's go for a walk."

Early signs of fall were in evidence. The air was crisp, leaves of the cottonwoods in front of the ranch house rustled with a song different from that of spring or summer, and the crickets no longer trilled in the night. They walked on the path leading up to the foothills under the full moon. "You mean a great deal to me, Joan. What we had in college was wonderful, and I won't forget that, but I'm not in love with you. I was hoping it was that way with you. Maybe I was wrong?"

Joan was silent for a moment. "Is there someone else?"

"Yes."

"Oh." Joan took her hand away. "Take me back please."

They turned and headed back. The moon ducked under a cloud. It became almost pitch black, and George took Joan's hand again to guide her as they walked. He could feel it tremble. They stopped, and he put his arm around her shoulders. "I've hurt you terribly. I guess I didn't handle this very well."

Joan, fighting back tears, was silent. They walked slowly toward the ranch house lights. Finally the moon came out from behind a cloud, clothing the surrounding country in eerie light. She made eye contact with Gorge. "You must have been suffering about this for some time. You cared enough to worry about my feelings, so you kept putting it off. When did you know?" Her voice was shaky, and she searched his eyes for some sign that he might be unsure. She found nothing.

"I met Betty several months ago."

"Is it because I'm not a western person?"

"No of course not, Joan. This just happened."

"I guess I should of come sooner. Before you fell in love with–."

"I don't think that would have changed anything."

They walked in silence, and in time started up the steps to the ranch house. Joan kept her face turned away, hiding her emotions, wanting now to be alone. George, uneasy and regretful said a soft good night.

The next morning, after a sleepless night, Joan found her way out to the cook shack. Mary Ellen had been up for hours preparing breakfast. She said a cheery good morning, then noticed the troubled look on Joan's face. "You don't look so hot, Joan, want to talk about it?"

Joan, not expecting empathy from anyone, smiled and said, "It's that obvious? I guess I'd better go fix up a bit."

"It sure is, honey, your red eyes tell me no sleep, and lots of pain."

Joan hesitated a moment, daubed her eyes with a handkerchief, thinking, "I certainly need someone to talk to." Then out loud, she said, "I'll see if I can change faces and come out and help you with the breakfast." When she returned she said to Mary Ellen, "You have probably guessed, but, George told me he didn't love me last night. I sort of half expected this, but could never face up to it. Somehow I always kept hoping that George would love me."

Mary Ellen came over to Joan and put her arm around her. "I'm so terribly sorry. Were you two engaged to get married?"

"No. George never did propose to me. And he didn't promise me anything either. I thought it was his shyness, and he really meant to. I guess I was wrong."

"What are you going to do now?"

"Well for starters, I want to see this ranch. George has been telling me about it for five years. In fact, I'd like to stay here in Wyoming for a while."

Joan stayed at the ranch for three days. She took part in as many ranch activities as she could. It was something new to her, and helped her recover some of her composure. She saw something honest and earthy about everyone she met. There was no phony-baloney here. No one put on a false front. You got what you saw.

Joan walked into Rosey's Cafe and found Rosey standing behind the counter sipping a cup of coffee. "Hi Rosey. Sorry I was gone so long. I hope you had some help while I was away."

Rosey looked over the top of her coffee mug. "That's all right Joan, I'm glad to see you. Tell me about your visit to the Arrow—B."

In the few short days Joan had known Rosey she learned to trust her as a friend, and this was a time when a friend was needed. "As far as the ranch is concerned, it was everything I expected and much more. As for my personal life, it wasn't that great. The man in my life told me he didn't love me. I guess what hurt even more, he said there was another woman in his life. Betty somebody. That was three days ago. I've recovered somewhat, but it will hurt for a long time."

Rosey thought of a time long ago when she lost her love. It wasn't a good time for her. Joan was alone, away from her family and friends. "Sweetie, I feel so sad for you. Best thing I can do is to tell you I'm your friend. This doesn't ease the pain much, but maybe you'll feel less alone."

"Thanks a lot, Rosey. Your friendship means a lot to me. I'm holding up pretty well, but George and I have had a thing going for nearly five years, and it's suddenly over. I'm sure I'll survive though. Do you know Betty?"

"Betty Harris and I have been friends for several years."

Joan was silent for a moment. "Must of been tough on you, Rosey, knowing that I was after your best friend's boyfriend."

"I made up my mind not to interfere, and that's the way it should be. What are you going to do now?"

"My first inclination was to move away. Run away, if you like. Now, after three days of looking at myself, I think I'm ready to go forward. Rosey, I kind of like it here. The distant vistas, the people I meet seem real and strong and forthright. I have a degree in animal husbandry and would like to be a veterinarian. Maybe there's a place for me here."

"I have to do some shopping. Would you care to come along?"

"Sounds good to me. Sitting here and feeling sorry for myself doesn't help a bit."

Joan and Rosey first went to the general store, where Rosey left her shopping list. From there they went to the livery stable, where Joan discussed riding lessons with the attendant. He said he would call when he found someone. The two women then went to the post office. Martha was leaning out the top half of the split door, her upper half filling the opening. "Martha, meet Joan LaCross. She's from Vermont. Joan, meet Martha."

"From Vermont. Well you must be the person who writes those pretty smelling letters to George Bentley. I mentioned it to him once, and he almost bit my head off. You must be very important to him."

"Uh huh, it's nice to know there's someone watching over my mail. You must be an expert at smelling letters."

Rosey thought the conversion hysterical. "Well that's a welcome change from horse and cow smells. Don't you find that so, Martha?"

"I don't see why everyone is so touchy about a smelly letter." She shifted her enormous topside back into the telephone booth-sized room. "Speaking of George Bentley, I have an air mail, special delivery letter from Marie Carpenter in Florida. If you see him in town, send him over. I think this is important."

Joan volunteered, "I just left the ranch. He didn't to my knowledge, have any plans to come into town. I can call him and let him know. When could it be delivered normally?"

"The next delivery out there would be day after tomorrow."

Rosey and Joan drove back to the general store. "Who's

Marie Carpenter, Rosey?"

"Marie was cook and housekeeper for the Bentleys for 35 years. She retired a couple of months ago."

Rosey entered the store first. She sighted a familiar figure at the counter talking to the proprietor, Betty Harris. Damn. Well there's no time like the present. Rosey managed to slide in between the two girls. "Joan, I want you to meet Betty. Betty, meet Joan. I think you have something in common. You both know George Bentley."

19 | ONE UNACCOUNTED FOR

Rosey backed away allowing the two women to face each other. Betty spoke first. "Joan LaCross isn't it? George told me you were in town. Where are you staying?" She extended her hand toward Joan.

Joan, taken by surprise, took Betty's hand, "I'm staying with Rosey, but I just spent three days out at the Arrow—B. Have you ever been there? It's a wonderful place."

Betty jerked her hand away. "You stayed at the Arrow—B Ranch for three days?"

"Yes, and I have never seen a more beautiful view of the mountain than from the bedroom window. It is gorgeous– you must be the Betty Herring, George mentioned."

Betty stood tall. Her eyes turned dark. "Aren't you a long way from home, dearie? You'd better run on back to wherever you came from before you get hurt. It's too tough here for the likes of you."

"No, I think I'm going to stay. I like this country. The rest of the people around here are mighty friendly. Are you from around here Miss Herring?"

"The name is Harris. A herring is some kind of a fish, but I wouldn't expect you to know that. Yes, I'm from around here." Betty studied the slim, well-rounded woman, dressed in tight-fitting western garb. "There's no demand here for girls that do your kind of work. Why don't you try Reno or Vegas?"

Rosey decided to intervene before this went any farther. She took Joan by the arm, and pulled her out the door. "Let's get back to the Cafe. The lunch crowd will be coming in soon."

"Hm, and we were just beginning to have fun." Rosey noticed a mischievous look on Joan's face.

Joan and Rosey were unloading the supplies into the cafe when Rosey spoke, "Betty is one of my oldest and best friends. Now I have Joan LaCross. You both mean a great deal to me–Joan, I will not interfere, nor will I become a mediator between you two–period!"

Joan, grimaced, and said, "Sorry Rosey, I didn't intend to cause you pain. You're right, this is between Betty and myself. It must be kept that way. I know that. We just happen to love the same man. I for one, don't intend to lie down like a puppy dog, you can depend on that."

Rosey smiled. "I didn't expect you would do anything else. He's some kind of man."

* * *

George hired another hand to help with the round-up. Each ranch hand found a niche in the routine of things. The days were long. The work was hard. George often finished his day well after dark. Two days after the "Betty and Joan meeting", a pile of mail arrived, and George was picking through bills, social notices and advertising when he found the letter from Marie Carpenter. He tore open the envelope and took out the letter.

Miami, Florida
10 September, 1952
Dear George,
Yesterday, while I was shopping in town, I saw Bob Gibson. I thought you would like to know,

as I remember you were looking for him before I left. I did not let him know that I saw him.

I miss the ranch a lot, but on the other hand it's nice to be away from the cold winters. I hope all is well with you. I remain, as always, your good friend.

Marie Carpenter.

George picked up the phone and called Bill at his home.

"Sheriff Williams here."

"Bill, guess what. Marie Carpenter just spotted Bob Gibson on a street in Miami."

"That's good news. Can you reach Marie by phone?"

"I don't have a number–I'll send her a telegram."

Bill said, "We need him here. That means extradition. I'll get with the State in the morning. In the meantime, let's hope he stays put. Tell Marie not to contact the suspect at all. This will be tricky. I'll have to find this guy, work with the police down there, and try to get the state of Florida to cooperate. All at the same time."

"You figurin' to go down there yourself?"

"I don't have a choice. Fortunately the Board of Supervisors came through, and I'm expecting two more patrol vehicles, and four seasoned officers in the morning. One of those will be assigned to respond to Arrow—B problems."

"That sounds nice. How seasoned? When do you expect to leave?"

"If I push the paper through, I expect it will take a week. Yours is not to worry. I'll check em out."

"I could make jokes about that remark, only it's not that funny."

"I'm not laughin' either. Call me if you hear from Marie again."

It was close to 3 a.m. when Tony came into George's bedroom and woke him up. "Mr. Bentley, I have a message from Sam.

"Mr. Bentley, please wake up. Sam just called on the radio. You told me to wake you if something happened."

"What's the message?"

"Some kind of car drove up the road that skirts the mountains to about three miles from the ranch. It stopped for a while, then turned back and took off."

"That's it?"

"That's all, I'll let you know if more comes in."

"That's fine, Tony. I'm going back to sleep. I'll check with you in the morning."

George lay back down, punched up his pillow, and closed his eyes. Sleep wouldn't come. There was something wrong. Why should a car come up that road at 3 o'clock in the morning, stop, then turn around and leave? He got up and went to where Tony sat, close to the radio. "Tony, see if you can get Sam again."

Tony called Sam back. He handed the mike to George.

"Sam, can you pin point where the car stopped?"

"Mr. Bentley I think it was somewhere near that great big boulder that sits off the road about three miles from the ranch."

"Thanks, Sam, you did great. Keep it up."

George turned to Tony, "Go wake up Pete, and tell him I want to see him, pronto."

Pete came, stuffing his plaid shirt under his belt. George filled him in. "Pete, I think that car let someone off. Maybe they'll try to shoot one of us, probably me. I'll take Nellie out that way at daybreak, and see if I can't surprise whoever it is. They'll be expecting a truck to come down the road. I'll ride up behind the rock. You drive out there about thirty minutes after daybreak. I'll be there about then. Be on alert, something's about to happen."

"Boss, I'd feel better if I rode along."

"Now that's right nice of you Pete, but I'll be okay."

* * *

The night was cold and crisp, and the moon was out, full and round. Nellie stepped lively, taking little twists and turns to avoid boulders and heavy underbrush, her keen senses reading the sounds and smells of the land. She walked quietly in the soft sand, making little sound.

The moon was just disappearing behind the mountains in the west when they stopped. The huge boulder, known as House Rock, was clearly visible about 150 yards ahead. George dismounted, studying the darkness as he waited for the dawn.

The whine of a far off truck broke the night-long quiet. That had to be Pete in the Rusty Bucket. George carefully searched the area ahead. He could see nothing. Could it be that this was another false alarm? He met Pete as he drove up. "We must have followed another bum lead."

Pete didn't answer. He got out of the truck studying the ground. The two men found the tire marks of the interloping vehicle in the sandy road. A sense of impending danger came over George. He ducked around the huge boulder, pulling Pete with him. A shot rang out. The bullet struck the rock about where George's head had been moments before. Nellie, who stood where George had left her, reared up and neighed. She trotted over to George. He reached up and retrieved his rifle from the scabbard tied to her saddle. He waved Pete over to the far side of the rock, positioning himself at the opposite end.

Daylight came quickly. George peered cautiously around the end of the rock. The ping of the bullet glancing off the rock pierced the silence of the morning. He looked over at Pete, then turned his attention back to the heavy underbrush all around. They waited. A half-hour went by. Not a sound. With their backs against the huge rock, they searched, constantly looking from one sector to another. Finally, they saw the barest of movements, like the waving of a mesquite branch in the wind, but there was no wind. With it came a slight rustle. The tiniest of sounds, audible to only the sharpest of ears. Nellie's ears stood up, and she turned her head a bit. George studied the surrounding area. He, very slowly, leveled his rifle in the direction of the sighting. Again nothing stirred. The two men waited, not moving, their eyes searching. Then it came again, like the sound of a side winder slithering in the sand. George tensed. He held up his hand to Pete, a sign to be quiet and to remain still. When the bush moved again, he fired. Three rounds, spread a few degrees apart. The echo of the shots continued in diminishing volume, and mingled with a human cry of pain. The two men moved forward, taking cover whenever possible.

Coming up on each side of their target, they approached with caution. There was a shape, lying alongside the bush. "Pete, check around, while I see what's here. I don't trust anything anymore. This is nasty stuff."

"You can say that again. Somebody sure wants you dead." Pete, with pistol drawn, peered around for any sign of a second person.

George leaned over and felt the pulse of the prone gunman. There wasn't any. He turned the body over. There was an ugly hole in the top of the man's head. A high powered rifle, with telescopic sight lay beside the body. An empty canteen stood in the sand. "I keep having to kill people to stay alive. I don't like that. Besides, it's difficult to get information from dead people." George went through the man's pockets. He found extra ammunition, a cover for the rifle scope, and a picture of George. There was a wallet with five one hundred dollar bills, and about seventy-five dollars in small bills. And of course, no identification. Strapped to his leg was a nasty looking knife.

Pete looked down at the body, "Wow, that rifle of yours sure knows which way to point." Pete shook his head, "I would think these people would get the message by now. We don't want 'em out here."

George said, "We've learned a couple of things, this is definitely Chicago mob related, and they have lots of money." He sighed, "Let's get the body in the truck. I'll drive into Walnut, and talk to the Sheriff. You ride Nellie back to the ranch. Get things going, but stay alert. They might have a back-up."

Pete shoved his pistol back into its holster, looked over at Nellie, "I ain't sure that hoss of yours will agree to me ridin' her, but I'll give 'er a try."

"Well just go over and talk to her for a few minutes, that'll help."

* * *

The Sheriff looked up from reading some papers on his desk. "Hi George, what's new?"

"I have something in the truck, I'd like you to see."

Bill got up and followed George outside to the truck. "Holy Christ, where'd he come from? You come up with more dead bodies then the Chicago morgue. I take it that's his rifle? That's high powered stuff."

"He has big money in his wallet too, and I think we're getting closer. How are you making out with the extradition business?"

"Bit too soon." Bill picked up the rifle and smelled the barrel. "I see it's been fired. People like this rarely miss. How close was it?"

"Too close. He came in for a second try, and would have made it if it weren't for Nellie. She has ears that point to sounds none of us humans can hear.

"I suspect his buddies will be by to pick 'im up in the next two to three nights. I didn't have time to look the area over. There might be some clues and for sure food and water someplace. How about you and I taking a look?"

"Sounds like a plan to me." The Sheriff turned to Leon, who was looking at the dead body, and seemed in a bit of a trance. "Go see if you can round up those two new officers. They might be over at Rosey's. Tell them to report to me pronto."

Leon, still looking at the body, asked, "What do you want to do with the body?"

"Let's take it inside, we'll put it in a cell for now." The Sheriff called the County Coroner and made arrangements for them to pick up the body. "We can leave as soon as those two officers report in."

George said, "You mind if I use the phone?"

"Be my guest."

"Hi Dorothy, please get me the Harris ranch."

"Sure Honey, just hold on."

Betty came on the line, "Hello, this is Betty Harris."

"Hello sweetheart, I'm glad to find you home. You've been hard to reach lately."

"Well, with all the company you have out there, I'm surprised you could find the time to call."

"Uh, are you mad or something?"

"Why should I be mad just because you had a woman live in your house for three days? The one you've never shared with anyone else but me."

"Don't I get a day in court?"

"Not this time." Betty hung up.

George stood there looking at the telephone for a minute, then hung up. The Sheriff came back into the office, looked over at George, and said, "I'm about ready to go. Did you make your phone call?"

"Yeah." George smiled wryly at his friend "This town must have the best communication system in the West. We don't need a newspaper or a town crier. Anything that happens just seems to be broadcast within minutes to everyone in or out of town."

The Sheriff guessed what the problem was, and decided this was not the time to get on George.

An hour later, the Sheriff and George arrived at House Rock and began a search of the area. From the tire tracks of the assassin's truck they found what they were looking for: Water and food supplies for a two or three day stay, and something else, "George, come over here." The Sheriff was looking down at the ground. "I see two distinct sets of footprints. What do you think?"

A cold chill crept over George. There's still someone out there. His mission, to kill. George was silent for a moment. "I agree, there have to be two, one is accounted for, and that leaves one. I tell you Bill, I'm getting tired of killing people to stay alive. Let's see now, this whole thing started in May. That's four months of murder, attempted murder, cattle rustling, arson, and harassment. And we still don't have an explanation or live suspect. Now I'm not sure I know how to protect myself from a man with a gun, hiding in the bushes until I make a mistake."

20 | A NEAR MISS

At six a.m., the day after the shooting at House Rock, the Sheriff put in a call to the Arrow—B. "Morning George. I hope I woke you up."

"You know better than that. What's on your mind?"

"I was wondering if there was any chance of getting a tracker from the Indian village?. I thought there might be something out there we missed. Maybe we can find this guy before he does his thing. If we hurry that is."

"Not a bad idea Bill, why don't you give the Chief a call."

"Hm, I thought you might be better at it than me."

"The Chief will want to see you face to face. Can you travel out there this morning?"

"I can be there in an hour."

"I'll call the Chief, and get right back to you."

After the Sheriff hung up, he leaned back in his chair and deliberated over the events of the last few days. He hadn't slept much during the night, but by morning he had thought out his strategy for defense against the criminals trying to invade his county. The phone on his desk gave two short bursts to break the silence and jar his thoughts from their depressed state.

"Hello, George?" the Sheriff guessed.

"The Chief will see you as soon as you can make it. I would suggest you approach it as a business deal. Ask to hire a professional tracker. When he asks what for, tell 'im."

Under an hour later, the Sheriff sat on the floor opposite Chief Running Deer. He looked into a kindly wrinkled face, commanded by two brilliant wide spaced eyes that seemed to see right through him. "Good of you to see me on such short notice, Chief."

"Welcome Sheriff. Your visit is long overdue."

"Thank you. I've come to ask a favor. And yes, this visit is long overdue."

"Tell me what I can do."

"I've a need for a professional tracker. The State of Wyoming will pay for the service."

"What risk is there to the tracker?"

"There is some risk. We're trying to track down a killer. He's somewhere in our county."

"You've come early; the need must be urgent. Can you tell me why?"

"For some months the Law has been dealing with a big city mob that wants to take over our county. At this time they 're bent on killing your grandson. We need to find this person before he kills."

The Chief registered surprise. "Red Fox did not mention this to me when he called." The kindly face turned hard. "There has been much trouble at the Arrow—B. It is the policy of our people to stay out of such conflicts. Now I'm asked to break that law, or look away when my grandson is in trouble." The Chief paused. He was outwardly disturbed. "I must consult with the Tribal Elders on this matter." The Chief rose, standing tall, looking down at the Sheriff with eyes of steel. Without another word he went out the door.

The Sheriff, a bit stunned, stood up and was about to leave, when a young Indian came in the door. "Chief Running Deer wishes you to wait. I am to see to your needs until he has an answer."

It was almost an hour before Chief Running Deer

reappeared. He came into the council chamber along with two others. "The decision has been to allow two of our tribe, skilled in the old ways, to accompany you. They will provide the necessary services. They are not to engage in any form of conflict, and will work with a representative of the Law at all times. We will accept the sum of one dollar each. This is to signify that they are working at the discretion and request of the Law. They will both require horses, equipment and supplies."

"I am grateful, Chief. George is one of my favorite people. He has earned the respect of most everyone in the valley." The Sheriff held steady the eyes of the older man standing before him. "The necessary horses and equipment will be made available, and they will be used as trackers and scouts only."

* * *

Early afternoon found the Sheriff accompanied by the two trackers from the Arapaho village examining the tracks around House Rock. This was the semi desert, with lots of mesquite and sage. Tumbleweed and patches of bushes dotted the landscape, with sandy passages winding in all directions. There had been little or no wind to disturb any tracks or clues.

The two trackers quickly identified the foot prints of the unaccounted for interloper, and traced his movements during the skirmish that took place thirty hours earlier. The Sheriff sat atop a saddle horse, borrowed from the Arrow—B, leading two others for the trackers who were on foot.

The trail of sign, some of which were totally invisible to the Sheriff, led through the low foothills at the base of the mountains, and turned left toward the ranch buildings. The Sheriff postulated the assailant would be looking for a vantage point overlooking the ranch buildings, and be within rifle range. The direction he was traveling would place him in just such a position.

A cold chill flashed through the Sheriff. George was at the ranch by now. Perhaps the killer had George in his sight right now! It was going to be close at any event. He fired three shots from his rifle, in hopes that George would hear the shots and guess it to be a warning. Both Indians mounted up, and the three riders raced for the ranch, the Sheriff leading at a full gallop.

Carl met the three riders, as they pulled into the ranch yard, "Howdy Sheriff, we heard some shots?"

"Those were mine. Is George here yet?"

"Got here about ten minutes ago. When he heard the shots he headed up to the water tank, where he could see things better. "Carl led the two ponies into the corral and said over his shoulder, "He's expecting you, Sheriff."

The Sheriff started up the narrow path leading to the ranch water tower, which was tucked into the side of the mountain, about 200 feet up from the ranch. He maneuvered around the first switchback, and was half way to the water tower when a shot rang out. He dug his spurs into the bay, urging her around the next switchback, and shelter. The Sheriff slid to the ground, pulling his rifle from its scabbard, and hugged the hillside.

A cleft in the mountains reached deep into the range. The higher area was covered with pine. Below the pine chaparral dwindled into sage brush, and then the land cleared, as the desert took hold. The shooter was most likely hiding in the chaparral. The Sheriff studied the terrain up ahead. There was little sound except for the soft whisper of the faraway pines. Finally he picked out Nellie, standing with head down, under a small pine that jutted out from the canyon wall. Cautiously, he made his way upward, until he was in position to see clearly across an open space to where Nellie stood. He would be exposed for about 50 yards if he went directly. The area had grown rough, with man-sized boulders dotting the landscape. By working his way around, he managed to draw within fifty feet of Nellie. He could see a body lying at Nellie's front feet.

He made a dash across the open area, drawing gunfire as he ran. Nellie snorted, as the Sheriff slid into the protected area; then dropped her head, nudging George with her snout.

The Sheriff knelt down to his friend. There was a nasty crease across George's temple. He felt his pulse. It was strong and steady. "George? George, can you hear me?" There was no response. He removed his jacket, and placed it under George's head, then turned his attention to the would-be assassin. One thing was certain; this was a vicious killer, who wouldn't hesitate to kill anyone in his way. The Sheriff knew it was essential to get George to a doctor as soon as possible, but getting him there dead was the worse of the two options. He peered around the corner of the rock wall, and a bullet slapped against the rock, ricocheting down the rocky hillside. Looking back toward the water tank, the Sheriff saw a lone horseman come out from behind the tank, and start up the trail. It was Don. There was no one he would rather see at this time. "Don, watch out, there's someone up above trying to pick us off. Get behind something fast."

"I hear you talkin' Sheriff. Is George up there?"

"He's here, and wounded. I shor am glad to see you." The Sheriff got on all fours and looked around the corner of the rock wall. Again he was met with the whine of a bullet, and chips of rock flying every which way. He could see Don hugging the side of the water tower, then slip behind and start up the other side.

Don climbed carefully, taking what shelter there was. In time, he placed himself in a vantage point, overlooking much of the interior of the mountain cleft. The Sheriff stuck his head out, and again drew fire. Don fired five times, aiming at the flash of the rifle.

Don worked his way uphill, trying to get above the enemy. The Sheriff stuck his head out again, but this time he didn't draw fire. In time Don reached the rock that had been used as a shield for the ambush. There was no one there. There were shell casings strewn about, and evidence of a person crouching. Foot and knee prints, plus a set of tracks trailing off, up the ravine. He called down to the Sheriff. "Come on up, Bill, he's out of range now."

The Sheriff and Don searched the area, but came up empty. They walked down to George, picked him up, and put him on Nellie. Don climbed up behind George and held him as they rode back to the ranch.

Pete picked up the phone, "Dorothy, we need Doc Morrison in a hurry."

"Sure, Pete, hold on a minute–he's not home. What's happened?"

"There's been a shooting out at the Arrow—B. George was shot in the head. We need Doc out here bad. See if you can find him, and tell him to hurry up out here."

"Okay Pete, I'll call around–is it bad?"

"Can't tell Dorothy."

Rosey picked up the ringing phone. "Rosey here."

"Rosey, have you seen Doc Morrison?"

"Sitting at the counter, Dorothy. I'll put him on."

'This is Doctor Morrison."

"Hi Doc, I just had a call from the Arrow—B. They need you out there fast."

"Thanks Dorothy, call them and tell them I'm on my way."

* * *

The ranch became a fortress. Each of the ranch hands armed themselves. The watch schedule now included daytime detail as well as night. Sam was sent to join Tony up on Leaning Mesa. Carl took over radio watch.

Mary Ellen was fussing around George, applying cold cloths to his forehead, when she noticed some movement. It wasn't much, just a bit of a shudder. She went and got Pete. They were both watching him when Doc Morrison came in carrying his little black bag. He took George's pulse, blood pressure, and breathing rate. George stirred under his touch. The Doctor examined the neat crease across the right temple;

then swabbed the area with Iodine.

"Holy Jesus." George opened his eyes, blinked, and looked at the faces around him. "Who did that?" He felt his head, looked at the doctor, and with a tortured grin on his face, said, "Oh, it's you Doc. I suppose you enjoy torturing people."

"Well not really, but if you'd rather I cauterize that wound you have in your head, I could do that too."

"Thanks, I'd just as soon you didn't." He dropped his head back down on the pillow.

The Doctor bandaged the wound, then stuffed his stethoscope back into his bag. "Pete try to keep this hard head down for a week. There's nothing I can do for him. He has a mild concussion, and will have a headache for a while."

"Hard head, you got that right. I'll try, but there's no guarantee that it'll work."

Pete picked up the ringing telephone. "Pete, this is Joan." Her voice was shaky. She fell silent, waiting for Pete to tell her something, anything, maybe what she didn't want to hear. "What's happened Pete?"

"We don't know Joan. Doc Morrison is in with George now. He's been shot in the head, but seems to be coming out of it."

Joan let the receiver fall. She turned to Rosey. "I'm going out there. Can I borrow your car?"

"Sure Honey, keys are in the ignition. Call me when you can."

The 30 minute drive to the Arrow—B seemed like three hours. Pulling up to the front of the ranch house, Joan turned off the ignition with a deliberate motion. She gathered her emotions into a neat numb bundle, stepped out of the car, walked up the steps to the front door, and prayed. Mary Ellen took one look at Joan's ashen face, took her arm, and said, "There's some good news Sweety, George just regained consciousness." She stepped aside to allow Joan to enter. "He's in the bedroom."

Joan entered the only place she had been denied access to

when she was a guest of the ranch. It had puzzled her at first, as the relationship they had together was anything but prudish. The three days she spent at the ranch were devoted to learning about the range, the people and the routines around the ranch. She slept with Mary Ellen, and as a matter of fact, saw very little of George. This only seemed to deepen her love, not turn her away. Her meeting with Betty was a surprise, but then again it seemed to sharpen her resolve. George was her man, and she was not loathe to show it–or about to give him up.

Doc Morrison was leaning over and in front of George, changing a bandage when Joan came in. She circled the foot of the bed, not knowing what to expect.

George looked up, managing a faint smile, "Hello darlin."

Joan dropped to her knees, touching him on the cheek, and looking deep into his eyes. "You scared me half to death. Does it hurt much?"

"Doc says I'll have a headache for a week."

* * *

Back at the café, Rosey stood at the front door, and watched Joan speed off. Concerned that Betty might not know about the shooting, she retrieved the phone which was still swinging back and forth where Joan had left it. She asked Dorothy for the Harris ranch.

Betty's strong confident voice answered. "Hello, Betty Harris speaking."

"Hi Bet, I have some news for you."

"Hi Rosey. What's going on?"

"There's been a shooting out at the Arrow—B. I thought you would want to know."

Betty was silent for a moment. Then, gathering her emotions, and reminding herself of her resolve to accept life as it came, "Rosey, tell it to me straight."

"Betty, all I know is that George has been shot, and Doc Morrison is out at the ranch."

"I'm going out there!. Bye Rosey, I'll call." Betty hung up, grabbed her coat and headed for the front door. As she passed her dad, she said, "George has been shot, I'm on my way out to the Arrow—B. I'll call you."

Betty ran out the house, slid under the wheel of the car, turned the key, and with squealing tires headed down the highway. The night was black, the air crisp, and she felt emotionally alone in an empty world. Her man had been shot. She drove in a sort of trance, not watching the road that much. The station wagon slid off onto the soft shoulder of the road, making a ripping sound. She snapped back from her state of oblivion, edging back onto the highway. She remembered what Rosey said many months ago. "Betty you 're a western lady. You must face things as a western woman, with the strengths that are yours."

The Arrow—B ranch house lights glittered in the distance. She gave a prayer that he would be okay, and drove on. By the time she made the turn onto the Arrow—B private road, she had settled down, prepared to face whatever fate had dealt her.

The Harris Ranch station wagon pulled into the ranch yard; Pete was there with a loaded shot gun. Betty shuddered. "It's that bad Pete?" She turned off the ignition, and ran into the house colliding with Doctor Morrison, sort of mutually holding each other up, Betty said, "Doctor, how bad is it?"

"Hi Betty, "Oh, he's OK. He'll be fine in about a week. Crossing to the bedroom door, which was ajar, Betty pushed it open and entered. She came up short when she saw Joan sitting alongside the bed. Taking in George, who was sitting up with a large white bandage wrapped around his head, she said, "Well, as usual, I'm the last to know, and I have to get my information from somebody else." Her dark eyes flashed. She looked at Joan, "Are you still here, Dearie, I thought you'd be gone by now. She turned back to George, "You obviously don't need me around. I'm leaving."

"Betty, you don't understand. I–"

"I understand perfectly. You need to get your women sorted out. Good-bye." Betty turned on her heel, and headed out the door. As she passed Pete in the yard, she slowed down enough to ask, "How'd this happen?"

"Someone took a potshot at him from up yonder in the hills."

She climbed into the station wagon and put her head out the window. "Would you do me a favor, Pete, call me if anything else happens." With that she drove off in a cloud of dust.

Joan looked after the closing bedroom door, "Wow, she sure is mad. I guess I sort of messed things up for you."

"It's not your fault. Betty's just a bit sensitive about not being informed when something happens to me." George's head sank back into the pillow. "Joan, I'm going to be fine , why don't you get a bite to eat and some rest. Go out and see Mary Ellen, and send Pete in to see me. I think I'll try to get a little sleep." With that he closed his eyes.

Joan got up and left. She knew her being there had made a sizable rift in the Betty/George relationship. She decided she better vamoose for now, and see if George could patch things up. From the way Betty exited the bedroom, she doubted it. Just maybe, if Betty stayed mad, she might have a shot at George.

Joan stopped to chat with Pete for a moment, "I guess George is coming out of this one with just a big headache. I'm going home now. If he should ask for me, I'll come out again–oh, he wants to see you." With that she drove off.

Pete entered the bedroom, "How you feeling boss?"

"I have several kinds of headaches, and the one on my head is the least painful. What's the status of things?"

"When we picked you up, Nellie was standing over you. I swear that horse was standing guard."

George managed a smile, "The guy out there would have got me if it weren't for Nellie. He's a pro, and has the right kind of equipment to do the job."

"Boss, that shooter was perched behind a boulder, way

above the water tower. Don went around after him, but he slipped out. We have the trackers out there now. The Sheriff's with them.

"All things are in place for meeting his pickup car. He's got to have planned to be picked up somehow."

"Sounds okay to me. I should be back in the saddle by tomorrow– tell the crew to be as careful as possible. Don't go out in the open unless necessary. This whole ranch isn't worth one life."

"Gotcha. The Doc said keep you down for a week."

"Yeah, well he doesn't know about my hard head. I'll be out and around by tomorrow."

21 | RENDEZVOUS

Pete left after promising to wake George should anything happen. About 2 a.m., Tony called from the top of Leaning Mesa. Carl took the message. A vehicle had entered the area, with lights out. The moon was full, and Sam and Tony spotted a small dust cloud, which turned into a pick-up truck, moving slowly along the road that skirted the mountains. Carl found Pete who hesitatingly went in and woke George.

George stirred, "Ow, my aching head." He listened to Pete, then, "This may be our chance, see if you can locate the Sheriff, fill him in, and send Don in to see me."

Pete went searching for Don. He found him in a poker game with Mary Ellen and Carl. "Don, the boss wants to see you."

Don had almost lost his shirt, with Mary Ellen about to wear it. He looked up at Pete, "I'm sitting on a hot hand, can he wait a minute?"

"I don't think so, he's got something special in mind that won't wait."

Don threw down his hand in disgust. "The way my luck has been, I ought to leave anyway."

George was sitting up when Don and Pete came in. "The shooter doesn't know that I lived, and probably thinks his job is finished. He for sure is going for his pick up rendezvous tonight. Tony, up on the mesa, tells us there is a vehicle sneaking along the foothill road headed this way. That's got to be it. The Sheriff can have one of his new patrol cars blocking off the exit to the highway. I want you two to travel out that way and set up an ambush somewhere near House Rock. As soon as we can locate the Sheriff, he'll be on his way to back you up.

"Don't engage this person if possible until the Sheriff gets there. Do not expose yourselves to his fire. He's deadly. Don't kill him if you can avoid it. We can't talk to a dead man. If he meets his pickup, let him get aboard. We've got him trapped.

"I'll stay here and watch the store."

"I don't suppose there's any use me mentioning what Doc said?"

"Thanks for the concern. I'm still a little woozy, but outside of this damn headache, I'm okay."

When Pete and Don left, George put some pants on, stepped outside with his rifle, and fired two shots, then paused and fired two more. He waited, listening, and heard a two shots reply. This told him the Sheriff would be returning to the ranch. He went inside and reloaded his rifle. Feeling kind of weak and woozy he sat down. That's where the Sheriff found him. "George, wake up, what's happening? You signaled?"

"Glad you're here, General. We had a call from Tony on the Mesa. They spotted a pick-up coming south on Foothill Road. I sent Pete and Don up ahead to set up an ambush."

The Sheriff shook his head, "You can't even be serious when you're shot in the head, and lying flat on your ass. How much of a lead do they have?"

"Maybe twenty minutes."

The Sheriff called his office, "Leon, locate those two new units and fast. Have them ready in ten minutes to set up a road block. You'll find a map in the top desk drawer in my office, get it, and find the junction of Foothill Road and

North County Boundary Road. That's in quadrant seven on the map. Tell Officer Carlton I want a road block at that intersection. Leon, time is everything. Move. When you have that going, high tail it out here." He looked over at George, I'm out of here. Stay put, you look weak as a pussy cat. We've got enough manpower to do this thing."

"Yes sir, General, good luck."

The Sheriff grinned at the title. Only George would keep his sense of humor at a time like this. He piled into his vehicle, and sped off toward House Rock. When he slowed, Don came out from the side of the road, and motioned him off the road into the bushes. The party doused all lights, took cover, and waited.

The moon went under a cloud, and it became almost pitch black. Ten minutes went by. It was Pete who first heard soft footsteps coming down the road. He touched Don, who reached over and prodded the Sheriff. They waited. The footsteps grew louder, and a figure loomed out of the black. The Sheriff reached in and turned on the truck headlights, and at the same time called out, "Stop right where you are. There are three rifles pointing your way. This is the Sheriff."

A man came into view. He looked startled, and raised his hands above his head. He maintained hold on the rifle in his right hand. "What's the problem Sheriff? Is it against the law to go out on a night hunt in this area?"

"Just ease that rifle to the ground. Don't make any fast moves. We are all good shots, and at this range, couldn't miss."

The gunman did as he was told, and then said, "You better have more than me walking in the dark at night. My lawyers will eat you alive."

The Sheriff placed hand cuffs on the suspect; then the two trucks with their prisoner, drove back to the Arrow—B. He stood the prisoner, and led him in to where George was. "Here's our man George." The Sheriff scratched his head, looked around the room, then, "Ah, George, do you suppose you could hold this prisoner here for, say–three hours? I have to see to that other matter."

"Congratulations General. Nice. I think three hours should just about do it."

The prisoner, looked from one to the other, "Who's this guy? Isn't he the Law?"

"No, just a concerned citizen. He'll take good care of you." The Sheriff turned, and went out the door. "See you in three hours or so, George."

"Pete, go get some rope, we need to tie this guy up. Handcuffs are not enough— let's hobble him, like we do horses that get in trouble all the time."

"Right Boss. Do you want me in here with you, or do you want to do it alone?"

"Some things a man has to do by himself. This is one of those things. You and Don had better get some food and rest. I suspect those idiots in Chicago won't know right off that their boy here failed. That gives us some much needed rest. That is assuming the Sheriff gets the pick up car. Oh, and while you're at it, bring me my scalping knife."

Pete looked inquisitively at George. "Where did you put it the last time you used it?"

"It should be in that cupboard in the bunk house."

Pete went out the door, returning shortly with a coil of rope and a sharp pointed knife. The prisoner was tied to a stout chair, still handcuffed. Pete handed a key to George. "The Sheriff told me to give you this handcuff key."

"Okay Pete, leave us alone for now." George got another chair and sat opposite the prisoner. He looked at a slender six foot Caucasian. Maybe 185 pounds, slim, and with biceps that filled the sleeves of a light leather jacket. "You almost made it up there. You sure did give me a headache.–Your buddy is lying in the morgue in Glencoe."

The face in front of him showed no emotion. It stared back, defiantly.

"Since you have no name, I'll give you one. Let's make it Lou. I wonder if you were told how many people have died trying to kill me in the last two months? Just in case you weren't, I'll tell you. First, two rummies were sent out to do the job about two months ago. They failed, and when they got back to Chicago, they died from their failure in a Chicago back alley, both with broken necks. Another man died trying to burnout the ranch house. Three more burned up in a car trying to shoot up the Sheriff, and kill one of your own. There's another man in a coma in the hospital. He'd expire, if ever your bosses could get at him. And we found another man dead from bullets out of my rifle in an abandoned stolen vehicle up north a bit.

"Now I don't give a shit if you die here and now. I've got nothing to lose. The Law around here would like to see you stretched out over an ant hill, naked and bleeding. My ancestors knew all about that stuff. Now you see this knife. I not only know how to remove a scalp with the owner still living, but it would be a pleasure. And if I should turn you over to my ancestors living just around the mountain, they would know other ways to do the job equally painful. The Sheriff, by the way, won't even fill out a report if he comes back and finds you dead.

"So let's talk business. You were caught doing attempted murder. You can get all the Chicago lawyers you want, but it won't help in Wyoming. Yes, we know about that judge that is on the take. We can prove that. Anyway the Syndicate would take care of you, long before you got to court. With a bullet.

"You're bluffing."

"You might feel that way about me, but you don't doubt what I said about the Syndicate. You forget, I've got nothing to lose. I've just been through three months of being shot at, and I don't intend to do another three months."

The prisoner squirmed around, testing the hand cuffs. He was calculating his chances with the man he faced. The Sheriff didn't seem to provide much protection either. He had heard that there were some casualties out here, but not that many. He heard about the car fire. But he didn't equate that with the Arrow—B job. The Syndicate had omitted quite a bit of information when they hired him. "So what do you want from me?"

"I need names and contacts."

"What will that buy me?"

"Your life."

The prisoner studied George, not saying anything, just looking.

"You have five minutes to make a decision."

George went out the door, and found Pete close by, in case he was needed.

"Do any good?"

"Not yet, but these types usually stand on what they are. I expect we'll have to use some physical stuff. He'll have to be hurting real bad before he opens his mouth."

Pete considered this for a moment. "You care to tell me what you had in mind?–If you are thinking of a nice friendly fist fight, I'll be glad to oblige. I don't think you should try it after that blow on your head."

"If I were considering that idea, I'd do my own fighting. Thanks for the offer. I could call Grandfather. He probably knows some of the old ways that would do the job. Unfortunately we have under three hours, and I suspect that Grandfather's 'old ways' require more time. I'm going in and see what the prisoner has decided."

"Ah, George, how mad do you think the Sheriff would get, if he weren't here when he got back?"

"Plenty, what did you have in mind?"

"How about the north line camp? It's close to the village."

"Not bad, Pete."

George entered the room to find the prisoner struggling against his bonds. "Make any decisions, Lou?"

"You go to hell."

George resisted the temptation to bust him in the face. He got up from the chair and went to the door, "Pete, come on in here. Let's move this guy out to the line camp you mentioned. It's a little more private there."

"Are you going to leave a note for the Sheriff?"

"Not on your life. If he wants this piss ass, he'll have to find him."

"Okay, I'll go saddle some horses."

"Better bring Don along. He might come in handy."

Four riders, one unwilling, with hands tied to the saddle horn, rode the winding eight mile trail to the Arrow—B line shack. The shack was built by Richard Bentley some twenty-five years ago to accommodate punchers out on the range. It was somewhat more than a shack, in fact it was quite sturdy. Made from field stone and heavy timbers, it looked like it could stand a frontal attack by a Sherman tank. Inside, the blackened stones above the mantle of the fireplace showed evidence of past fires. A cook stove stood in one corner, and the far side of the room contained four bunk beds. There was always plenty of food stored here, along with a huge pile of fire wood. Water came from a natural spring that the building was built over.

The four men entered. The prisoner was hobbled again, and then tied to a chair. George said. "I think I'll drop in to see the Chief. The Village is only a few miles from here. I should be back in a couple of hours. Put some grub together while I'm away."

George rode into the village about five in the evening. He went directly to the Chief's house, and soon found himself sitting opposite his Grandfather.

"Red Fox, this is a pleasant surprise. I hope it is good news that you bring."

"Grandfather, it is good to see you. I hope all is well with our nation."

"Yes it is Red Fox, but you didn't come a way out here to pass the time of day?'

George smiled at his Grandfather's quickness. "We have captured the person responsible for the attempt on my life. We have him in our line shack, a short distance from here. He's a professional killer, and will be prosecuted for attempted murder."

"By the looks of your head, he didn't miss by much."

George winced a bit, gingerly touching his still bandaged head. "I'm mad as hell, and I'm trying to keep from doing something irrational."

"Like what did you have in mind?"

"I thought if I rode over here, we might come up with some ideas; but then I convinced myself they wouldn't work anyway.–The suspect cannot be frightened. He's a professional killer with equipment to do the job. I suspect he can stand a whole lot of pain."

The old Chief considered this for a while, remembering things from his youth, when his people were warlike, and treated enemies in a different way.

"Who is behind all of this?"

"A powerful Chicago gang.–We need names, and witnesses that will stand up in court. I hoped to extract some of this from this person we have tied up in the line shack, but it's not working that way."

"Is the Sheriff aware that you have this prisoner?"

"Yes and he's out right now after the pick up vehicle. I expect him to have another suspect in tow when he gets to the ranch. Grandfather, there's something that puzzles me about all of this. These criminals seem to know an awful lot about our county for the average tenderfoot from the city. For example, the cleanup job they did at the place where Dad was killed, was phenomenal. Only one with the old skills could have done it so well. There are other signs too. Our desert is anything but friendly to outsiders. Yet they are able to move around the county with no trouble. This person traipsed all around the ranch with impunity. He knew what I looked like. He knew the lay of the land. I would think this unusual unless he had help."

"Do you have thoughts on this?"

"Well it's beginning to look like a contact was first made with a real estate broker, Charles Jones of Glencoe. When this became nonproductive, the Syndicate offered some sizable amount of money to the realtor. The money was enough to make a small town real estate broker greedy, and hire someone local to make things happen. It's just possible that the 'Someone Local' is innocent, or at least was not aware, of what was going on when he got into this thing. I'm sure he knows by now, but he's in too deep to pull out, and nobody gets out of organized crime unless they're horizontal. The big question is, who, in this County, has the necessary skills and the temperament to carry it out?" With just a touch of humor George continued, "It would be entertaining to get in on some of the dialogue going on in Syndicate headquarters when they hear about their latest failure."

"What you are saying, is that we may have an unfriendly right in our midst–perhaps in our village?"

"I did not want to put it that way Grandfather–I think, when we have all the facts we'll find a link to Bob Gibson, and someone in Walnut. By the way, we've found Bob. He's living in Miami, Florida, The Sheriff is all set to go down there and pick him up."

"I know Bob Gibson. He sometimes came to the Village when he was over this way tending Arrow—B stock. There may be a connection here in our village. I'll contact you on this matter."

George said, "I'm hoping to learn something from Bob. I believe he can explain a lot of what's going on. The man we have out at the line shack is strong, and I'm now convinced, won't break. Bob is another matter. Once he is faced with the threat of prison, he will tell us what we need to know." George stood up to leave. "I am going now. You have made me feel less alone."

The Chief considered that for a few moments. "Red Fox, you have had much trouble since your return. You may be getting close. Be cautious, as your enemies must be getting nervous."

"I am certain of that."

George waited for his Grandfather to continue. He knew it was expected of him to be patient and respectful. It was almost ten minutes before the Chief spoke.

"In the old days, I would have spent a night in the Kiwa. In the morning it would be clear to me. This custom is available to you, if you wish."

"I would be honored to partake of the Kiwa, but it will have to be some other time. I am responsible for those at the ranch with whom I have become good friends. I must return there very soon.–Your council has been good. The way ahead seems clear now." George rose to leave. He smiled at the fine old Arapaho Chief. "I guess you already know that I have found a woman?"

"I stopped in to speak to Rosey yesterday." The Chief rose slowly, to accommodate his aging, arthritic bones, looked at his grandson with a twinkle in his eye. "It is interesting that when the rains finally get here, they don't know when to stop. The way I hear it, you have two women. Have you sorted things out yet?"

"Grandfather, your source of information is sterling. I only wish I knew the who and where of my enemies with such aplomb. Yes, to your question, but I am having a hard time convincing these two. Neither you nor my father prepared me for women. These two seem to have the ability to complicate things."

The last traces of the Sun's rays were touching the tops of the mountains when George rode up to the line shack. The two guards were just sitting down to eat. George piled a plate with beans and corned beef, took a seat and looked over at the prisoner. "I guess you'd like to get at me and do your job. I'm considering giving you the chance. Somebody just like you killed my father, and I can hardly wait to get my bare hands on him." He stuck a fork into his plate of food. "You don't seem to understand what is about to happen to you. The least you could get for attempted murder is 25 to life. We have all the witnesses. There's nobody here to dispute our testimonies either. That leaves you out on a limb.

"You're not going to get much help from the Syndicate. They would kill you right now if they knew where you were, and that you failed to take me out. Oh, and as for that bogus judge, we have enough on him to make him harmless." George looked hard at the prisoner, perhaps looking for a weakness. He found none. This was a hard face. It belonged to a man of total discipline. His muscles were large, and there was no fat anywhere.

Pete and Don were silent. They were thinking much the same. They wondered what their boss's next move would be. The trip to the Line Shack was not paying off. Nobody was fooling anybody. Well before dawn, the four men found themselves on the trail back to the ranch. George could only hope that his prisoner would suffer from saddle sores for a long time. It was doubtful that he had ever been on a horse before… he'd have to turn this punk over to the Sheriff.

* * *

The Sheriff and Leon drove down Foothill Road heading north. The message coming from Tony up on Leaning Mesa told of a vehicle coming south on Foothill Road from its junction with North County Boundary Road. It would be expecting to gather up the two professional gunmen they had dropped off several days earlier. One of these had died from a bullet from George's rifle, and the other was now in custody. To let the pick up vehicle get away was not an option in the mind of the Sheriff. To cover all his bases, he called Chief Richardson at State Police headquarters and filled him in. The Chief, who was still stinging from having been part of the first two prisoners' release, was also very eager to get his hands on the criminals.

"What can I do to help, Bill?"

"Well for now, Chief, kind of stand by, I think I've got enough manpower to handle the situation, but you never can be too careful. This case is driving us all nuts out here, and I'm hoping this will clear up some of it."

"Did you ever get that dumb jail of yours put back to together?"

"Just finished it about a week ago. The Board of

Supervisors gave me a hard time over all the money it cost, then much to my surprise voted to beef it up a bit."

The Chief kind of laughed, "A considerable bit, I hope. If you need more space, I'll help out."

Bill considered this for a moment. "Thanks, that one I'll take under advisement."

He hung the phone on its hook on the dash board. "Leon, we must be getting close now. I think I'll turn off the headlights. I can see okay without them." They drove in silence for a few moments. They were driving slower now, both intently peering through the windshield. The moon came out from behind a cloud. Suddenly they were facing an oncoming car. The Sheriff flipped on the headlight switch, and slid the truck around sideways blocking the road. The oncoming vehicle skidded, and made a fast one- eighty, speeding off. The Sheriff and Leon piled out of the truck, firing their rifles at the tires of the receding car. The Sheriff retrieved the phone from its hook and called the units at the intersection, "Carlton, the suspect is coming your way. It looked like there were two persons aboard. They are armed and dangerous. Proceed with caution, but get these two. We're coming right behind them."

Officer Carlton took the call from Sheriff Williams. He turned and gave instructions to the three other officers. "Take your weapons and get out of the patrol cars. You better find good cover. I don't want any casualties." The two patrol cars, with lights off, totally blocked the road. The officers placed themselves behind rocks, with rifles ready.

The whine of the oncoming vehicles soon sounded through the night. And then they were there. With a screeching of brakes, the lead vehicle swung sharply to the right attempting to avoid the road block, careening down a slight slope, but unable to remain upright, toppled and slid further down the slope gradually coming to a halt. The four officers descended into the gully surrounding the disabled vehicle.

Sheriff Williams, close behind, pulled up and stopped. He

and Leon walked down to the crash scene. He asked one of the officers, "Are they both still inside?"

"They sure are, Sheriff."

The Sheriff called out, "This is the Sheriff. Are either of you injured in there?"

One of the two doors facing upward nudged open, A voice answered, "I hurt all over, and my partner is out cold. I think he hit his head on the window. For Christ sake, get us out of here."

"As fast as we can, remember we have six rifles, with the business ends pointing at your head. Move out slow and careful like.

The forward passenger side door of the vehicle edged upward, and a suspect climbed out, sliding to the ground, holding his arms upward when he could. The emerging figure was dressed in a black business suit. The shine of black patent leather shoes showed through the desert dust that billowed up as he landed. His black hair was ruffled, showing signs of much grooming earlier, he glared at the Sheriff. "You've got no right to do this to me. We were doing nothing but driving along a country road."

The Sheriff placed handcuffs on the suspect. "Don't make me laugh. We've got enough on you to put you in prison for life. This is Wyoming, not Chicago. And if the man inside your car dies, we'll pin that on you too." The Sheriff pushed the suspect inside one of the patrol cars. "And out here, that means a hanging."

The figure in black paled, and started to respond but thought better of it. The Sheriff read him like a book, and stored this in his mind.

The second occupant, still unconscious, was carefully lifted out of the car, and placed on the ground. He had a nasty bump growing on his right temple. He was a short squatty looking man, dressed in somewhat shabby clothes, wearing a billed, woolen cap. He was carrying a stubby handgun, and had a viscous looking knife strapped to his right leg.

The Sheriff called for an ambulance from his car radio, then called Chief Richardson in Glencoe. "We have our two suspects in custody, plus the one shooter we captured earlier. One of them is still out cold from bouncing off a car window. I think we'll jail them out here– for tonight anyway."

"Nice work, Bill. See if you can figure out where these guys spent their nights. I have a hunch they did a stay-over in my town somewhere. They sure didn't go back and forth to Chicago. Look in their pockets, in the car, and ask. I sure would like to check this out."

"Sounds reasonable. You'll be the first to know." The Sheriff left the mike open for half a minute or so.

Chief Richardson said, "Something else, Bill?"

"Well there kinda is. Is that offer to share your jail facilities still open?"

"Absolutely, and when you book them in, let me see the paperwork. I'm not going to have another screwup if I have to live down here."

"Great. By the way, what is the status of the man that was in the hospital unconscious?"

"I sent him up state to the prison hospital. It didn't look as if he'd ever wake up again, and it was putting quite a strain on my manpower here." The Chief followed with a kind of chuckle. "It would be nice if these new suspects of yours are at least breathing. You guys out there manage to permanently disable most of your criminals to the point that they can't even talk."

"I know what you mean. We have, as you say, two breathing and one out cold." That's better than our usual. Hmm–maybe you'd better at least take this out cold one over. I've called the Glencoe hospital. They are sending an ambulance out here to pick up the 'out cold one'. I'll send a black and white along with the ambulance. Can you have someone at the hospital to meet us?"

"I think so. When do you expect to be there with him?"

"I'd guess about two hours."

In time the ambulance from Glencoe arrived and the

prisoner was placed aboard, with a police officer riding along. One patrol car followed the ambulance back to the hospital in Glencoe. As soon as the two car convoy left, the Sheriff gathered his remaining forces, his one prisoner and headed back to the Arrow—B. The overturned vehicle had yielded little; however, the pockets of the black-suited suspect said a lot. A name, identification, eleven hundred dollars in his wallet, and a book of matches from the "End of the Line Motel" in Glencoe. It was late in the evening, but the Chief said he wished to be awakened if they found anything. The Sheriff's call roused a sleepy Chief Richardson. "This is the Chief."

"The information you want is the End Of The Line Motel. I'll call you from my office in the morning."

22 | MIAMI

The Sheriff did a lot of thinking on the way back to the Arrow—B. He had a twenty four year old Caucasian with a Chicago address [in his pocket]. He was not dressed like a mechanic, or a hoodlum from Crimesville. Maybe, just maybe, he was part of the Syndicate that was causing all this trouble. Eleven hundred dollars is a lot of money for a nobody to carry around. He's got to be somebody? The way he cried when he was trapped in the vehicle gave the sheriff the idea that he might tell all. And, should be easier to keep alive than the rest of this bunch.

Back at the ranch George, still in thought, plowed through a plate full of eggs, bacon and biscuits, and surveyed his crew. In the past several weeks they had become family. He knew a fast solution to the conflict with his enemies was imperative. Luck and watchfulness could not be successful forever. It is reasonable to expect a "friendly casualty" any day now. That must not happen. He turned to the Sheriff, "How's the Bob Gibson thing doing?"

The Sheriff came out of his muggy state. "The paper work is in progress, and I am thinking of a fast trip to Florida ASAP. The Sheriff got up from the table. "I'll be gone at least a week. Do you think you can house two officers here while I'm gone? I think that's the only way."

"Of course. They'll be damned welcome. When do you plan to leave?"

"I'll try for tomorrow morning. I think the timing is right, as it should take the boys in Chicago at least a week to get the news, and plan some other criminal act." The Sheriff continued, "I want to go to the DA with as much information as possible. I'd like to talk to both Gibson and this shiny-shoed character."

George said, "Bill, I also might have another person to interrogate besides these two, and I suspect the DA will subpoena Charles Jones from Jones Real estate for questioning. This should make a good package for the DA's office to work with.

Bill asked, "Who's the other person?"

"Can't tell you right now. You'll be the first to know."

The Sheriff sighed, "I suppose I should be upset with that, but I'm getting used to your surprises. Can I use your phone?"

"Be my guest."

The Sheriff called Chief Richardson, and when he came on the line, "Chief, if it's okay with you, I'd like to bring these two bums for jailing in your jail. I have to be gone for a week, and I'd feel a bit more comfortable if they were there."

"That's fine by me. Where you going?"

"Down to Florida to pick up a suspect. I'll keep in touch."

* * *

The Sheriff contacted Marie Carpenter before he left for Miami. Marie, an avid reader of detective stories, her favorite being Sam Spade tales, was glad to hear that he was coming. By now she was a bit tired of playing the role of stakeout as regards Bob Gibson. She had taken her job very seriously, and breathed a sigh of relief when the Sheriff called. Her strong confident voice greeted Sheriff Bill Williams' phone call.

"Yes Sheriff, I still see him from time to time, and I can finger the suspect."

The Sheriff grinned to himself, thinking, it's good to hear a little corn, when there seems so little sunshine surrounding this case. "That's just dandy Marie, you just sit tight until I get there." He hung up the phone and headed for the Walnut airfield.

On his way from the Miami airport, the Sheriff stopped to check in with the local police. He was led into the Chief's office, and met the chief, Ray Hope. Ray was a big person, looking like he had sat at a desk too long. He listened to his guest patiently, then offered to assist any way he could.

The Sheriff left the station and found a nearby motel, checked in, put on a clean shirt, and left for Marie's house. He drove up and parked in front of a modest one level house, with a veranda and two windows facing the front. The number 128 painted on the curb, and a nearby street sign told him this was it. The curtains were drawn, and the front door was closed, although it was a stifling 90 degrees. In response to his knock, a cautious "who is it" was whispered.

"Marie? This is Sheriff Bill Williams."

"Oh, just a minute." The door opened a crack, and the voice asked for the Sheriff's ID.

"Marie, you know who I am. You're expecting me."

"Yes, I recognize you now. One can't be too careful, you know." She opened the door, "Please come in Sheriff. Will you have a cup of tea?"

"Thank you Marie, that sounds fine."

From the kitchen, Marie said, "Tell me how things are with the ranch?"

"There's a lot of trouble, Marie, that's why I'm here. It's very important that I find Bob Gibson. He may be the key to what's going on."

Marie came bearing a teapot and two cups and saucers "Oh my goodness, I hope I can find him again. What kind of trouble?"

The Sheriff, growing uneasy over, "I hope I can find him again," stood up. "When did you see him last?"

"Well not for a week or so. I've needed to stay undercover, and haven't looked much since Mr. Bentley called. He asked me to not let Bob see me, and I have been careful to do just that."

"Well for a starter, here's a city map, can you point out where you saw him?"

"Oh yes Sheriff, let me show you." Marie spread out the map, and quickly found the intersection of Beach Blvd. and Third St.

"Can you tell me how he was dressed?"

"The suspect wore blue jeans, western boots and hat, and a Hawaiian type shirt. He kind of stuck out like a sore thumb among the others on the beach."

"How many times did you see him, Marie?"

"Just three times, Sheriff, then George called and asked me to lay low."

"Always in the same place?"

"Well yes, always around that big building on the corner."

"Marie, I think it will be all right for you to go out, just stay away from the beach for now. I'll keep in touch and inform you of any new developments."

Back in the motel, the Sheriff sat looking over the notes he had just made at Marie's house. They didn't tell him much. A long stint of a stakeout at this time was not in the cards. He had pictures of Bob, plus his record while at the ranch. The only meaningful information, "he likes to gamble."

Bill picked up the phone and called the police department, asking to talk to the Chief. When the Chief came on the line, Bill asked, "What goes on at Third and Beach in this town of yours?"

The Chief uttered a curse, "Where'd you get that one, Bill, I thought you just arrived in town, and have never been here before?" he paused, then, "That's bookie corner big time, and we've been trying to close it up for months. We know it, they know it, and we have our hands tied."

"Yeah, well it seems my man hangs out around there, and incidentally likes to gamble."

"That's the right place for him then. What can I do to help?"

"If you're still in your office, I'll come over, and we can hash this one out. Maybe there's something in this for both of us."

"Come ahead, do you need transportation?"

"No need, I got a rental. See you shortly."

It was hot, not like Wyoming, where the air was dry. At ninety-five in Wyoming, it was almost comfortable. Here, ninety-five was humid and miserable. Bill Williams sloughed into the Chief's office, and flopped into a hard straight-backed chair. Beads of perspiration resided across his forehead. The Chief noticed his guest's discomfort, and grinned. "Nice weather."

Bill grimaced, "Your Chamber of Commerce keeps this one to themselves. You don't believe in air conditioning?"

"You just hit a nerve, let's talk."

Bill Williams handed some pictures of Bob Gibson to the chief. "This guy disappeared from my area just about at the same time as an unsolved murder of one of our ranchers. That was four months ago. He's a prime suspect, plus we think he's tied up with a Chicago gang trying to muscle in on our county. He's been seen several times in and around Third St. and Beach Boulevard by a very reliable witness.

"Now I don't want to chase this guy underground. I don't have the time or the inclination to spend much time in this furnace of yours. I don't think a well-publicized APB etc. is the answer. Can we make plans based on this?"

The Chief wondered why the Sheriff hadn't sent a deputy or detective on this mission. Sitting before him was a solid looking officer, speaking bluntly and with considerable force. "Your concern is noted, we can treat it that way. You're asking for a stakeout. I can go with that, to a point. Let's hope it gets wrapped up fast."

"On my part, I think this guy might cave when faced with a murder charge up my way, and provide you with what you need down here."

The Chief responded tersely, "That would be nice."

Five days after the meeting with the Miami Chief of Police, Sheriff Bill Williams and an assigned officer of the Miami police force sat in the window of an upstairs hotel room at the corner of Third and Beach. It was a long, boring five days for the Sheriff. He had long since run out of patience, and wondered how a police officer could stand it. He was also concerned with things at home. He could not stay much longer.

The building they were watching contained a drug store, cleaners and a bakery, each of which enjoyed what seemed to be normal activity. Yet, there was something weird going on, as the same people came in view too frequently. There was also the fact that people would come and go without packages in their hands. Nothing illegal here, and no sign of the suspect. The Sheriff put in a call to the chief of police. "Ray, these guys do a recycle job of people. There seems to be a cadre of people coming and going. It looks busy and natural, but that's just a false front to make us think 'normal'.

"As for my suspect, no sign. My time's about up. I have to leave for home in a couple of days, no matter what happens."

"I hear you Bill. Let's hope something happens in the next two days then. With the problems you have, you don't need two trips." Chief Hope paused, then "I can spare another man for the next two days. Why don't you take a shot at our beach for a day or two before you leave. I read it's 32 up your way right now."

"That's an offer I can't refuse, Ray. Shall we say one day, and make it tomorrow?" I'll plan on leaving day after tomorrow. What beach do you suggest? I see there's quite a few."

"Sheriff, the one I go to is about 30 miles south of here. It's called Desolation Cove, and is off the beaten byway.

Take swimming suit and lunch. If anything happens, I know where to find you."

"That's mighty friendly, Chief. I think I'll just do that."

The following day found the Sheriff under an umbrella, and propped up against a beach chair, kind of watching the passers-by. He glanced down at the book in his lap, then said to himself, "This sure beats Wyoming." He closed his eyes, then dozed off. Sometime later he awoke. There was a new arrival, just to his left, wearing a wild Hawaiian shirt, and a broad-brimmed western hat. He looked again, then reached into his duffel bag, and pulled out a pair of hand cuffs.

Sheriff Williams walked into Chief Hope's office with Bob Gibson in tow. The Chief looked up. "I thought you were going to the beach. Where did you find this guy?"

"On the beach, of course. Sat down right next to me." He smiled, then, "Will you hold him for me until tomorrow? We're leaving for Wyoming tomorrow morning."

"Sure. You sure got lucky." He looked at the prisoner, who was wondering how fate could treat him this way, and had a real down look on his face. "Give you any trouble?"

"Not really. Said something about, losing all his money."

"That's nice, maybe I can learn something from him before you leave. I took your hint, and started to photograph the people going in and out of our building. There's no question, something is going on there. I'll have him ready for travel early tomorrow."

23 | TROUBLE IN THE VILLAGE

Roberts met the Sheriff and his prisoner at the Walnut air strip. They drove into Walnut, locked up the prisoner, and ordered dinner for three from Rosey's. The Sheriff called the Chief of Police in Glencoe. He filled him in, on the finding of Gibson, and then asked, "How you doing with Shiny-Shoes?

"Just fine; Papa, back in Chicago is giving me a hard time, but the new judge has said, no bail, and will stick to it. Are you bringing your prisoner over here?"

"Affirmative, Chief. See you about ten tomorrow." He hung up the phone, and turned to his deputy,

"Roberts, anything else happen while I was gone that I should know about?"

"No, just routine things, that I could handle. Oh, Chief Running Deer from the Indian Village called to speak with you. I didn't think it important enough to call you in Miami."

"Leon, you better tell me everything. Let me be the judge as to its importance." He picked up the phone, listened to Dorothy's "Where can I route your call," and asked for Chief Running Deer.

"Hello Chief, this is the Sheriff. You called?"

"Sheriff, I think I have found another link in your puzzle.

George has asked that I call and inform you that a member of our tribe may be involved."

The Sheriff was silent for a moment. He considered how difficult this call must have been for the fine old Arapaho chief. "Would you be able to come into Walnut today? You may stay tonight at my home, have dinner with Martha and me, then leave for your Village in the morning. We have plenty of room, and would be honored to have you stay with us." The Sheriff paused, then, "I will not be here tomorrow, and I am very anxious to meet with you."

"I could be there in an hour. Where shall we meet?"

"My office, if that's all right with you."

The Sheriff hung up the phone, and sat in thought for a moment. The enemy was hurting bad. This was a ruthless antagonist, not given to capitulation. Most assuredly he would attempt to upset any hearing or trial that might take place over his illicit activities. He picked up the phone, and asked Dorothy to call the Arrow—B. George answered the phone.

"I heard that you picked up our boy. Congratulations General."

"A bit of luck, my lad. Have you had any activity, or sign of something interesting to tell me about?"

"Negative, when can I see Bob?"

"He's in my jail right now, where I intend to spend the night. Tomorrow he goes to Glencoe jail, and will be held without bail. As to when can you see him, well knowing the high rate of fatalities surrounding this mess, it better be soon.

"I'm sticking with him until I see him in Richardson's jail. Would you join me? Why don't you come and spend the night here. Your grandfather will be here. In the morning we can interrogate, and take Bob into Glencoe."

"Sounds good to me. Is this an invite to dinner."

"That's the plan, but there's more, I don't trust anybody anymore, and I think I would like to see Don along with you; a bit of extra fire power would be nice. My jail house is going to be a bit crowded tonight, but I'll feel more comfortable with it that way."

"Can do. See you in an hour or so."

"Good, and might I suggest your crew be on alert tonight."

"Uh huh, see you later."

Sheriff Williams had been thinking long and hard of the upcoming events that should bring an end to his nightmare. There was plenty of hard evidence, suspects were in custody; now what could happen to screw this up? The Chicago Syndicate hadn't given up, that's for sure.

What would they do now? Road blocks would be in place, so it is doubtful they would try another invasion by motor vehicle. The prisoner he had in jail certainly would be dangerous to the mob. He must be eliminated. The Sheriff sat and stared at the wall. He asked himself, what if it were me? Would I try, walk-in? How about air? He sat up straight, his eyes staring but not seeing. That's the answer.

Leon came in with food for three. He placed a large platter full of Rosey's Pot Roast and mashed potatoes in front of the Sheriff, then turned to take another to the prisoner.

"Leon, where's the other patrol car?"

"I just met them goin' into Rosey's for dinner."

"Well that's nice." The Sheriff picked up the phone and asked for Rosey. When she came on the line, he asked to talk to his officers. Carlton came on the line, "Carlton, finish up there fast, and get your ass over to the air strip pronto. Check everyone that comes off any flight. You're looking for a man or two, heavily armed, and with the temperament to kill. Watch out, and keep me informed. He then called Chief Richardson in Glencoe. "Chief, you don't suppose the Chicago bunch will try coming in by air? I don't think they will try ground vehicles again."

"Bill, that seems reasonable. What did you have in mind?"

"I can watch the Walnut airstrip. How about you covering the one in Glencoe."

"Can do. I'll have someone out there in 10 minutes." The Chief paused then "Why don't you bring that prisoner over tonight? It might save another one of your famous fire-fights."

"Yah, well we only do what's necessary, however I think I'll take you up on that offer. Ah, I've got something important to do early evening, I'll call you later about timing etc. Speaking of air, how about that charter service you have up there. We could get Bob from here to there real fast and safe that way."

The chief muttered something like "Only dire need and circumstances would this be authorized by the city fathers. This fits those requirements pretty well." Aloud he said, "Sounds like a winner, I'll make arrangements and call you back."

The Sheriff sat and stared at the telephone for a moment, then picked up the receiver once more. Dorothy's all business-like voice came on the line: "What can I do for you Sheriff?"

"Dorothy, we are expecting unwelcome guests to arrive by small plane. Since there are lots of places they could land, like an open field somewhere, do you suppose you could spread the word around. Like if anyone hears or sees a plane, please give the Sheriff a call?"

"Can do, I'll start right now."

"Thanks Dorothy, that will be a big help."

* * *

The Sheriff was sipping a cold strong cup of this morning's coffee in his office when Chief Running Deer came through the door. He stood up, and offered the Chief a chair. "It is good to see you again, Chief. You honor me by coming. Would you like to discuss the matter you referred to now, or later after dinner?"

"Perhaps we should talk now, as it has been most on my mind for the last 24 hours. This is very painful for me." He paused, sitting silent for a moment, "Sheriff, a member of our tribe was responsible for much of the trouble concerning the Arrow—B. Let me tell you the story:

"Sometime earlier this year, a person I will call Little Crow, responded to a request from the realtor Mr. Jones, to tell him about the Arrow—B, its location, access roads, entrance into the mountains, ranch layout, and some other things. In fact, all the detail necessary for a stranger to move easily around the ranch. This seemed innocent enough to Little Crow, but was extremely useful to Mr. Jones' clients. Little Crow did not meet with anyone other than Mr. Jones. At the time of White Owl's death, Mr. Jones contacted Little Crow again, and asked him to assist in the cleanup of the area where the killing had taken place. Little Crow complied, but when he read the ground around where White Owl had been found, he decided that some wrongdoing had happened there. He indicated this to Mr. Jones, and a few days later, a man, unknown to Little Crow met with him and informed him that he was already involved, and that he must be quiet about what he found, or he would be in real trouble."

"When did this take place, Chief?"

"I cannot be sure, but I think it would be shortly after White Owl was killed."

"Do you or Little Crow know anything about this man?"

" I do not know any more than I have told you Sheriff."

"How soon can I talk to Little Crow Chief? I must talk to him direct."

The old chief shifted in his chair uneasily, and said, "We would like to discipline our wrong-doers ourselves. Is it imperative that you talk to him?"

The Sheriff hesitated, trying to find a way to honor the Chief's request, but found none. It was his responsibility to question the suspect, and he must do this. "This is something that is customary within law enforcement circles. Perhaps I could travel to your village and question him there?"

The Chief gave no answer until they were on their way to dinner at the Sheriff's house. "Will Little Crow be required to testify?"

"That I cannot answer until I have questioned him myself, Chief. I must use every bit of information I have to present to the district attorney before this case comes to trial."

* * *

Martha welcomed George at the front door. She went on with dinner preparations, and George sat at the kitchen table watching. Having company for dinner was a great event, and of course George was someone special to her. Her husband, Bill, was kind of tight-mouthed about much that was going on, and she sometimes had to get information elsewhere. Her questions covered all topics, and as a starter she wanted to know about his love life, which was one thing that George would rather not discuss. Martha, however, was quite persistent and didn't give up easily. "You haven't seen Betty all week?"

"Uh, Martha, I have been quite busy. I talked to her on the phone once."

"And Joan, has she left for the East or is she still out here?"

"The last I heard, Joan wants to live here permanently."

Martha was silent with her thoughts for a moment, then, "Things seem to be winding down into some kind of trial soon. What's been going on out at the Arrow—B?"

George was forming some kind of answer, when, mercifully, the Sheriff and Chief Running Deer come through the door. George took a long look at his Grandfather and said, "Grandfather, you don't look very good. Are you not feeling well?"

"Red Fox, I am well, but saddened by the betrayal of one of our tribe. I'm afraid it has caused you much trouble."

"Grandfather, it is better to think of how fine most of our people are as a whole. To have only one or two failing to uphold the honor of our nation is not all that bad. Have you talked to this person?"

"I have, and I have disclosed this to our Sheriff, along

with what information I have learned from Little Crow."

George looked from his Grandfather to the Sheriff. "Is there anything new, that we need to use in the forthcoming indictment? What are your thoughts Bill, you know this is difficult for our chief, and for that matter, for the whole tribe. I am certain that this matter will be discussed in council, and proper punishment will be meted out to the guilty one without our help."

"George, I intend to question this suspect, and determine just that. As you know there are lots of unanswered questions surrounding your father's death. The District Attorney will want all of the information available. He will be facing a strong legal task force from Chicago when this comes to trial. He will want answers, not guesses or conjecture. So far, all we have is a death certificate and a bunch of dead people. The witnesses are mostly hostile, and unlikely to admit to anything. I'm guessing that the involvement of one of your tribe was entirely innocent at first, but he found it hard to get uninvolved from this gang of hoodlums. I have had conversations with our DA. He doesn't think we will have a second chance. We have to get it right the first time."

The Sheriff answered the ringing telephone, "This is the Sheriff", then turning to George, said, "We're flying Bob Gibson to Glencoe tonight. We have to have him at the airfield in 30 minutes." He hung up the receiver, and told Martha that dinner would have to wait. Bob Gibson, the Sheriff, and the officer on duty got into a patrol car, and headed for the Walnut airstrip. When the twin Cessna arrived, a hand-cuffed Bob Gibson and the officer boarded the plane. On arrival at Glencoe Bob was transported to the Glencoe jail. The police chief of Glencoe saw the prisoner jailed then called Bill at his home informing him that all was well, the prisoner was in his jail, and would stay there, period. Chief Richardson now had Bob Gibson, a paid assassin, and two members of a Chicago syndicate, including Junior, the 25 year old son of the mob's boss in custody. The judge on the bench issued restraining orders, restricting both Mr. Jones of Jones Real Estate, and Little Crow of the nation of Arapaho from departing the area. It was time for the District Attorney to do his thing.

* * *

Dorothy, feeling the importance of her part in the unfolding drama, started calling the many ranches in the County. She knew each of the ranch owners by their first names, and hastened to inform each of them of the need for reporting anything they saw or heard. The general attitude in the County was hostile enough toward the invaders of their county to do anything necessary to get rid of them. They would all be on alert.

The two officers sat in a squad car alongside the hanger at Walnut's airfield. It had been a long night, and sleeping had not been an option, as the Sheriff had informed them of the need for vigilance. They had just about talked themselves out, and were about to call the Sheriff's home to report 'no activity' and to see if they could get some breakfast or relief out there somehow.

They heard it before they saw it. A high pitched whir, much like the sound of a house fly buzzing around in a hot hotel room or a seldom used front room while one was trying to read. Then, coming low over the land they spotted, at first, a tiny speck, and then the shape of a thin line, and finally a small aircraft. Each officer got out of the squad car and took cover, waiting for the craft to land. The aircraft flew low over the field. The occupants were clearly visible to the officers, looking out the window of the plane. Then the plane sped off. The two officers stood up again, and went to their vehicle and called the Sheriff.

Bill Williams took the call himself. He called Dorothy and asked her if she had spread the word around. She said she had been calling but was not quite done yet. "Dorothy, keep it up, something is about to happen." He then called the

Arrow—B. George answered the phone. "George, they're at it again, a small plane passed over the Walnut air strip. They saw the patrol car and sped off. I think they will find a level spot to land, and drop off another shooter."

"Thanks for the call, Bill, I'll take a look out the window now and then."

"One thing I can depend on is your sense of humor, which has nothing to do with someone shooting you in the head again. I figured you might take this one just a little bit more seriously." The Sheriff paused and then, "Your friend Dorothy is spreading the word around the county. We should get a call soon if they land anywhere."

"That's comforting, you seem to have things pretty well figured out, if you need any extra fire power, let me know."

The Sheriff sighed, and said, "Well keeping you alive is becoming more challenging all the time. I think if I get over this nightmare, I'll retire and take up knitting or something."

George laughed and said, "Somehow I can't see you in a rocking chair yet. We'll get you through this somehow."

Bill Williams shook his head in disgust. He had grown very fond of George in the last few months. He picked up the phone and asked to speak to Chief Richardson. When the crisp "This is Chief Richardson" came on the line, he filled him in on the small plane event.

The Chief said, "We're watching, like all over. These small planes have a, not-so-long-range, fuel capacity. They have to land somewhere soon. Keep in touch."

As predicted, Dorothy kept getting calls from various parts of the county, which she transferred to the Sheriff's office. By the end of the next hour the Sheriff had patterned the flight of said light plane on his special map. Several times the plane attempted to land, and because of terrain or the sight of police vehicles, veered off. In time it left the area altogether. With road blocks set up at all roads leading into the county, the Sheriff felt his county secure for the moment. He had done all he could.

24 | THE TRIALS

The Chicago Police had a vested interest in events taking place in Wyoming. For some time they had been plagued with illegal activities in their city, and chasing down those responsible had been somewhat of a challenge. Much money and effort was put into this, with disappointing results to say the least. The best they had come up with was the arrest of a few minor bums, who usually could tell them nothing.

When Bill Williams paid the Chicago morgue a visit to identify the two criminals that had died of broken necks, he confirmed that these two were indeed the same persons that had been released erroneously from Glencoe's jail earlier. In talking with Sheriff Williams, the Chicago Police recognized the Syndicate connection, but were a bit skeptical of the ability of western law to do much in the pursuit of capturing and convicting them, (sophisticated Chicago criminals). In fact there was a feeling of, "If we can't do it, how can we expect much from out there?" Nevertheless, they were watching. The Cook County District Attorney had likewise shown an interest, but soon filed the story away, as it was a long way out to Wyoming.

It was the Chicago Tribune that stirred things up. The story of the three hoodlums that perished in a car fire in an obscure corner of Wyoming found its way into the Tribune, which identified the three as having Syndicate connections, and publicly prodded the Chicago Police to take note of western law enforcement techniques. The Cook County DA put in a call to the Chicago Police Chief. The conversation was friendly but not friendly. The Chief did not like being told what or who to investigate. He put down the phone, and mumbled, something like, "Now I'm supposed to do something somewhere in Wyoming. Will someone tell me where I'm to get the money and manpower to cover this one?"

The Tribune didn't let it go. They picked up on the other killings and arrests associated with the Bentley case. The Chicago Police Department tried to ignore all this, and in fact became somewhat arrogant toward the hayseedy law enforcement people from the western countryside that were making the department look bad. The Cook County District Attorney called the Chicago Chief of Police and said, "Chief, I'd like to see you for lunch today, say 12:30 at Anthony's."

* * *

The District Attorney sitting across from the Chief of Police asked, "How come I hear all about this Bentley thing from the newspapers? Are we not picking up on this story, and who do you have assigned to its connection to the Black Mariah? Your department has spent five years and lots of bucks trying to get something on these guys and have come up with zilch. The way I hear it, this so called hayseed of a Sheriff is taking all the Syndicate can dish out, and in fact, is coming up with some hard evidence connecting these bums. Like killings, assassinations, conspiracy to do forceful coercion to citizens, to name a few. We sit back and aren't interested? You know we have been trying for years to put the kibosh on the Black Mariah bunch."

"Listen John, if I came up with as many dead bodies as that bunch out there, there'd be an investigation on police tactics and brutality." The Chief shifted his massive body, trying to look more commanding, then removed his glasses and wiped them. "Besides, I haven't the manpower or the money to waste on a maybe thing going on two thousand miles from my jurisdiction."

"I suggest that you find the manpower and the money but quick. Anything we can learn from that so called ragamuffin, hayseedy, dumb law enforcement bunch out in the backwoods of Wyoming seems appropriate. We have done diddly in nearly five years with our 'modern, sophisticated, expensive' police department. The media is making us look stupid and now the Mayor is on my back."

Neither the DA, nor the Chief ate any lunch.

* * *

Never before had the Contra County Court system had to deal with multiple crimes, or multiple criminal suspects. To further complicate things, out-of-state criminals and an Indian Nation were involved. Further, because of the interest the Chicago press was showing, it was headed for high profile status. When the District Attorney's office filed charges against Jon Ballant, and handed the court hierarchy the paperwork on the Bentley case, asking for a court date, the panel of two full time justices conferred, and discovered a mutual lack of knowledge concerning how to proceed. Consideration was given to appealing to the state courts for guidance, but both decided they didn't want the state screwing around in their bailiwick. They were still stinging from the errant part time judge that had taken a bribe for the release two prisoners earlier in this case. [He was no longer a sitting judge for Contra county]. So with some trepidation they came up with a court date of November 15. They considered that details would work themselves out as things moved along. This sort of put the onus on the District Attorney.

Chief Richardson had Bob Gibson, Joe Costello,

otherwise known as Shiny Shoes, a paid assassin, and a minor hood from Chicago, in his jail. Mr. Jones and Little Crow were told to make themselves available until further notice. The Chicago Police Department was advised of the forthcoming trials, and to expect requests for information concerning the activities of the Black Mariah Syndicate, and other related events such as the deaths of the two suspects released from Glencoe's jail earlier.

The District Attorney for Contra County, Claude Comstock, gathered all the information he could find on the Bentley case, and sequestered himself in his office to review his options. His first decision had to be "Try who for what?" There were so many crimes, and so much "aiding and abetting," going on, plus the out-of-state aspects that obviously had to be considered, and then there was the Indian Nation that fit in there somewhere? The DA scratched his head in disgust. He studied and restudied the pile of documents, which had grown to quite a heap, yanked off his glasses, and went out to lunch, muttering something about the idiotic judges that announced a trial date that was virtually impossible to meet. Not wanting to take the time to comb his hair, which was quite a doing, as he was still trying to cover up that saucer-sized bald spot growing toward the back of his head, he put on his baseball cap, which advertised the local hardware store, and walked out the door of the county building into a cold gusty world. He headed for Martha's place, about two blocks away. By the time he got in the door of the small café he was thoroughly chilled which seemed to exacerbate his problem, and his mood was gloom plus.

Martha looked at him and said, "D' ya want to talk about it?" She filled his coffee cup, and handed him a handwritten menu.

A little startled at how easily Martha could read a person, he grimaced and said, "Now Martha, you know I can't discuss matters concerning an ongoing investigation. Bring me one of your biggest hamburgers and some french fries."

"Sure Sweetie, but isn't this a bit off your diet? Yesterday you ordered me to keep you straightened out. Something about too much fat or something."

"Martha, just make me what I ordered."

Martha was considering a retort like You sure are in a tiff today, but thought it might not be the best of ideas, so she kept her mouth shut, and headed for the kitchen.

Martha's Cafe was a place where citizens came in to get warm and talk over the events of the moment. It was now the middle of October, and Martha had her storm doors and windows up. This helped a lot, but that cold gusty wind still got through whenever someone entered. The lunch time business had started, and each new arrival let in a new bunch of cold air. They would spot the DA, who was a well-known figure about town, greet him and then ask the same dumb questions: "How's the case coming? Will we win this one?" or, "When are you going to trial?" By the time his hamburger got there he was fit to be tied, finally, Chief Richardson came in, spotted him and sat down in the booth facing the DA.

"It's damn cold out there, Claude."

Claude nodded, and grunted out a "Hello Chief."

Martha came out and refilled the DA's coffee cup, and said, "What'll it be, Chief?"

"I kind of thought I'd try that steak 'n onions. Make it rare and hot." He turned to Claude, "CC, how's the case coming?"

"You don't wanta know."

Martha thought this sounded like fun and hung around to hear more. Claude glared her on her way, then called her back and asked for his bill. Turning to the Chief he said, "I had a nice quiet life here until this Bentley thing was dumped into my lap. I don't even know who to try or for what. The Court wants me to be ready by November 15th. I don't have the luxury of seven or eight assistants, and I share my secretary with the head of the Sanitation Department. Everybody asks me how the case is coming, including you." He shifted his over-sized bottom to the edge of the bench and said, "Hell, I don't even have a clue to any of these questions yet." He started for the front door, and zipped out without paying his check.

Martha came bringing Claude's check, and looking at the departing DA. She said to Chief Richardson, "Claude sure is in a foul mood today. What's got into him, anyway?"

The Chief sort of half laughed and said, "Oh Martha, he's probably trying to figure out how to handle a small legal problem he has to deal with right now. I suspect his mood will go on like this for some time. Here, gimmie that check, I'll pay it."

"Oh you don't need to do that Chief, I'll put it on 'is tab."

* * *

The Glencoe Chief of Police was sitting at his desk when the desk clerk called to inform him that there was a member of the Chicago Police Force waiting to see him. The Chief wondered why a visitor from 2,000 miles away wouldn't have called before making this long a trip. He said to the desk sergeant, "Tell him to have a seat. And pour 'im a cup of coffee. I'll see him in about thirty minutes." The Chief rang for his secretary. She came in, chewing gum as usual, and asked, "What can I do for you Chief?" The Chief looked at this 40ish year old spinster that reminded him of Eleanor Roosevelt, and had to remember that she may not look like much, but could do wondrous things when needed. "Pat, I've a visitor from Chicago waiting to see me. Before I see him I need to know the name of the Chicago Chief of Police, and some of that gobbledygook that's been coming out in the Chicago newspapers regarding the Bentley case, the Black Mariah Syndicate, and any other goodies you may think I should know."

"When do you want all this, Chief?"

"How about as much as you can give me in say thirty minutes and the rest after I start talking with this guy."

"Sounds unreasonable, but I'll try."

Patricia hurried out to her desk, and the Chief put in a call to the DA's office. He found Claude in and said, "I have a member of the Chicago Police in my office. Do you want to talk to him when we're through?"

"Hm, I suspect this is a small potato person, but maybe I'd better see him… send him over when you're through, fine, but give him good transportation to make sure he gets here."

"Roger, CC. Will do."

Some thirty minutes later, Pat walked in on the Chief, and said, "Here's what I have: The Chief's name is Tom Wrightwood, he is in the fifth year of a six year term. They have been trying to get something solid against the Black Mariah bunch for five years, and 'ave come up empty. He wishes to be re-elected next year, and the media is looking to crucify him over the news from here. Both the Mayor and the Police Commissioner are on his case, and this guy is desperate. The investigating officer sent out here is a last ditch attempt to save the department's neck. That's all I have so far, Chief."

Chief Richardson smiled, and said, "This department would have trouble functioning without you, Pat." As she left the office, he told her to send the guest in. Shortly, Pat opened the door and ushered in Officer Crawford, currently attached to the Chicago Vice Squad. The Chief told him to be seated, and asked, "What can I do for you Officer?"

"My visit is in response to your message that there will be a trial in which there is a possible link to the Black Mariah Syndicate. We have a vested interested in this bunch, and will help where we can."

The Chief grinned, and said, "The way I hear it you have more than just a vested interest. This bunch, as you call them, is making your Chicago Police Force look awful bad, and is drawing a 'bunch' of flak from the Chicago Tribune." The Chief paused for a moment, and then, "You've been sent out here to take some of the heat off your boss. That's plain and simple. In the first place, I would have expected a call from Chief Wrightwood before you came out. Now, we are expecting more than a mere vice squad detective. If the Chicago Police Force really wants our cooperation in this matter, they had better send out a heavyweight with lots of help and some authority. The Syndicate, I assure you, will have lots of manpower, authority, and money. Please convey my remarks to Chief Wrightwood."

The Chief rose from his seat to indicate that the interview was over and said, "We have set up a meeting for you with our District Attorney. You are due there in fifteen minutes. I have arranged for a police vehicle to take you there." He rang for Pat. When she stuck her head in the door, he said, "Pat, there's a patrol car out front, see that Officer Crawford gets in and heads for the DA's office."

Chief Richardson waited until Crawford was gone, then dialed the DA. When Claude came on the line, he said, "Sonny Boy's on his way. I cut him down a bit. Told him to inform his boss, Chief Tom Wrightwood, that if he wants information, or wants to help, send out a heavyweight and some legal people. You can take it from there."

"Thanks Chief. How far did you cut him down?"

"I told him that he won't get information one from us until Tom Wrightwood has the courtesy to call me, and send some upper level people or legal beagles out here."

Claude laughed and said, "Oh, that was nice and friendly like, and now you dump him in my lap. Thanks a lot."

"Don't mention it. That was fun."

The DA groaned as he hung up the phone.

Shortly thereafter Officer Crawford found himself sitting opposite the District Attorney of Contra County. The DA spoke first, "What can we do for you officer?"

"It is our understanding that you will soon be prosecuting certain persons, and possibly one from Chicago, for crimes against the Bentley Ranch and/or George Bentley."

"And?"

The detective squirmed in his chair, thinking to himself: This sure is an unfriendly town. Jeez, I hope I get orders to go back home, like today. "We would like to be included in any information developed during your investigations, pertinent to the activities of the Black Mariah Syndicate."

"That's nice, I suggest you take yourself on home, and have your DA's office request this, in writing. Also inform him that a qualified representative from his office on-site might be acceptable."

The Chicago officer left after saying a very insincere, "Thank you for seeing me."

Claude Comstock had been a local attorney serving his friends and neighbors before his election to County District Attorney. This was his second term as DA, and he was well liked and respected about town. During World War II, he served on the local draft board, and gained a reputation for fairness, and seemed to know personally each of the thousands of young men that passed through his office. Now in his late sixties, he looked the part of a senior citizen, but had retained that sharpness of mind, and quickness of response that had marked his younger life. Past experiences gave him that sense of preparedness needed in dealing with complex legal problems. The Bentley case was shaping up to be one of those things. To Claude, this was an opportunity. He would gripe a lot about the extra work, but love every minute of it. For three days he buried himself in the pile of complaints, evidence, history, newspaper articles and any and all aspects of the crime spree that had spread through Contra County. He subscribed to the Chicago newspapers. He reviewed each crime, each killing, each subsequent investigation, and what steps had been taken to prevent further illegal happenings. In short, he prepared himself to execute a successful prosecution, and identify the killer of Richard Bentley.

John Blake, the District Attorney of Cook County, Illinois, called, with apologies for not having gotten in touch sooner. He said, "It is my intention to cooperate fully with your office. Please consider this telephone call as a request for us to place a temporary representative from our office onto your staff at our expense. He would report directly to you, and at the same time keep my office informed of pertinent aspects of the case. Yes, we are interested in the Black Mariah aspects here, but we are not limiting it to that. I'll put all this in a letter and it should arrive in a day or two."

Claude Comstock hung up the phone, deep in thought. He was not enamored with the idea of advertising how small his "staff" actually was to the big Cook County person, however, having a free legal aide at his disposal at this time sure sounded good. Perhaps I'd better tell it as it is from the start, and accept this offer. The man at the other end of the phone sounded plenty cooperative and sincere.

He picked up the phone and asked the operator to connect him with the Bentley Ranch. In time, George Bentley came to the phone. "This is George."

"Mr. Bentley, this is Claude Comstock, the Contra County District Attorney. I would like to meet with you ASAP. When could that be?"

"I've been expecting your call, Claude, where and when? I'll accommodate."

"Can you make it to my office by 10 tomorrow? I'm buying lunch."

"Can do, see you there."

The DA's office was located in an old city-owned brick building that hadn't been revitalized for 50 years. Most of the city dignitaries had offices here, and would put up with it as long as the climate inside was okay: good air conditioning, and good heat when needed. There weren't many out of town people to impress, so this was okay with everyone, and the city saved a lot of money. Claude Comstock had spent his own money, however, to spruce up his office complex, which included a small outer office and waiting area where a secretary, when he had one, would reign supreme, and a rather commodious office where CC had his desk. Claude's desk had several stand-up pictures of his family, and a cigar humidor on one corner. George found the DA at his desk, deep in thought, staring at a six inch stack of paper resting on a messy blotter. The handshakes were firm, and told much to each about the other.

Claude said, "Welcome, have a seat."

"Hello to you, Claude, I've been hearing a bit here and there about our District Attorney. You sure have made a great name for yourself around these parts. You're kind of a local icon from what I hear. When did you get the case?"

"About a week ago. I'd have called you sooner, but it's taken me some time to get on board enough to ask intelligent questions. From what I hear, you have more of the answers than anyone else does. As for all that icon stuff, it's all baloney.

"A lot of what's been going on is well documented here." He pointed to the pile of papers on his desk, and continued, "So I'd like you to talk away about your thoughts and instincts. I see reference to the lone ponderosa on top of a mesa, will you start from there. Oh, and call me CC, everyone else does."

Most officials in Contra County were cattlemen first, and filled in on community jobs as sort of a duty. Claude Comstock was different; he was an official first and not a cattleman or miner. George looked at a strong face which told of a positive attitude and someone very sincere. He said, "Sounds like a winner, I'll keep it as abbreviated as possible. My father was killed sometime Monday morning the tenth of May. His body was found that afternoon by Peter White, a long time ranch foreman for the Arrow—B, and trusted good friend. I arrived at the ranch late May 11th. After the funeral and burial rites were over, I found time to go out to the crime scene. That would be May 17th.

"When Pete picked up Dad's body, he looked all around but couldn't find Dad's rifle, yet the Sheriff found it in plain sight three days later. According to the first conclusion from the Sheriff's office, my father fired his rifle at something or someone, fell off his horse, and broke his neck. The broken neck didn't make sense to me, so I concluded that someone or something else than falling off a horse was responsible.

Subsequently, Pete and I found rope burns on the lower limb of that lone ponderosa you spoke of. My conclusion: someone or something had swung from that limb recently. In time I contacted a Chicago pathologist and asked him whether there would be any identifiable difference between a broken neck resulting from a falling body, and one broken from a fall from a gallows. He said probably, and suggested the body be exhumed for an autopsy. I have not done that yet. I am suggesting that this might possibly be a place for you to begin. You have, I see, lots of documentation on this case. It is hard for me to preempt hard documented facts with memory. I believe it would serve both of us better if you led with questions, and I answered, with comments."

The District Attorney said, "I suppose you are right, that is, if I have done all my homework, and I'm still working at it. You have answered one of my questions already; however, the murder of your father is the place to start. From what I've read and from talking with you, I'm convinced that there has been foul play. People don't do criminal acts without reason. I think we must determine who is to gain what from the acquisition of a remote ranch in southern Wyoming." Claude continued, "Now I see the out-of-state Black Mariah Syndicate is allegedly involved. Why? I think when we get the answer to that one we might have half a chance of cutting into some of the illicit activities of that organization. So let's talk about the value of your real estate holdings to someone else. What's so valuable that they will kill and spend lots of money to get? If we rule out the value as a place to ranch and earn a profit raising cattle, that leaves possibly some unknown mineral deposits. Or perhaps a place for concealment. How about a place that has access to mineral deposits?

"George, I need some help. Start thinking in terms of why. The who, seems apparent. Look thoroughly through your father's records. Look for mineral assays, evidence of surveys performed on your properties. Examine the ranch tax records."

George hesitated for a moment, "This I have already given

a lot of thought to. So far I've come up empty. You are holding one suspect that might have the answer. He is the son of Frank Costello, the top man of the Syndicate. He's hurting plenty bad, and frightened for his life. Maybe, just maybe, he'll give us some answers," George paused, then looking straight at the man he sat across from, "with a little bit of persuasion that is."

The District Attorney offered a wry grin and head shake, and said, "Yes, well we have to handle that one strictly by the book. How frightened is he?"

"Plenty. He cried when we caught 'im."

The DA said, "Some of the stuff we're holding these people on is plenty weak. His is a case in point. Until we can prove a more serious crime than driving at night in our county with live weapons, we're in danger of having to release him on bail. That we do not want to do. I've already spoken to County Judicial about this matter. They cautioned me to hurry up with arraignment, and keep things moving, on the premise that denial of bail may bring motions and mountains of paperwork. So time is of an essence.

"We can argue that there are several ways to get a broken neck: by hanging, by forcing the head backward until the spinal structures are destroyed, or by a fall where a person actually lands on his head. We should know the answer to this.

"How about I should contact the county coroner, and have him prepare the paperwork to do that autopsy you had in mind. Let's get a look at that broken neck. I read about those two bums, that hit you on the head, ending up with broken necks. I agree with you, there must be some connection here."

"Okay Claude, have the paperwork sent to me and I'll sign what's needed to exhume my Dad's body. By the way, he's buried on ranch property.

"Now, I have an idea that there's someone, perhaps within the Chicago Mafia, very experienced in the art of breaking necks, huge, strong, and probably dumb. He is often used in lieu of bullets that can be traced. Because of his size, he probably does a good job of frightening too."

"Good thought, George, I'll contact Wrightwood in Chicago and see if he has anybody with that profile on his list.

" Do ya want a job George?"

George laughed and said, "You're kidding of course. No!"

" Let's go to lunch."

"Sounds like a winner to me. People on ranches eat kind of early, say like 4:30 A.M., and I could easily digest half a cow at this point. Your secretary on vacation or just resting for the day?"

"You just hit a nerve, my part-time secretary is great when I have her. What you see is what you get. And yes, I'm short-handed. Right now there's half a secretary and me, which condition I'll have to change or this case is dead. I'm in contact with Cheyenne and hope to get some help from the State. I asked the County Board of Supervisors for money to put on extra help to handle this thing. It seems that Sheriff Williams has already given them a pretty good idea of what's going on, softened them up so to speak, so they are already considering coming up with some bucks to help support this office during the prosecution."

The lunch was small by Rosey's standards, but healthy. George stood up to leave, and said, "Well, I've got a ranch to run, and this is shaping up to be a tough winter on the range. I sure hope any new interlopers sent out by the Mob freeze their butts off."

Claude Comstock watched George drive away amid thoughts and memories of himself as a young attorney, learning quickly about the real world, and at the same time trying to retain his idealism and enthusiasm. This young man conveyed a sense of honor and integrity while being subjected to a whole lot of trouble, uncompromising when he felt it right to do so, but at the same time understanding the human persona and all its foibles. This was unusual for one his age. I need to do the best job of my life for this young man. He flipped through his phone index box and found the name John Blake. It took a little doing, but in time he was speaking with John. "Claude Comstock, DA of Contra County, Wyoming here."

"Hello Claude, I'm glad you called, I've been wanting to have a chat with you about a mutual problem we have. What can I do for you?"

"Likewise here, John, I think we should meet some time soon, however there is one thing I need right now."

"Just name it, and if I can do, I will."

"I'm looking for someone, very large, very strong, probably not very bright, and possibly good at breaking necks. Also you might review the case of two bums who died of broken necks in Chicago a couple of months ago. These two were arrested on a charge of attempted murder here last August. They were released on $200,000 bail by, we think, a judge on the take. I thought it might be better if I asked you rather than Tom. This way, you will be kept informed of activity out here better."

"Not a bad idea, Claude, I'll find out if Tom has anyone that fits this profile on his books.

"That man I promised you should arrive tomorrow. He's young, but seems to have lots of savvy."

Claude said, "He will sure be welcome, this thing is going to keep me plenty busy for the next few months."

"You're alone, Claude?"

"For the time being, yes, I hope to do something about that soon. Thanks for the support."

John said, "Okay, I'll get back to you when I have something."

Claude Comstock hung up the phone feeling a little less alone.

* * *

The legal staff of the Syndicate began arriving in town soon after the capture of Junior and established its base in a rented office located in an old brick building that used to be part of the high school. It was about a block from the courthouse, and not too far from their motel. They quickly filed a motion with the court asking that their client be released on bail. This action had been expected, and the court set a date for a hearing on the matter for January 15. There was a lot of complaining about the timing of this one by the defense, claiming their client would be no threat to society, and that he should not be treated to two months in jail without just cause. The court stated that the holiday season was approaching, and that time was needed to review the suspect's background before a bail hearing could be held.

Bob Gibson turned out to be totally indigent, and unable to afford counsel. He was being held on charges of fraud against the Arrow—B Ranch, possible implication with the murder of Richard Bentley, and as a material witness. The Court appointed a defense counsel for Bob.

The matter of defense counsel for both the hired assassin, and the minor hood from the Chicago area was a real headache for the Syndicate. They were trying their best to distance themselves from either of these two; however, they didn't want to ignore them either for fear that one or the other might expose some of the illegal activities of the Syndicate.

Mr. Jones of Jones Realty decided to seek counsel in that there was a good chance that he would become implicated in 'aiding or abetting' a criminal act. He began to look at his "friends" with the possibility of conspiracy against the Arrow—B showing up.

The Indian Nation council met and took up the matter of Little Crow's involvement in the death of White Owl. No decision was made as to how to protect tribal interests and sacred rites and, at the same time condemn the wrongdoing of one of their own. Chief Running Deer pointed out that it was imperative that the council resolve this problem quickly or their white brothers would do it for them. The issue would be taken up again the following day.

Without waiting for the Contra County Board of Directors to formally allocate funds for another attorney to assist the DA, Claude put out inquiries to find one. There weren't that many legal types available in this part of the world, so he decided to settle for someone who could do research, make inquiries by telephone, and generally act as a super secretary. This would leave all court appearance responsibility on his own shoulders, which was okay with him.

Most of the City's hierarchy, including the County DA usually attended the Glencoe Rotary Club meetings, which took place on Mondays at noon. After a blue plate special lunch, Club members settled down to discussions of current issues and opportunities facing the City Government. Since the majority of the members were business owners, the term "opportunities" usually meant the opportunity to fix a problem, or to help the business community improve its money-making abilities. City officials, including the Mayor, generally attended and joined with "the boys", to find out what was going on. At one of these meetings Claude, sitting next to the Mayor, said, "Fred, it looks like the Bentley case is coming to fruition, and will be in court sometime next month."

The Mayor put down his fork, made a half turn to face Claude, and said, "Rumor has it that this is shaping up to be big time for our City. D'ya mind filling me in a bit?"

"Right Fred, How about tomorrow around nine? We can't cover it here."

"Claude, I've got some time this afternoon, could we do it right after lunch?"

"Okay. Your office or mine?"

The Mayor said, "It better be yours, mine is being redecorated."

It was just on 2 p.m. when the Mayor sat down opposite the County District Attorney. Claude Comstock spoke first. "Fred, I think the rumors you heard are right on, this town of ours is going to get national attention over this one. Certainly, the press is working us up to that level. The courthouse will be too small, our one hotel will be filled, to overflowing and we don't have enough space in motels to handle all the people that will want to be here. Food services will also be taxed to the limit to provide meals."

The Mayor smiled and said, "Well I see a challenge here, but there are going to be lots of happy people in town. How long do you think the trials will last?"

"Three months, give or take a couple of weeks, and it could be longer if we put every person guilty of criminal actions to trial. This is an incredibly complex combination of criminal acts by lots of people, some of whom are truly greedy, and some that have just been duped into doing criminal things. Sorting all this out is my job, and I don't begin to have enough staff to handle it at this point."

"The way I see it, you don't even have a 'staff'."

"Yes, well I'm working on that one right now. By the way I need someone to do research, make phone calls and in general act like a super secretary. Can you think of someone like that?"

The Mayor hesitated for a moment then asked; "Do you know Priscilla over at the library?"

"Are you serious? I don't need someone to sort and file papers."

"Priscilla has a masters in both Political Science, and Library Science. I found this out when I was running for office. She was very helpful as a campaign assistant and very bright. Why don't you talk to her at least?"

"Okay Fred, I'll check her out on your recommendation; in the meantime, see if you can divert some money from the city coffers to help out here. I'm already spending some of my own money to get started. Can't you rationalize a few bucks to be spent on attracting business to our city or something?"

"Claude, let me chew that one over a bit. In the interim keep me informed of your progress so I can plan out the next few months."

The Mayor got up to leave then said, "Claude, we go back

a long way. I see your problem, and I'll help all I can. Keep in touch."

Claude Comstock watched his friend climb into his pickup. *It sure is good to have friends when you need them, and I sure could use as many of those things as I can get.* He stood up, put on his ball cap and jacket, then headed for the library. It was now late in the afternoon, and getting colder. He hunched over, drew his jacket tightly around his neck, and stoically plodded on. He entered the library and approached the librarian at the checkout desk. "I'd like to speak to Priscilla if I may."

The clerk said, "Priscilla is in the basement repairing some distressed books, may I help?"

The DA reached in his pocket and withdrew a business card. "I don't think so; please hand her my card, and tell her it is urgent."

The clerk looked at the card handed to her, and said, "Oh, just a minute Mr. Comstock." She turned and descended the stairs, soon returning with a pretty woman in her late twenties. She was wearing a white blouse with sleeves rolled up. She had a wisp of auburn hair hanging over her left eye. Her skirt was short for this time of year, showing long slim beautifully proportioned legs. Her smile made Claude stumble over his words.

"You are Priscilla?"

She smiled, and answered, "That's my name; is there something I can do for you?"

Claude said, "Priscilla", and he chuckled, "I somehow was expecting someone a bit older. The Mayor didn't tell me much other than that you might be just right for a project I have in mind. Could we sit somewhere so I can explain?"

"Of course, come into my office."

They moved into the small library office. Claude outlined the details of what he had in mind to the young lady in front of him. He said, "The Mayor told me that he could make you available for the next few months, if it was okay with you. I can assure you, the work will be hard, with lots of late nights and missed meals."

"Gosh, Mr. Comstock, you sure don't make it very attractive. It's funny, but that's what happened when I worked for Fred. He worked me to death." She looked Claude straight in the eye and said, "I loved every minute of it. When do I start?"

"By tomorrow I'll have a desk and some file cabinets moved into your office space. How about tomorrow morning at eight?"

"Sounds great, I'll be there."

Claude called the local hardware store and got the owner, Jack, "How soon can you come up with a couple of standard five foot desks, a couple of swivel chairs to match and about three five-drawer filing cabinets?"

Jack answered, "About two weeks, I guess. Is there any hurry Claude?"

"Yes, well can you fix up something temporary?"

"How about a couple of standard doors on saw horses and porch chairs to match?"

Claude chuckled, "Can you get them over here this afternoon? You better make it three instead of two, and bring some bricks and boards to make a bookcase out of."

"Will do, see you in about an hour."

Claude Comstock arrived at his office about six the next morning. The added 'furniture' made it look like the inside of a barn expecting some physical activity. He had called the phone company the night before, and ordered two extra phones. The installers were due at seven. The law library was located in the secretary's area. He decided to move them directly into his office.

At a quarter to eight, the phone rang. A strong male voice stated that he had arrived and was sitting on his duff, twiddling his thumbs at the airport, waiting to be picked up.

Claude said someone would pick him up directly.

Priscilla arrived, looking expectantly for a place to put her things. Claude said, "Well yes, we don't look like much right now, but give me a week or two. Ah, there is a man from

Chicago waiting at the airport. Please go pick him up."

By noon, the offices were put together enough to function, and all three went out to a quickie lunch. At one o'clock sharp, Claude declared the D.A.'s office was open for business. The man from Cook County was Edward Hunt. He was already acquainted with much of the known information about the Syndicate. Priscilla took notes, and started to get on board. She absorbed things quickly, and the team, including the part-time secretary, was formed.

The coroner called to say that arrangements were made to exhume the body of Richard Bentley tomorrow. The casket, with its contents would be taken to the lab in Glencoe, the body would be autopsied, and then returned to the ranch for re-burial.

Claude called John Blake, in Chicago. "John, Claude Comstock out in Wyoming."

"Hello Claude, what's on your mind?"

Claude said, "John, we're having Richard Bentley's body exhumed to take a look at that broken neck. Would you consider doing the same on one of those two rummies that died last fall of broken necks out your way? I think we need to tie the two events together."

John said, "That's not an easy thing to do here; however, I'll do my best to get that one going. I agree with you, it's too much of a coincidence not to tie in. Anything else, Claude?"

"Well yes, I'm sending you pictures of all four suspects we have in jail out here. Call me if something comes to mind, or any of them are on one of your lists; and thanks for the help. Your man arrived this morning. Many thanks."

Claude sat and considered some of the evidence, or lack of it that is. There were a lot of events that have been recorded, but little tangible evidence against any of the suspects in custody. Many of the participants involved were dead. The remaining were going to be hard to get anything out of. He called the Arrow—B. When George came on the line he said, "George, I need to visit with you on the ranch. I need to look at the crime scenes and get a feel for what went on.

Is tomorrow okay, or would you rather wait until the coroner is finished doing his thing?"

"Come tomorrow, CC, I know time is running out. I can handle the other."

"There'll be two of us. Is that okay?"

"Claude, as long as you keep focused on the main issue, you can do whatever you feel is necessary. Don't bring sack lunches, I just butchered a steer that broke a leg."

Claude turned to his two associates and said, "Ed, I want you to run the office tomorrow. Priscilla and I are going to be gone the better part of the day. We'll be at the Arrow—B. If you need me, just ask the operator to connect you to the Arrow—B Ranch. You will have our secretary with you tomorrow. Priscilla, you and I are going out to the ranch. It's going to be cold, so dress warm. Let's plan on leaving here at 8 am. By the way, Priscilla, do you have a nick-name?"

"Uh huh, most everyone calls me Pril. You can if you wish."

Claude and Pril found themselves driving under the weathered board announcing the entrance to the Arrow—B Ranch and crossing the temporary plywood bridge about 10 a.m. They drove the quarter mile ranch road into the yard, and sat in their seats while Charlie barked his head off. Mary Ellen came out from the cook shack, and shushed him up, and welcomed them to the ranch. "I'm Mary Ellen, the do-anything person around here. Come right on in, we've been expecting you. George is out on the range, but will return shortly. How about a cup of coffee?"

"That sounds fine Mary Ellen, I'm Claude, and this is Pril."

Mary Ellen said, "The cook shack is the warmest place on the ranch, let's go in there."

Shortly, the sound of a pickup entering the ranch yard, and a woof-woof from Charlie announced the arrival of George. He stuck his head in the cook shack and said, "Hello, I see you have already met Mary Ellen. He came in, poured himself a cup of coffee, sat down, and said, "Where do you want to start Mr. District Attorney? You have the floor."

"George, meet Priscilla. We all call her Pril. She is doing research etc. for the case. I kinda thought we could break us in two, Pril spend the day with Mary Ellen, and I stay with you. How does that sound?"

George said, "Sounds like a winner, Mary Ellen's been here almost from the start, and can fill Pril in fine. You and I can tromp to your heart's content. How cold do you want to get?"

Claude did a shiver and said, "Yes, well we don't have the luxury of waiting till spring is here. I guess I can suffer a bit. Let's start with the place your dad was killed."

"How good are you at riding horses?"

"You're serious about this?"

"Uh-huh."

"Do you have something slow and gentle?"

"We do, honest injun."

Claude screwed up his nose and said, "Somehow that remark is suspect, but I've run out of options. Let's go."

In time, the double horse trailer which was occupied by Nellie and, what looked like a placid slow pokey steed, was hooked up to the ranch pickup. Claude and George drove to the bottom of Portal Mesa, mounted up, and started up the trail. At the first switchback Claude looked down over the side of his mount, and nearly fainted. George, riding behind, noted the insecure look on Claude's face, laughed to himself, but admired the courage of his companion, and instinctively knew this person would prevail in the challenge that he faced. Riding up this steep trail on a horse for a person that doesn't ride, must be scary. In time they reached the top.

The two men walked their horses up the trail to the crime scene area, dismounted, and George laid out the events, and where they took place. Claude took notes and made drawings. He had a tape measure with him, and at the end of an hour, was well on his way to understanding the sequence of events. He commented that this was too hard a place to get to, for ordinary city folks, and that it seems evident that some local people were involved and therefore might be suspected of complicity.

The return trip was slow, as Claude needed to dismount several times because of his rear end. He wondered if he would ever recover? "It seems we need to stay over for another day, George. I can sleep in the bunk house. Can you find a place for Pril?"

"Can do, and then I can use up some of that beef I butchered yesterday."

Claude said, "I'm not sure I can sit down at this point, can I eat standing up?"

"The good news, Claude, is that we can reach all the other spots by pickup."

The next morning, George and Claude visited the other places where events had taken place. In the meantime, Mary Ellen and Pril hit it off very well, and by the time Claude and George returned, Pril was well informed of events.

On the return trip to Glencoe, Claude and Pril stopped in to see Sheriff Williams.

The Sheriff showed the evidence envelopes to Claude. Arrangements were made to borrow those items he would need for the trials.

The next morning the three members of the legal staff were together again in the office. The material they had gathered was shared and filed. Claude said, "The way I see it there have to be at least three separate trials. I think they should be sequenced like this, first Jon Balante, the mechanic, then Bob Gibson, and Peterson maybe together, then the Black Mariah itself."

Ed said, "I take it you would handle Jones Realty, Muscles, and our Indian friend within the Black Mariah trial?"

"Yes, and there might be others that we will have to slip into that trial."

Ed said, "I believe that when we expose some of the lesser players the Judge will hand out suitable penalties.

Pril asked, "Will there be a jury for any of these trials?"

"The defense has the right to have it either way."

Ed said, "I believe security is going to be an issue. There's a nasty looking bunch floating around town. We need security on all this data we are collecting?"

Claude said, "Good point, Ed. We really need extra copies of everything, and put them in several places."

Pril said, "I suspect that's where I come in. This is a lot of grubby work, but it has to be done. I'll start right in."

"Well we'll all help when we can, and Alice out front too."

John Blake, the Cook County DA called. "Hello Claude."

"Hello John, I see it's snowing out your way. What's on your mind?"

"Yah, it's snowing alright, but good. The kids are ecstatic. It took me two hours to get to work this morning. Say, you've been asking the right questions. I have a make on that hit man you have in custody. His name is Jon Ballant. He's international, and is a wanted fugitive in at least three states. He is also an escape artist. Please pass that information on to your police department. Muscles is a Chicago hood, often suspected of brutal crimes, but never convicted. Up to now he's been local Chicago. I sure hope you can come up with something on this guy. We can get hold of him, with the proper paper work."

Claude laughed and said, "That's gonna be fun; from what I've heard, you'll need a regiment to collar 'im. I'll try to tie him in to the broken neck issue. We have exhumed Richard Bentley's body, and have neck pictures. We'll have an autopsy report soon. How are you doing on that issue there?"

John Blake answered, "Sometimes I'm jealous of you guys out there, you can get from here to there just like that. Me, I've got a whole bunch of red tape plus line of command to go through. I do have the process started though, and I'll let you know when I have something."

"Gee John, I sure thank you for the information. We're going to prosecute the hit man first. I did the arraignment yesterday. Keep warm."

Claude hung up the phone. He turned to Ed and said, "Ed, that was John Blake; he came up with a name for the hit man, and there is a man called Muscles that might fit the broken neck theory. I'd like you to follow up on that end. Cover the Bentley X-ray thing, and coordinate with your Chicago office about the progress there.

"Pril, we need pictures of House Rock, where the first ambush took place, also, go with Don up the mountain above the water tower, where the suspect fired at George. I want all the info we can get about that sequence. Leave this morning, and you better take an overnight bag along. I'll coordinate all this with George. Before you leave, review all the documents we have on this attempted murder, and be sure to take a camera with you. Sheriff Williams will be with you. He's a good source of information. Spend some time with him. If you get an invite to dinner or overnight from his wife, Martha, accept. She is also a great person to find out things from."

Pril said, "I was wondering when the late nights and missed meals would start. I just got my answer. Does everyone know I'm coming?"

Claude laughed and said, "No, well I'll call them now."

The secretary out front rang, and Claude picked up the phone. "Comstock here."

"Mr. Comstock, this is Agnes, the court clerk, I just had a visitor; he is a registered attorney in Cook County and his name is Harold Hoople. He will be representing Jon Ballant."

"Thanks Agnes, find out if he can practice in this state without a special permit. For that matter cover me on that one for any lawyer type that might show up."

"You got it, I'll be in touch."

Claude hung up the phone and sat for a bit. He buzzed for his secretary. When she came in he said, "I need you to write to John Blake, Cook County District Attorney. As follows: Jon Ballant is being represented by a Harold Hoople, registered to practice in your County. I would like to tie him into the Black Mariah bunch. Talk to you soon. Sign it with my name, and get it off pronto, like in thirty minutes. You can catch the afternoon mail that way."

"I gotcha Claude."

"Thanks Alice."

Pril gathered what she needed for an overnight stay, bought a camera, extra film, notebook and such case information as she would need, and headed for Walnut. She arrived in Walnut about noon, so she dropped in at Rosey's for lunch. There was only one customer in the diner when she got there. Rosey, looked out through the kitchen pass-through, saw Pril, and came around with the coffee pot and a mug. She came over to Pril, said hello, handed her a menu and filled the coffee cup. It took less than a minute for the two to become acquainted and involved in a credible conversation. And, it took just under five minutes to finish up the small talk and get to George Red Fox Bentley, which was what Pril wanted to talk about in the first place.

Of course when two single women get together, the question has to be "Is he married?" Now Rosey has been juggling her affections between her two best friends, Betty and Joan, for the past six months. She has said she is neutral about this thing, but it's hard. Now here sits a rather good looking 27 year old asking if George is married. She can see the humor in this question only because she has watched, and been involved in this happening before, that is, two women both in love with the same man. She was also aware of the pain that must be going on with both Betty and Joan. For this she is sad. Rosey, however, was never one to pussy-foot around about things, and said, "No Pril, but he has, I think, fallen in love, and talks like they might get married soon." Rosey eyed her other customer, noticed his empty coffee cup, and got up to fill it. When she returned, she said, "That was, of course, before the shooting."

Well Pril was there to gather information, so she said, "Tell me about the shooting, Rosey. I need all the information I can find. The District Attorney wants me to walk the walk, take pictures, do interviews, and especially with you Rosey."

Rosey kind of smiled and said, "I didn't know my fame had traveled so far," then asked, "What can I tell you that you don't already know?"

"Well, why don't you tell me when you first learned about George being shot. Then, we can go on from there."

"Okay, Pril, I was here in the kitchen when the phone call came in. Doc Morrison took the message from Dorothy, the telephone operator. Joan, one of my helpers, was out front waiting on a customer. When she heard the news, she became very upset, and asked to borrow my car. I said yes, of course, and handed her the key. She rushed out of here like a bullet. Climbed into the car, and sped off. I went right to the phone and called Betty, George's lady friend at her father's ranch, and told her about George. Now anything else I could tell you would be hearsay. I suggest you go out and see Betty for more information. You can use my phone to arrange a visit with her. The last name is Harris. Joan is off today. She will be here tomorrow, and if you wish to stay over tonight, you can see her then."

"I'd like to do that Rosey; well I see you're getting busy. When should I come back to continue our conversation?"

Rosey said, "Three this afternoon, or tomorrow at ten would be fine."

Priscilla reached for the phone, and asked for the Harris Ranch. Betty Harris answered, "Hello, this is Betty."

"Miss Harris, this is Priscilla Beckman, the librarian at the Glencoe Library. I'm kind of helping our District Attorney, who is prosecuting the bad guys that have been involved in the Bentley saga. I would like to ask you some questions concerning the crimes against the Arrow—B. Could I come out and see you?"

Betty sounded a bit cool when she said, "Priscilla, I have very little knowledge of things that happened. I think you would be wasting your time. I have always been the last to hear about things, and all I know would be what someone else told me."

"Well, hearsay is good, that's about all I have right now. I was instructed to learn what our County's residents believe. Can you tell me your instincts and insight on this matter?"

"I guess I can do that much; where are you calling from?"

"I'm at Rosey's Café in Walnut."

"Can you come now? It's about a thirty minute drive from there."

"Fine, I'll be there." She hung up the phone and turned to Rosey and said, "Betty will see me, although she didn't sound that enthusiastic about the idea. Can you tell me how to get to the Harris Ranch?"

* * *

Betty met Priscilla at the ranch gate. She welcomed her guest, and said. "Come right on in, do you care for a cup of coffee?"

"That will be fine. Would you mind calling me Pril, everyone else does."

"Sure Pril, and I'm Betty, that's much easier."

"Betty, the County District Attorney is putting a case together against each of the perpetrators of the many crimes committed here in the last six months, and I am helping with the investigation. It's not open and shut by any means, as most of the evidence will be circumstantial. It is therefore essential that we know as much about these crimes as possible. Today we filed papers against Jon Ballant, who is an international killer, for attempted murder. He is the man we think shot George Bentley in the head. That's what I want to talk about today. Please tell me what you know, in your own words about the shooting."

"Pril, the first I heard about George being shot is when Rosey called me. I rushed over to the Arrow—B, and found George sitting up with a big bandage around his head. There were lots of people around him already; he didn't seem to need me, so I turned around and left."

"You didn't stay around to talk to him then? Who were the other people that were there?"

"Well, there was Doc Morrison, Pete, the Arrow—B foreman, Mary Ellen, oh and there was a Joan somebody."

"Well Betty, Rosey told me how Joan got the news, and rushed out to the ranch."

"How did she get the news?"

"According to Rosey, the telephone operator, Dorothy, called looking for Doc Morrison. He was sitting at a table having some pie, so Rosey handed him the phone. He listened, then quickly hung up the phone and started for the door. As he went out he said, There's been a shooting out at the Arrow—B, and he was gone. Rosey now called Dorothy back and asked what happened. She said that George had been shot in the head. Joan, who was waiting table, gasped, and said, Rosey, can I borrow your car, I'm going out there."

Betty was quiet, having her own thoughts, she was going over the bedroom scene at the Arrow—B Ranch. Maybe she had been a bit hasty. It was such a shock to see Joan caressing George. It appears that George couldn't help what happened. She knew that where George was concerned, she was a little crazy, a bit jealous, and not really rational at times. Her father told her to trust her instincts—sometimes that didn't work, and this was a case in point. She had rejected George, refused to listen to him, and in fact had been bitchy to the nth degree.

Pril waited for a response. She sensed the need to be patient, that there was something private happening here.

Betty finally spoke, "You have just told me something I didn't know and very important to me. Thank you for that. Of course, I will give you any information I have, which isn't much. George is very special to me. Unfortunately, I always seem to be the last person to hear about things that happen to him."

"Betty, I didn't mean to infringe on your privacy. I'm beginning to understand some of the pain and concern going on in this County. I hope you will consider me a friend.

"When the DA goes to trial, he will face a bunch of high priced lawyers who have been there before. Since the evidence in this case is mainly circumstantial, getting convictions will be difficult."

Betty took her time to answer; she kind of had her mind on how to make up to the man she loved. Pril, waited. Betty finally said, "Pril, you didn't infringe on my privacy. Have you talked to George yet?"

"Kind of, I spent a day with Mary Ellen, while Claude questioned George."

"Are you staying overnight?"

"I guess so, I have a lot of people to see."

"Why don't you spend the night here, I'd love the company."

"That's very generous, you sure you don't mind?"

"Of course not, get your things from your car, we have a spare bedroom that needs using

Pril spent the evening with Betty and her dad. In time Betty spoke of the death of her first love, and the return to her father's ranch. Pril was silent for a moment, then asked, "How did you meet George, Betty?"

"At Rosey's, Pril. I was having a cup of coffee when George walked in. Rosey had just talked to me about starting to live again. I had been in sort of a funk since Paul died."

"Thanks, Betty for sharing this with me." Pril stood up and said, "I'd better call the ranch, and ask Mr. Bentley if I can see him in the morning." As she headed for the telephone she said, "Betty, can I help you with the dinner?"

"Betty smiled and said, "Pril that's nice of you, yes, and we can talk some more."

Pril picked up the receiver, listened to Dorothy's, what number would you like, and replied, "Please connect me with the Arrow—B Ranch."

George's strong voice came on the line, "This is George Bentley"

Mr. Bentley, this is Priscilla Beckman, would it be OK if I come tomorrow morning, I need to take some pictures, and gather as much evidence as I can."

"That'll be fine, Pril. Do you know how to get here?"

"Well, I'm at the Harris Ranch, and I'm sure Betty or her dad can give me directions."

George said, "Oh. . . may I speak to Betty?"

Betty came on the phone, "Hello George, you haven't called me for over a week."

"You haven't allowed me to talk to you for over three weeks."

"I think it's time you surprised me with another trip up the trail to the lone ponderosa." She covered the transmitter with her hand, turned to Pril and her dad and asked if they would leave and allow her some privacy. They nodded and left the room. "George, I wasn't very nice to you, I'm sorry."

"Sweetheart, I love you so much. I've been very sad. Of course I would like to take a trip up the mountain again. That's where I fell in love with you. I'll call you as soon as I finish with Pril—Better yet, why don't you drive over with Pril in the morning?"

"I guess that will be okay, goodnight. Love you."

"Goodnight, Sweetheart."

Pril and Betty driving separate cars drove into the Arrow—B driveway just at nine the next morning. It was still bitter cold from a below zero night. The frosty looking sun wasn't doing much to warm things up yet either. Mary Ellen came out from the cook shack and welcomed the two women, then led them up the porch steps and into the house. There was a beautiful fire feeding on a huge log which cheered everyone. She said, " Get yourselves warm, I'll go get a pot of coffee. George should be back in fifteen minutes or so."

In time, George came in, stomping off snow and slush from his boots. He came over to Betty, kissed her, and whispered, "I love you. Why don't you stay and sit in on this?" Pril pretended not to notice, and Mary Ellen disappeared out toward the cook shack. He turned to Pril and asked, "Where do you want to start?"

"Mr. Bentley, I need pictures and locations of all the events that took place the day you were shot. The trial of the professional killer, Jon Ballant, who was responsible for that act will be the first of several, and I need to take photographs from where he knelt and shot at you as well as pictures of the spot you were found and space in between. I need to know the time of day it happened, and pictures of your horse standing guard."

"We can do that, Pril. How do you want it, hiking boots or horses? It's drier from a horse."

Pril smiled, and said "Horses will do, I'm not much on hiking in the snow." She spent the early part of the day with Don, who was there when the shooting took place. By the time lunch was being served on the long table inside the cook shack, she had covered the crime scene pretty well. She called Sheriff Williams, and made an appointment for the afternoon.

Pril found the Sheriff's office and was just beginning a discourse with Sheriff Williams when the phone rang. The call was from Claude Comstock. "Bill this is the Contra County DA. Is Pril there?"

"Sure is, d 'you want to talk to her?"

"Right, stay on the line if you can. Pril, how soon will you finish up with the 'shot-in-the-head' sequence?"

"I'm just about finished, Claude. I walked the real estate, and talked to George, Don, Mary Ellen, Pete, and have yet to speak to Doctor Morrison and the Sheriff. I've got a bunch of pictures and have made the measurements you asked for."

"That's great Pril. Place all evidence you have up to now in the Sheriff's office safe. I want to be sure it gets from there to here safely. I repeat, do not bring evidence. Leave it with the Sheriff. You come on back as soon as you finish with Doc Morrison. Put the Sheriff back on the line.

"Bill, two things, first: I'm getting a little paranoid about the Chicago connection, and I would like to see a squad car follow Pril home; second I need all the evidence here and under tight security. Besides that evidence that Pril has, I need what your office is holding. If you need authorization to release said evidence, let me know and I will approach the judicial, and get right back to you."

"Claude, we're kind of used to being paranoid about such matters, it happens all the time here. Sure, I agree we need to do an escort thing on both Pril and the evidence. I'll release what I have on your phone request, please follow-up with a written. And let's do it this afternoon. You better call Richardson and fill him in. We'll leave here in about an hour."

"Bill, we have four shady looking lawyers camping in town, and there are several seedy characters hanging around as well. I talk to Richardson several times a day, and I would say he's getting a sort of harried look about him. When you come into town go right to police headquarters. They have a fairly secure evidence lockup. I'll call him and tell him you're coming."

The District Attorney hung up the phone. He called Chief Richardson and filled him in on the transfer of evidence, and also advised him that the prisoner, Jon Ballant, was an international killer.

After Pril and Betty left, George went back out on the range. The temperature had dropped to a chilly five below zero. He wore everything he owned, including long johns, but still shivered, and squelched down in the saddle to get as close to Nellie as he could. The big bay with her winter coat on bounced along, happy to be out. George found the small herd that were missing earlier, and pushed them out and over to the bales of hay Pete had dropped off earlier. There was water nearby and George broke the ice so the eight animals could drink. They would eat and drink, then huddle together for warmth. These were hardy creatures, but when the weather got too cold, and the ground was covered with snow they became a bit befuddled. Pete and Don had been out most of the day doing the same kind of duty.

As always, when he was alone on the range he had time to ruminate over the oncoming events, and often placed himself in the District Attorney's shoes, as if he were one of those things. It was five P.M. when he unsaddled Nellie, gave her a short session with the brush, and went into the ranch house. He called the DA.

"Claude, I'm thinking you will need the two Indians that tracked this scum ball as he crept up the hill to where he could do a murder."

"Yes, well I've been sort of putting off asking you about that one. I thought you might be a bit sensitive on that issue, however, since you mentioned it, I sure think it will help to have them there. Ah, can you discuss this with your grandfather?"

"Knowing the Chief as I do, I think you would be better advised to do that one. Do you think you can traipse out to the Village and chat with the Chief about this?"

Claude said, "Sure, will you make the arrangements or should I just call?"

"It's better that you do it. My grandfather would be honored to have you call."

The call to the Indian Village found Chief Running Deer in Walnut. The telephone operator, Dorothy, located the Chief at Rosey's. "This is Chief Running Deer."

"Chief, this is Claude Comstock the District Attorney. I'm preparing cases related to the prosecution of the criminals who attacked your grandson. I need to talk with you as soon as possible. We can do this here in my office or in the Village. When and where would this be convenient ?"

"Mr. Comstock, I've been expecting your call and I'm anxious to meet you. Would this afternoon be acceptable? I can come to your office."

"That will be fine, Chief. My office is on the second floor of the old office building in the center of Glencoe. I'll see you soon then."

The District Attorney sat facing the Arapaho Chief. Their handshake had been firm and spoke of a mutual respect for the other. "It's good of you to come Chief. Please call me Claude. There is much we need to talk about. We have four persons in jail here that we will be dealing with. The evidence against these four is all circumstantial, and it will be difficult to get convictions. Today I am concerned particularly with a Jon Ballant, who is a killer hired by a Chicago Syndicate to kill your grandson. He was captured with the offending fire arm, trying to depart this area. In this sequence your Nation provided two trackers who successfully followed this person when he approached the Arrow—B. Chief, I need to put these two on the witness stand to tell the court their story."

"Mr. Comstock, it has been our wish to remain invisible if possible." The piercing hazel eyes of the chief bored into those of the District Attorney, and he continued: "How serious is this need?"

"Very, Chief, I must establish a time line, and the movement of this suspect needs to be tracked as accurately as possible. In order to do that, I must have some person or persons describe and identify to the court what they saw or heard. The Court will not take hearsay. They will want evidence from credible witnesses."

"It seems then, we don't have much choice. I will discuss this matter with the Council."

"Chief, I would ask that you go forward with this as soon as possible. I don't have much time before the trial is to begin."

"How long will they be asked to be available to the court?"

"I can't answer that exactly, Chief, but I suspect it will be the better part of a week. The County will provide housing and meals for them while they are here. If they were not to respond to this request, the law could subpoena them to appear and testify."

Chief Running Deer was silent for a time, then, "Our people have learned not to interact with other Americans because of things like this. When we do, we are sometimes treated as vermin. We will be telling events we have witnessed. It will be embarrassing if our words are not accepted. And your subpoenas have no effect on our reservation." The old Chief paused, then, "I will give you an answer after our council meeting tomorrow."

Claude Comstock sat in thought for a long time after the departure of Chief Running Deer. Putting himself in the position of a defense attorney, he postulated arguments he himself would use. Reflecting on the last words the Chief uttered, It will be embarrassing if our words are not accepted. Yes, I certainly would argue that point. As a defense attorney, I would question the veracity of any witness claiming to be qualified as an expert i.e. tracking a person through several miles of underbrush, rocks and rubble. He turned to Pril, "You took a hike up the mountain to where the shooter knelt as he took a pot-shot at George. Did it seem plausible that a person could leave enough sign as he passed to be followed?"

"Claude, I couldn't follow any kind of a trail in that stuff. It's done all the time in fiction stories, but this isn't fiction. Can't we ask the trackers to demonstrate to the Court an example of their skills?"

"What did you have in mind, Pril?"

"Suppose we have a rabbit take a trip through the wilderness some place, going from point A to Point B. The trackers would not know where point B is."

"I can fill in the blanks. Good thinking Pril. I'll approach the court with a plan."

In time the DA was able to reach an agreement with the court on the matter of tracker skill and the proof thereof, and to conduct such an exercise that would both show the skills of the 'Old ways tracker' and a plausible scenario of the events of attempted murder by the accused, Jon Ballant.

In the name of the accused, the defense attorney, Harold Hoople, waived the right of a trial by jury. A request by the defense for a change in venue was denied. The prosecution provided a witness list to the defense, and the trial began.

25 | THE MECHANIC

The trial of Jon Ballant began on the 14th of November, 1952. Representing the accused was Harold Hoople, an attorney licensed to practice in the State of Illinois. A Wyoming judge granted Hoople a pro hac vice petition to practice law, in this case only. The prosecution team consisted of District Attorney Claude Comstock, Edward Hunt, the attorney on loan from Cook County, Illinois, and Priscilla Beckman. The presiding judge was His Honor Ralph Hastings.

The accused, Jon Ballant, was brought into the courtroom under heavy guard and manacled. Chief Richardson insisted on security checks on any strangers coming into the courtroom. The courtroom was filled to capacity, and the city was jammed with newspaper reporters, out of state lawmen with arrest warrants out on the prisoner, and onlookers.

The court clerk announced the arrival of the judge, "All rise, His Honor Ralph Hastings presiding."

The judge asked the prosecution to proceed with their opening statement.

The DA addressed the court, "There have been several attempts to kill George Bentley going back to mid-1952. This trial concerns just one of those attempts. The State intends to prove that the accused, Jon Ballant, a known assassin, did willfully, and with malice of forethought attempt to murder George Bentley, as he rode his horse up a trail on the Arrow—B Ranch, on the afternoon of October fifteenth nineteen hundred and fifty two. The evidence will show that the accused, Jon Ballant, fired shots at George Bentley with the intent to kill. The evidence will also show that this act was done for money, and not for self-defense, or accidentally. The accused is wanted in several states for other crimes and killings."

Judge Hastings instructed the defense to make its opening statement.

"Your Honor, the defense will make its opening statement later."

Judge Hastings said, "Claude, present your case against the accused."

The District Attorney said, "I call George Bentley to the stand."

After George was sworn in, Claude asked George to relate the events of the fifteenth of October, 1952.

George began his narration with the call from the lookout atop Leaning Mesa. The DA asked, "What caused you to post a watchman in such a place several miles from the ranch complex?"

"In the past few weeks the Arrow—B Ranch has been literally under siege. In an effort to assist law enforcement to protect ranch employees and others in our county, a ranch employee was posted on the highest location in the county, and a system of communication with the Sheriff was established."

The witness continued, "Some days later we received a call from our lookout. He reported that a strange vehicle had entered ranch property. The lookout said that the car drove to House Rock, stopped for a few minutes, then turned around and left the same way they had driven in. As it was three o'clock in the morning, and in view of recent criminal activity in our county, I decided to have a look. Peter White, my ranch foreman, drove our pickup and I rode my horse Nellie. I left orders with the cook, who was already up and starting breakfast preparations, to call Sheriff Williams and inform him of what we were doing. Peter and I met at House Rock where the intruding vehicle had stopped.

"Early that morning as Peter White and I stood talking together, a shot was fired by a concealed gunman. The would-be assassin would have been successful had it not been for my horse. She sensed something and warned us of the hidden threat. I returned fire which resulted in the death of the wood-be assassin. We loaded the body of the gunman and his weapon onto the pickup. I drove the pickup into town and to the Sheriff's office. Peter rode Nellie back to the ranch."

The District Attorney then asked, "What did you do next?"

"The following morning the Sheriff and I traveled out to the crime scene. We searched the area of the shooting, and found a second set of footprints, leading off in the direction of the Arrow—B Ranch. It appeared to me that there was another person still out there, programmed to kill."

The defense attorney jumped up, "Objection, this is pure speculation, Your Honor."

"I think I'll let it stand. Proceed."

The DA said, "Continue with your story, Mr. Bentley."

"I conveyed this feeling to Sheriff Williams, and he agreed that this might be so."

"Objection. Hearsay."

Judge Hastings said, "Yes well this can be corroborated, I'm sure, by the Sheriff. In the interest of moving this trial along, I'll let it stand. You may continue Mr. Bentley."

"I felt cold chills creeping up my back, having the thought that there was still someone out there dedicated to killing me."

The District Attorney then asked, "What did you do next?"

"After the Sheriff had measured and drawn a picture of the footprints, I headed for the Arrow—B."

The District Attorney turned to the judge and said, "I'm through with the witness for now, Your Honor, but I would like to reserve the right to recall him for further questioning later."

The Judge agreed, and said to the defense, "Your witness Mr. Hoople."

The defense attorney approached the witness stand and asked, "Were you alone when you shot and killed the alleged intruder?"

"No, Peter White was with me."

"What reason did you have for taking a human life? In your mind is the act of entering private property a crime punishable by murder?"

The prosecution objected on the basis that the witness was not on trial.

The Judge agreed, and said to the court clerk, "Strike all of the last question from the record."

The defense attorney then said, "Your Honor, I was merely trying to establish a trend of actions by this witness. It is a documented fact that he and some of his employees have taken matters into their own hands. Matters that should have been handled by law enforcement. Your Honor, this witness has been through much stress in the last several months, and I question the value of his testimony. The fact is, and the record will show, that this witness has often failed to allow law enforcement to do its job. I believe this shooting is a case in point."

The prosecuting attorney said, "The people object to this line of questioning, as the defense has made many assumptive statements. He will have to establish a basis for these unsubstantiated remarks."

The Judge said, "I concur, the defense has not established a proper foundation, objection sustained. The court clerk will remove these remarks from the record. Do you have any further questions for this witness?"

"Yes Your Honor, I wish to continue."

"Well get on with it, and try not to prattle on about things you have no proof of."

"Mr. Bentley, you said that the Sheriff made drawings of the footprints found at the location where the first shooting took place. Is this correct?"

"Yes, that is correct."

"And is there a likeness between my client's shoes and these shoe prints?"

"That question will have to be answered by Sheriff Williams."

"Well, considering that the answer would be yes, can you tell the court how this ties into my client, considering there are thousands of people wearing the same make and size shoes?"

Judge Hastings snapped, "Claude, are you going to let that one go by?"

Claude a bit caught off guard, said "Objection, that's an argument, not a question."

"Objection sustained. Hoople, If you don't have any further questions for the witness, go sit down so we can move this trial along. The court clerk will remove that last gibberish from the record."

"Your honor, we have a witness who has killed, and in fact, been the center of a number of killings. This is a witness who states he was shot at twice, and a witness who has repeatedly made aggressive moves toward others he states were trying to kill him. I submit, Your Honor, this witness is not qualified to be objective in any way concerning the charges against my client. I have no further questions Your Honor."

Claude Comstock stood up and asked, "May we have a word with you, Your Honor?"

Judge Hastings nodded. The DA spoke first, "Your Honor, there have been many crimes committed here. I wish to deal with this one here and now. There are reliable witnesses who will be called to deal with the alleged killings.

This witness is not on trial. If the defense wishes to discredit the witness, I suggest he wait until the court has had a chance to hear sworn testimony from these other witnesses."

The defense attorney said, "Your Honor, the prosecution has made several uncorroborated statements. I have the right to question these."

The Judge glared down at the defense attorney, then said, "Mr. Hoople, I'm losing my patience. Let the prosecution present its case, then do your thing. At this rate we'll never get started. Do you have any further questions for this witness?"

"No, Your Honor."

The DA said, "I call Dr. Morrison to the stand." After the witness was sworn in, the DA asked him "Did you receive a call from the Arrow—B Ranch on the 15th of October,1952?"

"Yes, Dorothy, the telephone operator, found me at Rosey's Café. She told me of the shooting, and I went right out to the ranch."

"Just what did you find when you arrived there?"

"I found George just beginning to recover from an injury to his head."

"I assume you are referring to George Bentley. Now what, in your opinion caused, that injury?"

Dr. Morrison answered, "It was obviously a bullet bouncing off his hard head. There was a neat crease across the top of his head. It could not have been anything else. Take a look at the scar on George's head."

The audience in the Courtroom laughed over the hard head bit. Claude asked the Judge to observe the scar resulting from the near miss bullet. The Judge agreed, suppressing a laugh of his own. Claude asked George to show his scar to the Judge.

George complied, parting his hair to make it visible. There was an amused expression on his face, until he remembered the pain of that day, and the worry that the shooter would probably try again.

Claude's next witness was Peter White, who was sworn in, and introduced as the longtime foreman of the Arrow—B Ranch. The DA said, "Tell us in your own words what happened on the 15th of October, 1952."

"Tony woke me up at 3 a.m., and told me that George wanted to see me right away. I put on some clothes, an' my boots, then I left the bunkhouse, and headed up the hill to the ranch house. George, fully dressed, met me at the door and said, 'We've just received a message from Sam up on the mesa. He told me that a strange vehicle had entered ranch property, driven to House Rock, then turned around and headed back to where it came from, and then he said, we'd better go see what's goin' on." I drove the ranch truck, and George rode on Nellie, George's horse. We both met at House Rock. George got off' n Nellie, and I climbed outa the truck. About then, Nellie snorted. George grabbed my arm, pulled me 'round the end of the rock, just as a bullet whined past my head. I figger that hoss heard somethin with them keen ears a hers.

"Wal, we waited, George, me and Nellie. After a while, George heard a rustle in the bushes, and he aimed his rifle in that direction. The sounds came again and George fired three shots. There was a cry of pain, and then silence. In time we crept up to the spot where the cry had come from, and found a dead body. Along with the body was a 30-aught six rifle fitted with a scope."

"And what happened next?"

"We loaded the body and his rifle onto the truck. George drove the truck to the Sheriff's office in Walnut. I rode Nellie back to the Ranch."

Claude went over to the prosecution table, picked up the aforementioned rifle, and entered it as Exhibit B, then turned to the Judge and said, "I have no further questions for this witness."

Judge Hastings asked the defense attorney if he wished to cross.

Hoople stood and said. "Yes, Your Honor." He turned

and faced the witness, then, "How long have you been employed by the Bentley family?"

"For the last 35 years."

"You must have a great fondness and loyalty toward the Bentleys. Isn't this so Mr. White?"

"That is certainly true."

"You wouldn't want anything to happen to this family. Is that not true Mr. White?"

"Yes, that's true."

The attorney turned to the judge, "I submit, Your Honor, this witness could never be objective. His testimony must always be in question. I request that the testimony just given be thrown out, as the witness has a vested interest in the proceedings here."

The Judge turned to the DA and said, "Claude, what's your response to that?"

"I'm not sure about the character of witnesses in the Midwest, but, this is Wyoming. Folks who are placed on the stand here, and take an oath to tell the truth, and nothing but the truth, usually do. I assume that everyone is aware of the penalty for doing perjury. Most of what Peter White is telling us has already been corroborated, and I expect the rest will be proven as correct also."

Judge Hastings glared at the defense attorney and said, "Request denied. Call your next witness Mr. Comstock."

Claude said, "I call Sheriff Williams to the stand."

The Sheriff took his seat and was sworn in. The District Attorney asked, "Sheriff, how long have you known George Bentley?"

"I first met George around the middle of May of this year."

"Tell the Court what you know about the shooting at House Rock."

"Early on the 15th of October, 1952, George came to my office with the body of a man, and a 30 aught six rifle fitted with a scope. He told me that the man had shot at him from some bushes near House Rock, and that he had returned fire.

According to Mr. Bentley, he and Peter White searched the bushes and found the body of the apparent shooter. Upon examination, the body was found to have a bullet in his head, and was dead.

"The next morning George and I returned to the scene of the shooting, and examined the surrounding area. We found the footprints of the shooter, and a second set of footprints, which could only mean that the shooter did not act alone. The second set of tracks led away from the area where the shooting took place and toward the Arrow—B ranch house. We found cartridge casings that matched the caliber of the rifle that has been entered as Exhibit B. We also found supplies, which included food, water and extra cartridges, which were the right ammunition for the aforesaid rifle, and a case for a second scope. In addition, we found a picture of George. When we examined the signs on the ground, they indicated that the individual departed quickly."

The DA indicated a plastic bag containing several cartridges, " Would these be those cartridges?"

"Yes, my initials are across the seal."

The prosecuting attorney held up a second envelope containing a scope case, and asked, "Would this be that extra scope case.?"

"Yes, that is the one."

The DA said, "I would like to enter these two items as Exhibits C and D. What did you think, and do next, Sheriff?"

"We both came to the same conclusion; there must be another shooter, and he was still out there."

The District Attorney then asked the witness. "What then did you do?"

"I decided to hire a tracker, and try to determine where the suspect was headed. I called Mr. Bentley, who advised me to contact Chief Running Deer myself."

"And did you in fact meet with the Chief?"

"I did, and was able to secure the services of two Indian trackers who had been trained in the old ways of the Arapaho people."

Lawyer Hoople jumped up and said, "Objection, Your Honor, I question the indicated skills of said trackers. Let's see some proof that they are qualified to follow a trail across the desert."

The Judge grimaced a bit then turned to the prosecuting attorney and asked, "Are you able to identify anyone as a "professional" tracker? That is, can you produce any kind of a degree, certificate, or life experience to this effect?"

Claude said, "No your honor, but I am prepared to demonstrate to the court the skill of some individuals in this art."

"Just how do you propose to do this?"

"With the Court's permission, a person, acceptable to the defense, would travel by foot for a five mile stretch through our countryside. He is to conceal said trail to the best of his ability. The trackers would be expected to follow the test route."

Judge Hastings turned to the defense and asked, "Are you in tune with this idea; and do you have any further objections?"

Mr. Hoople responded, "Only if I can review the process of selecting the site of testing and the test results."

The Judge glared at the defense attorney and said, "As you will, Hoople, but don't test me too often." He turned to the DA and said "Get on with your demonstration Claude. How long will this take?"

"We should set the stage in a day, and run the demonstration the day after. I expect the defense will want to verify everything, so let's give him a day. That's about three days."

The Judge said, "Does the defense have any objections to a postponement until Friday?"

The defense attorney answered, "Your Honor, this is putting an undue burden on my client. He has already spent unwarranted time incarcerated. Under the Con—-"

At this point the Judge interrupted the defense, "Mr. Hoople, I know what the Constitution says. Are you through?" He looked at his desk calendar, and said, "Objection overruled. Do you have any other questions for the witness?"

"No, your honor."

The Judge said, "Claude, do you have any further questions?"

"Not at this time, Your Honor, but I would like to reserve the right to recall this witness for further questions later."

"Judge Hastings said, You may step down Sheriff; the court stands adjourned until 9 a.m. Friday." He motioned to the DA and the defense attorney to join him in his chambers. In chambers the Judge asked Claude to outline his plan to demonstrate the skill of a "professional" tracker.

"Your honor, I suggest the defense, with perhaps, the help of such local persons acquainted with our countryside, lay out the route to be followed. You, of course, would have to oversee test preparations and/or appoint a neutral person to do so." Claude continued, "A person or persons would travel from point A to point B over a route of five miles or more. The defense is to establish said route with the approval of the court, and specifically kept unknown to the prosecution. A person or persons from the local Arapaho village will attempt to follow said trail, and demonstrate the skill."

The defense attorney looked like he was about to choke said, "Your Honor, this is so filled with fraud I must object."

"So what do you object to, be specific."

"Finding someone who is not biased against my client in this county is not possible. How do you expect to keep the destination of the tracker secret. I agree we would need to use the services of a local person, and that would negate the results of any plan the prosecution comes up with."

"Claude, what is your response to this objection?"

Claude Comstock chuckled and said, "Well, Judge, the ease with which the defendant and his cohorts have been moving around our county, day or night, makes me wonder why the defense doesn't call on one of them to help. Anyway you discredit the Court when you question their integrity in this manner."

Judge Hastings glanced over at Claude and said, "Shut up Claude, when I need your help in defending the court I'll let you know, and besides I haven't heard any testimony yet that confirms the presence of said 'cohorts'." He turned to the defense attorney and said, "Objection noted, but denied. Let's see this demonstration first and then you can make your statements in regards to the alleged misconduct of the prosecution. Claude, get on with it. Keep me informed, and do what you can to satisfy the defense."

Claude returned to the prosecution table and said to Pril, "Find George, and Bill Williams and ask them to join us for lunch. Pete's Café will do, and ASAP."

Claude, seated at a corner table in Pete's café, was into his second cup of coffee when Pril arrived with George and Sheriff Williams. Ed Hunt came a few moments later.

George smiled and said, "I was in the courtroom when you were doing your thing. I think you will need to talk to my grandfather. I'll find him for you."

The DA gave George a nod and said to the air, "I must be getting weak in the head. I just let George tell me how to run this investigation."

Sheriff Williams, who was standing nearby chuckled and said, "Join the crowd Claude, he's been doing that to me for three months. I got used to it, and I expect you will too."

The lunch party at Pete's place put two tables together next to the pool table which was not in use. Pete came out from the kitchen with a hand full of menus, and said, "Hi Claude, my out front help is sick, but me and the cook can do the job. What d'ya wanta eat?"

Claude said, "Coffee all around, and bring us a flock of those lead sinkers of yours. We're on a short fuse Pete." He then said to Pril, "I would like you to go over to the End Of The Line Motel and see what you can find out. Stay overnight if you need to. According to Chief Richardson, one or some of these crumb-bums have stayed there several times. Talk to people. Ed, we need to take a look at the registration records of that place. Talk to Judge Hastings. See if he will give you a search warrant to commandeer those records, quickly and quietly, before they have time to cover up something.

"George, please do set up something with your grandfather. Since time is of an essence, yesterday will do. Any comments or questions?"

Defense attorney Hoople left the courtroom a bit uneasy about the so-called test of Arapaho skills. By the time he reached his motel room he decided he couldn't win this one anyway, as the prosecution sounded awfully assured of success. On top of that, he was directly challenging the court by questioning its integrity in the matter, and that was never a good idea. Still, if he did not question the de facto presence of Jon Ballant at the shooting site, he would have to switch his defense to another strategy. He didn't have many choices. After ruminating most of the night over this one, he decided to deep-six the testing idea, and to accept, without proof, that in fact his client could have traveled to the shooting site. He reasoned that the prosecution had to prove that it was Jon Ballant who fired the bullet that grazed George's head.

Court convened at 9 a.m. Friday, and after the ritual formalities had taken place, the judge said, "Continue with your case, Mr. Comstock."

Claude said, "Your Honor, in as much as the defense has conceded that it is possible to track a man through our wilderness, the prosecution considers the matter of testing moot. I call Sheriff Williams back to the stand."

The Judge reminded the witness that he was still under oath. "Go on with your questioning, Claude."

"Sheriff, after you determined that the defendant was headed for the Arrow—B , what did you do?"

"The following day I contacted Chief Running Deer by phone, and subsequently proceeded out to the village and met with the Chief. He agreed to provide two tribe members for the purpose of following the alleged assassin."

"And did you use the services of these persons for the purpose of following the suspect's trail?"

"I did, and the trail led off toward the Arrow—B ranch house. I fired three shots in the air as a warning to George. We then hurried on to the ranch. George fired two shots in return. We arrived at the ranch a short time later to find that George had already left, and was headed up the mountainside on Nellie. We heard a shot and Don and I started on up, taking cover as we went. I was looking around from behind a rock when a bullet whined past my head. After awhile I saw Don inching his way around the water tank, and also, looking to the right I made out a horse standing over a body lying on the ground at its feet. I proceeded forward, taking cover, and as I came up to about fifty feet from the horse, I recognized George Bentley's Nellie. I could see no movement from the body. I then made a dash for Nellie and the person at her feet, drawing fire from above. I made it across without injury and knelt to check George. He was alive. A short time later Don called to me from above stating that the threat was over. The shooter had departed. Don joined me then, and we put George on Nellie, and we all returned to the ranch house."

Claude said, "Your witness Mr. Hoople."

The defense attorney stood and approached the witness stand, "Sheriff, did you ever see the alleged shooter?"

"I did not."

"Then it is only an assumption that places the accused at the shooting sight. Is it not a fact that anybody could have fired those shots?"

"Well, I suppose so, but this is a largely unoccupied area, and short of people that would show up and take potshots at someone."

Hoople paused for a moment, and asked, "Did you track the defendant all the way to the shooting sight?"

"Well no, we broke off our tracking when we knew the quarry was headed toward the ranch house."

The defense attorney stepped back and turned to the

Judge and said, "I'm through with the witness your Honor."

The Judge told Bill Williams to step down from the witness chair, and asked the DA to call his next witness.

"I call Don Jones to the stand."

After Don had taken his seat, and was duly sworn in, the district attorney said, "Mr. Jones, tell us in your own words what you know about the attempted murder of George Bentley."

"After the shootin' at House Rock, all of us at the Arrow—B were on alert for any intruders. There had been several attacks agin us at the ranch, and we were all gittin a mite gun-shy, so when the Sheriff fired them three warnin shots I headed up the canyon to cover George, who'd rode up ahead on Nellie. Just about then the Sheriff joined me, and we heard the shot. I seen the Sheriff dart across the open space to get to George, and a bullet splattered on a rock near his head as he ran. He made it to George and Nellie, and I sidled on up the canyon on t'other side. I took a couple a shots at where I thought the shots were comin' from, and they stopped comin'. I climbed up to where the shootin were comin' from, an found no one home. I called to Bill to come on up, all was clear. He came up, and we found shell casings strewn about, an' knee prints where someone had knelt to shoot." Don paused, then said, "We hiked on down, picked George up, put 'im on Nellie, and hauled him on down to the ranch."

Claude said, "I have no further questions for this witness, Your Honor."

Judge Hastings said, "Does the defense wish to question this witness?"

"Yes, Your Honor."

"Well proceed."

"Mr. Jones, did you ever see the suspected ambusher?"

"No, I did not."

Attorney Hoople said, "I have no further questions for this witness, Your Honor."

The Judge said, "The witness may step down. Claude, call

your next witness."

"Your Honor, I would like to recall Sheriff Bill Williams to the stand."

"So be it, the witness is reminded that he is still under oath."

"Sheriff, what did you do after you took the injured George to the ranch house?"

The Sheriff answered, "I returned to the site where the shooter knelt and fired at Mr. Bentley. I collected several cartridge cases, put them in a plastic bag and sealed the bag, writing my initials across the seal."

"Would these be those cartridges?"

"Yes, I see my initials and the seal is still intact."

"Your Honor, I wish to enter these cartridges as Exhibit E, I also ask the court to unseal both this exhibit and Exhibit C. I wish to show that the same gun was used to fire both. I ask that this be done under the eyes of the Court, and the defense if they so desire."

The Judge answered, "I think we can do that; does the defense have any difficulty with this plan?"

"No, Your Honor, as long as you are there to supervise."

"All right then, we meet in my chambers at the end of this court session to carry out this process, continue with your examination of the witness, Mr. Comstock."

"Sheriff, what other actions did you take at the shooting site?"

"I found depressions in the sand, where a person must have knelt to fire a weapon, and I saw footprints leading to and leaving from the site. I made plaster molds of both."

"I have these molds on the prosecution table, Your Honor. May I ask the witness to step down and identify said molds?"

The Judge said, "Make it so, Sheriff, and then return to the witness stand."

The Sheriff complied, and identified the plaster molds as those he had made at the crime site.

Claude said, 'Your Honor, I wish to enter these molds as

Exhibit F."

The judge nodded and said, "Continue Claude."

"Sheriff, did you return to the site of the injury to Mr. Bentley, and what did you find?"

"I did, and after a careful examination of the surrounding area I dug a bullet out of a tree trunk about six feet off the ground."

"Would this be that bullet?"

"Yes, I see my initials across the seal."

Claude said, "Your Honor, I wish to enter this item into evidence as exhibit G. I'm through questioning this witness."

The judge said, "Do so. Any cross, Hoople?"

"No, Your Honor."

The Judge said, "The witness may step down." He looked at his watch and said, "It's almost lunch time; this court is adjourned until 2 o'clock." He banged his gavel on its pad, and got up to leave.

The defendant, manacled and escorted by two burly deputies, was scurried away to some place not obvious to the public.

Among the exiting spectators were four men, dressed in business suits which stood out from the casual wear of western folk in the courtroom. Two other personages, trying to look invisible in western-like garb, stood out, as their clothes seemed new and stiff like. Their offish demeanor chilling. The procession of peoples bulged out the courtroom double doors mingling with the outside crowd seeking some word of the proceedings. The media seemed like everywhere and was rushing to telephones, of which there were too few.

The prosecution team headed for Pete's place, and settled into their corner. A short time later the Mayor showed up. He pulled up a chair and ordered coffee. A bit surprised, Claude said, "Hi Fred"; then did introductions all around. "Join us for lunch?"

"No thanks, I just wanted to remind you that there are some weird-looking characters lurking around town. I think you‘ve attracted a bunch of oddballs. Watch out. By the way, it sounds good in there. How long do you think this thing will go on?"

"No idea, I hope it will be finished soon, as there's a touchy time element involved."

"Claude, be sure to coordinate with Chief Richardson about security. We don't need any surprises." The Mayor got up to leave, and said, "You sure don't need me here. I'm leaving."

* * *

Hoople left the courtroom a bit concerned. He was hired by the Syndicate to defend an almost un-defendable client. The Syndicate wasn't that kind to those who failed to do what they wanted. The Judge wouldn't put up with much stuff either. 'Catch 22'? So far the prosecution was not making many mistakes, and there wasn't much he could argue with. *Oh God, why did I take this case in the first place?*

He turned to see where his employers were, and they were gone. That was scary. Earlier, when he had checked into the End of The Line Motel, he found his bill was paid in advance… The Syndicate owned him!… He really didn't feel much like lunch so he got in his rental car, pulled a flask from his inside pocket and took a long swig, then drove to a side street close to the courthouse, and pondered about his plight.

* * *

The seven members of the Syndicate, which included Junior's father, the two mob legal minds, and four close associates, retired to their hotel suite, and ordered food to be sent up. The conversation began as soon as they closed the door.

Frank said, "Hoople seems with no tongue. How much are we paying him anyway?"

"Like a grand a day plus expenses, Frank. But we

discussed all this, and decided to write off Ballant anyway. What's the big deal?"

"I'll tell you what's the big deal, we need someone to defend Junior, and Hoople looks hopeless. I could care less for Jon Ballant."

"What about the tie-in between Ballant and us?"

Frank said "These hit men never rat, however it would be nice if Ballant were dead or something. Anybody got any ideas?"

One of the four Syndicate members present said, "Frank, the security around that courthouse is so tight that we couldn't get an eighty-year-old grandmother that was blind and deaf in there."

Frank got that frustrated look he was noted for when he thought everyone around him were idiots. Some of the Syndicate members were not so sure how long they wanted to be classified as idiots, and there was a pointed pause in the conversation, then another of the seven said. "You know Frank, this is your caper, you figure it out."

Frank glowered, and said, "We'd better get back to the courthouse; it's almost time for things to start again."

* * *

Court convened right at 2, as directed, and Judge Hastings asked, "Claude, do you have any other witnesses?"

"Your Honor, I would like to recall Sheriff Williams to the stand."

Sheriff Bill Williams seated himself in the witness chair, and Claude said, "Tell the court about the first time you saw the defendant."

"Having established the probable route the defendant would take to exit the area, we, including George Bentley, Don Jones, and myself, waited in the dark. In time the defendant appeared, and we captured him. He was carrying a fully loaded 30 aught six rifle, with a scope."

The DA picked up a rifle from off the prosecution table

and asked "Would this be that rifle?"

The Sheriff examined the sealed plastic bag, and said, "Yes, I see my initials on the seal."

The DA asked that the rifle be entered into evidence as Exhibit H, and then said, "I have no further questions for this witness, Your Honor."

The judge said, "Do you wish to cross, Mr. Hoople?"

"Yes, Your Honor."

The defense attorney asked, "What led you to believe the defendant would choose that particular spot in a large open country to appear?"

"We knew he had been dropped off by motor car at that spot, and we were sure he would be picked up at the same place."

"Did he tell you where he had been?"

"He said he had been hunting, and stayed a bit longer that he intended."

"So, I take it that you didn't buy that. Is that not true, Sheriff?"

"That is certainly true."

The defense attorney went over to the defense table, and picked up a folder. He extracted a single sheet from the folder and said, "You testified earlier that you had not seen the suspect until he appeared out of the night. You further stated that you arrested a man walking in the country at night carrying a loaded rifle. Would you please explain to the court why. Certainly it is not against the law to go hunting and stay later than one planned."

"The arrest of Jon Ballant was based on his movements, the time of day, the weapon he carried, and intuition. I would always play it on the safe side, and considering the circumstances, it was evident that he was not what he represented to be, and that further investigation was called for."

"What did you do with the prisoner?"

"I placed him in the custody of George Bentley."

The defense attorney stared at the paper in his hand, then

asked, "Isn't this a little unusual, to turn a prisoner over to a non-lawman?"

"In as much as the prisoner is still safely in custody, I feel your question is moot."

"All right then, when did you regain custody of the suspect?"

"Perhaps six hours later."

"Why so long?"

"Other matters more urgent were taking place that required my attention."

"Are you aware that during that six hours the defendant was subjected to threats and coercion?"

"There was no physical evidence of this, and the prisoner didn't mention it when I picked him up."

The defense attorney said, "I have no further questions for this witness, Your Honor."

The judge said, "You may step down Sheriff. Mr. Comstock, call your next witness."

"Your Honor, the prosecution rests. I am ready to make my closing statement."

"Mr. Hoople, do you have any witnesses you wish to present to the court?"

"No Your Honor, but I would like a court recess until tomorrow morning in order to prepare my closing statement."

"Since it is late in the day, I think that is prudent. The court stands adjourned until 9 a.m. tomorrow morning."

Pril spent the night in the End of The Line Motel. The night clerk, who checked her in as Mary somebody, was more interested in her looks, which were quite something, than her entry into the motel log. He stared, which Pril pretended she didn't see. When he asked her if she was planning to have dinner somewhere, she asked him where he would suggest. Of course, the next move was to offer to take her to his favorite spot. She accepted eagerly, and the clerk said he would be available at seven. She acquiesced, and the clerk, whose name was Joe, escorted Pril to her room. He then went back to his station, and phoned a friend, asking him to handle the night shift at the motel. He was so excited that he almost slobbered to his friend over the telephone. Joe picked up Pril at seven and they proceeded to the middle scale coffee shop and were seated in a corner booth. The small talk included the weather, local beef prices, and such mundane subjects as the coming county fair.

Pril said, "You have such an interesting job. I bet you have met some very fascinating people."

"I sure have, Pril. This is one of only three motels in town, and the first one you see when you drive in."

"Tell me about some of the strangest people you have met."

"Well, I guess the weirdest ever was a great big man, signed his name with a slanted X, and ordered six dinners sent up to his room. He apparently ate them all, as I saw the empty plates outside his room."

"Wow, how long did he stay."

"He was here for three days, and then one of the other guests paid his bill, and escorted him out."

"That's very interesting Joe, did he eat for six every day?"

"Yes, and the other guest must have picked up his meal ticket also, as I didn't hear any complaints from my friend Antonio, who runs the restaurant."

"Oh, that's this restaurant then?"

"The very same."

Pril asked, "What was his friend like?"

"He was sort of cold, dressed in black, and did the paying sort of indifferently."

"Did he also stay in the End of The Line?"

"Yes, he stayed in unit nine, and the big man was in ten."

Their meals came, and there was little conversation for the next half hour, then the tab came and Pril reached for it. Joe didn't argue much, but was thinking, "Boy this is the best I ever had, she even pays for the date!" They got into his car, and he was just about to ask her, your room or mine, when Pril said;

"Joe, this is not really a good time, please take me back to my room."

Joe's silence was deafening, and his uplifted spirits dropped to bottom somewhere. Pril's voice was solid, and left no room for discussion. He did as he was told. The night passed without incident, and in the morning, while Pril was completing her diary [of the events of the last 12 hours], the maid knocked on the door. Pril said she would soon vacate, but would she come in for a moment. The maid said, hesitatingly, "Well, I've finished all but yours, I guess it'll be OK."

"My name is Pril, it's a nickname my mom gave me when I was small. What's yours?"

"They call me Marge, it's short for Marjorie."

"That's a nice name, are you married; or have any boyfriends you like a lot?"

The girl blushed a bit and said, "I have a boyfriend named Jimmie. We plan on getting married as soon as he finishes school."

"When will that be?"

"In June."

"Have you worked here long?"

"Almost two years."

"You must have met some interesting people then."

"I suppose so, but I mostly clean up empty rooms."

"Did you get to meet that great big bruiser that was here a few months ago?"

"You must mean Muscles. He was huge. He seemed to take a liking to me."

"Did he stay in his room all day?"

"All except the second day. A man dressed in black came and got him in the morning, and brought him back in the afternoon. I was running late that day, and was still cleaning the last room when they came back. He was nice to me, I was sorry to see him go."

Pril checked out after that, and left for the court house. She arrived in time for the court session to begin.

Ed Hunt, in the meantime, made an afterhours call on Judge Hastings. With some grumbling the judge agreed to a fifteen minute conversation.

"Are we discussing the case currently before the court, if so, then this conversion is over."

"Well it is and it is not. May I indulge Your Honor for just a moment?"

"All right, get on with it."

"As you know, the Syndicate from Chicago is involved here. We think that the records at the End of The Line Motel contain information pertinent to the case on the docket. We would like to subpoena those records before the Syndicate people get there and destroy said records. We need a writ from you to do so."

"This is a little late to be coming up with more evidence. How come you waited so long?"

A bit embarrassed, the attorney said, "Call it hindsight, whatever, the need is there, and it may improve the time line of this case."

"I suppose you want this yesterday, and I'll have to be late for dinner to do this thing. All right, give me an hour. You can pick it up at 6 P.M."

At a little after 6, Ed Hunt gave Claude a call. "Claude, I have the writ we need to subpoena the End of The Line register."

"Great, Ed, I'll call Richardson, and get right back to you. What's your number there?"

"I'm in a phone booth outside the courthouse. The number here is 7892. Hope you don't take too long, I don't like it here much with that black-suited bunch around."

"Gotcha Ed, you're on the corner of Birch and Main I take it?"

"Right."

Claude called and talked to the night duty man at the police station. The Chief was between the station and his home. Claude got into his car and drove over to where Ed was and picked him up himself. It was dark now, and Ed was downright relieved to see Claude. In time Claude reached Chief Richardson, "Chief, Claude here. I have a writ from the judge to pick up the records from the End of The Line Motel. I need to do it, like now, and before the syndicate bunch does. Can you dig up a likely crew at this hour?"

"Uh huh, where are you now?"

"Down town, across from the courthouse."

"Stay there; I'll send a crew over, and we'll all drive out to the End of The Line together."

A short time later, the Chief came along with some muscle. The two cars drove to the End of The Line Motel. Out in front the Chief gave orders to cover the back entrance, and sent an officer in to commandeer the motel records.

Claude smiled and said, "Chief, to what do I owe the honor of your presence?"

The Chief answered, "I couldn't find anyone else at this hour. Didja have any trouble with Hastings?"

"Well, he did say something about missing his dinner etc., but saw our point in the end. I think he's like the rest of us, leery of all the outside attention this thing is getting, and a bit concerned that something violent seems to be in the offing."

"Uh huh, me too, and my bunch are good but not nearly enough in numbers to match up with what's in town. I have no way to check any of them, let alone what artillery they've brought in with 'em."

"If it's any consolation to you Chief, this trial is about over, and I don't think this mob is really interested. When I get into the next one, I'm sure you will have some problems. That one will strike a little too close to home."

"Claude, are you trying to tell me something, like you are going after the Chicago Syndicate. Can't you keep this a little more local?"

"In order to find and prosecute the killer of Richard Bentley, I'm going to have to dig pretty deep. The chips will have to fall where they may."

"I thought you might take that attitude. I guess I'd better

call up Stateside and see if I can get some outside help."

Court convened at nine sharp, and after the usual formalities, the prosecution faced the judge, and began its closing statement.

"Jon Ballant, a known assassin, took part in the October fifteenth, 1952 shooting at House Rock. He then traveled up to a vantage point above the Arrow—B Ranch and shot George Bentley in the head, just missing a fatal killing. We have the gun he used in each location, we have the empty shell casings, we have matching bullets in both places, and we have trail signs, foot and knee prints to substantiate the connection between the two crime scenes. The equipment that this criminal carried was designed to kill at long distances, and rarely owned by honest citizens. The defendant, beyond a doubt, is guilty on the count of attempted murder of George Bentley as he rode his horse up a trail above the Arrow—B Ranch house. The prosecution rests, Your Honor."

Judge Hastings said, "Mr. Hoople, you may make your close."

The defense attorney stood and said, "Testimony has shown that the accused was never seen at or near the crime scene. There is no direct evidence that he was the one to pull the trigger that sent the bullet at George Bentley. The prosecution's case is based entirely on circumstantial evidence. The defense rests, Your Honor."

Judge Hastings said, "This court is in recess until 4 p.m." He got up and retired to his chambers. The courtroom buzzed, stirred, and gradually emptied.

Court reconvened at 4 p.m. The court clerk said, "All rise, His Honor Judge Hastings presiding. The Judge entered, and when the assemblage had quieted down, he said, "It is the decision of this court that the defendant is guilty as charged. He is to be incarcerated in the state penitentiary for a period of twenty years."

The defense attorney closed his briefcase, and tried to look small as he exited the courtroom. The media rushed to their respective phones to call their offices, and the courtroom emptied.

26 | BOB GIBSON

District Attorney Claude Comstock knew he had some of the nation's best legal minds looking at what he was doing in this remote corner of Wyoming. He also was deeply loyal to those locals that put him in office, and he loved his position in Contra County.

During the trial of Jon Ballant Claude filed papers toward prosecuting Bob Gibson for fraud and associated complicity in the crimes being committed in Contra County. His mind-set was to prosecute the little foul-ups, gather information as he went along, and then go after the Syndicate. He felt that a direct attack against the Syndicate without this preparation would surely fail. Failure was not an option here, because to let the bad guys off would not only be a travesty of justice, but physically dangerous. He saw an uphill battle ahead, and he loved it.

Law enforcement in Cook County, and in Chicago itself, became less skeptical than at first. As events moved along, and the trial of Jon Ballant came to a successful conclusion, interest in happenings away out there in Wyoming blossomed, and of course the media, particularly the Chicago Tribune, had a field day at the expense of local law enforcement. The Cook County District Attorney's office sent another body out west for a week to more directly view what was going on, and augment the role of Ed Hunt.

The Syndicate, observing all of this, was weighing its options, both legal and otherwise. With Frank's son Junior (Joe Costello) incarcerated in a western jail, with western lawmen looming around every corner, strong-arm stuff didn't seem practical. Gloom prevailed among the members of the Syndicate that had made the trip out to Wyoming, and more and more thoughts were to step over the line and try some good old big city coercion. Like maybe, hold someone hostage for a little blackmail and squeeze out a plea bargain, then get out of town fast. Junior, of course would be the prize. The question of who out here would succumb to that kind of pressure needed to be answered.

From the start the Syndicate had a source of information in the area. It was time to tap that source again. A meeting was set up in the usual way that carefully shielded the informant. The Syndicate legal beagle spoke first, using the agreed upon, code name Freddie. "Freddie, you do like the extra money that's been finding its way over to you?"

"Shor do Mr., it's helped me a lot to pay for Ma's operation."

"Well then, would you mind helping us out with a little information?"

"Anythin' I c'n do Mr."

"You know all those good people out at the Arrow—'B Ranch pretty well don't you?"

"Shor do."

"Well, we'd like to know them better, tell us about the ranch foreman."

"Pete, he's a real nice fellow, he always been kind to me. Been there for as long as I can 'member."

"Gee that's nice, do you have any other ranch friends out there?"

Freddie thought for a minute then, "Oh yes, George is my favorite, and I like him most."

"Really, does everyone like George?"

"Oh I reckon so, he's a real nice fellow."

"Tell us about some of his friends."

"He has lots of `em, especially Betty."

"Tell us about Betty."

Freddie blushed a bit and said, "She's his girlfriend."

"Does he like Betty a lot?"

"She's his girlfriend!"

Frank said, "Thank you for helping us out Freddie. Here's another hundred dollars to help with your Ma."

* * *

The day after the conclusion of the Jon Ballant trial found the DA pressing the court for a trial date for the Bob Gibson case. He wanted it sooner rather than later, as the holiday season was coming up fast. Most of the material and data he needed to prosecute Gibson was already on file. The Las Vegas connection was the exception, and he pondered over this one for a full day. He also had the problem of how long he could keep key witnesses under lock and key without breaking the law by denying them their civil rights. It was now the first of December, and it would be a tactical boo-boo to run into the holiday season. He turned to Ed Hunt and said, "Ed, you had better check on progress toward getting Muscles out here. I filed extradition papers last week, and that needs follow-up."

"Got your message Claude, I'll get right on it."

Claude next called Chief Richardson, "Good morning, how's law enforcement doing these days?"

"I don't get much sleep any more, and I dream of total annihilation by little black dressed gnomes running around with Tommy guns shooting up everything in sight."

Claude tried not to laugh out loud, but didn't quite make it. "Gee Chief, that's terrible, what brought all this on?"

"You know damn well what brought all that on, Claude, and I suspect this phone call is going to add more to my miseries."

"Gosh Chief, I'll try not to add to your demise, I just need a little information this time."

"So what information from me, who knows nothing, could you possibly want?"

"Do you have any friends in Las Vegas?"

"Claude, you know that subject is like hush-hush with my types." There was a short pause, and then, "So what do you need?"

"Well it's this way, I'm sure you know about Bob Gibson and his being into one of the Las Vegas boys for lots of bucks. I need to know a little about that, and for about how much. I figured you might have a fellow law enforcement type there who would know how to come by that info."

"Yeah, well I might, but the relationship between Vegas law enforcement and the wagering type is a bit touchy. How bad is the need?"

"I figure that the guy in Vegas understands that you can't get blood out of a turnip anyway, and would like us to nail Bob but good. Call it revenge, they get to see Gibson hung up, without doing the strong-arm thing."

"Your logic sounds good on paper, but how it would play out in the real world is something else maybe. OK, I'll give it a try. When do you need this?"

"Like yesterday, which means ASAP. Thanks Chief."

December 7th, a Monday was not a day to start anything in this country, so the court came up with Tuesday the 8th to start the trial of Bob Gibson. In his brief, the District Attorney cited criminal actions committed by Bob Gibson against the Arrow—B Ranch, and possible involvement in the Richard Bentley murder. He wanted to start tying the civil action of fraud into the criminal action of murder. In as much as the prime purpose of these investigations was to find the killer or killers of Richard Bentley, all matters relating to, and going on around the time of said murder were pertinent to this case.

The Jon Ballant prosecution team left the court together, and headed for Martha's Café. Claude spotted George, and invited him to come along. Martha saw Claude enter, and came out from behind the counter with a handful of menus. Claude said, "Martha, could you put us in that back room of yours. We need some talking space while we eat."

"Sure Claude, follow me."

Claude said, "George, we need information relating to the fraud perpetrated by Bob Gibson against the Ranch. Will you gather such evidence as you have and get it to me as soon as you can."

"Yes, well I figured you might need something like that, so I brought it with me. It's all here in this folder." George handed the folder over to the DA, and said, "I think you will eventually be able to tap Bob for information, as he seems plenty scared. You will want to talk to Peterson in Walnut, as he aided and abetted. He runs the local general store, and I'm not sure why, but he didn't like my dad much. I kind of think it was something about Indians maybe?"

Claude asked, "What does that mean George?"

"When I first landed here from college, I did a thing about town, and found a not so friendly attitude. I stopped in to see Rosey at her restaurant. She explained that my father created quite a stir when he married an Indian, my mother, and that I would have to stand up to these folks just like my father had done 25 years earlier. Most everyone here finally got over it after 20 years or so. Peterson, and a few others never changed their attitude towards my ancestors. I think Peterson is so bigoted that he might have entered into an agreement with Bob, just to defraud dad. Certainly Bob had to have help from someone to steal for over two years without being caught."

Claude asked, "How did they pull it off, George?"

"As near as I can figure out, Peterson was doing the billing, Bob took delivery of half of what the ranch paid for. It was hard to notice in the short run, but when I studied ranch records over a five year stretch, I found considerably more winter feed paid for in the last two years than in the previous three. I think dad figured this out and fired Bob.

He also cut off Bob's retirement money which he had set up for each of the employees.

"I was alerted to the Las Vegas connection by what I learned from Pete and Marie. They told me that Bob was often gone for a holiday to some place, but nobody seemed to know where. On one of these trips he was seen in Vegas."

About that time Martha came in, and just in time to hear some of it. She poured coffee all around, and sort of stood there until Claude eyed her out. She said, "I guess you're not ready to order yet–call me when you are."

Claude said, "George, will you stay in Glencoe for the next few days, you seem to have answers for most of my questions before I ask them. I find it somewhat scary you getting into my head that way. You sure you don't want a job?"

"No, I just want to run a ranch."

Claude turned to Ed, "Do you think it would be of any value to subpoena the records from Peterson's store?"

"Probably not, from what George has told us. I hate bigots like Peterson. I wish there was something I could come up with. I think our best bet is to break down Bob Gibson. He's the link we have to Peterson."

Claude said, "I'd like to know a little more about Peterson. Pril, why don't you go on out to Walnut, and have another visit with Rosey. Then stop in at Peterson's General Store, buy some nails or something. Get an idea how people feel about this man. Nose around out there for a day, you seem to do this sort of thing pretty well."

"Gotcha, Chief, I might get an invite from Rosey to stay overnight."

Claude said, "George, I keep trying to tie Bob into your dad's murder. Do you think all that money he owed the gamblers might have caused him to help them around the county, etc.?"

"That's kind of a stretch with no evidence like you like to have. I feel we still have to determine the 'why' of all this stuff. Bob's gambling debts might be part of it, but by no means all of it. Claude, you once asked me to review all that paper that dad left scattered about the house, and see if there wasn't some indication of why, that we might have missed. I've already done that, and have come up with zilch. I think we must get hold of both county assay records and those of Jones Realty.

"This thing all started with Jones, seeing some mighty big bucks coming his way if he could sell the Arrow—B. Take 6% of a million dollars and you have sixty grand commission. That's a lot of money to a small town real estate broker."

* * *

Pril arrived in Walnut early, and dropped into Rosey's for breakfast. Rosey saw her from the kitchen, and when Joan brought a menu and coffee out to the table, she joined in. They were alone in the café, so the three girls sat together sipping coffee and chatting, as women do. Small talk came easy for these three, and when that was over Rosey asked, "Pril, you didn't come out here to have breakfast, what brings you out to this end of the road?"

"Uh huh, Claude needs some special info, and I like seeing you anyway."

Rosey said, "So what does he wanta know now?"

Pril sort of looked at Joan, and Rosey said, "Joan is an OK type, and anything you say won't go anywhere but here."

"What we have is a jailed Bob Gibson, some evidence, and lots of supposition-ing. George thinks that Bob conspired with Peterson, the owner of the general store in town, to defraud the Arrow—B of many bucks. We think that Peterson double billed the Arrow—B, then Bob in the name of the Arrow—B, took delivery of only half of what was billed. Bob and Peterson would then split the profits.

"Richard Bentley had turned the job of purchasing for the ranch over to his foreman, Peter White. Pete was not very good at arithmetic, as he had not gone past the 3rd grade in school. He was embarrassed about this, and assigned Bob that duty, without saying anything to his boss."

Joan sort of half laughed and said, "I'm beginning to see why George is a bit paranoid about his ranch. He not only has the Mafia after him, but he has this thing going on."

Rosey said, "Peterson's never been one of my favorite people anyway, and I sure think he's capable of doing a caper like this. When's Bob's trial coming up?"

"It starts December 8th. We need to get it over with before the holiday season. The biggie is that the court won't let us hold our suspects for much longer without just cause, and we are running out of time."

"What is your next move, Pril?"

"I thought I'd drift over to Peterson's and get acquainted, so to speak, with the man himself. Claude thinks he might have a weak spot somewhere, and I might be able to find out what it is. In any case I can't hurt anything by trying. We kind of don't have much of a leg to stand on at this point."

"Good luck, Dearie, he's cautious and penurious and probably is immune to 'people' too."

Pril got up to go, and said, "Thanks Rosey, I'll see you two later."

Rosey said, "Aren't you going to have any breakfast? You'll need lots of energy and guile to get anything out of that character."

"Yes, well you're probably right, but I've been with this George Bentley thing for several weeks now, and my adrenalin is kicking into high. I'll catch up on food later. Bye."

Joan said wryly, "There seems to be more females looking out after George's welfare than my dog has fleas. I'm beginning to hate that man."

Rosey said, "Now Joan, who's kidding who?"

Pril walked the four blocks down the street to Peterson's. She had been going over in her mind how to go about getting into Peterson's head and confidence. The man had to do something with the extra money he made when the caper was going on. He didn't seem to have many friends in town according to Rosey, but most loners didn't anyway, and he sure was one of those things. This is a small town for a small town. Nothing ever went on that everybody didn't know about.

It was easy for Peterson to be a non-person, and still prosper in the general store business, as it was the only one for a hundred miles. Still, there must be something or someway to find out what went on during the time he and Bob did their thing. She stepped up into the store. The owner looked up from behind his cash drawer where he was setting up for the day's business. Pril had put on a western style blouse, a tight fitting pair of jeans and no hat. Her hair was shoulder length framing a pretty face with a pair of opalescent eyes peering out beguilingly. In other words, she was strikingly beautiful.

Peterson, sort of gasped, as he usually did business with ranch women with scarves over their heads or who were wearing men's hats, and not too great looking. This was something different. He said, "Good morning, are you new to Walnut? I don't remember seeing you before."

Pril said, "Well kind of, gee this is a nice little town. I almost wish I lived here. Every one is sure swell here."

"My name is Ralph Peterson. How can I help you?"

"Oh, I'm Pril. You must be the owner of this store."

"That's right, it's the only one in town."

"How long have you owned this store; it seems such a big part of this town?"

"Just on ten years."

"Oh, it must take a lot of money to stock a store like this one. Do you make keys. My spare car key is broken in half."

"Sure, let me see your pieces."

"Well I threw them away. I do have the regular one for you."

The store owner moved over to his key making area, and began looking for a blank that was like the one in his hand. He found what he was looking for, then fitted the blank alongside the original into a bench vice. He looked up at Pril, and said, “I’ll have your copy done in five minutes, is there anything else you need?”

”Oh, I don’t think so.” She paused and then, “Well, could you tell me where I can find a lunchroom?”

Ralph Peterson said, “Rosey’s Café is about four blocks south of here.”

“Oh, I am so dumb, I don’t know where south is.”

Ralph said, kind of greedily, “If you can wait a few minutes, I’ll be going there myself and I can show you.”

“That’s very kind of you, but I really don’t want to put you out.”

“You’re not, I have to eat too. Would you like to join me, I would like that?”

“Oh, a luncheon date. That sounds like fun.” Pril put on one of her most beguiling smiles. Ralph, hung an out-to-lunch sign on his front door and with Pril on his arm, walked down to Rosey’s Café. Rosey and Joan both caught Pril’s eye, and pretended not to know her. The two luncheon customers were seated in a booth under the storied rams head. Joan handed out two menus, and said hello to Ralph, then filled two huge cups with coffee, and moved away, promising to return when the guests had decided on their choice of lunch.

At Ralph’s suggestion, Pril decided on today’s blue plate special. Joan came back, took their order and left again.

Pril said, “You have such a nice store, did you start out as big as it is?”

“Oh no, I struggled at the start. Later I paid off the mortgage, and I now own the building.”

“Did it take very long to become successful?”

Ralph, who was now on an ego trip, would tell Pril anything she asked for, said, “Just for the first eight years, then it was all go.”

Pril judged Ralph to be about 55, and guessed what was going through his mind. She laughed to herself, at the same time kept focused on what she was there to do. “Most successful men have a good woman back of them. Are you married Ralph?"

"Oh my no, my dear, I've been much too busy to think of marriage."

"I guess, now that you are successful you might though?"

"Well, there is that girl that works at the bank."

"How did you meet her?"

"When I make my deposits, I see her."

"What's her name Ralph?"

"Helen."

Joan brought their lunch out from the kitchen, asked if they wanted ketchup and retreated to behind the counter. She was having trouble keeping a straight face considering the moon-faced middle aged man drooling over a pretty woman who was trying to extract information. She was sure that Pril was up to the job.

Ralph Peterson paid for both meals. Then said, "I must get back to the store, Pril. Can you find your way back?"

"Sure, thanks for the lunch Ralph, I'll see you in a little bit."

Pril lingered until Ralph was well along toward his store. She got up and went to the kitchen pass-through and said, "I see what you mean Rosey, this guy seems to love money, and sounds plenty greedy. I think that's the answer, he did conspire with Gibson. May I use your phone?"

"Sure honey, be my guest."

Pril picked up the phone and listened to Dorothy's "How may I help you Rosey?"

"Dorothy, this is Pril, not Rosey. You know me as the librarian in Glencoe. Can you connect me to Claude Comstock's office."

"Sure Pril, just a minute."

Claude came on the line and Pril said, "Chief, I just spent an hour with Peterson, and guess what, he paid off the mortgage on his store in the last two years. Can't you get into his bank account and see if he made big deposits or something? I think he had to get the money somewhere. Maybe County Hall of Records might tell us something. He bought the store, land and everything."

"Great work Pril, and a good idea. Come on back now, you did what we needed."

"Thanks, see you soon."

* * *

Claude called Judge Hastings. He found him at home, and got a rather gruff "Now what do you want so bad that you can't wait until tomorrow when I'm at my office?"

"Sorry about that Judge, something's come up that is pertinent to the forthcoming Gibson trial, and there is so little time before trial date, that I thought you might not mind if I called."

"Well you've already messed up my day at home anyway so you might as well go ahead and get on with it."

"We have a business owner that looks like he conspired with Bob Gibson to defraud the Arrow—B Ranch. I have some evidence to this scenario but not enough to hang my hat on."

"So what illegal thing do you want me to OK."

"Really Judge, I wouldn't think of doing something not exactly on the up and up."

"Uh huh, that statement makes me sure that it's something wiggly. Spell it out."

"I thought you might allow me to read Peterson's bank statements for the past three years, that's all."

"Oh yes, that's about as outside as it can get. Just what am I supposed to use to justify that kind of stuff?"

"Well, we have Gibson, who we know was fired by the diseased Richard Bentley for some reason outside normal issues. A man who was with the Arrow—B for 25 years. We know he did some money juggling to pay off gambling debts, and we know he disappeared down to Florida and would have stayed there invisible except for a fluke. The tie-in with Peterson is that Peterson was the sole supplier of ranch material needs, including winter feed. A closed loop, so to speak. We have paper evidence of that."

"So you want me to open up a man's bank account in order to prosecute him. That's pretty wild Claude."

"Judge, we're trying to bring to justice some criminals that have done serious damage to our community in the last six months. I think we have to use every tool we have to accomplish this. So, what if Peterson is innocent? The world won't know what we did anyway."

"So what bank is it, Claude?"

"Farmers Security, Judge."

"Can you do your thing in one of the back rooms of the bank?"

"Sure."

"OK then, I do business there myself. I'll call Sumner the president, and you come meet me at the courthouse. I'll have the papers ready when you get there."

"Thanks."

Claude put down the telephone receiver, and turned around to look at Ed Hunt, who had heard only one side of the conversation. Ed had a bit of wonder on his face. "I guess he went for it Claude, that was a neat bit of work. We could never get away with that in Cook County."

Claude said, "Ed, that's only half the job, we have to find something yet. I want you to go over to the county Hall of Records, and look up Peterson's mortgage, and when it was paid off. Now is a good time!"

"I gotcha, I'll go."

Claude got up from his chair, grabbed his brief case and headed for the courthouse. He found the judge in chambers, and waited as he finished preparing a subpoena to allow access to Ralph Peterson's bank account. A short time later he found himself reviewing five years of bank statements. He copied what data was pertinent onto a long yellow legal pad, handed the pile of monthly bank statements back to the bank official, and returned to his office.

Ed Hunt had a bit of trouble finding the records of mortgages as county records were spread out wherever there was available free space. In time he found what he was looking for in one of the off rooms of the city hall. Plans for a records depository had been in the mill for some time, waiting for funds to build the building. The records were filed by category in fireproof containers. It took him several hours to find the specific document pertaining to Peterson's purchase of the land and buildings known as Peterson's Store. Ed asked and received official copies of those documents he needed, and returned to the office.

Pril walked into the DA's office, and found Ed and Claude discussing the next move. Claude put in a call to George, who had spent the night at Chief Richardson's house. "Good morning George, glad I found you. Can you come over to my office before you go to the ranch?"

"Can do, see you shortly."

"Is the Chief at home?"

"Yeah, I'm here, if it's about LV, no news yet."

"Thanks, did I tell you, the trial is set for Dec. 8th?"

The Chief sighed, and said, "That's pressing my end of this thing, but I'll do the best I can. My LV contact is working on our problem. He should have something soon and call me. I'll let you know post haste."

George walked in and asked, "What can I do for you Claude?"

"George, I've been going over that wad of paper you handed me a few days ago, and I agree with your concept of what went on. I think we can get a conviction. I'm still hazy, however about the arithmetic of this thing, and I feel there has to be a tie-in with the murder of your father. I need to connect this fraud with the other crimes that have transpired around here. The numbers need to add up in a way that a jury can understand. Help me out on this one."

George said, "In a nutshell, dad was spending an average of $3,000.00 a year for winter feed for the ranch. This jumped to almost 6,000 dollars in 1950 and 1951. My foreman, Peter White, feels that the ranch has been overcharged around 3,000 a year. I remember Dad doing his books once a year around tax time. Somehow he missed the first out-of-line billings, but he sure noticed it early in 1952. Shortly after that, like March, he uncharacteristically fired Bob and took away his pension. Bob had worked for my Dad for 25 years. Dad must have been plenty mad to do that.

"Now the tie-in between the fraud going on and the killing of my father has yet to be established in my mind. I am hoping that this can be determined in the forthcoming trials."

"Yes, well the trial date has been set, and we have only six days left to prepare. Bob has no money for an attorney, so I expect the court will appoint one for him. I'm going over to the jail to talk to Bob. He's probably not too happy to be this close to the Syndicate types in town, and might be seeking friends. Finding a loose attorney to represent him in these parts might take a bit of imagination." Claude sort of got a wry expression on his face, and said, "Judge Hastings is a little antsy lately, he claims I'm edging a bit outside the law all the time, and giving him the ethical jitters. Now I need to ask him to figure out a way to keep all the suspects in jail until they can be brought to trial, which may be as long as another month. I know he's going to scream at me! So here goes."

Pril, who saw the humor in all of this, said, "Gee boss, you seem to be good at this kind of thing, I think you should go right over and talk to him now."

"That's cute, Pril, I'll remember that one."

The meeting with Judge Hastings was cordial. The Judge said, "Claude, so far we've not heard a lot of squawking about the issue of suspect's rights, but that might change soon. The Syndicate has been talking upstate, and I'm bound to hear about it." He gave Claude a sideways peak, "Claude, get this thing moving, I don't want to face the problem of being forced to release anyone."

The next morning Claude called the Judge, "Good morning Judge, Claude here."

"As if I didn't know. Who else would I be getting phone calls from at 7:30 AM. Now what twisted, controversial problem, which probably calls for some slightly illegal action on my part, has our DA come up with?"

"Now Judge, you know that I don't like things that aren't on the up-and-up."

"Alright Claude, cut the bull and come out with it."

"The thought has occurred to me that Bob Gibson is really small potatoes, which brings me to the question: Since he must be plenty scared, and I think he is sitting on information that will be of much value later, how much plea bargaining is too much in your mind to extract a bit of what he knows?"

"I hate this, the DA is asking me about limits. That's entirely in your bailiwick, you're running the investigation, not me."

"Well it's this way, I can't try all of these transgressors at once, and I need the flexibility to move from one trial to another. For example I hope to show information we get from Bob into another trial, say that of Joe Costello when I bring him to trial. When the jury provides us with a verdict, I want to capture such info that is pertinent from that trial, and use it in one of the following trials. Do you get what I'm driving at?"

"So what do you want from me?"

"There's no one in this county that didn't like Richard Bentley. There's also no one living in this county that doesn't want to see Bob Gibson hung out to dry. We're, none of us, going to be very popular if we let Bob off with a light sentence. But think of this scenario. Bob is tried for fraud, and is convicted. He gets a sentence tuned to the action of fraud. Later he is found to be implicated in the killing of Richard Bentley. Like aiding and abetting. Will we have to open up a new trial, can we, for that matter, try him for the more serious crime of aid/abet?"

"That's a lot of hypothetical, Claude. Do you see it going this way?"

"I kind of do, Judge. The only link I have between Bob Gibson and the killing of Richard Bentley is the money that Bob owed some gambling interests in Las Vegas. I am, however, hoping for a link-up when I get an answer from Las Vegas. Then I'll know more."

"So who do you know in Las Vegas?"

"That you're not to know."

"All right, let me see, you want several trials to look like one, that would be a neat trick, and a bit cavalier. I suggest that you finish one, hold the convicted individual, or individuals in tank until you need him. Then face the problem."

"That's nice, Judge, I assume that I will get all kinds of flak from the black suits in town. I'll just pass them on to you."

* * *

The court began jury selection on the 2nd of December. It took about a week to complete the process, and said jury was ready to be seated.

Whereas there were Syndicate members present they noticeably took no part in the trial of Bob Gibson. Their main interest was in Joe Costello, and would be heard from for sure when Joe's trial came up. In the meantime, Frank had been trying to get to his son, but seemed to run into road blocks everywhere he turned. If things were taking place in Chicago it would be a whole lot easier. This judge had no intention of allowing a change of venue, although the defense had asked for one. Plans were discussed relative to buying a juror when Junior's trial came up. Finding another mouthpiece to replace Hoople was also discussed, but that idea was nixed as a feeler put out indicated the court would do a veto on that one.

In the meantime, Claude made a visit to the jail to see Bob Gibson. The jailor, a Joe somebody, said, "Hello Claude, the Chief said you were coming. He told me to put you in the cell with Bob. He seems awfully cautious lately."

"Uh huh, well he's worried that something mean might take place in his town and on his watch. Just put me in, lock me up, and I'll yell when I want out."

The DA sat at a small table and motioned for Bob to sit on the bed. He said, "Bob, I'm Claude Comstock, the DA for the county of Contra. I will be prosecuting you for fraud against the Arrow—B Ranch, and possible involvement in the death of Richard Bentley. The court is in the process of procuring a counselor for your defense. Your trial is to start on December 8th, and I will stand as prosecuting attorney. I think we need to talk. You are to know that you are considered a prime suspect, or at least that you aided and abetted in the death of Richard Bentley. This trial will deal with the criminal act of defrauding the Arrow—B, and evidence of wrong doing that might have abetted the killers of Richard Bentley.

"We know that you gambled in Las Vegas big time, and we know that Richard Bentley discovered your stealing from the ranch and fired you. You are also suspected of providing information to others that led to the death of Richard Bentley." Claude paused, then, "You are in deep trouble."

Bob said, "When do I get to see my lawyer?"

"Probably in the next two to three days. The court hasn't found one that's willing to take your case yet."

"What happens next?"

"Your trial will begin on December 8th as scheduled."

After several minutes of silence, Bob said, "I swear that I had nothing to do with Dick's death. You can't pin that one me."

"The DA said, "Don't be so sure about that, the money you owe gambling interests in Las Vegas, and the timing of Mr. Bentley's death along with your flight to Florida will give any jury pause."

Bob groaned, and then said, "I don't see how the Sheriff found me in Florida. I thought no one knew where I was. How could I be so unlucky?"

"The here and now, Bob, is that you have no friends left in this county. I am the best chance you have. It is my sworn duty to protect the rights of all our citizens, even yours. Your defense attorney is appointed, and may not like to defend a hopeless case such as yours." Claude paused, "Tell me what happened Bob."

The prisoner was silent, and after a time, Claude stood up to leave, and he said, "Bob, you think this over for a bit. If you make a decision, tell the jailor, and he will call me."

Back in the office, Claude sat at his desk outlining his forthcoming court proceedings. He first made an outline of the coming events along a time line that starts the morning of December eighth and ends with the reading of the verdict, and the sentencing of Bob Gibson. Next he wrote his opening statement. Third, Claude started listing such evidence he felt would prove his case. He was just about ready to start on arguments when Ed Hunt walked in. "Hi Ed, what's the good word, and where's Pril?"

"The extra body my office promised won't be here until the Syndicate issue comes up, and I haven't seen Pril all day. I guess she's following up on one of those hunches she gets."

Claude laughed and said, "Yes, you're probably right, Pril seems to be able to think ahead and come up with some surprises. How are you doing with the deed to Peterson's store?"

"I found the deed, and it was cleared sometime last January with a final payment to the mortgage holder of $1,500.00."

"And?"

"The money was paid to our esteemed attorney Emery Forbes of Walnut. Vintage the 1890s."

"That's interesting. I know him. You don't suppose that old man is in this thing too?"

Ed said, "I don't think so, I don't think he's smart enough to try a caper like this."

"Nevertheless, check Forbes out. I'd like to get to the source of each action that took place."

* * *

Pril was sitting on a stool in Antonio's coffee shop. She

was sipping a cup of coffee, and chatting with Antonio. The conversations had gotten down to a Tony and Pril stage, and Pril said, "Oh Tony, were you around when that seven foot monster was in town? I heard that his meals came from here."

"I was here, but he never came in here."

"Oh, how did he get his meals, I heard that he ate six dinners at a time?"

Tony said, "His friend came in, ordered food, then took the meals over to the motel room."

"Well, that seems nice, was his friend a relative or something?"

"I don't know, of course, but I don't think so. He wore a black business suit, and had a hard look about him. One time, when he leaned over I saw the butt of a pistol inside his coat. Not that this was so strange for around these parts, but we usually have our hardware in sight. It kind of gave me the shivers."

"Gee that sounds kind of gangster like, did he always come in alone?"

"No, sometimes he came in with two others, and once he had several more."

"How long did he stay?"

"Something like two weeks, but the large man was only there for three days."

Pril finished her coffee, paid her check, and said, "So long Tony, I'll be by in a day or two, when I have another call to make over this way."

Tony said, "Why don't you try me for dinner sometime, Mama does the cooking, and she has everyone in Glencoe going ga-ga over her food."

Pril turned on one of her best smiles and said, "I'd like that Tony, and I love Italian food. Sounds yummy, I might just do that. See you."

Pril found her way back to the office to find Claude with a long yellow legal pad scribbling away, and not even looking up when she came in. She finally said, "Hello, how'd you make out with Gibson?"

Nothing happened, and Pril reached over and touched his shoulder. "I'm here Claude."

"Hi Pril, how long have you been here?"

"Just got here. You seem to be somewhere else, can I help?"

Claude took off his glasses, put them on the desk, and said, "Was I that dense Pril?"

Pril looked at the pile of notes, and legal papers scattered all over his oversized desk, laughed, and said, "You had me a bit worried, not being aware that I came in, but I can see why now. Why don't you try a bit of shut-eye on that couch over in the corner?"

"Honey, you sound like my mother, but you sure don't look the part. Why are all the women in my life trying to take care of me? Even Martha watches my diet, and tries to make me eat sensibly."

"Well you deserve it. Now that you are back from nowhere, how did it go at the jail?"

"Not that great. What have you been up to?"

"The coffee shop owner where Muscles got his food when he stayed at the End of The Line Motel had an interesting story to tell. His name is Antonio. We shortened it to Tony."

"Now you have my attention. Tell me the story."

"There's really not much to tell, but he might help you verify the presence of Muscles and some of his Black Mariah friends."

"Anything that I might use in trial?"

"I would guess that you will have to subpoena, as volunteering anything might be hazardous to the health."

"Good job Pril, write it up with a copy for me; you're right, I'm beat. Let's get outa here."

Claude Comstock climbed into bed and died. He had been doing his thing for 48 hours, and was getting waxy. Thoughts and ideas had begun to mix with facts. He dreamed of a judge with a monster head, testing his mettle, endurance and integrity. In the end, and just as he awoke some ten hours later, he found himself in today's world and in a cold sweat, foggy, and a nervous wreck. He dressed, looked at his shadowed face contemplating shaving, then decided not to. And so he found his way to the office, to find a bright, smiling, and apparently unsympathetic woman filing her nails. Now he knew better, but he couldn't keep from climbing all over Pril for not doing something productive, or routine or something else. "Pril, must you do that at the office? And where's Ed?"

Pril, still in her cheery mode said, "Gee Chief, was I supposed to be doing something that I missed? And Ed called from the police station. He's been talking to Richardson about prison visitors."

Claude looked hard at Pril, then said to the air, "This job must be getting to me, I just scolded Pril." He sighed, then said, "Pril, I'm in a lousy mood, I'm sorry. Would you find me a cup of coffee, and some donuts. Maybe that will get me back on track again."

"Sure, I'll be back in a minute or so" She exited, and a few moments later returned with an oversized cup of coffee. "The donuts are on the way. Why the lousy attitude Claude?"

"We have a weak case, not enough time, and I had a terrible dream."

"Claude, this is a new day, it is different from yesterday. Trust it for what it can bring. You did great on the Ballant trial. We all trust in you, and the successful conclusion of this one. So, no more negative stuff. It won't help." Pril picked up the ringing phone. She listened, and then handed the receiver over to Claude. The call was from the jail. Bob Gibson asked to talk to the District Attorney.

The donuts came, and Claude with a cup of coffee in one hand and a couple of raised donuts squeezed into his jacket pocket climbed into his car and headed for the police station. The duty officer looked up from his desk, reached for a ring full of keys hanging from a hook on the back wall and led Claude to the secured area where the jail cells were. He turned the area alarm off, and let Claude into Bob Gibson's cell and closed and locked the cell door.

"Hi Bob, you called, what can I do for you?"

Bob sat back down on the cot in his cell, and looked up at Claude. "Mr. Comstock, you said that you would protect my rights as a citizen. Is that true?"

"That's true, Bob. But keep in mind that, as your district attorney, I must also seek a conviction for the fraud charges."

"You said that I might be implicated in the murder of Richard Bentley. If I plead guilty to the charges of fraud, will this get me off the hook on the murder of Richard?"

"No Bob, it won't. I am going to use every tool I have to bring to justice the ones responsible for the murder of Richard Bentley. If you have a role in this murder, whether intentional or otherwise, you will be called to account. There will be consequences."

"Do I have any choices or way out?"

"Not really, but it would make it a whole lot easier for myself and the court to understand your point of view, and perhaps be more lenient in the end, if you told us what happened. We know that you conspired with Peterson. We know about the gambling in Las Vegas, and we know that Richard Bentley found out about the theft of ranch monies to pay off your gambling debts."

"Should I choose to do this thing, will the law protect me from gorillas who would kill me should I not come up with the money I owe?"

"The law will intervene where the law is broken. You will be expected to make good on your debts. Something can be worked out to satisfy your debtors. Bob, you're no good to them dead. That is a separate issue."

"What about Peterson?"

"I expect Mr. Bentley will take Peterson to civil court to recover his losses plus punitive damages the court will impose. Your testimony, and other information we have will make this guy pay in full.'

There was a long pause before Bob spoke again, then,

"Alright, how do I do this thing?"

* * *

The trial started at nine a.m. on the 8th of December, 1952. The jury was seated, and Judge Hastings entered the courtroom. He sounded his gavel announcing that the court was now in session and the trial of Bob Gibson should begin. Seated at the prosecution table were Claude Comstock, Priscilla Beckman, and Ed Hunt. At the defense table Bob Gibson, and his court appointed attorney, Jerry Brooks. The judge said, "Will the prosecution make its opening statement."

The DA rose and faced the jury. "Your Honor and members of the jury, the troubles in our County began with the act of fraud against the Arrow—B Ranch. The accused, in conjunction with others conspired to defraud the owner, Richard Bentley, a long time rancher and respected citizen, of our community. The exact amount of money related to this fraud is not known, but is in the neighborhood of $6,000.00. It should be noted that this trial is not necessarily for the purpose of recovering Mr. Bentley's losses, which can be handled through a civil suit between George Bentley and Ralph Peterson, but is endemic to the ultimate discovery of who killed Richard Bentley, and hopefully why. During this trial, the prosecution will present evidence and provide reliable witnesses that will prove our case. I'm finished, Your Honor."

Judge Hasting said, "Will the defense make its opening statement."

The defense attorney stood, and faced the jury. "Your Honor, and members of the jury, the defense prefers not to make an opening statement at this time."

The Judge turned to the DA and said, Mr. Comstock, you may begin your case."

The DA said, "I call George Bentley to the stand."

George approached the bench and was duly sworn in. He

took his seat in the witness chair, and the DA asked his first question. "What was your reaction and what did you do after you returned from college, and learned that the accused had left the ranch after twenty five years of service?"

"After my dad's funeral, I started to handle affairs of the ranch. In time I was able to enter dad's safety deposit box in the bank in Glencoe. When I opened it I found among other things, a note which read, 'I, Bob Gibson, do hereby relinquish all claims to the Bentley Ranch or other Bentley holdings, stocks, bonds or cash and bank accounts'. The note was dated March 13, 1952. It was signed by Bob Gibson, and bore the seal of a notary public registered in the state of Wyoming."

The DA handed a note to George. "Is this the note you referred to?"

"Yes, that is the note."

The DA took the note over to the material table. "I would like this to be entered as Exhibit one." He turned back to the witness, and said, "Continue Mr. Bentley."

"I became very busy with ranch matters, but in time I learned more about the absence of the accused from Peter White, my ranch foreman, and from Marie Carpenter, the ranch cook."

"And what did you learn?"

"First that Dad had set up a retirement fund for all his employees, and that when he fired Bob Gibson, he cancelled that fund for Bob. That and the Exhibit #1 note got my attention. This was totally out of character for my dad."

"What did you do next?"

"Soon after that, I went through the papers in dad's desk. My purpose was to learn about the running of the ranch finances and such. I gathered the records of expenses for the last five years, and discovered that the winter feed costs had climbed to double for the last two years. I talked to Pete about this. He said that since his arithmetic was so bad, he had turned the buying of all ranch needs over to Bob Gibson. He saw no reason for the disparity found in the financial records referred to."

"And who was the recipient of these monies?"

"Mr. Peterson, the owner of Peterson's General Store of Walnut."

The DA turned to the judge and said, "May we approach the bench, Your Honor?"

The judge nodded assent; and motioned to the defense to join.

The DA said, "Your Honor, it appears that we have a co-conspirator in this case. I wish to question Ralph Peterson regards his knowledge of the matter at hand. I request that we bring Mr. Peterson into court. If he is implicated, he needs to be here to defend himself. If he is not, he should still be here for the same reason."

The judge asked, "Mr. Brooks, do you have any objections to bringing Mr. Peterson in to testify?"

"No, Your Honor."

"Claude, how long will it take to bring Peterson in?"

"Judge, I expect we will need the rest of today to subpoena him, and allow him to prepare as a witness."

The judge took a long look at his desk calendar, and said, "That's fine, but keep in mind that I won't tolerate too many delays in this trial." He then turned to the courtroom and said, 'This court stands adjourned until 9 a.m. tomorrow morning."

Claude returned to the prosecution table. Pril leaned over, and said, "Boss, I just saw Peterson leave the courtroom. Can't we grab him?"

Claude said, "Oops, let's try; Ed, see if you can follow him, and I'll go for the Sheriff, he's also in the courtroom. Pril, you contact Richardson. Tell him what's going on."

Claude found Sheriff Williams about four rows back, just getting up to leave. "Bill, we need Peterson. There will be a subpoena issued directly. He just left the courtroom. Pick him up before he vanishes."

"I get your message, get me that subpoena ASAP, I'm on my way."

Judge Hastings was just leaving the bench when Claude said, "Judge, we need a subpoena to pick up Peterson, kind of like a few minutes ago. Can we do this ASAP, as he is here, and reachable."

"Sure, come into chambers with me."

Sheriff Williams got into his pickup, spotted Ed Hunt chasing Peterson. He was just getting into his car. The Sheriff slid to a stop just in front of Peterson's car, and walked over to the open car window. "Not so fast Pete, you're needed right here."

Pete Peterson said, "Sheriff, you're out of order, you have no right to stop me unless I'm breaking the law, which I'm not."

Ed's face and shoulders appeared in the right hand window. He said, "Mr. Peterson, a subpoena is being written at this moment. I suggest you comply with the Sheriff's requests."

"What are the charges?"

Ed said, "They will be read to you as soon as you appear before Judge Hastings. Now come along like a nice little boy, park, and get in with the nice Sheriff. He's bigger than you."

Peterson did as he was asked, and said, "My lawyer will make you two pay. This is akin to kidnapping."

"Well that's just fine, Pete, we're going to see the DA right now, and you can tell him about your mistreatment." The three drove the short distance to the court parking lot, entered the court, and were ushered into the judge's chambers by the bailiff. Peterson continued to make noises, even in chambers. The judge said, "Shut up Peterson, or you will be cited for contempt."

The DA said, "Sworn testimony indicates that you have knowledge pertinent to the ongoing trial of Bob Gibson. I suggest you seek counsel; and you will be expected to testify in court tomorrow."

The judge said, "Peterson, you can spend tonight as a guest of the state with the Glencoe police dept., or post bail, but you still have to be here for questioning at nine tomorrow. Sheriff, will you see that this citizen is on hand at nine A.M. tomorrow."

The Sheriff said, "Yes, Your Honor." He handcuffed Peterson, then got on the phone and called Chief Richardson. "Hi Chief, Bill Williams here. Do you have room for an overnight guest?"

"So who are you sending over?"

"Peterson, the owner of Peterson's General store in Walnut."

* * *

Court convened as directed on schedule, with George reseated in the witness chair. He was reminded that he was still under oath. Ralph Peterson had spent the night in jail was seated in the front row, waiting to testify. Since Peterson had been unable to procure counsel on such short notice, the court ordered Bob's defense counsel to represent both Bob Gibson and Peterson.

The DA said, "Mr. Bentley, in our last session, you stated that billing was done from Petersons General Store in Walnut, is that correct?"

"Yes, that is correct."

The DA picked up a handful of five by seven lined sheets of paper filled with numerical entries, and calculations. He handed them to the witness, and asked, "Do you recognize these?"

George thumbed through, and said, "Yes, these represent billings from Petersons, they have Peterson's name and logo at the top. Claude walked over to the material table, and asked that they be placed in the evidence box, as Exhibit two. "Did you find evidence that indicated that any other person, or concern might have supplied winter feed to the Arrow—B?"

"I did not."

"What did you do next?"

"I met with Sheriff Williams, and we discussed the

possible mishandling of ranch finances, specifically where winter feed transactions were concerned."

"And as a result of that meeting?"

"I filed a complaint with the Sheriff's office."

"Claude then said, "I'm through with this witness, Your Honor."

"Judge Hastings said, "Your witness, Mr. Brooks."

Jerry Brooks, the court appointed attorney for the defendant, strolled up to the witness chair. He said, Mr. Bentley, would you please explain to the court your reasons for selecting Bob Gibson to file your complaint against."

"I think I have already explained that adequately; however, the sudden disappearance of Bob from the area has to further implicate him. Sheriff Williams agreed with me, that Bob Gibson should be located and brought into court."

"Thank you Mr. Bentley, that will be all."

"Any re-direct, Mr. Comstock?"

"No, Your Honor."

"Well, call your next witness."

"I call Sheriff Williams to the stand."

After the Sheriff was duly sworn in, Claude asked, "Sheriff, when George presented you with information concerning alleged fraud against the Arrow—B Ranch, what did you do?"

"I asked him to file a complaint."

Claude handed the witness a copy of the complaint. Is this a copy of that complaint?"

"Yes, that is it."

The DA walked over to the material desk, and asked that the complaint be entered into the material box as Exhibit three.

"Thank you Sheriff, that's all the questions I have at this time."

The Judge said, "Your witness, Mr. Brooks."

"I have no questions for this witness, Your Honor."

The Judge said, "It's almost time for lunch, this court is adjourned until 2 p.m." He rapped his gavel once, and left the bench.

The prosecution team was just walking into Martha's place, when a police officer walked up to Claude, and said, "Mr. Comstock, Chief Richardson wants you to call him. He said it was important. You can use the radio in my car."

Claude thanked the officer, followed him, and was connected up to the Chief.

"Claude here Chief, what's up?"

"Will you have time to stop at my office before you go back to court?"

"I could I guess." Claude sat for a moment. The Chief must have something important on his mind to make a request like that. He pressed the mike button, and said "Sure, I'll see you in ten minutes." Turning to the others, he instructed them to proceed with lunch and return to the courthouse ASAP.

Claude walked into the police station, and was ushered into the Chief of Police's office. "What's on your mind, Chief?"

"Hi Claude, you better sit down for this one. I just had a call from my L V connection. Guess what, Bob's contract was sold to the Black Mariah Syndicate in April of 1950. It was for 30 thou, plus interest, which never stops with these types. I think Bob Gibson is in more trouble than a little fraud."

Claude said, "I have suspected such, and I think there is our tie-in. Thanks Chief, this should help a lot."

"Claude, watch your back, these are nasty people. They want Bob, but they want the Arrow—B more. I figure Gibson has made some promises he couldn't keep."

"I'm sure you are right Chief, thanks for the warning." Claude got up and headed for the courthouse.

The Chief picked up his phone, called the duty officer and said, "Have an officer follow the DA. See that he gets there in one piece, and stick around the courthouse. I want the prosecution team to have protection from now on." He then called the Mayor, "Fred, Richardson here, have you got a minute?"

"A minute I have, but not much more, what's on your mind?"

"Some complications are showing up, and I would feel more comfortable with more of us. Do you suppose we could beef us up a bit until this trial stuff gets over?"

"What you're saying makes sense, but we've got some hard heads on the Board of Supervisors that think the city government should be all volunteer, and your department is already too big. Hell, go ahead and hire what you need. I'll take some heat, but by the time the naysayers get around to action, maybe the trials will be over, and things will go back to normal."

Chief Richardson hung up the phone. He sat still for a moment, then buzzed for his secretary. "Peggy, get me through to State police in Cheyenne."

Court reconvened at two. The judge said, "Claude, continue with your case."

Claude stood and said, "Your Honor, if it please the court, I will accede to the defense; I think they have a thing of import to tell us."

"So be it, Mr. Brooks, the floor is yours."

The attorney for the defense stood and said, "Your Honor, the defendant, Mr. Gibson, wishes to change his plea of innocent to 'guilty as charged' pertaining to the fraud portion of the charges against him. As regards the matter of the aid/abet charge, the not guilty plea stands. He further states that he will be available as a witness if the court should desire."

The judge said, "The court accepts the new plea of 'guilty as charged' for the fraud portion of these charges. However, the aid/abet charges are still in effect. Any further testimony in the case against Mr. Gibson which concerns the fraud charges are moot. The matter of sentencing Mr. Gibson will be taken up later. Are there any comments or questions from either the prosecution or the defense?"

Claude said, "Your Honor, the prosecution has just

received new evidence concerning the gambling debt incurred by the defendant, Robert Gibson. We now feel that Mr. Gibson has been an unwitting participant in crimes related to the death of Richard Bentley. In view of his change of plea, we feel that justice would best be served by dismissal of all aid/abet charges against Mr. Gibson, however, he may have information that is pertinent to the successful prosecution of the killers of Richard Bentley, and other related crimes. It is therefore requested that Mr. Gibson make himself available for questioning as a witness in the forthcoming trial of Joe Costello.

"This action will close out this trial, and allow us to move forward quickly into the next. As regards the new information, I hold an affidavit to the affect that the gambling debt that the defendant owed to a Las Vegas group was sold to the Black Maria Syndicate of Chicago Illinois early last year. This explains the interest that a Chicago based Syndicate has in our County.

"In light of this, the prosecution requests that this trial be terminated, and that the court proceed with the sentencing of the accused as far as the fraud is concerned. If it please the court, the prosecution will drop the aid/abet charges against the defendant, so this trial can end."

The Judge asked of the defense attorney, "What is your comment on this, Mr. Brooks?"

"Your Honor, the defense is pleased with this line of action."

"So be it then, This trial is ended. Mr. Gibson is ordered to make himself available for questioning as needed." He turned to the jury and sad said, "The Jury is dismissed and the court thanks you for your participation."

* * *

Members of the Syndicate gathered after the trial was ended for the evening. Among those present were Frank Costello, attorney Hoople, and four other members of the

Syndicate. Frank spoke first, "This is not getting Joe out of jail. This prosecuting attorney is trying to choke us to death. He hasn't mentioned Joe one time. He will. What are you legal beagles doing? Nothing. Where did he get all his information from? How did he find out about Muscles? Let's not be stupid, this guy is smart. Chicago is a long way off, but it's my bet that he's going to end up there, and that we can't afford. In Chicago, we could buy our way out of something like this. Nobody likes money out here. Now I'd like to know if Joe gets a thumb down from the jury, what will they do to him?"

"Frank, Joe is charged with aiding and abetting in an attempted murder case. If the jury comes back 'guilty as charged', he could get five to ten years.

"Well that's just peachy. Let's reconsider some of that strong-armed stuff we've been talking about."

"Frank, we're already in much trouble out here, if we try and fail, it'll put us in so much shit we'll never get out. I think we'd better be real careful about breaking laws in this state."

Frank said, "Uh huh, well we're not going to abandon Joe. From my view, they haven't anything more on Joe than driving at night on a country road. Now you smart legal people figure a way out of this."

"Frank, we can't defend Joe until the prosecution attacks him. And this they haven't done yet."

Frank said, "I know that Hoople is useless, which one of you two legal types are telling him what to do or say?"

"We both are Frank, but to date there hasn't been anything to argue on. Just as soon as he starts to include Joe in the prosecution agenda, maybe we can do something."

"Maybe! You guys are frightening me. I don't like maybes. I hear that the prosecution is prepared to give its closing statement. Are we?"

"Yes but don't expect much. The prosecution has nearly all of the testimony backed up pretty well." In the interest of the defendant, nit-picking sworn testimony will only make us look bad. I expect our major asset is the lack of actual evidence…on the part of the prosecution, and, of course, the fact that the entire case for the prosecution is based on supposition and circumstantial evidence. Frank, that's the best we can do. Yes, we will run the show, not Hoople. He does what we tell him to do."

27 | THE BLACK MARIAH

The day after the end of the Gibson trial, Claude Comstock filed charges with the court against the Black Maria Syndicate and its de facto leader, Frank Costello. He also stipulated the inclusion of other Syndicate members that might be shown to be culpable in killings and other criminal acts. To prevent the flight of Frank, a closed hearing was held in the judge's chambers. Judge Hastings signed an order for the arrest of Frank Costello.

Claude Comstock reached Chief Richardson at his office, "Hello Chief, how's policing these days?"

"It's been good up until now. You don't usually call just to pass the time of day, what nice little thing do you want from me this time?"

"Nothing much really Chief, I have a warrant for the arrest of Frank Costello."

"Oh shit, that bunch all carry small cannons under their coats, and never are caught out alone. You come up with some doozies, Claude, and as far as Hastings is concerned, he just sits there and scribbles on a piece of paper. I have to do the tough stuff."

"Well Chief, you're good at this kind of thing. We don't want you to get bored."

The DA and Judge Hastings had managed to streamline procedures and paper work such that the Black Mariah legal minds were caught unprepared. Frank was picked up the night before as he was leaving Howard Johnsons, where he had his evening meal. He was all bundled up against the bitter below zero temperature. Chief Richardson had sent plenty of manpower to be sure of no firefights. Frank began to scream when he was picked up, and didn't stop all night. In the morning, and in front of Judge Hastings he started to chirp all over again, which, of course, didn't help his case a bit. He was charged with conspiracy to commit murder, instituting plans to take possession of private property illegally, and coercion of local citizens.

The trial of the Black Mariah Syndicate, and its leaders was aimed at bringing to justice those responsible for the series of criminal acts that had taken place in Contra County. The prosecution had been gathering data and information concerning events, clandestine or otherwise, leading up to the culmination of the Gibson/Peterson trial. The arraignment of Frank and Joe Costello took place on a wintry day in January 1953. The trial date was set for January 26, 1953. The Black Mariah Syndicate lawyers asked once more for a bail hearing, this time, for both Frank and Joe. Judge Hastings refused bail, based on the proximity of the upcoming trial. He felt a hearing was moot at this time in as much as the defendants would be needed in court directly. The District Attorney provided the defense with a witness list, and the witnesses had all been advised. Chief Running Deer was told of the need for Charlie Little Crow to testify, and after much consultation with the council, he agreed to allow this.

After much blustering by the defense, a jury of twelve men and women were selected from the monthly jury pool, and duly accepted by both the prosecution and defense. As soon as the trial of the Syndicate was announced, the media and other interested parties showed up again, after having lost interest during the Gibson trial.

The trial began, as scheduled with the prosecution

represented by Claude Comstock, Ed Hunt, Priscilla Beckman, and a new arrival from the Cook County district attorney's office. Present were reps from the Chicago Police Department as well. The courtroom was jammed and the city's bedrooms were once again filled, with some persons having to share.

Representing the defense were two from the Syndicate's stock of sleazy Chicago lawyers, and Harold Hoople, who was the only one of the three licensed to practice law in Wyoming. The Syndicate would have a difficult time replacing him for that reason. They postulated that he would be easy to manipulate anyway.

As soon as the jury was seated the judge said, "Mr. Comstock, make your opening statement."

"Your Honor, and members of the jury, the State intends to prove that the Black Mariah Syndicate of Chicago, Illinois has been responsible for many criminal acts within the County of Contra. This organization, headed by the accused, Frank Costello, has deliberately, and with malice of forethought orchestrated attempted murder, coercion, and attempted illegal takeover of properties within Contra County. Indeed, this organization has shown little regard for human lives or private property, and has been willing to spend large sums of money to execute its intended goals. The state will provide both factual and circumstantial evidence to prove the guilt of the Mr. Frank Costello. Additionally, Mr. Costello's son, Joe Costello, will be tried as a co-defendant on aid and abet charges relating to the aforesaid crimes. I am finished Your Honor."

The judge said, "Will the defense make its opening statement."

The defense attorney rose and said, "The defense intends to prove that the allegations against the Black Mariah Syndicate, and specifically, Frank and Joe Costello are entirely false, and are a figment of the imagination of the District Attorney. I am finished, Your Honor."

"Mr. District Attorney, present your case."

The DA said, "I call Bob Gibson to the stand."

Bob took the witness stand, and was dully sworn in.

Claude began, "Mr. Gibson, you were fired by Richard Bentley, your employer for twenty-five years, sometime in March of 1952, is this not true?"

"Yes, that is true."

"Will you tell us why?"

"Mr. Bentley suspected me of stealing money from the ranch."

The DA handed the witness the note found in the ranch safety deposit box which had been previously entered as Exhibit I, "Do you recognize this note, and is that your signature at the bottom?"

"Yes, that is my signature."

"Alright, please read this note out loud to the jury."

Bob, looking forlorn, took the note and read, "I Bob Gibson do hereby relinquish all claims to the Bentley Ranch or other Bentley holdings, stocks, bonds, cash or bank accounts."

The DA said, "This note was duly certified by a Wyoming State notary public." He then handed the note over to the clerk at the material table.

"Your employer of twenty five-years fires you, and divests you of any of your retirement money. Is that correct Mr. Gibson?"

"Yes."

"How do you explain that?"

"Mr. Bentley was very good to me, I don't hold anything against him. I made a mistake when I mismanaged the accounts with Peterson's general store."

"Just how did you make a mistake?"

"I needed money. One day while I was picking up a load of winter feed hay from Petersons, I told Peterson about my trips to Las Vegas. He seemed interested, and asked me to play $5.00 for him. I'm not sure, but I think we won on that bet. One day I didn't do that well, and I lost a considerable amount of money. I continued to try to win back what I had lost, but instead I lost even more. The next time I saw Mr. Peterson, I talked this over with him. That's when we hatched the plan to double bill the Arrow—B, and we would split the profit. I considered taking money from the ranch as a loan, and I would to pay it back when I won in Las Vegas."

"Was this a mutually decided plan, or did you decide on your own?"

"As I said, Mr. Peterson suggested the plan, and I went for it."

"And, in your opinion, that's why Mr. Bentley fired you?"

"Yes."

"Alright Bob, can you tell us what options your creditors offered."

"Either come up with the cash or something of equal value. Sometime toward the end of 1951, a man paid me a visit to discuss the debt. He was very big and very strong looking. He frightened me."

"This man knew you had no money, he also knew that you would be no good to him dead. He knew that your salary, as a ranch hand would never pay up the money you owed. Tell us, Mr. Gibson, just what did he offer? What kept you alive?"

There was a long silence from the witness. Claude repeated his question, "What kept you alive Mr. Gibson?"

"He questioned me about the Arrow—B Ranch, and when I think about it, about the land itself."

"You mean the mines, the mountains, the ranchers, be specific."

"He asked about access into the mountains, and never stopped asking for information about the Arrow—B."

"Such as?"

"Where does the water come from, and how much. Information on hunting, are there any mines on ranch property. He asked me several times about how close was the nearest ranch to the Arrow—B."

"Could you identify this person if you saw him again?"

"I don't think so, it's been almost a year, and he didn't show his face much when we talked. I might recognize his voice though. It was strange and tough."

"Let's see, sometime toward the end of 1951, you met with a stranger who seemingly represented your creditors. A month or so later, Jones Realty of Glencoe, approached Richard Bentley with an offer on the ranch. Did you put said stranger in touch with Jones Realty?"

"Mr. Comstock, he asked me if there was someone in the area that dealt in land sales. I saw no harm in telling him about Jones Realty."

"During the period that you were profiteering at the expense of the Arrow—B, did you in fact repay any of the debts you incurred due to your gambling?"

"I did, but every time I paid something on my debts the total I owed went up, due, I was told, to interest."

Claude asked, "How many times did you meet with this mystery man?"

"Just three times."

"What else did you talk about?"

Again there was a long pause. Finally Judge Hastings said, "Mr. Gibson, you must answer the question, and remember you are under oath. Wrong answers could get you cited for perjury."

Bob Gibson had been a cowhand most of his adult life. The ranch fed him, housed him, clothed him, and paid him a fair wage. He had never been required to manage his own life. Now, sitting in the witness stand in the courthouse in Glencoe, and in the presence of his peers, the law, and the world through the news media, he must tell of his misdeeds against the Arrow—B, and its owner Richard Bentley. He coughed, cleared his throat and started in. "We talked of ranch things, like how many ranch hands there were. Was Mr. Bentley wealthy, or did he have to struggle each year to make it. Were there ever any visitors to the ranch, and how does one get up into the mountains? When he finally left, I had a feeling that I had betrayed Mr. Bentley, and those I had been working with for most of my life."

"Was there ever any discussion concerning, or about, the

local Arapaho village or for that matter, persons considered to be Arapaho Tribal Members?"

"Thinking back to the meetings, I recall him asking where and how could he procure a guide for a trip into the mountains."

Claude asked, "And did you accede to this request?"

"I saw nothing wrong in putting him in touch with a member of the Tribe that I knew."

"Do you know if he did, in fact, make contact with your Arapaho friend?"

"I do not, as shortly afterwards, I left for Florida."

"Your Honor, the new evidence I wish to show is in the form of an affidavit, and I wish to enter this into the record as Exhibit II. The contents of this Exhibit is a transfer of Mr. Gibson's gambling debt from a Las Vegas group to the Black Mariah Syndicate of Chicago. This action took place in April of 1950. This explains the presence and interest of the Syndicate in the proceedings going on here." The affidavit was handed to the jury foreman, and duly passed around to the jury members. "Your Honor, I have no further questions for this witness."

The judge asked the defense attorney if he wished to cross.

"Yes, Your Honor." He stood and approached the witness, "You have testified that the man that called on you, let's call him Mystery Man, looked threatening. Did he verbally threaten you?"

"Yes, on all three visits."

"Can you tell us what he said, and how he said it?"

"It was said clearly and distinctly, and included either/or. I soon concluded that my life depended on giving him the information he asked for."

"Did you ever see a firearm or knife on the "Mystery Man?"

"Yes, once on his third visit, I saw the butt of a pistol under his coat."

"I have no further questions for this witness, Your Honor."

The Judge said, "You may step down Mr. Gibson." He turned to the DA and said, "Claude, call your next witness."

"I call Ralph Peterson to the stand."

Ralph Peterson had not had time, and didn't want to spend the money, to hire an attorney. Before he was sworn in, he said to the judge, "I wish to make it clear that I am not here voluntarily."

"Your objection is duly noted. You are required to be sworn in however, and will enjoy all of the requirements and benefits of all the other witnesses." With that, Ralph Peterson was duly sworn in.

Claude said, "Your Honor, these proceedings have shown that Mr. Peterson may share equal responsibility with Bob Gibson for the crime cited in this trial. I wish to question him as a hostile witness."

The judge took a moment, then said, "I think I'll allow this as long as you treat the witness as such, and not as a suspect. Remember, he has not been charged with any crime."

"Mr. Peterson, you heard Mr. Gibson testify that you and he entered into a pact to defraud the Arrow—B Ranch; is that not true?"

"There was no such agreement. What Bob did was strictly on his own."

The DA walked over to the prosecution table, and picked up a folder. He faced the witness and said, "I have here a review of your bank statements. They reveal deposits and withdrawals for the past five years. Would you explain why your deposits were considerably higher in the past two years than in the previous two?"

Peterson said. "I'm a business man. I often deposit different amounts. I don't feel the court has the right to my account information."

"Alright, I see where you paid Bob Gibson by way of a check in the amount of $500.00 on the 15th of November, 1951. Can you explain that Mr. Peterson?"

"This information is, in fact, personal and confidential to myself and Mr. Gibson. This should not have been revealed.

I shall pursue legal assistance to bring suit against you, and the court Mr. Comstock."

"Mr. Peterson, you are required to answer the question."

"If you must know, it was a loan."

"This seems a little unusual, a business man in a small town loaning a cowhand this much money. What did he use for collateral?"

"That is also confidential between two persons."

"Were you aware that Mr. Gibson owed a large sum of money to some Las Vegas gambling interests?"

"I was not."

The DA looked at his notes and said, "I see that you paid off the mortgage on your store late last December. Is that correct Mr. Peterson?"

"That is correct, and I see you have been illegally nosing around into my private affairs."

"Not that it matters Peterson, that is a matter of public record. Where did that money come from, Mr. Peterson?"

"Since you have been given access to my bank account, I'm sure you noticed that the money came directly from that account."

Judge Hastings intervened and said, "Please answer the questions without the embellishments. Will the clerk remove most of that from the record. Claude, you're getting close to off base. Where is this line of questioning leading?"

"Your Honor, this whole six months of criminal acts started when Bob Gibson committed fraudulent acts against the Arrow—B Ranch. It appears that Ralph Peterson knew of this. Mr. Gibson has been relieved of the fraud portion of his charges, and the prosecution has dropped his aid/abet charges, on the grounds that he took an unwitting part in involvement here. I suspect that the witness, Ralph Peterson, would also be so treated were he charged. It is not the intent of the prosecution to prosecute the witness on either count. The matter of fraud against the Arrow—B will have to be handled in civil courts. I have no further questions for this witness, Your Honor."

The Judge said, "The witness may step down."

The DA said, "I would like to recall Mr. Gibson to the stand."

"So be it, proceed Mr. Comstock."

"Mr. Gibson, you are reminded that you are still under oath. Now you testified that you had a verbal contract with Mr. Peterson to over-bill the Arrow—B and share the proceeds. Do I have that right?"

"Yes that's right."

"How was your share to be paid?"

"In cash, and directly after the Arrow—B accounts payable were received."

"Why, then was some of it paid by check?"

"Mr. Peterson told me that he needed his available cash to complete his mortgage payment. He gave me that check, and told me not to cash it for a full month. I agreed, and cashed it one month later."

Claude turned to the judge, "May I have a few moments to confer with my staff?"

"Okay Claude, but make it fast."

Claude returned to the prosecution table, opened the Peterson folder, and found the $500.00 check. He faced the jury, and handed the cashed check to the jury foreman. He said, "Notice that the cancellation date on this check substantiates the witness's testimony."

The check was passed around for the jury members to review, then entered as Exhibit III.

Claude said, "Mr. Gibson, it has been shown that Mr. Peterson gave you a check for $500.00. He claims it was a loan. What, if any, did you give him for collateral?"

"There was never any talk of it being a loan. It was money he owed me."

"You're saying that the $500.00 was your portion of the swindle money?"

"Yes, that was one payment."

Claude said, "I have no further questions for this witness."

The judge said, "The witness may step down." He paused,

looked at his watch and said, since it is late in the day, the court is adjourned until tomorrow at nine."

Nine A.M. the next morning found all the principals present, and most everyone shedding scarves, galoshes, overcoats and sweaters. The judge, who had moved from the south, didn't like the cold weather one bit. He was grumpy and impatient. He said, "Alright Claude do what you have to do to get this thing started."

"Yes, Your Honor, I call Charles Jones to the stand."

A sullen Charles Jones seated at the prosecution table, rose and took his seat in the witness chair. He was duly sworn in and Claude began "Mr. Jones, you are on record as having made an unsolicited offer to Richard Bentley for the sale of the Arrow—B ranch. You are also on record of making an offer on said property, subsequent to the death of Richard Bentley to his son, George Bentley. Do you confirm that this is so?"

Jones shifted around in the witness chair, and said, "That is the truth, I was merely following the law, which requires that I present all offers to buy property to the property owner."

"And in both cases, I understand, your offers were turned down. Is that correct, Mr. Jones?"

"That is correct."

"Now, I have a copy of the Jones Real Estate offer that was made to Richard Bentley. The offer was for one million dollars for the ranch. Doesn't that seem a bit high Mr. Jones?"

"Seems to me."

"Well, what would you say would be a good price for a ranch of that size in this area?"

The witness was silent for a moment, finally when the prosecution asked if he heard the question he said, "I am not qualified to appraise real estate."

"Alright, then who did put a price on this particular piece of Wyoming?"

"The prospective buyer made an offer, which was refused

by Mr. Bentley, and then the offer was doubled."

"So, Mr. Jones, the first offer must have been for $500,000.00, is that about the way it was?"

"Yes, that is the way it was."

"Now, tell the court the name of the person or consortium that made these offers?"

There was a time of silence from the witness, and then, "I refuse to answer that question, as it violates the agent-client relationship." After another short pause, "I take the 5th amendment to the Constitution."

Claude turned from the witness and said, "Your Honor, we need to know the identity of the person or organization that made this inflated offer to buy the Arrow—B Ranch. This witness obviously knows the answer to this question, and the district attorney's office respectfully requests that the court use its powers, as needed, to learn the answer. By taking the 5th this witness has indicated involvement. As such, he should be held over for further questioning, and possible charges."

Judge Hastings said, "I concur. Mr. Jones, I suggest you obtain counsel; and, you are to make yourself available to this court until the court is satisfied. Claude, do you have any further questions for this witness?"

"No, Your Honor."

"The witness may step down. Call your next witness."

The district attorney said, "I call Charlie Little Crow to the stand."

Charlie Little Crow was seated in the witness chair, and duly sworn in. He looked uncertain and somewhat frightened, not knowing what was to come.

The DA said, "Mr. Little Crow, you've known Mr. Jones for some time. Is that not true?"

"Yes, that's right."

"How did you first meet?"

"We met at the county fair."

"And when was this?"

"October of 1951."

"Tell the court about that meeting."

"Me and Mr. Jones talked of sheep. And what I was doin' for the Village at the fair. He ast if I knew anything about the Arrow—B spread. I said yes, as I often took our flock into the hills around the ranch. He ast me if I could learn him somethin' about the area."

"And did these questions seem to center around the Arrow—B Ranch area?"

"Yes, they seemed to. I kinda thought about that later."

"Now Mr. Little Crow, did you see Mr. Jones again, after the meeting at the county fair?" "Yes, I saw 'im once more. He called me at the Village, askin' me to meet 'im on the highway near there."

"Tell us about that meeting."

"Wal, when I got to the meeting place, there was another man there instead of Mr. Jones."

"Can you tell us when this was?"

"It musta been the day after White Owl died."

"I assume you are referring to Richard Bentley."

"Yes, we in the Village always called him by his Indian name 'White Owl'."

"Was that date May 11, 1952?"

"Yes, I guess that was the date."

"Tell us about your meeting with this mystery man."

"He tol' me he needed me to do some work in the mountains. He said it would only take an hour or two, and he'd take me there."

"And did you, in fact, go with him into the mountains?"

"Yes, he took me in his car to the bottom of Portal Mesa, and we climbed up to the top."

The District Attorney looked up in surprise and said, "Mr. Little Crow, that's a long uphill climb, and not one that the average city person is capable of. Did this man seem to have any trouble making it up to the top?"

"No sir, he acted like he had done that kinda thing before."

"Alright, what did the man ask you to do when you

reached the top of Portal Mesa?"

"There was a big mess all around the lone ponderosa that stands at the end of the mesa. He ast me to clean things up and make it as natural as I could."

"Mr. Little Crow, didn't this seem a strange request, the stranger asking you to erase footprints and other signs high up in the mountains?"

"It did, and I ast the man about this. He took out a big pistol and pointed it right at my face. So I had to do what he ast me too."

"Were there other signs there besides those of the passing elk herd?"

"Yes, there was signs of several horses, men's footprints, and some kind of a struggle. I did what the man with the pistol wanted."

"Mr. Little Crow, to the best of your memory, can you recall anything special about those signs that you removed?"

"The one thing that was strange was a set of footprints that were large."

"How large, can you give us an estimate?"

"Wal, I put my foot in one of the footprints, and it only filled half of the big print."

"Your Honor, may we take the time to measure Mr. Little Crow's foot?"

The defense attorney jumped up and yelled, "Objection, Your Honor, this is not testimony, this will be a guess by a questionable witness, and can in no way be verified by the defense."

Judge Hastings paused for a moment then said, "Well, the witness could have said, large, very large, huge, or any of a number of adjectives to describe a footprint. He was obviously under stress, and certainly not in a position to measure something. I think I'll let it stand. Proceed with the measuring Mr. Comstock."

The bailiff somehow found a yardstick, and the witness' foot was measured. With shoes on it measured nine inches. The DA said, "Your Honor, I would like the record to show that, based on the measurement of the witness' foot, the footprints found at the scene must have been somewhere in the neighborhood of 18 inches long."

"I guess that will be alright, as long as it is shown as an estimate. Continue with your questioning the witness."

"Mr. Little Crow, was that the end of it, or did the man just take you back to the Village and leave? Tell us what happened."

"The two of us went down the trail to his car. He tol me not to say anything about this, that I was part of it now. He also said he would be watchin'. He took out his pistol and stuck it at my head again."

"Mr. Little Crow, would you recognize this person if you saw him again?"

"He kept his face away or covered when we were together, so the answer has to be no. I would remember his voice, however, as it had an unusually nasal tone to it.

"I'm through with this witness, Your Honor."

"Does the defense wish to question the witness?"

"Your Honor, may I have a few moments to consult with my colleagues?"

The Judge nodded, looked at his watch and said, "It's almost time for lunch, this court is adjourned until two P.M. this afternoon."

The prosecution team filed out, and headed for Martha's place. George joined the group. Martha came and took orders. Claude turned to Ed, and asked, "How are we coming with getting Muscles out here?"

"Haven't heard, but I'll check this afternoon."

Claude said, "George, you seem a bit quiet and thoughtful, what's on your mind?"

"Well, as long as you asked, I'm trying to figure out how they got Muscles up on that mesa. I'm convinced he was up there, the foot-prints and the broken neck, etc. But you will need to show how. If we rule out his climbing up that trail on the basis of his size and weight, riding horses would have been too visible as it would have left sign of passing. Aircraft is out as there is no landing spot, that leaves a car of some kind. We know something happened but how has to be answered. If we rule out walking, riding, and air; then it has to be by car. I think we need to look around for another access into the mountains.

"Claude, you have asked me twice to search the ranch for clues, which I have done. The only thing I found was a reference to a government sponsored search for uranium, which resulted in none being found in these mountains. The search was discontinued sometime in 1948. Now you know the government types would not like walking much anywhere. They must have their cars."

Claude said, "I think you've got that one right, however we are in the middle of a trial, and I don't think Hastings will give us the time we need to look. Unless you can come up with a quick way to search three hundred miles of county roads, we're dead on that one."

"Yes, well I think it's time to talk to grandfather again. He would know the answer. I'll find him this afternoon and ask. In the meantime, Claude, can you slow things down a bit?"

"The judge isn't prone to be that nice to slow moves by either side. He's already been on my back to keep things moving. But I'll try."

Pril asked, "Who's our next witness, Claude?"

"The End Of The Line motel owner, why do you ask, Pril?"

"The thought has occurred to me that it was quite a coincidence that Muscles was in the mountains at the exact time that he was needed. Someone must have told someone that Richard was on his way into the mountains."

Claude looked at Pril and said, "I wish you would come up with these ideas of yours a little sooner. Why now?"

"Well, when I was talking to Sheriff Williams he mentioned that Dorothy the telephone operator had been passing information in a friendly manner to her Glencoe counterpart."

"Your point is well taken, I missed that one. Let's get

Dorothy on the witness stand. I'll get back to court, and sort of drag things a bit. Ed, make tracks for Hastings. Tell him we have a surprise witness to add to the witness list, and notify the defense, of course. Good job, Pril. Now you find out from Dorothy who her Glencoe friend is, and do your thing with her."

The court convened at 2 P.M. with Little Crow again seated in the witness stand. The judge said, "Will the defense continue its cross."

Mr. Hoople rose, and said, "Little Crow, you stated that Mr. Jones asked you to meet him on the road near the Village. Is that correct?"

"Yes."

"Did he call you on the phone, or how did he contact you?"

Little Crow sat silent for several minutes. The judge finally said, "Little Crow, you must answer the question."

"A friend in the Village told me that Mr. Jones wanted to talk to me."

"So, how did you talk to Mr. Jones?"

"I called him on the telephone."

The defense attorney looked up in surprise. "Do you have a telephone Mr. Little Crow?"

"No, I used the village phone."

"Oh, is this phone the only one in the Village?"

"Yes, that is the only one."

"Does every member of your tribe have access to that phone?"

"No, only Chief Running Deer."

"Well, how did you get to use it?"

Again there was a long silence, finally Little Crow said, "I used it when the Chief wasn't there."

"So you broke the rules of your village, do you break village rules often?"

The DA said, "Objection Your Honor, the conduct of the witness within the lands of the Indian Nation is not in the jurisdiction of this court."

The judge said, "Objection sustained, the court clerk is to remove all reference to in-village activities. Continue, Mr. Hoople."

"How long is the road adjacent to the village, that you were to meet Mr. Jones?"

"It is a long road. I don't know how long."

"Well make a guess, one mile, five?"

The DA said, "Objection your honor, the witness has already stated that he didn't know how long."

"Objection sustained. Continue Mr. Hoople."

"Alright, Little Crow, how did this mystery man know where on a long road to pick you up?"

"I don't know, he just spotted me at the side of the road, and picked me up."

"Can you give us an idea as to what the so-called mystery man looked like?"

"He was taller than me, he wore large dark glasses, black city-like clothes and a baseball hat. I really didn't see much of his face."

"You said, in your earlier testimony, that he climbed the trail leading up to Portal Mesa with ease. Is this true Mr. Little Crow?"

"Yes."

"Have you ever climbed up that slope before?"

"No."

"Was it a tough climb for you?"

"No, I am used to climbing hills."

"I have no more questions for this witness, Your Honor."

"The witness may step down; call your next witness, Mr. Comstock."

"I call Joe Fisher to the stand."

When the witness was seated and sworn in, the DA said, "Mr. Fisher, what is your occupation?"

"I'm the manager of the End of The Line Motel."

The DA went over to the prosecution table and picked up a folder. Returning to face the witness he said, "According to the motel register, you checked in several persons including a very large man, all who came together on the 8th of May, 1952. I also see that they all came from Chicago. I see that one of them signed in with a sort of slanted X. I'd like to talk about the big man that signed as X. Did he ever leave his room?"

"Not to my knowledge."

"Can you recall anything special about the large man that checked in with several friends?"

"Only that he said very little, and seemed to let his friends do the signing in and paying the bills."

"Didn't you see him when he went out to eat?"

"To my knowledge, he had all his meals in his room."

"Mr. Fisher, we're interested in the 10th of May, 1952, are you sure the big man did not leave his room that day?"

"Well I can't watch out the window all day to check on who leaves or who stays."

"Your Honor, I am finished with the witness for now, however, I would like to recall him at a later date."

"So be it, since it is Friday, and near the close of the day, this court is adjourned until 9 A. M. Monday." The Judge rapped his gavel, and the courtroom gradually emptied.

* * *

Priscilla found Dorothy at the telephone switchboard. "Hi, I'm Priscilla Beckman, I think we've met at the library— you seem quite busy— can we talk a bit?"

"Sure honey, I'm off in five minutes. What's it all about?"

"Dorothy, I'm helping our DA on the Bentley case. I have a few questions to ask you; and would you call me Pril, everyone else does."

"Pril, I have already squared this thing away with the Sheriff. He knows everything I can tell you."

"I know, the Sheriff filled me in pretty well, however, hearsay is not that great in court. The court doesn't want to hear from the Sheriff as to what happened. The court wants to hear it from you. Your testimony will help explain how information about Richard Bentley's whereabouts was obtained by the bad guys."

"And?"

"Your switchboards are the only link to the outside world."

"I see your point, Pril, I didn't know at the time what I was doing. When the Sheriff explained what was happening, I stopped. When will you need me?"

"This is kind of an ASAP thing. Can you get off the rest of today, and all day tomorrow?"

"I'll have to."

"Also, Dorothy, we need to know the name of the switchboard operator in Glencoe that you talked to. She has to be the tie-in with the Syndicate people."

"We've been kind of friends for a long time. I sure don't like to get her in trouble. Is there any other way?"

"Dorothy, if your friend is guilty in some way, I'm sure you would want the truth to come out. We need to find out how information about Richard Bentley's whereabouts on the day he was killed was obtained by the bad guys."

There was a long pause, then, "Her name is Gladys. I really don't think she would be capable of knowingly informing or telling anything that would harm George. We all like him, and worry that he might be hurt. There must be another answer. Why don't you talk to her yourself? I can call her, and tell her you are coming by."

"That sounds like a winner, Dorothy, would you call her now, time is of an essence. Can you come with me? Maybe when the three of us get together, we can come up with some answers."

"Sure, why not, I'll do whatever it takes if it will help George."

Gladys was waiting for them, just outside the door of the telephone building in Glencoe. The three introduced each other, and they found a nearby coffee shop, ordered coffee, and retreated to a rear booth. Dorothy said, "Gladys, Pril is working for the County District Attorney, and has some nitty-gritty questions to ask us. Pril, tell both of us what's been happening in court, and what is needed to help. What can we do?"

Pril said, "The hoods here, from Chicago, seem to know everything that goes on in our county like instantly. They apparently have a way to hear our conversations over the phone, or perhaps they have someone in town that is less than nice, and is informing the Syndicate of everything that is going on out here. It seems something more than a coincidence that the day Richard Bentley happened to go hunting up in the mountains, someone or perhaps several people just happened to be there waiting for him to show up. In other words, somebody told somebody that he was coming. And where. Since there are no other ways for information to move around this county except through the telephone lines, it seems logical that the fact that he was going hunting must have traveled over your lines.

"Now if we rule out any one of us, then who did the dirty work? Uh, girls, how secure are your switchboards?"

Dorothy said, "Gee I never gave that any thought. How about you Gladys?"

"I have no idea about that, we do have a 'fix everything' guy that you maybe should talk to. His name is Stanley somebody. Are you suggesting that someone might have tapped into my switchboard and hears everything?"

"Well that's a new thought. How do we get in touch with Stanley–somebody?"

Gladys said, "I can get him for you, Pril, give me a minute. I'll call him at his home."

Stanley joined the three women in about 20 minutes. He was introduced all around, and apprised of the problem. He said, "Sure, it's easy to tap into your circuits. I can sit up on top of a nearby crosstree, and tap in from the lines that are coming out from your switchboards. I do this all the time to locate open or misdirected circuits. Now if you ask me if a stranger coming from somewhere away from our area could do this, the answer is, yes if he has the knowhow."

Pril asked, "Do we have any lines near the End of The Line Motel?"

"Runs right along the back of the End of The Line,"

"Can you tell if any of those lines have been tapped?"

"Maybe."

Pril said, "Stanley, will you take a look? We're in court now, and every bit of information we can give the DA will be helpful."

"Yes, well I need my truck, it has my climbing cleats and other stuff that I'll need. Do you want to follow me over there?"

"You're on Stan, let's go."

* * *

George found his grandfather in the Village. "Grandfather, do you know of a road, perhaps through our lands, that leads into the mountains?"

There was a long silence, then, "This is something off limits to discuss. Why do you ask?"

"Grandfather, we have determined that White Owl was killed by someone coming out of the mountains. The question is, how did they get into the mountains in the first place? Without this information, it will be difficult to prosecute the wrongdoers, as we can't show that they were even there."

"Red Fox, we have long had sacred lands in the mountains. A few years back these special and spiritual lands were invaded by the government to search for uranium ore. The damage done was sadly serious to our nation. The access you are looking for is through sacred lands. The road was abandoned, and hopefully, forgotten."

"Grandfather, unfortunately it appears that this abandoned road has been discovered, and used for more than just curiosity. I'm calling from Glencoe, and don't have the luxury of coming to the Village right now. Could you have someone check and see if that road has had recent use. The need of this information is great and urgent. You can reach me through the DA's office here in Glencoe."

"Red Fox, that I can do." He sighed, and said, "I'll call you in about two hours."

* * *

The prosecution team gathered once more at Martha's Place, ordered dinner, and began discussing the court session of today. The phone call from the Village came when they were half way through dinner. Martha handed George the phone.

Gladys said, "George Bentley?"

"This is George."

"I've had a hard time finding you. You have an incoming call from the Village, stand by and I'll connect you."

"Grandfather, did you find anything?"

"Yes, Red Fox, the old road has been used recently."

"Grandfather, this explains a lot of things." George paused then, "would you consider a trip up that road with me? We need to see what's been happening up there, and I would need your wisdom and expertise."

"That I can do Red Fox. When do you wish to do this?"

"The need is for now; could we do this tomorrow morning, say a 9 A.M. departure from the Village?"

"I will be ready. Be careful, evil things have been happening, and I don't think they're finished yet."

George returned to his seat and said, "It would appear that the Syndicate found an abandoned road into the mountains. Which brings up another question; how would a Chicago person find a convenient long abandoned road in a remote part of Wyoming two thousand miles away?"

There was a stunned silence around the table. Pril was the first to speak, "Add this to the man that knew his way up to Portal Mesa, was strong enough to walk it and never got noticeably tired."

Claude said, "That's a good observation, Pril, I think there must be a local criminal, and whose identity is unknown."

George drove in the ranch pickup out to the Village. Chief Running Deer was waiting and standing alongside his favorite mount. Another horse stood close by, and was saddled and ready. George said, "It's a long tough ride Grandfather. Are you sure it's not too hard for you?"

"It's the only way. I don't like driving a car across our sacred lands. I'll be fine."

George knew better than to take issue with the Chief. He parked the truck he came in, retrieved his rifle from the front seat, and mounted up alongside the chief. The two horsemen started out from the Village, and in time found a faint set of tire tracks leading up into the highlands. Snow had fallen the night before, and covered the trail with a two inch layer of the powdery white. The sun was trying to warm things up a bit with little success. It was a full two hours travel to the top where the land leveled off, and George was getting colder by the minute. He kept checking on his grandfather, who was apparently immune to the 20 degree weather.

George was proud of his grandfather, and his heritage. As they rode together, not speaking, but knowing much between them, his thoughts ran to the many times he spent, as he grew, with this man. They passed through Arapaho sacred grounds, and continued to follow trail signs leading south toward Portal Mesa. The road ended in an area of huge tumbled rock, and somewhere close to Portal Mesa. The two men dismounted, picketed the horses, and started off afoot. It had been a long three hour ride. George was concerned for his grandfather, and watched carefully for signs of fatigue from the Chief. There were none. They walked to the south following a path that wound around huge, bus-sized rocks. Signs of abandoned mining activity caught the eye, and completely shrouded by ridges and rock formations was a small shack. The two men entered, and were treated to evidence of recent occupation.

"Grandfather, did you know this was here?"

"Yes, but I was not aware that anyone else did, or that it

was in use. Let's walk on further and see where the path leads to. I think we have more surprises in store."

Advancing beyond the shack they came to a solid wall of rock. They moved to the right, and found a fissure in the wall running straight up the rock face, and wide enough to slide through. The two men exited onto a lea, sloping off toward Portal Mesa. They proceeded forward, and found tracks of the local elk herd. Looking back, they could see no evidence of the cleft in the rock, and concluded it explained why no one knew of the passage. It was completely invisible from this side of the ridge.

Chief Running Deer said, "I have long forbidden our people to pass through our sacred lands to this area. We therefore knew little of this. I think this is the answer you are looking for."

"Yes, Grandfather, but now I must find out who knew about this. The trial against the Syndicate is moving along and we don't have lots of time to do it. It's getting late, and we had better get started for home fast."

The trip back to the Village found darkness enshrouding the valley, while the departing sun plied the upper peaks with an iridescent glow that made George feel the mystery of the sacred lands they had passed through. He had never been there before! The sky darkened as an eerie fog covered an icy moon coaxing the travelers to hurry. In time they reached the Village, and eventually warmth.

George was now certain that there was a mystery person, probably known to most locals, and most likely bigoted toward the Native Americans of the area. His thoughts ran over the events of the last eight months, and of those persons he had met since his return from college. The person he was looking for must have some kind of connection with the Chicago Syndicate.

He turned to his grandfather and said, "there has to be some outsider who knows his way around our county, or someone who is a member of our nation, and at the same time has a connection with the world beyond the Village."

After a long pause the Chief said, "Red Fox, there is only one outside person that has access to tribal activities, or talents. He represents the Bureau of Indian Affairs, and is knowledgeable of the land around here." The old Chief grimaced, and said, "He's supposed to be on our side."

George was silent for a moment, then, "Tell me about him, grandfather."

"There's not too much to tell; he calls on the Village about twice a month. We discuss matters that are related to tribal activities and interaction with the whites that live close to the Village. I have no reason to suspect that he would do harm to our people."

"Do you like him?"

"Not that much. Red Fox, it is not my position to like this person. I must communicate here, not anything more."

"Grandfather, you have been very successful at doing just that. You have been a good leader of our people, however, you have never spoken with a forked tongue either. I need to know your true feelings."

"I don't like him, and I don't trust him."

"Can I reach him by phone?"

"Most of the time I have to wait for him to return my call."

"What's his name, grandfather?"

"John Fowler, and you just ask Dorothy to find him for you."

George went to the telephone, picked up the receiver, and when Dorothy came on, said, "Dorothy, will you see if you can find Claude Comstock for me. He might still be at the courthouse, or maybe at his home. I need to talk to him."

"Sure honey, I'll get back to you as soon as I can."

George stayed with his grandfather for almost an hour. They talked about the earlier times, and about how much each of them missed George's father, Richard, and his mother, White Dove. In time the telephone rang. George answered, "George Bentley here."

Dorothy came on and said, 'Here's Claude for you

George."

"Hi Claude, how's the trial coming?"

"Lousy, what's new with you?"

"I just came out of the mountains with the chief. We found out how they did it, and why no one saw the killers enter the mountain area. Claude, I think there's one more person involved. One that we hadn't expected. This person had to know a good deal about our land, and was the person who really set up the killing."

"That's nice, when do I get to hear the whole story, and do you have any clues as to who this bad guy of yours is?"

"Yes, well I think I better traipse on over there and fill you in, like tonight. I'm a bit gun-shy about using the phone on this one. I'm at the Village, and it will take me about an hour or so to get there. In the meantime see if you can find the whereabouts of John Fowler, the Bureau of Indian Affairs man. Where are you, by the way?"

"Meet me at my office. I'll see what I can do to find John."

"Say Claude, he's not to know we're interested. I feel we might need him, and I don't want him to slip away somehow."

"I get the picture. See you soon."

George pulled up in front of the city office building, parked, and climbed the stairs up to Claude's office. Claude had the coffee pot on, and George poured himself a cup and sat down. Claude said, "I found Fowler. Tell me the story."

"Going up the back way, we found tire tracks, a shack, stocked with lots of food, and I suspect, lots of fingerprints. There's also a path leading through solid rock headed for Portal Mesa. The passage through the rock is completely invisible to the eye from either side. I took pictures. Can we stir up the local photo shop, and maybe get these developed, like tonight?"

"Wow, that's answering a bunch of questions." Claude picked up the telephone, "Gladys, would you see if you can reach Ed at the photo shop, or wherever he is. I need to get a roll of film developed tonight. Have him call me here at my office." He said to George, "Now tell me about Fowler."

"Yes well, there's only one person that is allowed to visit our Village. That person could also have connections to the outside world. Grandfather doesn't like him, or trust him. I think he is the man we are looking for."

"You are talking about John Fowler?"

"Uh huh."

"We need a tie-in, got any ideas?"

"This guy has a plushy job that is usually politically appointed. He gets paid by the government to make two trips to the Village a month, and send in reports. It doesn't pay very much, but gives him access to the country around the Village. I suspect he was recruited by the Syndicate some time ago when they first decided to invade our county. This would place him somewhere in the Cook County area. Why not start there?"

"Wouldn't Little Crow recognize him?"

George hesitated a moment, then, "I think that's worth a try. How soon do you expect Muscles?"

"Any day now, that's been kept as quiet as possible. We don't want the Black Mariah to find out until we put him on the witness stand. Wrightwood in Chicago agrees, and we don't even talk about it on the telephone. I sent Ed back to do this mouth to mouth. No documentation."

"You need to know everything about Fowler. I suspect he's cheated on my people too, so I'm very interested!"

"Got any place to sleep tonight?"

"Not really, is this an invitation?"

"Uh huh, let's go home."

The phone rang. Gladys came on and said, "I have Ed from the photo shop on the line."

"Ed, this is Claude Comstock. I need a great favor of you."

"Just name it. If I can, I'll do what you need."

"How long would it take you to develop a roll of 35 mm film."

"About an hour."

"How about right now?"

"Can do, I'll meet you at the shop."

Claude next called Chief Richardson,

"Chief, Claude here, I need some muscle down at Ed's Photo Shop for a couple of hours, starting now."

"You sure have crazy hours on that job of yours, don't you ever sleep?...Sure, I'll send a patrol car with two officers. Let me know when this, 'alleged emergency' is over."

"Will do Chief."

George and Claude arrived at Claude's house, and after dinner spread out the pictures on the kitchen table. Ed, at the photo shop had made two sets of prints. Claude also had the negatives. He called the Chief. "Thanks for the back-up. I have one more thing to ask. I have a package that needs to be in your safe place at the station. Could you have someone stop by my house and pick it up?"

"You mean, like tonight?"

"Uh huh."

"Okay, that's nine or ten you owe me, you are going to bed for the night, I hope."

"Chief, I'm just trying to save you some police work, later on."

"Even that sounds phony. My jail is full. I have hoods from Chicago trying to take over my town. The news people are driving me crazy, and you call usually after working hours."

"It's that bad huh? Goodnight, Chief."

When the patrol car pulled up in front of the house, Claude handed over the negatives and one set of prints in a sealed envelope with his signature and date over the sealed flap. After food, Claude laid out the pictures on the dining room table. George and he viewed the pictures, made some diagrams, and talked for the rest of the evening. As a result, they became of one mind as to who was the missing link in the puzzle. Claude made notes, and plans for the next day.

Claude's first call was to Judge Hastings at his home.

"For God sakes Claude, can't this wait for an hour until we get into court? This is pushing it too far. It's not only lousing up my home life, but this call is illegal. Now make it fast. It better be good."

"Judge, I have a new suspect. We know who he is. He is available, but would vanish in a second if he thought he might be suspected. I need to contain this person for sure and fast."

"So on what grounds am I to authorize a pick-up?"

"I need an innovative idea on that one, all I have at this point is logic, opportunity, intuition."

The judge exploded, and then, "Why don't you ask Richardson to break the law, not me. I'm not going to do it!"

"Judge, may I remind you that the results of this trial may determine whether we remain in control or some Chicago gangsters do. The new evidence and this new suspect will help a lot. I need this man to testify. I need him as a suspect, and I need time to prepare."

"Did I hear right? You also want a trial delay?"

"Well…yes Your Honor."

"How much of a delay?"

"Well, I was thinking three."

"Alright, I maybe can do the trial delay, but the other, you'll have to work something out with Richardson. You and he seem to be buddies, and get away with all kinds of cuties, which I usually don't hear about until you have accomplished your objectives. Damn, if Upstate ever hears about some of this, my ass is in deep trouble."

Claude's next phone call was to Chief Richardson, also at his home. "Sorry to wake you Chief, something's come up that needs your delicate hand, and kind of can't wait much."

"Am I to remember my vow to uphold the law at all costs etc., or am I supposed to ignore all that rubbish when dealing with the DA? I already smell something wiggly coming from you. Why else would I get a phone call before breakfast, and at home?"

"Notwithstanding your warm attitude, what I have to ask

is simple, and entirely above board."

"Now you have my attention, this has to be a first for you, what do you need?

"Remember our conversation in your office yesterday, we talked about a certain individual? No name please."

"Yes, what about him?"

"I need you to pick him up."

"Fine, just bring the court order down to the station."

"Ah, there isn't going to be one."

"This is beginning to sound like your old self Claude, I thought for a minute you had reformed. So what do I use for cause?"

"There must be something, disturbing the peace, drunk driving, or something. How about resisting arrest. Which I'm sure will happen?"

Next, Claude left his office, and from a nearby phone booth, called John Blake, the Cook County DA, "John, I need to know everything I can about a John Fowler, especially any connection he might have to the Black Mariah Syndicate. John is the Bureau of Indian Affairs rep for this area. I'm sending Ed back to explain and help any way he can. Security is paramount, as we don't want the rabbit to vanish. Timing is like I need something yesterday."

"So what details on this guy can you give me?"

"Only that without him the killing of Richard Bentley last year could not happen. Someone had to plan and execute. Someone needed to know a lot about this country, and someone knew place and time. This rabbit fits the bill perfectly."

John Blake laughed out loud. "I hear you are now in court, with the Syndicate itself, facing relatively weak charges. We've been through all that out here, and end up chewing on our lower lips. I sure hope you can come up with something strong enough to get some kind of a conviction. Sure, I'll help all I can. Where can I call you if I run into something?"

"Let's try Richardson's office. Everything else seems to be bugged, including my own phone. I'm calling from a phone booth now. Hastings is absent but his associate should be there. I'll call you."

Claude entered the courthouse building, and found the presiding judge. "Your Honor, we have John Fowler in custody, and I would like to keep him there until I can put him on the stand as a material witness."

The judge said, "I would hope that you have sufficient cause for this action."

"Indeed I do, Your Honor, this suspect is crucial to the case before the court. He is found to be the only person with both the knowledge and opportunity to have carried out the killing of Richard Bentley."

"In other words, he is only a suspect, and you have no real evidence on which to base your assumption?"

"In essence, Your Honor, that is true, however circumstantial evidence is piling up against this suspect. I'm certain he is guilty of aid and abet at least."

"Alright, I'll issue, but I warn you, don't abuse."

Muscles arrived. He came both manacled and handcuffed, accompanied with not one but two burly Chicago policemen. Chief Richardson was there to sign off the extradition papers. The Chief was visibly relieved when the prisoner was locked up in a jail cell. He called Claude, "Claude, the big man is here. Do you have any time frame as to when you'll need him in court?"

"Sometime after next Wednesday. You sound kind of nervous Chief?"

"Yes well, so would you be if you could see this one. He's too big to fit on an ordinary cell cot and, I've already had a visit from the Syndicate types."

"Chief, he probably won't be any trouble. Oh by the way, feed him well, say about six times what you or I might eat. That should keep him quiet."

"Thanks."

For the next five days, the DA worked on his case. He had more witnesses to call, a summation, or closing statement to write, and there was the legal staff of the Syndicate in town to consider. He was certain they were about to be heard from. He considered what he would do if he were a defense attorney and faced with their situation. He expected, and did receive counsel from interested Upstate legal types. He was also aware of the risky situation in which he had placed Judge Hastings. As he wrote his agenda for the forthcoming week of trial activities, he referenced back through the sworn testimony already given. He tried to anticipate, and prepared answers for a host of questions the defense might ask. He consulted with his colleagues and made sure that everyone was on board.

Ed Hunt returned from his trip to Chicago on Sunday afternoon. He walked into the office with a smile on his face. "Hello all, how are things?"

Court convened at 9 a.m. Wednesday. Judge Hastings said, "Claude, call your next witness."

"I call John Fowler to the stand." After the witness was sworn in and seated, the District Attorney asked the witness to state his name, residence and occupation.

"My name is John Fowler, I am the designated representative from the Bureau of Indian Affairs for Contra County."

"Your residence?"

"1600 Fargo avenue, Chicago. Illinois."

"Mr. Fowler, will you explain how you are able to work in Contra County and live in Illinois?"

"I commute."

"In the pursuit of your assigned duties do you often visit areas within Contra County. The Indian Village, for example?"

"That's my job."

"Have you ever been in areas of the county other than the Indian Village?"

"Yes, I have traveled some of the county roads."

"Were these trips purposeful or were you just driving to look at the scenery?"

"This is interesting country, I guess I have explored a bit."

"Have you ever been up into the High Country?"

The witness remained silent trying to form an answer, finally the Judge said, "The witness must answer the question."

The defense attorney rose and said, "Your Honor, we object to this line of questioning. The movements of this witness seem a long way from the charges that are currently leveled against my clients."

The judge said, "Mr. Comstock, will you show us what the connection is."

"Your Honor, I wish to show that this witness has more than a casual knowledge of the geography of our County. The perpetrators of the crimes committed here in Contra County needed a fairly detailed geographical picture of this area to carry out their crimes. Time and time again, outsiders have found their way around this area, sometimes even in the dark. This witness has such knowledge. Furthermore, he was the only outside person to have access to Indian lands herein."

"Do you consider Mr. Fowler a hostile witness?"

"Yes, Your Honor, I do."

"Objection overruled. You may proceed Mr. Comstock. The witness must answer the question."

"Yes, I have been in the mountains. I often take hikes to where I can do some climbing."

"Mr. Fowler, I have information to the effect that you often spend time in the Blackstone Hotel in Chicago. I also see that you rarely spend much time in your stated address on Fargo Avenue. The Blackstone Hotel is an expensive address. Would you mind telling the court who paid for those extended stays at the Blackstone?"

"I have always paid my own bills."

"You have an address and stated it to be your primary residence, yet you spend sometimes weeks at a time in a hotel, just ten miles distant. Now according to your tax records, your sole income is from your job as a representative of the Bureau of Indian Affairs. Please explain how you were able to spend extended times in an expensive hotel, Mr. Fowler."

"I repeat, I pay my own way."

The District Attorney studied some papers he held, then, "I have some of the hotel charges. They are far higher than your salary as a BIA Rep could handle. Explain where the rest of the money came from. We also know of your connection with the Black Mariah Syndicate. Mr. Fowler, did the Syndicate pick up the tab while you stayed at the Blackstone?"

"No, that's not true."

The District Attorney turned to the Judge and said, "Your Honor, in that this witness refuses to answer questions pertinent to this case, I request he be held over for further questioning, and possible charges of aiding and abetting the crime of murder."

The judge said, "I concur. Bailiff, place this man in custody. Claude, call your next witness."

"Your Honor, my next witness is still in the court retention cell. We will be bringing him out shortly. As he is a very large person, he will not fit in the witness chair, so I have taken the liberty to provide a large bench for that person. The piece is out in the hall."

"Well, bring him and his bench in."

The double doors leading into the court house opened wide and a man entered escorted by two deputies. He stood over seven feet tall, and must have tipped the scale at over 300 pounds. He was both manacled and handcuffed. There was a gasp from the courtroom spectators. He was taken to the witness bench and seated. It was evident that the Syndicate persons present were completely taken by surprise.

The defense attorney jumped up and screamed, "Your Honor, the prosecution keeps injecting new witnesses. The defense needs to have some advance notice of this, and we object to this kind of trickery."

The Judge said, "Calm down Hoople, we have good hearing here. We don't need to be screamed at. Well Mr.

District Attorney, how about that? I think the defense has a point here."

"Your Honor, the extradition, transporting and arrival of this witness was kept quiet in the interest of his safety. The bad guys have already killed twice to stifle the voices of witnesses. I am convinced that had it not been done this way, he would be dead by now. This case is about truth. We can't get the truth out of dead people."

The Judge said, "Well as long as you've gone to all this trouble to get him here, I'll let him testify. The defense will have its chance to comment on his testimony anyway. Start your examination Claude."

"Muscles, you have friends out there among the spectators. Isn't that true?"

"Oh yes, I see several men that I know. They have been very nice to me."

"Just how have they been nice to you?"

"They been real nice to me, they take me to the café in Chicago and buy me a nice dinner. Sometimes they buy me things too."

"What do they buy you, Muscles."

"Lots a things, shoes, clothes, and games."

"You must want to thank them; how do you pay them back for being so nice to you?"

"Oh, I keep them from being hurt sometimes."

"How do you do that, Muscles?"

"Oh I just do, I won't let anyone hurt my friends."

"You came out here last May, Muscles, was that one of the times you kept your friends from being hurt?"

"That's a long time ago, it's hard for me to remember."

"I'll help you. You stayed in the End of The Line Motel. While you were there you ate your meals in your motel room, and sometime on the 10th of May you were driven up a bad road to a shack in the highlands. Do you remember that?"

The defense attorney jumped up, "Objection your honor, the prosecution is leading the witness."

"So he is, I'd like to see where he's going. I think I'll let it stand. Continue, Mr. District Attorney."

"I repeat, do you remember being driven up into the high country?"

"Oh, I'm not supposed to talk about that."

"You are not supposed to talk about what?"

"About the mountains."

"Who told you not to talk about the mountains, Muscles?"

"Oh, my friends."

"Muscles, we know you went into the mountains, now, is this a place where you wouldn't let your friends be hurt?"

"I can't talk about the mountains."

"Your Honor, it appears that any further questioning of this witness concerning his activities in the mountains is futile. I am through questioning him at this time, but I would like to reserve the right to question him further at a later date and time."

"Request so noted, are you through with him for today then?"

"I am, Your Honor"

"Does the defense wish to cross?"

"No, Your Honor."

"Then, will the bailiff return the witness to a secured area. Call your next witness, Claude."

"I call Marjorie Clark to the stand."

When Miss Clark was seated, and took the oath of a witness the DA asked, "Miss Clark, please tell the court where you work, and your job there."

I work for the End of The Line Motel. I make up the rooms after they have been used."

"Do you recall seeing this person, Muscles, when he stayed in your motel?"

"Yes, he stayed in the motel for several days."

"While he was there at the motel, did he ever leave his room?"

"Yes, he was gone for a whole day, the man that paid for his stay came and took him away for the day."

"And what day was that Miss Clark?"

"It was Tuesday, May 10th, 1952."

"Are you sure of that date?"

"Yes, I'm sure. That happens to be my birthday, and also it was the day that Mr. Bentley died. I won't ever forget that date."

"Your Honor, I'm through with this witness."

"Does the defense wish to cross?"

Attorney Hoople responded, "No, Your Honor, I have no questions for this witness, but I ask again, what does this testimony have to do with the guilt or innocence of my client? We seem to be skirting the issue of my client's innocence, which I think is the purpose of this trial? If the prosecution would stick to the issue at hand, we, the defense feel justice would be better served. My client has suffered long enough."

Judge Hastings turned to the DA and said, "Claude, I also am confused with the direction this trial is taking. You'd better tie all this in soon. Do you have any more witnesses?"

"Yes, Your Honor, the prosecution has one last witness, his name is Bob, and we have been unable to find a last name for him."

"Are you asking me to let you put someone on the stand, and you can't even tell the court who he is?"

"Well Your Honor, it's not exactly like that. We caught him with the defendant, Joe Costello. He was driving the car that was to pick up the hired killer, Jon Ballant."

"Claude, are you asking for him to be a witness as well as a defendant?"

"Your Honor, I would like to have him be a witness at this time. The matter of his being a defendant will come later."

"Alright, I will hear this person as a witness only, however, the matter of the case at hand must be carried forward in an expeditious manner."

"I call Bob to the stand."

After the witness was sworn in, Claude said, "Bob, please state your residence."

"I live in Chicago."

"Give street and number in Chicago."

"I don't have one at this time."

"What is your occupation?"

The witness hesitated then, "I do things for people, like driving them, or carrying things, like messages."

"Alright, I ask you to describe what happened when you were arrested?"

"I was driving Joe and we skidded into a ravine. I must have hit my head on the steering wheel. The next thing I knew was that of waking up in jail with a headache."

"Where were you going when you skidded off the road?"

"I was driving to where Joe told me."

"And where did Joe tell you to take him?"

"I was told to drive to a rendezvous place."

"And where was that?"

"At the corner of Foothill Road and the County road."

"And that's where you skidded off the road?"

"Yes."

"Did you receive compensation for driving to the rendezvous place?"

"Yes, Joe was to pay me when the job was done."

"Can you tell us what the job was that took you all the way from Chicago to Contra County in a remote area of Wyoming?"

"I wasn't told anything except that I would be driving on some unpaved roads."

"You were armed. You had not only a pistol, but a long nasty knife strapped to your left leg. What were these for?"

"I live in a rough part of town. I need these things for my own protection."

"Have you known Joe Costello long?"

"No, this is the first time that I met him."

"You mean when he hired you for this driving assignment?"

"That's right."

"Were you aware that Joe Costello is the son of the top boss of the organization known as the Black Mariah

Syndicate?"

"No, I didn't know that."

"Alright, didn't you also drop someone off at the alleged rendezvous site, two days earlier?"

"Yes, we did."

"And was this person, in fact, Jon Ballant?"

"I was never told his name."

The DA walked over to the prosecution table, picked up a folder, and returned to the stand. He selected a photo from the folder, and handed it to the witness. "Isn't this the man you dropped off at the rendezvous site?"

The witness studied the photo, then said, "Yes, this is the man."

"Your Honor, I'm through questioning this witness."

The judge said, "Does the defense wish to question this witness?"

"No, Your Honor."

"Claude, do you have any more witnesses?"

Claude spotted a breathless Pril sliding into her chair at the prosecution table. She beckoned with a nod. He turned to the judge and said, "May I have a moment to consult with my colleague?"

"Alright, make it fast."

Returning to the prosecution table he bent down to hear Pril say, "The telephone switchboard was tapped at the End of The Line, and all conversations between the Walnut operator and the Glencoe operator were available to the Syndicate people. The trunk line from Walnut to Glencoe passes right behind the End o The Line, and that's where the tap took place."

"Pril, that's a tie-in that we needed, thanks." He turned to the judge and said, "Due to some new information just received, I need additional time to consult with my colleagues."

"Alright, there will be a 20 minute pause in these proceedings. Mr. Comstock, do your thing, but don't hold us up. We need to move along here!"

Claude returned to the table and asked Pril to fill him in on the wiretap. She did, and said, "Dorothy, Gladys, and Stanley are available out in the hall if you need them."

"Great, Pril, ask Stanley to come in." He turned to the bench and said, "Your Honor, we have found another witness that I wish to put on the stand. He is here and will testify to information pertinent to this case. May I do so?"

"As long as it is pertinent."

Yes, Your Honor, I call Stanley Cooke to the stand."

When Stanley was seated and duly sworn in, the District Attorney asked, "Stanley, what is your occupation?"

"I am the telephone lineman for the city of Glencoe."

"As such, what are your duties?"

"I maintain the Glencoe telephone equipment, lines, and I handle any special requests concerning the equipment."

"You must know this equipment quite well, is that true, Mr. Cooke?"

"Yes, I know this system very well."

"Alright, please tell the court what you found when you examined the trunk line connection on the telephone pole at the rear of the End of The Line Motel."

"I found that someone had tapped into the trunk line between Glencoe and Walnut."

"Are you saying that someone could listen in on all the calls that were made between Glencoe and Walnut?"

Stanley said, "Yes and any calls made on other city lines."

"That pole at the rear of the End Of The Line motel, have you done work on that specific telephone pole before?"

"Yes, that one in particular. I often have requests to add additional service to accommodate motel clients."

The District Attorney then asked, "I understand that you climbed that specific pole earlier today, is that correct?"

"Yes, that is true."

"And that's when you found the lines had been tampered with?"

"Yes, the configuration of wire bundling had been altered from my style. I knew that some other person had moved wires around. I noticed that the trunk line to and from the Glencoe switchboard and that in Walnut was lifted out of the bundle, bared, and taped."

"How did you identify that particular wire?"

"That line is slightly larger, and it is cobalt blue in color."

"In your opinion Mr. Cooke, would you say that someone tapped that line, for the purpose of listening to conversations?"

The defense jumped up, and said, "Objection, Your Honor, this calls for a conclusion by the witness."

"Objection sustained, continue Mr. Comstock."

"I have no further questions for this witness Your Honor."

"Does the defense wish to cross?"

"Yes Your Honor."

"Proceed."

Defense Counsel Hoople asked, "Mr. Cooke, what made you investigate this particular telephone pole? There must be hundreds like it in this city."

"Miss Beckman, in the name of the DA, requested I do so."

"Your Honor, this is a blatant example of this district attorney's effort to promote his theory of how a crime went down. This type of fishing expedition into the unknown is not getting my client cleared or otherwise."

The judge sighed and said, "Mr. Comstock, where are we going?"

"Your Honor, this is more circumstantial evidence and will be shown as pertinent downstream. After all, no one saw anyone kill anyone, and no one heard the alleged conspiracy being discussed. It is my intention to provide the Jury with sufficient information upon which they can make a well informed decision."

"Alright, the defense objection is noted, but denied, proceed Claude."

"I have no further questions for this witness, Your Honor."

"The witness may step down. Anything else, Mr. Comstock?

"Yes, Your Honor, I wish to recall George Bentley to the Stand."

"Will this one be short? If not, since it is near the end of the day, we'll adjourn, and pick it up tomorrow at nine."

"Your Honor, I anticipate an hour or more with this witness."

"Alright then, this court is adjourned until 9 AM tomorrow."

Court reconvened on schedule at nine, with George Bentley seated in the witness chair. He was reminded that he was still under oath, and the DA said. "Mr. Bentley, please tell the court about your recent travels into the mountains."

George began, "In the company of my Grandfather, Chief Running Deer, I followed tire tracks that led up into the mountains. From the snow conditions on the ground, it was obvious these tracks had been made recently.

"In the upper reaches of the mountains we found a small shack, well hidden, and well stocked with food and water. There were signs of recent activity everywhere. The same large footprints observed around the site where my father was killed, were present. We followed a foot path, and in time came to a natural rock wall. We followed along the face of the wall and found a fisher or slit, well hidden, but wide enough to walk through. On the other side of the wall was a path, leading directly down to Portal Mesa. We took pictures as we went along. These have been turned over to the District Attorney."

The District Attorney said, "I have these pictures, and would like them to be passed out for the jury to review, and then entered into evidence as Exhibit IV.

"May it please the court, I am finished with the interrogation of this witness. I wish to recall Sheriff Williams to the stand."

The judge said, "Mr. Comstock, it is difficult for the Court to function on any kind of a schedule or order if you continue to come up with more witnesses. Have you cleared this one with the defense?"

"Well, yes Your Honor, this is just a recall, the defense was advised upon his earlier testimony. However, if the court will allow, this is really the last one... so far."

"You mean, there may be more?"

"I'm sure that if something that will help us learn the truth came up, you would insist that it be heard."

"Uh huh, Mr. Hoople, are you comfortable with this?"

"Not really, Your Honor, the defense objects to these entire proceedings. The prosecution keeps telling us he is looking for the truth. We're all doing that. The fact is that the prosecution's case is built on suppositions, and has little relationship to the truth. At this time we have received no notices of more witnesses, and would object strenuously to any additional persons testifying."

"Okay, I'll allow this on the basis that it is recall. We will reconsider a long time, however, were the prosecution to come up with more witnesses. Proceed Mr. Comstock."

When Sheriff Williams was seated and reminded that he was still under oath, the DA asked, "Did you receive a call from George Bentley yesterday?"

"Yes, that is correct."

"Please tell the court about that phone call and the action you took subsequent to that call."

"Mr. Bentley requested that I examine a certain area in the mountains, and officially collect evidence in and around an abandoned shack. He gave me the location, and how to get there."

"And did you, in fact, find said shack, and did you collect evidence?"

"I did, and made a report on my findings. I have since turned the report over to the district attorney."

The DA handed the report to the Sheriff and asked, "Sheriff, is this that report?"

"Yes."

The District Attorney handed the report to the jury

foreman, and asked that after the jury had finished its review, it be entered into evidence as Exhibit V, then turned to the judge and said, "I'm finished with this witness, Your Honor, and have concluded the case for the prosecution. I would like some time to prepare my closing statement."

The Judge asked, "Does the defense have any witnesses to present?"

"No, Your Honor, but I wish to make a statement on behalf of my client at this time, and I too would like time to prepare."

"Proceed."

Mr. Hoople faced the jury and said, "My clients were wrongfully detained, and as a matter of fact, Joe Costello was placed in a great deal of physical danger, when elements of the local law enforcement forced his car off the road. During this trial, the prosecution has failed to present any evidence to show that either of my clients broke any laws."

"Alright, we meet again tomorrow at nine A.M." With that the judge rapped his gavel, and retired to his chambers.

The courtroom crowd emptied in a raucous display of hurrying humanity, each pursuing his own goal of the moment.

Court convened at 9 a.m., and after all parties were seated, Claude Comstock began his summation. "Ladies and gentlemen of the jury, it became painfully evident back in May of 1952 that criminal elements from outside our county, albeit, from outside our state, were attempting to take control in Contra County. Indeed in the last eight months criminal actions here in Contra County have been frequent and sometimes deadly.

"Two gunmen from the Chicago area kidnapped George Bentley, brutally beat him over the head, and dumped him in the desert to die. Mr. Bentley didn't die. The suspects were captured. A Wyoming district judge accepted $200,000.00 bail, posted in cash and directed they be released. This is a lot of money, and indicates powerful criminal elements were involved. These same two suspects were found dead with broken necks in a back alley in Chicago.

"Late in the fall of last year another attempt was made to kill George Bentley. The perpetrator escaped into the high country, but was later captured while attempting to escape in the getaway car. This hired killer, Jon Ballant, was successfully prosecuted for attempted murder. He did not however, divulge information on those who hired him. Jon Ballant is wanted in several other states. Extradition proceedings are in the pipeline as we speak. Another indication that big time crime organizations are involved.

"Three persons died attempting to kill an injured suspect. These three were obviously big city criminals. They carried automatic weapons, and used them. One more person was injured while he and his accomplice attempted to destroy the Arrow—B ranch house. A fire caused the destruction of the ranch truck.

"Sworn testimony and forensic evidence indicate that the co-defendant, Joe Costello, was implicated as a passenger in the car intended to pick up Jon Ballant, when he was finished with the deadly task of killing George Bentley.

"The defendant, Joe Costello, is the son of the leader of the Chicago-based Black Mariah Syndicate, co-defendant Frank Costello. This organization is known by Chicago law enforcement as a gang of hoodlums, coercing and sometimes doing acts of violence against city residents. Cook County courts have wrestled with this, and to date have come up with insufficient evidence to convict, but are fully aware of the illicit activities engaged in by the Syndicate.

"We might ask, what are they doing in a remote area of Wyoming? Certainly, an armed Joe along with an armed accomplice negotiating a lonely dirt road in the middle of the night seems strange. Their weapons were not hunting type that a local might use, but pistols with silencers. The knife that Joe's accomplice carried strapped to his leg was long and vicious.

"You have heard evidence that the Bureau of Indian Affairs representative for this area has close ties with the

Syndicate. It is obvious that the Syndicate availed themselves of the local knowledge gained from this relationship. The defendant, Joe Costello, was found in a vehicle at night on a seldom used road in our county. This required prior knowledge of the area. Where did he come by this information?

"Evidence has shown that elements of the Syndicate knew about a long abandoned road into our local mountains. Muscles, in his testimony, told us by denial, that he had been into the mountains. The death of Richard Bentley took place on May 10th of 1952. Just incidentally, Muscles was absent from his motel room for the entire day of that date. He fails to tell us 'about the mountains.' We have tied Muscles into the Syndicate. Forensic evidence connects the death of Richard Bentley, by way of a broken neck, with two hoodlums who died of the same cause in a Chicago alley. Muscles is now under investigation for the murder of all three. We have shown you evidence that the defendant's cohort driving the getaway car was employed by the Syndicate.

"The road into the mountains leads to a well-supplied cabin. Footprints in and around this cabin match those of Muscles. Earlier, those same footprints were observed at the Richard Bentley killing site. These footprints are easily distinguished from any others, as they were some 18 inches long, the size of Muscles' feet.

"Further evidence within the cabin shows that he was there. Muscles stated several times that he always protected his friends, and his friends told him 'Not to talk about the mountains.' From what we have found, Muscles' friends were Black Mariah Syndicate members.

"Black Mariah members have often stayed in the End of The Line Motel. Examination by the local telephone lineman shows that there was a wiretap placed on a telephone pole crosstree and run down into one of the motel rooms that the Syndicate usually occupied. This allowed a listener to hear everything that takes place in the county. It is apparent that these people have more than a casual interest in our piece of real estate.

"Why all this interest in the Arrow—B Ranch? Let's take a look back to the recently concluded trial of Bob Gibson. Bob managed to get into debt with some Las Vegas people. He couldn't pay up, and they didn't like it. In time the Black Mariah Syndicate bought his debt from the Las Vegas group. Bob stole from the Arrow—B Ranch to pay off his debts. He didn't make it. Bob disappeared down to Florida.

"Bob Gibson told the Syndicate about the Arrow—B to get them off his back. The Syndicate was looking to break into the lucrative gambling business in Las Vegas. The Arrow—B properties offered a good place to launch their bid for entry into this business. It was remote enough to conceal their activities, and not make someone curious. The Ranch location also gave them easy access to the mountains. They figured to make the ranch and its upper reaches into a game park for Syndicate members and friends. It would become a place for target practice, and a readymade place of concealment for those getting in trouble with the law.

"Richard Bentley refused to sell to the Syndicate. Muscles was called in to frighten Bentley into selling the ranch to them. He got carried away and broke his neck.

"George Bentley, Richard Bentley's son, was found equally difficult to buy the ranch from. The Syndicate, acting through Jones Realty of Glencoe, offered one million dollars for the Arrow—B Ranch. This offer was turned down by George Bentley. The Syndicate got stubborn and tried several times to coerce George into caving in to their wishes. He didn't.

"Now we are faced with a killing, several attempted killings, and the deaths of several others trying to carry out the wishes of the Syndicate. This trial is, in effect, trying the Syndicate for its part in this saga. They are the real criminals. They don't dirty their hands with most of this stuff. They pay others to do that. It was not, however intended that the codefendant, Joe Costello, take a fall for the Syndicate.

Although Joe Costello is certainly guilty of aiding and abetting the would-be killer of George Bentley in his attempt to escape, he is no more guilty than each and every member of the Black Mariah gang. Evidence shows that the hierarchy of the Syndicate directed the defendant to 'do whatever it takes'. There is certainly sufficient evidence to convict the defendant of the pending charges. In your deliberations it is incumbent upon you to make pointed recommendations to the Court regarding the Black Mariah Syndicate itself."

Judge Hastings interrupted the District Attorney, "Claude, the court will tell the jury as to what is incumbent for them to do, and what is not. I suggest that you follow normal procedures like bring charges etc. Now proceed with your statement without telling the jury what to do."

"Members of the jury, you are reminded that the codefendants, Joe Costello and his father Frank are family members of the Black Mariah Syndicate. By right of family ascendancy, Frank is the leader of this illicit organization, and as such has directed others to conduct these heinous acts. Justice requires that you provide a 'guilty as charged' verdict.

"In this trial we have uncovered much information that will ultimately help solve the crime of Richard Bentley's murder.

"The prosecution rests, Your Honor."

"Mr. Hoople, is the defense ready with its case summary?"

"Yes, Your Honor."

"Well proceed then."

"Gentlemen of the jury, you have listened to the prosecution make statement after statement concerning the alleged guilt of the defendants. You are reminded that much of this dialogue is assumptive. Solid evidence is totally lacking. If you come in with a 'guilty as charged' verdict, you will be convicting on circumstantial evidence mixed with much speculation, and romantic rhetorical gibberish. The suggested scenario by the prosecution fails to place the co-defendant, Joe Costello, anywhere near the shooting site above the water tower on the Arrow—B Ranch. As to the unsubstantiated claim by the prosecution that the vehicle, driven by the man from Chicago, and containing the co-defendant Joe Costello, was, in fact, a 'getaway car'– this has yet to be proven. Specific details relating to the death of Richard Bentley and other illicit or lawless activities cited by the prosecution are not pertinent to this trial, yet the District Attorney seems to want to involve my clients in an olio of alleged crimes. Solid evidence as indicated by the prosecution, when examined carefully, sort of dissolves.

"The involvement of the Black Mariah Syndicate in the alleged crime that my clients are charged with, is equally irrelevant to this trial.

"The prosecution informs us that we are here to determine the truth. What is the truth? We have heard, not evidence supporting the truth, but a story dreamed up by the District Attorney."

"The defense rests, Your Honor."

The Judge asked the District Attorney, "Do you wish to refute any of the defense arguments?"

Claude said, "Yes, indeed I do, Your Honor." Then turning to the jury he said, "The prosecution has stated from the start that this case must be judged on the basis of circumstantial evidence alone. Throughout this trial the prosecution has provided sufficient evidence to support the suggested scenario. Fact: The defendant, Joe, was caught by law enforcement in the act of trying to assist the shooter, Jon Ballant, in his attempt to get away. Fact: The co-defendant, Joe, was armed with weapons used only for criminal activities. Fact: The defendant's companion revealed that they had a job to do, and upon completion he would be paid. Fact: Bob, the driver of the getaway vehicle, in open testimony referred to 'dropping off' Jon Ballant at the rendezvous site. Fact: The defendant, Joe, provided no logical reason for being in this remote part of Wyoming at two A. M. And, Fact: The co-defendant, Joe, resisted arrest.

"The defendant's position within the Black Mariah Syndicate, by virtue of his birthright, makes him a number one suspect in other illicit activities engaged in by the Syndicate. The prosecution does not intend to pursue these at this time, but certainly as more evidence comes to light, new charges will be made. We all might wonder how the son of the head of the Black Mariah Syndicate could be so innocent as the defense would like us to believe?

"A verdict of 'not guilty' would allow the illicit gang of hoodlums known as the Black Mariah Syndicate to continue its reign of terror against our citizens." The District Attorney turned to face the judge. "Your Honor, the prosecution rests."

The judge said, "Will the defense present its closing arguments?"

"Yes, Your Honor, may I have fifteen minutes to consult with my associates before I begin?"

"That'll be fine."

The three attorneys for the defense sat and conferred regarding strategy. Judge Hastings fidgeted, twirling his pencil, and looking at the courtroom clock to his left. After twenty minutes had passed he said, "Mr. Hoople, either begin your arguments or waive your rights to one."

"Your Honor, we are ready now." He stood up and faced the jury, "Gentlemen of the jury, you are about to begin deliberation on the guilt or innocence of the two defendants. If you render a 'guilty as charged' verdict you will be condemning two innocent men. You have been treated with a fictitious dissertation concerning the conduct of the defendants by your eloquent district attorney. He has repeatedly advanced his theory as to why the defendants must be guilty. Remember, his rhetoric is a theory only, and in no way proves the defendants guilty. Your gilt-tongued District Attorney has also told you that you must judge on circumstantial evidence only. In this statement he is also telling you that there is no real hard evidence that the defendants participated in the charged crimes.

"Your instructions from the court will be, 'without reasonable doubt', and the charges filed against the defendants are certainly doubtful.

"The defense rests, Your Honor."

Judge Hastings said, "Since it is almost noon, this court is in recess until two P.M. this afternoon." The judge motioned for the two attorneys to join him in chambers, and together they hammered out jury instructions. The key element insisted on by the defense: stiff requirements for the use of circumstantial evidence toward conviction. The prosecution worried over the same issue, only from another viewpoint. The judge finally said, "Thanks people, I'll finish this one alone and get you copies for this afternoon's session."

* * *

Two P.M. found the courtroom filled to capacity. The media, which had lost some of their enthusiasm of late, were there in force. Outside the courtroom, parked as close as they could get, were several media vehicles, and there were law enforcement persons all over.

Judge Hastings said to the jury, "Notwithstanding the instructions handed out by both the defense and the prosecution, the court issues instructions to juries! You are to consider all of the testimony given in this trial. Your deliberations are to be thorough, considering all aspects of the allegations made by the prosecution, and all of the defense arguments. The value and worth of circumstantial evidence is to be discussed fully. The court feels that circumstantial evidence needs to be overwhelming to decide the fate of anyone. You are to render a verdict based on 'without reasonable doubt' and the verdict is to be a unanimous vote of the jury. To convict, then be sure to meet these parameters. I remand the trial of Frank and Joe Costello to the jury."

The jurors rose and filed out of the courtroom and into the jury room. The heretofore selected jury foreman took his place at the head of the long table and said, "Let's go around the table one time. Each of us can make such comments concerning the trial as each of us sees it. Speak your thoughts!"

Each of the twelve jurors spoke a bit about their feelings regarding the trial. There were both pros and cons, with the 'guilty as charged' in the lead. When it came to the foreman, he said, "I think everyone here would like to crucify the entire Syndicate organization. There's no doubt in my mind as to their initiating this crime wave. They have come out here and tried to force our neighbors and friends to do their will. Now our DA has done a great job in showing the Syndicate connection. The application of this connection to the trials of Joe and Frank Costello is pertinent, as is the application of the abundance of circumstantial evidence shown in the trial.

"It is easy for us to come in with a guilty as charged verdict, as these bums have given us much trouble in the last eight months. Has the circumstantial evidence been overwhelming? Has it been enough to qualify, as 'beyond reasonable doubt'? Now I would like to clear my mind of the Black Mariah Syndicate for the moment, and be sure and judge only on the guilt or innocence of the defendants. That's what the indictment instructs us to do. Other wrongdoers will be indicted separately." The jury foreman rose, and pointed at the wall clock. "It's five, people. Let's retire for the night. We meet here at nine A.M. tomorrow morning."

* * *

Frank Costello rose from his seat in court. As he stood waiting to be ushered to his jail cell, he studied the faces of the twelve jurors that were now filing past and entering the jury room. They looked fearsome and determined to exact severe punishment upon the accused. Frank's mood was certainly somber, and full of frustrations concerning the probable fate of himself and his son. Joe was likewise miserable, and now wondering what his father was going to do about this one. In a way he was almost glad to see his father fail for a change. He had been afraid of his father for most of his life, and now that fear was lifted a bit.

This caper into Wyoming had backfired, and now Frank was faced with a possible prison sentence. He said to his attorney who was standing close by, "Hoople, have one of the boys see me in jail… like right now."

Harold Hoople did as he was told, and shortly thereafter Frank and one of his 'cousins' were facing each other in one of the two holding cells located in the courthouse building. Joe Costello occupied the other. Frank said, "This is not good. What are you legal types doing besides sitting on your asses?"

"Frank, there's nothing legal we can do. This district attorney doesn't seem to make any mistakes. Both the judge and the jury as a whole don't like us. This place is not Chicago. Money doesn't buy anything here.

"As long as this judge won't hold bail hearings, we're screwed. I went up state and talked to judicial hierarchy about bail. They seem to be hard of hearing. Anything soft ain't working, Frank."

"How about some rough stuff then?"

"That's a possibility Frank, but I warn you, if it doesn't work, you're down the tubes along with the rest of us."

"You better go after Bentley's woman then. He seems nuts about her."

"Okay then Frank, I'll put things in motion."

* * *

It was early evening when George received the phone call. It was simple and straight to the point. The caller said, "Bentley, we have Betty Harris, and we will exchange her for Frank and Joe. Make a decision fast, or you won't see her alive. We expect to see Frank and Joe, out of jail by tomorrow at nine. There is to be no police anywhere when we leave town."

Stunned, George looked at the receiver in his hand, cursed

quietly to himself, and struggled to keep his mind focused. Anger flared up and almost made him lose control. In a moment he lifted the receiver and said to the operator, "Please get me the Harris Ranch."

Shortly Gladys came back, "Mr. Bentley, the lines to the ranch are down. I'll report it, and get back to you."

George next called Claude, "CC, we've got a problem. Our friends the Black Mariah have Betty somewhere, and are holding her for ransom. The price is the defendants out of jail. They want no police follow-up, while they exit town."

Claude said, "This is sure bad news. Don't those idiots know that the law can't make those kinds of deals with anyone. Any idea where they have her?"

"None yet, but I'll work on it. In the meantime, contact Richardson and Williams and fill them in. I'll make some calls, and find out if there has been any unusual activity in the Harris Ranch area. This thing sure happened fast. I suspect this is the trump card they planned to use if the jury comes in with guilty as charged. I think Frank saw the light this afternoon, and figured it was hopeless. That's when he decided to pull out all the stops and do the rough stuff. I'm going after Betty. When I find her, there's liable to be some bloodshed."

Claude was silent for a moment, then, "George, you must be right on the edge on this one. Hold it in as best you can. You must be feeling pain big time, and don't need any sympathies or platitudes. Good luck, and if there's anything I can do, just name it."

"Thank you for that, Claude, I have to find Betty before they kill. There's no way they will let her live to testify against them. On the positive side if they fail this time they'll be in so deep they'll never get out, and you'll have your linchpin to the Syndicate."

George next called his grandfather, "Grandfather, Betty has been taken hostage by the Syndicate. I need to know if they have taken her into the mountains. Will you check for me? I'll call you back in an hour."

"Of course, Red Fox. These are evil people! Watch out for your own life in the trials you're about to face."

George next called Dorothy at the switchboard. "Dorothy, this is George, can you tell me about a call I received about an hour ago? I think it went through your switchboard."

"Sure, George, it came from the Harris Ranch."

"Thanks Dorothy, that's what I needed to know. The line to the Harris Ranch has been cut. Will you check the other lines out that way and see how close to the ranch you can get. I need to find Steve and Spike fast. I'll check with you later." He then called the Arrow—B. Mary Ellen answered. "Mary Ellen, is Pete available. If so, put him on the line."

"Yah, he's here. I'll get 'im. You sound mad or something. Is there something wrong?"

"Sure, just get Pete pronto."

Pete came on the line, "What's goin' on boss?"

Pete, the Syndicate has Betty, and is holding her hostage. I need to know where they are holding her. Do whatever it takes to locate them. Start with the Harris Ranch, find out what happened to Steve and Spike. The phone line's been cut, find out where, and fix it if you can. Use everyone, I'll call you in an hour."

George had checked into a downtown motel. He managed to come into Glencoe via a neighboring rancher, leaving the ranch pickup at the ranch for use by Pete and crew. It was now close to 9 P.M.., and the voice on the phone had said, if…by 9 A.M. That gave him just 12 hours to find Betty, and extract her from her captors. He called Claude back, "Claude, I need transportation. Can you dig me up something?"

"Will do, George, where are you?"

"I'm at the Glencoe Motel."

"Okay, sit tight, I'll have something there ASAP."

George sat and considered his options. They weren't many. He kind of guessed that the cabin in the mountains would be the most likely place. It was cold out. The

Syndicate surely would pick a spot that could be heated. Unless they commandeered a ranch building somewhere, the cabin in the mountains would be the selected spot. There was no telephone there, of course, so some communication problems would arise. He postulated that the Syndicate would try to bluff it, without producing Betty for exchange. It was just approaching zero outside, so it was essential that they have heat. By the time the promised vehicle arrived, George had changed into long johns, and had his sheepskin jacket and lined gloves handy. He made his call to the Village.

"Chief Running Deer here."

"This is George, any news, grandfather?"

"George, it doesn't appear that anyone has traveled into our mountains by way of the road we found. I have someone out watching, and I'll let you know if we see anything."

"Thank you, for that, grandfather. Call the DA if you see anything. He'll always know where I am."

George put down the receiver and pondered. He felt both sad and angry. What else could he do? If they hadn't used the mountain shack, where were they" He picked up the phone and called Dorothy at the switchboard. "Dorothy, do you know of any rancher that has gone south for the winter?"

"Hi George, I heard the news, that's terrible. Let me think—well yes, the Wellingtons usually take a trip at this time of year. Last year they took a month long trip back to England to see their folks."

"Thanks Dorothy, can you think of any other?"

"Not right now, but I'll think about it, and call you. Where can I reach you?"

"Try the DA's office. He'll always know where I am." George sat for a moment. He had a picture in his mind of the Wellington spread. It was located just south of the Harris ranch, and off the same road. That had to be it. He considered calling the Sheriff, but decided in favor of doing it himself as it would have to be done 'whatever it took', and very carefully! He called the Arrow—B. Pete answered.

"Boss, we found Steve and Spike. They were out on the range spreading feed when Betty was taken. They're okay."

"Pete, I'm going out to the Wellington's spread. I think that's where they have Betty. Call the Sheriff in about an hour, then take Don and drift out that way, I may need help, but I want to go in alone at first."

"George, I get your message. Good luck, and take care."

George Red Fox Bentley was able to drive with the lights out most of the way as there was a full moon. He stopped about a quarter mile from the Wellington ranch buildings, then started off afoot, walking softly in the sandy soil, taking what cover there was, and in time came close to the ranch house. His heart did a thump as he saw lights in the windows, and smoke coming out of the chimney. There was a car parked in the ranch-yard. He studied the area around the building for some time, and finally found the outside guard, sitting on a porch swing, close to the door. He had a blanket wrapped around and over his shoulders, and looked miserable and cold. George was standing right above him when he looked up. That was too late! An iron fist slammed into his jaw. He slumped sideways onto the swing, totally out. George disarmed the unconscious would-be outside guard, and moved to one of the lighted windows. Peering in he saw Betty, her hands and feet tied, lying on a bunk, One of the guards was asleep in a second bunk, and the other sat at the table reading a newspaper. There was a potbellied stove in the middle of the room, and a pile of firewood nearby. An automatic weapon lay across the top of the table, and no doubt, a pistol would be worn by each of the guards.

George didn't have a lot of options. What had to be done was best done now. He needed to move fast. The element of surprise was his only ally. He looked closely at the door, and decided that it was not locked. Walking softly he tested the door. It was unlocked. He burst into the room, heading for the seated gunman. The man rose, yelled, and reached for his pistol. He never had a chance. George's fist came fast and hard. The man went down smashing the chair, and making a lot of noise. The man in the bunk came awake, reached for his weapon, and swept it toward George. In an instant, George was there, knocking the man's pistol aside, then came that iron fist again. George disarmed both men, then turned to Betty.

"George, at least this time I don't have to get the news from somebody else. What took you so long?"

George untied Betty's wrists and feet, he smiled at her bit of humor "I guess you know how frightened I was when I found out what happened," then taking her in his arms, he kissed her.

Bill Williams appeared in the doorway, surveyed the room and said, "There you go again, George, taking the law in your own hands." He shook his head, "I like this guy more all the time." He and Leon put handcuffs on the three suspects. Betty and George hardly knew they were there.

* * *

In the jury room, and seated, a dozen Wyoming townspeople, ranchers and miners, sat sipping coffee, and eating doughnuts. These were all sincere citizens, looking to carry out their duty as jurymen. They all had been ruminating over the unfolding drama of the trial, most of the evening before. The first to speak was a man from town, "Perhaps I missed it, but what penalty will the defendants face if we find them guilty?"

The jury foreman said, "I think we must confine our efforts to determining 'guilt or innocence' as charged. That should be black or white. But I will ask." He went to the door spoke to the bailiff, and in a few moments he came back with the answer. "The judge said, 'That information is irrelevant, and should not affect the jury's decision'."

The foreman then said, "Let's see how we stand. Those who are for conviction, raise your hand." Eight hands rose to be counted. "How many for acquittal?" Two hands were raised. "Okay, two undecided, I guess. Let's hear from one of the jurors for acquittal. Why do you think the defendants are not guilty?"

Juror number two said, "I'm uncomfortable with it being all circumstantial. We don't have anyone seeing Joe Costello in the act of picking up and dropping off the shooter, or do we have any proof that Frank directed the illicit acts that have been going on."

The jury foreman said, "Alright, let's hear from someone for conviction."

Juror number three said, "We have a car with two armed suspects driving in the middle of the night with lights out. We have a shooter headed to meet the car with the two suspects inside. They expected to meet and exit the area. There is no other logical explanation for them being there. There is no possibility that this was all innocent or coincidental. I think the DA has it right. The shooter missed his mark by a hair. He didn't know that he had missed. He has been successfully prosecuted for the crime of attempted murder. We know that planning all the various acts of violence that have occurred came from within the ranks of the Black Mariah Syndicate. Frank Costello represents the Syndicate. It is he that has the final word, and it is he that is responsible in the end. I feel the circumstantial evidence is overwhelming!"

The jury foreman said, "That is pretty convincing to me. Let's hear from the other juror that votes for acquittal."

Juror number six said, "Law enforcement collected the suspected shooter quite a long distance from the alleged getaway car. I would like to see the actual contact. All we have is a guess that they were headed for a rendezvous."

"Your point is well taken." The foreman sort of paused then, "I too would be more comfortable with a closer connection between the attempted murderer and the alleged getaway car."

Another juror said, "The timing is right. It's too much of a coincidence that a car with two persons, armed with killing tools attuned to gang-like activities just happened to be driving on a deserted unpaved road at the right time to meet Jon Ballant in his attempt to fly the coop. I don't think there's reasonable doubt."

After a few moments of silence, the foreman asked, "Does anyone else care to share his thoughts."

Juror number three said, "I think that we should be looking at the Syndicate connection here. Our DA has laid it out, given us enough information so to speak, pretty conclusively. The defendants are certainly members of a destructive and evil organization. They come from a family identified as carrying out illicit acts in the big city. What are they doing out here in our land anyway? Glencoe is host to a bunch of these crooks, and I want them out of here." He paused for a moment then, "These vermin are not here for their health."

Another juror said, "Did anyone else but me notice the look that went between Frank and Muscles when he took the stand?"

The jury foreman said, "I did. I think the tie-in is Muscles. He is obviously well acquainted with the defendant, and other members of the gang. The DA is going to prosecute Muscles for the murder of Richard Bentley."

Another juror asked, "Where did you hear that?"

"I overheard the DA instructing one of the prosecuting team to file charges against Muscles."

"So you think Frank is guilty by virtue of the fact that he is friendly with Muscles?"

The jury foreman said, "Not necessarily, but it adds one more item to my thinking 'guilty'. Alright, it's time for another vote. Those in favor of acquittal, raise your hands." One hand was raised. "All those in favor of conviction?" Eleven jurors raised their hands. The foreman said, "eleven to one for conviction. That means it's time to go to work." Turning to the dissenting juror, "Tell us why you feel the defendants are innocent."

"I'm not sure that the defendant Joe Costello is innocent per se, however the thought that we might be sending an innocent man to prison worries me. Has the prosecution been diligent in its effort to find any other cause for Joe to be in that place at night? That act isn't illegal anyway. Has the prosecution proven that Frank is really the kingpin of the Syndicate?"

The foreman asked, "Does anyone wish to answer to that?"

Another juror said, "I have felt the defendant, Joe Costello, guilty from the start. He has that family connection to the organization that has been responsible for much trouble in our county. Their presence here in Glencoe is certainly not in the best interest of anyone living here! The Syndicate provided counsel for Jon Ballant, the man who shot George Bentley in the head. This was not brought out in the trial. It is one more reason for conviction. Joe did what he was told to do by Frank. Frank is the one most responsible."

The foreman said, "That is a good point, I guess our DA missed that one. Does anyone else wish to comment before we take another vote?"

There were no more comments by the jury. A vote was taken, and a unanimous decision to convict was recorded. The jury foreman went to the door and handed a note to the bailiff who took it to Judge Hastings.

The members of the jury were seated when the judge read the verdict aloud: "We, the jury, by a unanimous vote, find the defendants guilty of all charges. Besides the sentences that will be awarded by the court, we recommend that fines to cover the expenses incurred by the State of Wyoming, the County of Contra, and others that have cause, be considered. Further, we recommend that the injured parties be awarded punitive damages in an amount felt appropriate by the court."

The Judge said, the court accepts the verdict from the jury, however the matter of compensation to injured parties will be determined through lawful petitions, and in civil court actions. This court session will recess for two hours while I consider sentences that are to be imposed on the convicted. I wish to see the attorneys for the prosecution and the defense in my chambers. This court is in recess."

Judge Hastings was seated across from Claude Comstock and Harold Hoople. He said, "This case has become unique in several ways. Imposing sentences on the two codefendants is simple. Identifying the members of the offending organization and imposing meaningful penalties on said, is another thing. Claude, do you have any thoughts on this matter?"

"Judge, the verdict submitted by the jury gives us a place to start. We can only deal with actions that took place in this jurisdiction. My office is in direct contact with the Cook County District Attorney. They have a vested interest in this drama. There will be extradition requests to remove the convicted to Chicago, and requests for information gained during this trial.

"My office needs at least forty eight hours to develop a figure that represents the losses incurred in this jurisdiction. We will also suggest punitive damages be levied that the prosecution feels reasonable.

"Additionally, the matter of Muscles must be dealt with. He is charged with the murder of Richard Bentley. He is also a de facto member of the Syndicate, and in time will be extradited to Cook County to stand trial for other murders. It will be shown that he is psychologically incapable of standing trial, and therefore not wholly responsible for his actions. In as much as he was directed to do harm to Mr. Bentley by members of the Black Mariah Syndicate, his misdeeds really were those of the Syndicate. He cannot be turned loose into society however."

The judge said, "Hoople, give us your thoughts."

"Your Honor, the prosecution is assuming that the entire Black Mariah Syndicate is responsible here. I would hope that this organization will not be required to pay for any of the actions described in this trial. By the same token, most of the offences indicated in this trial occurred while my clients weren't even in this State. As for Muscles, there has been no proof that he is a member of the indicated organization."

Judge Hastings thanked the two attorneys for their comments and said, "I will announce judgment before the end of the day."

Members of the press rushed to inform their home offices of the verdict. Electricity seemed to flow everywhere. This was news, big time. The all-powerful had been challenged, and lost.

John Blake, the Cook County district attorney, had flown out from Chicago to watch, and listen to final arguments, and the judge's charge to the jury. He waited through jury deliberations, and heard the sentencing of the defendants. As the courtroom emptied, he came up to the prosecution table to congratulate Claude Comstock. He said, with a smile, "CC, that was a great job, you wouldn't want a job in the big city?"

"Thanks no, John, besides, I have Muscles to deal with, and I'm at home here."

"You know, CC, I hope to see Frank when you get finished with him out here. I assume you will make your notes etc. available to me."

"Of course, John." Claude smiled and said, "You and I both know I got away with stuff here, that you couldn't do out your way. I guess the media will give Wrightwood a lot of flak, which is too bad. I kind of feel sorry for him."

"Well that's politics, which we have a lot of in Chi. Take care, and let me know if I can help in any way."

"Well, as long as you ask, can you leave Ed out here for a while longer, besides, I think he's fallen in love with Pril, and I'm not sure you're going to get him back anyway."

"Claude, you're holding all the winning cards dammit. Maybe they'll get married and come back to Chicago. Did you ever think of that? Yes, I guess you can keep him, at least until you're completely through with the Black Mariah."

Claude smiled, and said, "Join us for a victory dinner tonight? Howard Johnson's at seven."

28 | KIDNAPPING

Sheriff Williams delivered three totally miserable suspects to the Glencoe police headquarters. The desk sergeant looked up in surprise, picked up the phone, and called his boss. "Chief, you'd better come out here, Sheriff Williams is back."

"So what else is new, just send 'im in."

"What do I do with the three suspects he has in tow?"

"Waaat, I'll be right out." The Chief swung his 220 pounds off his desk chair, thinking. This has to end sometime. I'm expected to do all kinds of off center stuff, and now I'm expected to have an expanding jail to boot. He turned the corner to face a grinning Sheriff Williams. "Where'd these come from, and why me?"

"Hello Chief, these three were caught in the act of kidnapping. Claude wants them held over for trial. I expect he'll be along soon to file charges."

"So where do I put 'em, The only space left is my office, oh shit," he turned to the desk sergeant, "Book 'em, I'll figure out something. Put manacles on all three, leave the handcuffs on, and put them in the storage room. Call one of the patrol units and have them come on in. We need more manpower here. Come on into my office Bill, I want to hear about this one."

Bill said, "You know about the George and Betty thing, well last night Betty gets picked up by the Syndicate gang. The boys put in a call to George asking to free Joe and Frank, or Betty would die. George disappears, figures out where they had her, overcomes three armed criminals with his bare hands, frees Betty, and leaves me the job of escorting the three bums to jail. One of them had a broken jaw, the other two were in shock. And now he acts like it's a normal day's work. Ain't love grand?"

"You're kidding, of course."

"No, he's been doing this kind of thing for the last eight months, nothing new here. He came here from college questioning my judgment, telling me to do my job and investigate his father's murder. Not our best time together. In time I believed him, and we became good friends. Claude is putting Muscles on the stand soon, and I believe will prosecute him for the murder of Richard Bentley. That's been George's goal all along, find the killer of his dad."

Claude Comstock entered the building, and joined the Chief and the Sheriff. He too was wearing a huge smile, "Hi Chief, how's jailing these days?"

"Everyone seems so happy around here. Me, I'm ecstatic, I've finally filled all of my jail cells. And now I'll have a surplus of applicants, all eager to spend the night, so I can't sleep at all, and have bad dreams about jail breaks, with little black suited gnomes, their beady little eyes peering at me. And my two friends grinning like they're happy to see me in this crappy fix."

The Sheriff said, "Gee Chief, I thought I was doing you a favor, taking three criminals off the streets. What else can I do to make you happy?"

"Well for starters you might tell me that it's all a myth."

Claude said, "Hmm, Hastings mentioned that you were having a jail problem, but then he said that you usually found a way out of these kinds of situations. How bad is your problem?"

"Well I'm considering finding a spot in the old building, the one you have your office in, until you can get rid of a few. When do you think that will happen?"

Claude said, "Just as soon as I sign off on Muscles, which may be this week. I'll have a place for some of them as fast as I can Chief."

"How long will we keep these three?"

"Their trial will be sometime down the line. Muscles comes first, and will start in a week if Hastings goes along with it. That gives you no relief for at least ten days. How do you intend to provide security for the county if you put people outside the jail building?"

"That's a problem, especially since we have a town full of their buddies, looking for a way to bust them out. Just try to keep me informed enough so I can plan enough ahead of time to transport people somewhere when you are through with them."

"That I will do, Chief."

EPILOGUE

Judge Hastings sentenced Joe Costello to five years in the State penitentiary. Frank Costello received ten years, and the Syndicate itself was ordered to pay damages incurred by state and county institutions and individuals, plus punitive damages in the amount of five million dollars. This penalty was designed to bankrupt the Syndicate.

With the information gained from the Wyoming trials, the Cook County District Attorney's office successfully prosecuted the Syndicate for crimes committed in Illinois.

Claude provided the court with evidence to support the charges against Muscles, and he was indicted to be tried. Claude also asked that the defendant be examined by a psychiatrist to determine his ability to defend himself. A trial was held, and Muscles was convicted of second degree murder of Richard Bentley, he was sentenced to the state mental institution where he could be cared for. In time, Muscles was extradited to Chicago, and was tried and convicted for the killings in that jurisdiction. He lived out his life in an Illinois institution.

The three who forcefully took Betty Harris from her home were tried and convicted of kidnapping, one count each, and each received ten to twenty years in the Wyoming state penitentiary.

Ralph Peterson was sued in Civil court for his part in fraud against the Arrow—B. The Arrow—B ranch was awarded said losses.

ABOUT THE AUTHOR

From the start Jack F. Kirkeby's interests have been of the West. He grew up in an era of strong Western stories and movies. Later in life, then, his writings would be of the West. Jack's motto, "Look behind you, there's no one there," is his way of reminding folks to accept personal responsibility for their successes and failures as adults. His principal characters embody this theme in their actions on the easily turned pages of his books. He has written two full length novels, and is well into his third.

Before he was twelve years old, Jack F. Kirkeby had lived in a plethora of homes and places as the product of fractured family conditions. Very early on this gave the author a desire to succeed and foster something more. Ultimately a sense of personal responsibility and gritty determination oozed from the tall, six foot, four inch young man. In 1933 he entered Hollywood High School, where he joined the ROTC.

In 1935, mother and son Jack moved to Lake Geneva Wisconsin where he finished high school, graduating in June of 1936. Then it was on to live with his brother in Chicago where he worked through the depression years while he continued his education attending after-hours college classes.

On June 9th of 1941 Jack enlisted in the United States Army Air Force, and served in the Pacific theater for two years as an enlisted man, later returning to America where he entered officer training.

In December, 1943, the author worked as a service manager for an appliance and radio firm while he continued his education. He eventually entered the aerospace industry. His job with Northrop Corporation, later Northrop Grumman, included Quality Control, Contract Administration and Configuration Management. His duties included customer and government quality control issues, contract interpretation and technical writing.

Jack has attended and earned credits at several colleges, including Oklahoma A&M, Saddleback Junior College, Long Beach State and Fullerton Junior College. He currently lives in Mission Viejo, California, where he remains active in his community and works tirelessly on his next novel. In addition to his novels, Jack also writes situational poetry. Here's a taste--

Today is now
Full and rich
Unlike any other
Not to be wasted
For tomorrow it is gone

****

Tomorrow is promise
Another chance
Different from today
What will it bring?
Trust and respect it
For what it can be